JOAN JOHNSTON

TEXAS WOMAN

A DELL BOOK

TEXAS WOMAN
A Dell Book

Published by Bantam Dell
A Division of Random House, Inc.
New York, New York

All rights reserved
Copyright © 1989 by Joan Mertens Johnston

ISBN 0-7394-3817-4

Manufactured in the United States of America

For my sister
Joyce Evelyn Mertens

Singleminded, softhearted.

TEXAS
WOMAN

Prologue

IN HIS DREAMS, RIP STEWART ENVISIONED three sons sweating shoulder to shoulder with him as his cotton plantation along the Brazos River blossomed in concert with the new Texas frontier. He had his sons' names already picked out before he ever married Amelia, chosen as his bride because she was the only daughter in a nearby Scots family of seven healthy children.

His eldest son would be named Sloan. Sloan would be strong and brave, a proud, capable heir to take Rip's place. Bayleigh would be Rip's surety. He would be the educated one, bred to be a loyal and steadfast help to his elder brother. Rip's youngest son would be named Creighton. Creighton would be the child of Rip's heart, the child he played with, and indulged, and lavished with his love. Creighton would be fiery-tempered and bold, demanding everything the Texas frontier had to offer a man, and getting it.

Unfortunately, Amelia gave Rip three daughters. That did not deter Rip Stewart. He named the eldest Sloan, the second Bayleigh, and the youngest Creighton. Then he set out to make his dreams come true.

Chapter 1

REPUBLIC OF TEXAS
1844

"I SEE YOU'VE TAKEN YOUR BROTHER'S WHORE for your woman, Don Cruz. Is she as hot-blooded as Antonio boasted she was?"

"Keep your tongue to yourself or I'll cut it out, Alejandro."

Sloan Stewart blanched at the malicious words that had been spoken by the grizzle-faced Mexican bandido bound hand and foot in the stinking San Antonio jail cell, and the equally savage retort from the tall, lean Castilian Spaniard who stood rigidly at her side. Humiliation drew the skin tight over her cheekbones as she restrained the bitter denial that sought voice. Yet what could she say in her defense?

She could not deny that she had been Antonio Guerrero's lover. In fact, she had borne Tonio's bastard son. Nor could she deny that Tonio's elder brother Cruz desired her, and had sought—without success so far—to possess her. But it was a hideous thing to hear her relationship with the two brothers put in such contemptible terms.

She laid a hand on Cruz's arm and felt the corded muscles of a feral animal tighten and form beneath the layers of fashionable cloth.

A narrow strip of sunlight flashed off the wide silver-and-turquoise bracelet Alejandro wore on his right wrist, drawing Sloan's attention once more to the man before them. "Are you sure this bandido is the same man who murdered Tonio four years ago?" she asked Cruz.

"The same."

"Antonio Guerrero was a traitor and a fool!" Alejandro snarled. "If I had not shot him, the Texas Rangers would have hung him for plotting with the Mexican government to overthrow the Republic."

"You are going to hang, Alejandro. If not for murdering my brother, then for stealing my cattle and my horses and for raping the women of my pueblo," Cruz said.

The bandido's hostile eyes glittered in the darkened cell. "I admit to nothing—except that I enjoy the first tearing thrust into virgin flesh." He eyed Sloan and added, "You are not, it seems, nearly so fastidious, Don Cruz."

"Enough!" Cruz said from between clenched teeth.

Sloan unconsciously backed away from the bandido's malevolent stare until she felt Cruz's implacable strength behind her. She straightened her shoulders and said with outward calm, "I'm ready to leave. I've seen all I need to see."

Alejandro nodded his head in mock obeisance to her. "*Adiós, puta.* Until we meet again."

Sloan recoiled from the cruel smile on Alejandro's sharp-boned face. His pitiless eyes undressed her, exposing the full breasts with dusky nipples he would pinch and fondle, the slender waist and wide, child-bearing hips he would mount, the triangle of dark curls at the juncture of slim, strong legs that would grip his hairy thighs.

She closed her eyes to shut out his visual rape of her, but the sound of Alejandro's low, grating laugh forced them open again. She shivered as his eyes insolently skimmed her body one last time.

"I will not be here long enough to hang," he promised. "I will escape, as I escaped from the Rangers four years ago. And when I do, I will see for myself whether Antonio spoke the truth about his whore."

Sloan didn't wait to hear Cruz's response to the bandido's taunt. She left the dank room of tiny cells filled with frontier riffraff, murderers and thieves and walked outside onto San Antonio's dusty central square. She squinted her eyes against the sun's midday glare and leaned her hand against the rough brown adobe building, fighting the dizziness that overtook her.

She inhaled a deep breath of air to clear her nostrils of the stench of the jail. The smells outside were equally pungent, but not so offensive—*frijoles* cooking, a freshly laid pattern of horse dung, tiny wild roses climbing the adobe jail wall, and overlaying it all, the tangy smell of sweat from humans and horses.

Sloan froze as a rigid-backed Spanish woman passed by, tugging along a dark-haired little boy dressed in short pants. For an instant Sloan thought it was Cruz's mother Doña Lucia with Cisco—Sloan's now three-year-old son.

But it wasn't.

Sloan slumped back against the adobe wall, fearful her legs wouldn't support her, as memories of Tonio, of her pregnancy, and of the birth of her son came flooding back.

It was hard to remember why she had first been attracted to Antonio Guerrero, but she supposed it must have been his smile. It was charming and rakish and tilted up at one corner more than the other. Or it might have been his dark eyes sparkling with devilry that had captured her heart. But it was his voice to which she had succumbed, a voice that was low and smooth and coaxing in a way she hadn't been able to resist.

She had felt foolish when she realized she had fallen in love with Tonio. As the future heir to Three Oaks, she had been trained by Rip Stewart to make calm, rational decisions, and there was nothing the least bit calm or rational about falling head over heels in love. Especially when she had been raised from birth to understand that her destiny lay with Three Oaks—not as the wife of the younger son of a Spanish don.

She didn't dare admit her feelings to her father, for fear he'd think her clabber-headed. So she had kept her thoughts to herself. And made some terrible mistakes.

Sloan picked at a callus on the palm of her hand. Tonio hadn't liked her hands, she remembered. She held them out in front of her and looked at them. Raising cotton was dirty work. Her fingernails were broken to the quick, and not a little grimy. Calluses adorned her fingertips and the palms of her hands. They were small hands, but there was nothing dainty about them, she thought with a grimace.

Yet she had full breasts and hips, a shape a man might admire if he could ever see beyond the planter's clothes she usually wore. Sloan glanced at her dusty Wellington boots, at her stained osnaburg trousers, at the visible ring of sweat at her armpits on the gingham shirt she wore, at the unraveling threads on the second button of her waistcoat, which had been nearly yanked off when it got caught on the cotton gin. Her lips curved in a rueful, self-deprecating grin. Right now she looked a mess!

She hadn't been near a mirror this morning, but she could imagine her face also showed signs of her hurried journey from Three Oaks to San Antonio. Her one vanity, her waist-length sable-brown hair, was tied at her nape in a

single tail with a piece of crumpled ribbon that had once
been pale yellow.

There was nothing about her normal working-day appearance to entice a man as handsome as Antonio Guerrero to fall in love with her. She should have realized from
the beginning that he'd had other reasons for what he had
said and done.

Sloan felt her stomach roil with the disgust she felt
every time she thought of how the man she had loved had
so coldly and calculatedly used that love to get from her
what he had wanted.

She would have done anything for him. He had used her
to further his sordid plot with the Mexican government to
invade Texas, giving her secret messages to carry to his co-
horts. She had done his bidding without questioning him,
because she had loved and trusted him. How gullible she
had been! How stupid!

It was hard to remember the initial joy she had felt at
finding out she was pregnant with Tonio's child. Hard to
remember the hours when she had pressed her hands
against her belly and thought with wonder of their child
growing within her. She should have realized something
was wrong when Tonio did not immediately offer to marry
her when she told him she was pregnant.

"We must wait, *chiquita*," he had said. "There will be
time enough to marry and give the child a name."

Of course, he had never intended to marry her. It had
been devastating to discover he was a traitor, that he had
been murdered by one of his own men, Alejandro Sanchez,
and that she must somehow bear all on her own the sorrow
of his death, the shock of his betrayal and the shame of being pregnant and unwed.

It had not taken long for sorrow and shock and shame to

become hate and anger and resolution. She had thought it out, weighing every detail, and made the only rational decision possible: She would not keep Tonio's child.

She was bitter and angry for what Tonio had done. She did not think she could love the child of such a man, or even maintain indifference to it. She was afraid she would blame the child for the sins of the father, and she feared the hateful emotions she felt whenever she thought of Tonio and the bastard child she was to bear him.

To spare the innocent child, she had sought out Tonio's elder brother, Cruz, and they had come to an agreement.

Sloan sighed and shook her head. She still could not believe she had acted as she had. She could only blame her actions on the turbulent emotions she had felt at the time. She could vividly recall the disbelieving look on Cruz's face when she told him what she wanted to do.

"You will give away your own child?" he had exclaimed in horror.

"It would bring back too many memories to keep Tonio's baby," she had replied.

"Surely in time the memories will fade," he had said, "and you will want your son or daughter—"

"I will never forget Tonio. Or what he—"

"You loved him, then," Cruz had said, his voice harsh.

"I did," she admitted. "More than my life," she finished in a whisper. That was what had made his betrayal so painful. It did not occur to her that Cruz would not realize her love for his brother had died with Tonio.

She had watched Cruz's lips flatten to a thin line, watched him frown as he came to his decision.

"Very well. I will take the child. But he must have a name."

"You may call him whatever you wish," she said, in a rush to have it all done and over.

"My brother's son must have his name."

"If you wish to call the child Antonio—"

"You misunderstand me," Cruz interrupted brusquely. "My family possesses a noble Spanish heritage. My brother's child must bear the Guerrero name."

Sloan had not imagined how difficult it was going to be to go through with her plan. She swallowed over the painful lump in her throat and said, "If you wish to adopt the child as your own, I will agree."

"That is not at all my intention," Cruz said.

She felt the warm touch of Cruz's fingers as he lifted her chin, forcing her to meet his gaze.

His blue eyes were dark with some emotion she refused to acknowledge. He could not feel that way about her, not when she had been his brother's woman. What she could not accept, she ignored.

His gaze held hers captive as he said, "My brother's child will bear the Guerrero name because you will be my wife."

"That's ridiculous," she blurted, pulling away from him.

"Not at all," he countered. "If you wish me to take the child and raise it as my own, you will marry me."

"That's blackmail! I won't do it."

"Then find another solution to your problem, Señorita Sloan."

The tall Spaniard had already turned on his booted heel before she found her voice. "Wait! There must be some way we can work this out."

He pivoted back to her, determination etched in his features. "I have stated my condition for taking the child."

His arrogance infuriated her, and she clasped her hands

to keep herself from attacking him. She held her anger in check, knowing that however satisfying it would be to feel the skin of his cheek under her palm, it would be a useless gesture. She had nowhere else to turn.

"All right," she said. "I will marry you."

Before his triumphant smile had a chance to form fully, she continued, "But it will be a marriage in name only. I will not live with you."

"That is hardly a proper marriage, señorita."

She snorted. "I don't care a worm's worth about a proper marriage. I'm trying to find a way to compromise with you."

"As my wife, you will live with me," Cruz announced in a commanding voice.

"If I marry you, I'll live at Three Oaks," she retorted.

"Unfortunately, that would make it quite impossible for us to have the children I desire."

Sloan flushed. "I won't live with you."

"Then we can come to no agreement."

Once again, Sloan was forced to halt his departure. "Wait—"

"You agree, then?"

Sloan raked her mind for some way to put off the inevitable and came up with an idea. "I'll agree to marry you. But I'll live with you as your wife only after Alejandro Sanchez is brought to justice."

Cruz grimaced in frustration. "My brother's murderer may never be caught."

"I know," Sloan replied. "But that is *my* condition." She said it with the same intractability he had used when he laid down his own demands.

"I agree to your suggestion," Cruz said at last. "We will be married now, and I will take the child when it is born and raise it as my own. Ours will be a marriage in name only—until such time as Alejandro Sanchez shall be brought to justice."

It was obvious to Sloan when she shook hands with Cruz to seal their bargain that he expected to find Alejandro within days. But her luck had held. Alejandro had remained elusive, and she had remained at Three Oaks.

Over the years, while Cruz had hunted diligently for the bandido, he had kept their bargain and raised her son as his own. Now, at long last, Cruz had found Alejandro. Now, at long last, the arrogant Spaniard would expect her to fulfill her part of their bargain.

For reasons she could never explain to him, Sloan knew she could not do it.

She jumped away from the adobe wall as Cruz's voice startled her from her reverie.

"I should have killed him when I had the chance."

"The law will avenge Tonio's death," she said.

"Only if Alejandro is still in jail when the time comes to hang him."

A frisson of alarm skittered down Sloan's spine. "You don't seriously believe he can escape, do you? He's tied hand and foot, and he'll be guarded by Texas Rangers."

"He is treacherous and cunning. He must be clever to have stayed free this long. And there are those who would help him escape."

"But—"

Cruz thrust a restless hand through his thick black hair. "But, as you say, I am worrying needlessly. We will surely see him hang tomorrow."

"I won't be staying for the hanging," Sloan admitted. "I dropped everything and left in the middle of the cotton harvest when I got your message that Alejandro had been caught. My responsibilities as overseer can't wait. And I have enough nightmares to disturb my sleep without adding one more."

"Do you still see Tonio's face at night, Cebellina?"

Sloan whirled on Cruz, keeping her voice low to avoid drawing the attention of those who passed by them. "Don't speak to me of Tonio. And don't speak to me a name intended for a *novia*. I'm not your sweetheart, Cruz, and I never will be."

With a strength and quickness Sloan knew he was capable of, but had never seen for herself, Cruz grabbed her by the waist and carried her the few steps to a nearby alley. He pressed her up against the adobe wall and held her there with the length of his hard, sinewy body.

Sloan saw a ferocity in Cruz's blue eyes, a harshness in his aristocratic features, an intransigence in the jutting chin rent by a shallow cleft, that she hadn't seen since the grim day they had sealed their bargain.

There was nothing of the daring Spanish cavalier in the face of the man who held her, only brute strength, iron will and the knowledge of unrequited love.

"What do you expect from me, Cebellina?" With a hand that trembled under the force of the control he exerted, he caressed a wayward strand of the sable hair that had fostered his nickname for her.

His gaze touched her heart-shaped face, her large, intelligent brown eyes topped by delicately arched brows, her short, straight nose, the angled cheekbones leading to her confident chin, and finally her full, inviting pink lips, the lower of which she held clasped between her teeth.

When he spoke again, his rumbling voice held the fervor of someone who has reached the limit of his patience and will not be denied. "I have waited to claim you until

Tonio's murderer could be brought to justice. For four long years I have waited!

"I have kept my part of the bargain we made when you came to me swollen with my brother's child and asked for my help. I accepted Tonio's son from your arms when he was born and took him to Rancho Dolorosa to raise him as my own.

"And though I was often tempted, I did not ask of you my soul's desire. I did not take from you that for which my body hungered. I waited. And I hunted down my brother's murderer.

"Now you must keep your part of the bargain. I want you for my wife, Cebellina. And I will have you. Whether you see my brother's face in your dreams or not!"

His mouth came down to claim Sloan's, his touch rough with need, his teeth breaking the skin of her lip so she tasted blood. His hands freely roamed her body, commanding a response from her.

Sloan felt the insidious tingling sensation begin deep inside her, felt her lips softening under his, felt her mouth open for his searching tongue that ravaged her, mimicking the movement of his hips against her belly. She felt the rush of passion, felt the desire for him, for the joining of their bodies, begin to well and grow within her, as unwelcome as a weevil in cotton.

She could not allow this. She would *not* let herself be used by any man again! She shoved against Cruz's chest, but she managed only to break the contact between their mouths.

"Stop it," she hissed. "Let me go!"

Her hand rose up between them to cover Cruz's lips. When she felt the wetness on his lips, it caused a shiver of desire within her so fierce that she felt compelled to deny it in words. "I don't want you. I'll never want you. And you can't want me. I was your brother's *puta*. Your brother's *whore!*"

Abruptly, Cruz released her. His blue eyes had become chips of ice. The veins stood out along his neck, and his hands were balled into tightly clenched fists. "Never, *never* call yourself whore. Do you understand me?"

Sloan flinched when he raised his hand, afraid he would strike her. But she stood her ground, waiting. She was Rip Stewart's daughter. It would not be the first time she had been struck in anger. She was no coward; she would not run from him.

His fist unfurled like a tight bud that finally flowers, and his callused fingertips smoothed over her freckled cheekbone in a caress as surprisingly soft as a cactus blossom. "Do you hate me so much, Cebellina?"

"I don't hate you at all."

"Then why do you resist me?"

"I can never love you, Cruz. A true marriage between us would only cause unhappiness for us both."

"I will be the judge of what will make me happy."

"Will you also judge what will please me?"

"Only tell me what I can do to please you and it shall be done. What do you want, Cebellina?"

"I *don't* want or need a husband."

His mouth tightened and a flush rose across his cheekbones. "Nevertheless, when Alejandro hangs, you will fulfill our bargain and become my wife."

"I'm going home to Three Oaks, Cruz."

"Go. But know this: When my brother's murder is avenged at last, I will come for you."

"Let me pass. I want to go to Ranger headquarters before I leave."

"Is there some problem at Three Oaks?" Cruz asked.

"I only want to thank Luke Summers for his part in capturing Alejandro," she replied, annoyed at his assumption that their bargain gave him the right to know about her affairs.

Cruz's eyes narrowed. It was said that Luke Summers drew women like a Texas marsh drew mallards. It took Cruz no time at all to make up his mind what he should do. "I'll come with you."

Sloan started to object, then shrugged. "I can't very well stop you."

Cruz stepped away from her, and she had never been so aware of his great height or her own more feminine stature. She slipped past him and out of the alley into the warm September sunshine.

Her heart was racing, and she took several deep breaths in an attempt to calm herself before she headed purposefully toward the adobe building where she knew she would find the young Texas Ranger lieutenant. Cruz followed, a shadow by her side.

The shutters on the windows of Ranger headquarters had been closed to keep the interior cool. Sloan had to wait for her eyes to adjust to the dimness before she saw Luke sitting on the edge of a spur-scarred wooden desk. He kept a well-worn lariat circling two inches above the dirt floor with no more effort than the gentle flick of his wrist.

She had first met Luke Summers when he had come to provide protection against the Comanches who had once threatened Three Oaks.

Although you couldn't tell it to look at him, slouched against the desk as he was, Luke was tall and rangy. His dark brown hair was streaked with blond from the year he had spent at hard labor in a Mexican prison after he had been captured at the Battle of Mier. He had high cheek-bones and a narrow nose over a wide, full mouth.

His eyes were hazel, but she had seen them look green or gold at various times, depending on his mood. She guessed he was about her age, twenty-two or -three, but his eyes bespoke a life filled with some unutterable sadness.

With another flick of his wrist, Luke collected the lariat in his hand. As he shaped the rope in small, even loops, he said, "Howdy, Sloan. What's troubling you?"

He was also far too perceptive for her peace of mind. "Nothing worth mentioning," she said, slanting a glance at Cruz. "Before I leave town, I wanted to thank you for your help in capturing Alejandro Sanchez."

"You're leaving? The hanging's not until tomorrow."

"I know. I don't plan to stick around for it. Anyway, thanks."

"Just doing my job." Luke stood up and gestured toward the ladder-back chair across from the desk. "You want to set a spell, Sloan?"

"No, I need to get started home. I don't want to leave Rip alone too long."

"I thought your father was completely recovered from his stroke," Luke said.

"Oh, he is," Sloan was quick to reassure him. "Except for having to use a cane to get around, he's back to being his same ornery self. But he pushes himself too hard. If I'm not there, he's liable to do more than he should. Why don't you come for a visit and see for yourself how well he's recovered?"

"I just may do that when Captain Hays returns and I'm not tied to this desk taking care of Ranger business. Are you traveling back to Three Oaks by yourself?"

"I came by myself," Sloan said, as though that answered his question.

"But you are not riding back alone," Cruz said.

Sloan's eyes narrowed.

Luke looked from Sloan to Cruz and back again. "Between Comanches, bandidos and immigrants anxious to stake a claim before Texas gets herself annexed by the Union, the Republic isn't the safest place to travel these days. Maybe you ought to let me send some Rangers along for the ride."

"I can take care of myself."

Luke gauged Cruz's temper and said, "Josey and Frank are shoving down some vittles at Ferguson's Hotel, but I know they'd enjoy the ride. Shall I give them a holler?"

"No," Sloan said.

"Yes," Cruz said.

Sloan stood toe to toe with Cruz and poked her finger against his unyielding chest to emphasize her speech. "I don't need *anyone* to follow me home. I take care of *myself*. Do you *understand*?" She pivoted on her heel and marched out of the office, slamming the door behind her.

Luke fought the smile that threatened. "I'll send Josey and Frank after her."

"Be sure you do."

Cruz slipped off his boots and settled onto the soft feather bed in Ferguson's Hotel. He lit a cheroot and let the sweet smell of tobacco swirl around him as he waited for dawn. One step at a time, he was slowly but surely clearing the devastation left upon his brother's death—a woman despoiled, a son orphaned, a country betrayed. Each deserved something beyond the legacy of selfishness and greed that Antonio had bequeathed them.

Cruz had to admit that taking Sloan Stewart as his wife was proving to be more of a challenge than he had expected.

He had not ever thought he would marry again after watching his very young wife Valeria die during childbirth. His parents had arranged the match, and he had not objected because Valeria was comely and compliant and he had wanted a home and children of his own.

Before long he had discovered his pretty wife was obedient because she had no thoughts of her own. He had ceased to feel any fond emotion for her long before she had died shrieking with the agony of birthing their stillborn son.

At her death, guilt smote him that he had made her short life less happy than it could have been. He had sworn he would never marry again until he found a woman who could engage both his heart and mind.

That had not proved a simple feat. Indeed, he had turned away many offers of marriage to the daughters of neighboring *rancheros* over the past ten years.

Then, in the course of one brief conversation with Sloan Stewart, he had found what he had been seeking. She possessed a mind and a will that challenged his own. He had looked deep into her large, liquid-brown eyes and discovered an inner fire that burned far more brightly than in any other woman he had ever known. At last, he had found the woman he would spend the rest of his life loving.

It had been a shattering experience to discover that the woman he wanted to make his wife had already given her heart—and her body—to his brother. God help him, he had envied Tonio.

And when he had seen Sloan's pain upon learning of Tonio's betrayal, he had hated his brother for the cruel theft of her innocence.

Over the years, he had come to understand that the spirit he so admired in Sloan also kept her at arm's distance. He did not understand her need for independence or her desire to play the man's part or her rejection of his offer of a husband's protection.

But he had convinced himself that once he and Sloan were living together as husband and wife, once she was carrying his child, those issues would resolve themselves. Soon, that belief would be put to the test.

Dawn came on slow, tired feet, dragging the huge Texas sun behind it. Cruz felt the weight of the day as he left the hotel and walked toward the dusty central square. This would be a day of endings . . . and a day of beginnings.

Two men were flogged in the plaza before Alejandro's turn came to meet the hangman. Two Texas Rangers escorted the bandido to the raised platform and secured the black bag in place over his head with the hangman's noose. The bright Texas sun glinted off Alejandro's silver-and-turquoise bracelet as his hands were tied behind his back.

The bandido's bold threats of escape had come to naught, Cruz thought. This morning he would die.

Cruz scarcely noticed when Luke came to stand beside him. He heard the murmured incantations of the priest at the gallows and, a moment later, the abrupt crack of the trapdoor as it dropped open, leaving Alejandro kicking his legs frantically against the pull of the noose.

Cruz felt the bile rising in his throat. The bandido took a long time to die. The smell of urine pinched Cruz's nostrils, and the thought of Alejandro's grizzled face beneath the mask, his tongue purple and swollen, his eyes white-rimmed with fear, nearly made him gag. At last the bandido stopped fighting, and the smell of death rose up to suffocate Cruz.

"Let us leave this place," he said to Luke.

Cruz headed for the stable where he had left his powerful *bayo* stallion. The palomino whickered when he saw Cruz and sidestepped impatiently. Cruz quickly bridled him and led him from the stall.

Luke reached out to run his hand along the palomino's flank. "He's a beauty."

"Yes, he is." Cruz grabbed a striped wool blanket and slung it on the palomino's back, then added a black leather saddle that was beautifully inlaid with silver and edged with tiny silver trinkets that jingled when he rode.

"You seem in a godawful hurry," Luke noted.

"I am." Cruz led the *bayo* out of the stable and mounted him in a single agile move. Once mounted, he fit the high-cantled saddle as though he had been born in it. He pulled his flat-brimmed black hat down low to shade his eyes, then met Luke's solemn, hazel-eyed stare. "*Hasta luego, mi amigo.*"

"Hey! Where you headed?" Luke shouted as Cruz spurred the *bayo* into a distance-eating lope.

Cruz called back over his shoulder, "I am going to collect on a bargain."

Chapter 2

"I HAVE COME FOR MY WIFE."

Rip Stewart leaned back in his rocker on the front porch of Three Oaks until the floorboards creaked. His flinty gray eyes never left the tall, proud Spaniard who stood spread-legged, fists on hips, confronting him. Cruz Guerrero wasn't a man to be crossed. "And who might that be?" Rip inquired.

"Your daughter Sloan."

Rip threw back his head and bellowed with laughter. "You want to back up and try that again?"

"You did not mistake me. I have come to take Sloan to Rancho Dolorosa as my wife."

Rip's auburn hair, tinged now with silver, fell in careless hanks over his brow as he shook his head in disbelief. "There's been some mistake here, son. Sloan didn't say anything to me this morning about going anywhere with you—not as your wife or otherwise.

"I'll admit I made plans with your father before he died to have you marry my youngest girl Cricket. But my eldest daughter Sloan was never part of the bargain. Besides, Juan Carlos called off the deal himself when Cricket ran off and married that Texas Ranger Jarrett Creed. What's this all about?"

"Sloan has agreed to come live at Rancho Dolorosa."

"Like hell she has! Sloan's hip-deep in cotton right now, and that's where she's going to stay. She's already taken off on one wild goose chase this week without a word of explanation, and that's enough. Come back when the cotton's been baled and sent down the Brazos to Galveston, and maybe she'll have time to see you."

Cruz's dominating stance remained as unyielding as granite. "She will come home with me today."

"You care to tell me what makes you so all-fired sure of that?"

"Perhaps it would be best to explain when Sloan is here to answer your questions."

"Perhaps it would be best to explain right now," Rip said, all humor gone from his voice.

Cruz met Rip's stern gaze with icy blue eyes that revealed nothing.

Rip cursed the stroke that had made it awkward for him to rise from his chair with any kind of grace. He wanted to give this young pup his comeuppance. But the stroke had happened, and while Rip could stand with the aid of his oak cane, he chose instead to rely on his imposing physical presence and his sober stare to force the younger man to yield.

The two men faced one another in unspoken challenge, neither backing down.

"Where is she?" Cruz demanded.

For a moment it appeared Rip wouldn't answer. Finally, he said, "Where you might expect my overseer to be. She's out in the cotton fields, making sure the snatching gets done in good time. She'll be back along about sundown."

Rip squinted into the lowering ball of golden fire along the horizon. "It may be a while yet."

"I will wait."

Rip shook his head again. The man had spleen, all right. He had to admit his curiosity was aroused. Why was Cruz Guerrero making such an outrageous claim? When Sloan arrived, the fur was sure to fly. He looked forward to the coming confrontation between this bullheaded man and his strong-willed daughter. "If you're determined to wait, you might as well find yourself a seat."

Cruz looked from the weathered wooden swing that hung on ropes from the porch ceiling, to the rocker that sat next to Rip's. Then he settled himself on the highest of the three porch steps, his long legs stretched out before him. He braced his back against the round pillar that supported the upper-gallery porch.

His gaze narrowed as he sought out Sloan on horseback in the distant cotton fields. If she was out there, she was too far away to be seen with the naked eye. Cruz took a thin cheroot from a pocket in his jacket and lit it, then leaned back to wait.

The only sounds were the creaking of Rip's rocker, the buzz of flies, and the faint harmony of Negro voices that drifted to them on the warm September breeze.

Rip wasn't uncomfortable with the silence, but he had been isolated from his friends during the months he had spent recuperating from his stroke and yearned for the give and take of conversation.

"How was your trip to Spain this past summer?" he asked, smoothly sidestepping the issue of Sloan.

Cruz pulled his rapt attention from the fields and turned to the older man. "I accomplished what I set out to do. I have copies of the royal Spanish decree granting land in

Texas to the Guerrero family. Rancho Dolorosa's claim cannot be challenged now if Texas is annexed by the United States."

"It'll be annexed, all right. Don't you ever doubt it. We've got men in Washington right now convincing legislators it's the right thing to do."

"They have not been very successful so far."

"The American Senate will be voting again soon, and they won't make the same mistake they did in June. Next time they'll ask Texas to become a state of the Union. They have too much to gain and nothing to lose if they do."

"I thought you stood against annexation—that you favored Texas remaining an independent Republic," Cruz said.

Rip harrumphed, uneasy with being caught in any change of opinion, especially one as monumental as this. "I'm entitled to have a change of heart."

"That must mean you think Texas has something to gain from statehood."

"We get federal troops to control those murdering Comanches," Rip spat, "and the protection of the United States against those Mexican bastards who keep testing our southern border!"

Rip felt renewed fury at the memory of how his middle daughter Bay had been stolen by marauding Comanches. She had spent three long years living in a *Quohadi* village as a Comanche war chief's prize possession before she had been rescued by Long Quiet, the half-breed Comanche who had become her husband.

He fairly sputtered when he recalled the tragedy that had struck when Antonio Guerrero had involved Sloan in a plot with the Mexicans to invade Texas. Six months after Antonio's death, Sloan had borne Antonio's bastard son and, to Rip's everlasting fury, had given the child to the Guerrero family to raise.

Rip stared at the Spaniard who had come to lay claim to Sloan. Cruz Guerrero already had his grandson Cisco. He wasn't about to hand over his eldest daughter without a second thought. He took some comfort in the fact that Sloan wouldn't welcome the Spaniard's advances. She had loved his brother—before she had learned to hate him. Rip was certain she would never agree to marry Cruz.

Rip rubbed his square chin thoughtfully. Not that he wouldn't have been glad to have the Guerrero wealth and bloodlines in the family.

Cruz was descended from royal Castilian stock, and the Guerreros had prospered in the New World. Rancho Dolorosa, southeast of Three Oaks along the Brazos River, was the largest cattle ranch in Texas.

When Juan Carlos Guerrero had passed away three summers ago, Cruz had inherited the vast estate that included thousands of hectares of land and the Spanish longhorn cattle that populated it. Cruz might have made a good son-in-law—if his brother hadn't broken Sloan's heart.

In the uncomfortable silence, both men were acutely aware of one another, of the unspoken tragedy that lay between them, and of the tribulations yet to come. The strain increased as the sun slipped beyond the gently rolling landscape, revealing the silhouette of a rider loping toward them.

Cruz stood and ground out his cheroot in the grass at the foot of the steps. Tension thrummed through him as he waited to confront the woman he was ready, at last, to make his wife.

·   ·   ·

When Sloan recognized the tall figure standing in the shade of the moss-covered oaks that shrouded the white frame plantation house, her heart rose to her throat. She had known Cruz would come, but she had hoped it would not be so soon. She had not yet made up her mind what she was going to say to keep him at bay.

She was grateful for the help he had given her at a time when she hadn't known where else to turn. But she didn't want to repay him by becoming his wife—even if it was what she had promised him at the time.

She walked her horse the rest of the distance to the two-story house, taking the extra time to search for an answer she could give to Cruz's demand. It might not have been so bad if she felt nothing for the man. But, however much it chagrined her to admit it, she was attracted to Cruz. If she went to live with him at Dolorosa, she was deathly afraid her attraction might grow into something more.

She refused to take the chance of falling in love again. Love had made her foolish. Love had made her lose control of her life.

Moreover, she had learned enough about Cruz Guerrero to know he would expect his wife to follow his lead. Sloan was not, had never been, a follower.

Yet she knew from her experience with Tonio that a woman in love might do anything. A woman in love was vulnerable. A woman in love went a little crazy.

Sloan had no intention of repeating the experience. She would never give another man the chance to control her through love.

Sloan's eyes never left Cruz's face as she dismounted and walked the remaining few steps it took to reach him.

"Cruz, I—"

Before she had a chance to speak further, he reached out

and drew her into the possessive circle of his embrace. He smelled of soap and sweet tobacco, of horses and leather. She stiffened as her cheek grazed his soft ruffled shirt.

"Well, well, well."

Sloan whipped her head around at the sound of her father's mocking voice, seeing him for the first time in the shadow of the porch. When she tried to back away from Cruz, his powerful arms would not release her.

She put her hands flat against his chest to keep him from drawing her any closer. His heart pounded beneath her fingers, causing her own pulse to race.

She had hoped to avoid involving Rip in her confrontation with Cruz. Perhaps it was not yet too late if she chose her words carefully.

Rip had risen from his rocker and was leaning on his cane, his feet braced wide apart to hold himself steady. "You two look mighty friendly." His eyes narrowed as he added, "Cruz says he's come to take you back to Rancho Dolorosa—as his wife."

Sloan's eyes met Cruz's with an unspoken plea for discretion. "I thought we settled this in San Antonio."

"I said I would come for you," he said, "and I have. I will wait while you pack what you need, Cebellina."

Sloan jerked herself from Cruz's embrace. "I thought I made my feelings clear. I won't—"

"What the hell is this all about, Sloan?" Rip asked. "I want an explanation, and I want it now."

"This doesn't concern you," Sloan retorted.

"Sounds to me like Cruz is ready to cart my daughter off to Rancho Dolorosa—over his shoulder if necessary. That makes it my concern."

"I'm not going anywhere."

"You are my wife," Cruz said. "You will go where I tell you to go."

Sloan avoided the questioning look Rip gave her and said to Cruz, "I can't come with you. I . . . I . . . need more time."

His voice was equally quiet, but adamant. "My part of the bargain is met. Now you must meet yours."

Sloan sought desperately for some other excuse to deny his demand and blurted, "What about the young woman I heard you brought home from Spain with you?"

Cruz frowned. "Señorita Hidalgo?"

"That's the name I've heard."

"She is not your concern."

"Is Sloan your wife or not?" Rip demanded.

"She is."

"I'm not." *Exactly.*

Rip turned on Sloan, his patience gone. "What the hell is going on? And I want a damn straight answer!"

Sloan's lips flattened against making an explanation. "I've said all I have to say on the matter. I've got more work to do before it gets dark, so if you'll both excuse me—"

Cruz's sudden fierce grip on Sloan's arms cut her off. "I will not excuse you. I will not allow you to ignore me or to pretend nothing exists between us. We have an agreement. Alejandro is dead. The time has come for you to finish the bargain."

Sloan shivered, feeling something halfway between fear and anticipation at the words that were both a threat and a promise.

"Let go of my daughter."

Sloan froze when she realized Rip held a Navy Colt Patterson aimed at Cruz. She knew Cruz had seen the gun, but he tightened his hold rather than freeing her.

"I will have you for my wife, Cebellina," he said, his voice a harsh breath that fanned her ear. "Do not doubt it."

He released her and stepped back to meet Rip's dangerous stare with one of his own. "I expect Sloan to come to me within the week. If she does not, I will be back with my vaqueros to get her."

Cruz turned and threw himself onto his palomino stallion. He raked its belly with his spurs and the beast bounded away as though the hounds of hell were chasing him.

Sloan's body trembled with agitation as the dust settled. She was completely unaware of Rip until she heard him slump back into the rocker. She watched her father warily, wondering what he would say now that Cruz was no longer a buffer between them. She didn't have to wait long to find out.

"What kind of claim does he have on you, Sloan? What have you gotten yourself into this time?"

"I don't need you to judge me," she snapped. "I only did what I thought I had to do to get Cruz to take the baby."

"You should have kept the boy."

"It was Tonio's child!"

"It was your child—my grandchild."

"It was a child born of deceit. I would have hated Cisco, though he was faultless. Don't you understand? I couldn't keep him. I was too angry—"

"Peace!" Rip interrupted. "Peace, I say."

Sloan bit her tongue and slowly sank into the rocker next to Rip's. She leaned her head back against the varnished wood and began to rock gently back and forth. The steady creaking sound made by the two rockers soothed the tension between them as the deepening twilight claimed the land.

"Do you plan to go to Dolorosa?" Rip asked.

"I can't be his wife."

"He'll be back."

"I know. Don't worry. I can handle Cruz."

As darkness fell, Stephen, the slave who had managed Rip's household since Amelia's death, when Cricket was still a child, lit the lanterns inside the house. The bright yellow light spilled through the front windows, enabling Sloan and Rip to see each other's faces.

"It's too bad things worked out the way they did. I know you miss seeing your boy—"

Sloan felt her stomach begin to churn at the further mention of her son. "Please. I don't—"

"Don't interrupt me, girl. And don't contradict me!"

Sloan wrapped her arms tightly around herself, but she remained silent.

"I know your sister Bay finally got you and Cisco together this past year at her husband's ranch. I know that about the time you started letting yourself care for your son, he got hurt and nearly died. I also know that as soon as he got well again, you stopped seeing him. I'm sure you had your reasons for that."

Sloan's glance skittered off Rip as she recalled holding her three-year-old son for the first time since she'd handed her day-old baby to Cruz. Cisco's skin had been incredibly soft against her cheek. She had loved the feel of his chubby legs wrapped around her waist and his arms clinging to her neck as he murmured a mixture of English and Spanish childwords at her neck. She had suddenly felt the full brunt of what she had done.

It had been too easy to love her son. When he had been

attacked by a renegade Comanche and nearly killed, she had been thoroughly shaken to realize how devastated she would have been by such a loss.

It had been frightening to realize that even the tender love of a mother for her son was fraught with danger. It was better, she had decided, not to love at all. It seemed the only way to avoid the pain that seemed irrevocably to come along with loving.

"You can't keep ignoring the fact you've got a child," Rip continued. "When you're as old as I am, you realize you don't get a second chance in this life. If I had a son out there somewhere, you can believe he'd know I cared about him."

But he didn't have a son, Sloan mused, which was why she and her sisters had taken the place of sons in her father's dreams. How different things would have been if he'd had even one son instead of three daughters.

Sloan rarely let herself think what her life might have been like if she had not been her father's heir. Would she have been so ready to reject love if she had not been so sure she would always have the demands of Three Oaks to fill up the lonely hours?

Sloan realized she ought to seek out Cruz and speak with him, to settle this matter once and for all. His cause was hopeless. She would never allow herself to love him. And she could never be the willing and obedient wife she was sure he expected her to become.

He would do much better to marry the young woman he had brought home with him from Spain, the one who had a long Spanish name regal enough to be joined with his. She had heard the señorita was unbelievably beautiful . . . and most certainly a virgin.

She turned her head to tell Rip what she had decided

and realized he had fallen asleep. His body was no longer equal to the demands he put on it. The stroke had taken his strength and left him only his will.

In sleep he looked a gentle man, yet she knew he wasn't. He was as hard and uncompromising as the land he had fought to tame. And he had raised her in his image.

Her future was tied to Three Oaks. She loved the land, and it gave her joy to see its burgeoning harvest. Somehow she would convince Cruz Guerrero she had nothing left to give to a man.

Cruz had not anticipated, when he made a personal vow to repay the Republic of Texas for Antonio's treachery, that the Republic would recruit him as a double agent. But it had.

Because of his brother's previous connection to the Mexican government, it had been easy to convince the British government that he was willing to spy on the Republic in order to help Mexico in its dealings with Texas.

Recently, he had been ordered to find out what plans the British government was cooking up with Mexico to interfere with President Houston's plans to get Texas annexed by the United States. When necessary, he was to feed misleading information to the British.

While he was anxious to have Sloan in his household, having her around was going to complicate his work as a spy considerably. If he could have explained everything, he was sure she would have understood and approved his actions. Unfortunately, he was bound to secrecy.

After her experience with Antonio, Cruz was certain that if Sloan got an inkling of his activities, she would draw all the wrong conclusions. Therefore, he planned to speak today with the British agent he regularly dealt with and make certain that the man never came to Rancho Dolorosa again.

Cruz was careful not to be seen entering the upstairs hallway of Ferguson's Hotel. He quickly found the room where he was to meet with his contact, who reported directly to the British minister to Mexico. Cruz knocked twice, waited a moment, and knocked once more.

"Who's there?"

"The Hawk," he murmured, giving the code name the British government had assigned to him.

The door opened, revealing a short, rotund Englishman dressed foppishly in bright-colored silks and satins. Sir Giles Chapman had purposely adopted the foolish clothes as a disguise. Together with his bloodshot eyes and florid jowls, they had kept many a man from discovering the shrewd brain that resided beneath his shiny bald pate. Sir Giles gestured with beringed fingers for Cruz to enter, then checked the hall one last time before he closed the door behind him.

"Do you have your report for the minister with you?" Sir Giles asked, his British accent crisp and authoritative.

"I have written everything down."

Sir Giles nodded his head in distracted acknowledgment as he accepted the missive. He smiled as he finished reading the document. "So. President Houston is still leaning toward keeping Texas an independent nation rather than accepting the offer of annexation from the American government?"

"It appears that way from everything I have been able to learn."

Sir Giles snickered. "Thank goodness Houston hasn't changed his song over the summer. There were rumors . . .

Well, it's good to know that at least we don't have to concern ourselves with trying to delay an offer of annexation from the United States."

"I have not told you anything in this report that your own British chargé to Texas could not have found out for you," Cruz pointed out.

"Yes, but the official version of Texas policy given to our chargé might not have agreed with the version you've given us. And that, my good man, is where your true value lies. I will expect another report next month, or sooner if the political climate changes. Do you understand?"

"But of course."

"Is that all?"

"There is one thing more," Cruz said.

The Englishman raised an inquiring brow.

"I am taking a wife. Since her political sympathies are not precisely in accord with mine, I must ask that you no longer attempt to reach me at my hacienda."

The Englishman pursed his lips. "Can't you control your own wife, sir?"

Cruz ignored the scarcely veiled sarcasm and said, "I have made my wishes known to you. I expect you to abide by them."

"I make no promises," the Englishman said. "In this business, you understand, we must all make allowances for necessity."

"Then make sure it is never necessary to come again to my home," Cruz said. He nodded curtly to the Englishman, turned on his heel, and left the room.

Chapter 3

"YOU PROMISED YOUR FATHER YOU WOULD marry the Hidalgo girl, and now you tell me you cannot! Does the deathbed wish of a dying man mean so little to his eldest son?"

Cruz met his mother's imperious stare with one of his own. "I promised my father only that she would be well wed. And she will be. I will find a husband who will take good care of her."

"Bah! You are the husband for her. Refugia Adela Maria Tomasita Hidalgo carries the blood of kings in her veins, as you do, my son. She is a woman worthy of the Guerrero name."

"I cannot marry Tomasita," Cruz repeated quietly.

"You must get over this foolish notion that you are somehow responsible for Valeria's death, and take another wife. Many women die in childbirth. It is the way of things."

"That does not make it any less a tragedy, Mamá, as you must know."

He did not disabuse her of the notion that it was the memory of Valeria's death that kept him from marrying

Tomasita Hidalgo. He had chosen not to tell his mother about his marriage to Sloan Stewart until he was finally able to bring her to live at Dolorosa as his wife. That would be time enough to meet the objections to the marriage he knew his mother would voice.

Cruz pushed himself away from the mantel and turned to lean a shoulder against the cool, rough stone. He watched his mother's skin tighten unbecomingly across her patrician cheekbones.

Her hair, parted and held in its tight bun at her nape, was still black as a raven's wing and her body was slim and firm, without the gaunt, bony appearance that occurred in many tall women as they aged. Her creamy complexion was unwrinkled except at the corners of her eyes.

Doña Lucia Esmeralda Sandoval de Guerrero looked more youthful than her fifty-three years, too young to be a widow whose household would soon be the province of a younger woman.

He could not help thinking that part of Tomasita's suitability as his wife stemmed from her unresisting obedience to his mother's will. The girl was still very young, and had lived nowhere but El Convento del Sagrado Corazón, the Convent of the Sacred Heart, in Madrid, under the strict censure of the nuns.

Yet he had seen a smoldering streak of rebellion in Tomasita that he felt certain would burst forth in flame if it were fanned even a little. She was malleable now, and mayhap his mother could keep her that way if she became his wife. He doubted it, but he had no intention of finding out. The sooner Tomasita Hidalgo was married—to another man—the better.

"I will find a good husband for her," he said.

"And what of you? Will you not marry and breed up

heirs? Who better than Tomasita to be the mother of your children?" his mother demanded.

"Rancho Dolorosa has an heir. Have you forgotten my brother's son, Mamá? Tonio was your favorite. I have taken his son as my own. Is Cisco not heir enough for you?"

"He is also *that woman's* son," she spat.

Cruz's eyes narrowed to slits and his lips pressed flat in anger. "You will speak of Sloan Stewart with respect."

If Cruz had ever lifted a hand to his mother she might have been cowed by his fury, but although her son's voice was hard, she was willing enough to fight words with words. She dismissed his obdurate stare with an angry wave of her ivory fan.

"Something must be done about *that woman.*"

"She has a name, Mamá."

"I will not have it spoken in this house!"

"This house is mine," he said, his voice harsh with the effort it took to control his temper. "I decide what names will be spoken here."

"Of course," she replied, her pride bringing her chin up another notch. "I see I cannot expect any more consideration for my wishes than you have given to the wishes of your father."

Cruz refused to answer his mother's challenging words with the taunting response on the tip of his tongue. Since his father's death, he had found himself in almost constant conflict with his mother. She wasn't ready to concede the father's place to the son, any more than she was ready to concede her own place to a daughter-in-law.

He had told himself to be patient, that her abiding grief made her say things she did not mean, and that with time she would accept her new role in the household with grace. She needed his support and his solace in this time of change. He would not allow her to goad him into saying something now that he would regret later.

Instead of answering her accusation, he countered, "Are the plans completed for the *fandango* celebration to introduce Señorita Hidalgo to our neighbors?"

"All is in readiness, as you requested. I have invited all the noteworthy families in the area—including the Anglo planters from along the Brazos whom you added to the list—to come and welcome Tomasita."

Cruz noted the disdain with which his mother referred to the wealthy Anglo planters. In the eight years since Texas had won its independence from Mexico in the Battle of San Jacinto, she had not accepted the reality of Anglo dominance in Texas. She had always retained the hope that someday Spain would step in and reclaim Texas. That was never going to happen. Annexation by America was a far more likely fate for the Republic—unless England could somehow manage to forestall it.

For now, Texas was free of oppressive Mexican taxes and military rule. Cruz would do everything in his power to keep it that way for himself and for the children he hoped to have with Sloan Stewart . . . assuming he could bring her to his home and to his bed.

He had hoped to present Sloan as his wife at the *fandango*. His mother's enmity for *that woman* reminded him that she would not have been above "forgetting" to invite Sloan to the *fandango*.

"Did you send an invitation to the Stewart family?" he asked.

"If they were on the list—"

"You know they were on the list." He dug deep for the patience to treat his mother with the respect that was her due and in a calmer voice asked, "Did you send the invitation?"

"I cannot remember," she replied sullenly.

"Then perhaps you should check and make sure," he said, his words both a command and a warning.

Cruz swore under his breath as he felt his shoulders knot with tension. Even if Sloan received an invitation, she probably would prove her independence by staying away.

He reached out to touch the smooth blue Talavera jar that stood in one of the recessed arches found at intervals along the interior walls of his adobe hacienda. Sloan's skin was softer, smoother, than the finish on the delicate jar. He jerked his hand away from the glazed pottery and thrust it through his hair in what had become a habitual gesture of agitation.

His mother's attitude toward Sloan troubled him, yet nothing he said seemed to change it. As far as Doña Lucia was concerned, Sloan Stewart had given herself to a man beyond the bounds of marriage and borne a bastard child. She would never forgive Sloan that transgression, even though the man Sloan had taken to her bed had been her favorite son and the child born of that union was her own grandchild.

He should have told his mother long ago that he was not free to align himself with Tomasita Hidalgo. But he could not—would not—explain his agreement with Sloan to his mother. At the time Cruz had learned of the betrothal contract, Tomasita had still been a child. Cruz had thought he would settle the matter with Sloan long before Tomasita had reached an age to marry.

But things had not gone as he had planned.

Tomasita's father had died and his will had instructed

the Convent of the Sacred Heart to send for Don Cruz Almicar Guerrero to come and claim his bride.

Cruz regretted the circumstances that had kept his relationship with Sloan Stewart in abeyance, because now Doña Lucia had her heart set on becoming mother-in-law to the aristocratic young Spanish woman he had brought home with him from Madrid.

Fortunately, Tomasita knew nothing of the alliance that had been proposed by their fathers, and Cruz had sternly forbidden his mother to tell the girl about it. It was enough for Tomasita to know he was her guardian until she married. For, indeed, he was.

He had asked his mother to plan the *fandango* in the hope that a prospective bridegroom for Tomasita would show himself. After all, once word of Tomasita's beauty spread, he had no doubt the suitors would flock to his door. He planned to watch closely at the *fandango* to see if Tomasita favored any particular man.

Not that the girl could be allowed to make her own choice of husband, but perhaps she would show a preference for some suitable man. He was happy in his own choice of mate, and he wished Tomasita to be happy as well.

"You would be wise to make your claim on Señorita Hidalgo known at the *fandango,*" Doña Lucia said, demanding his attention.

"I have no claim to make."

The sound of running feet on the tile floor suspended their argument.

"Papa! Papa!"

Cruz opened his arms wide as the three-year-old he thought of as his son threw himself forward. He scooped Cisco up and hugged him hard.

"Diablito! What demon is chasing you?" Cruz asked.

"She is coming. Hide me. *Pronto!*" Cisco hid his face in Cruz's shoulder as though that could make his sturdy little body disappear as well.

"Who is coming?"

At that moment the beautiful young woman Doña Lucia wanted Cruz to wed skidded to a halt inside the arched doorway to the *sala*. "Holy Mary . . . I did not know . . . I did not expect . . . we were only . . . Holy Mary . . ."

Cruz watched as the seventeen-year-old he had brought from Spain blushed from her neck to her hairline. She had folded the sleeves up on her elegant blue silk day dress, exposing slender arms. Several buttons had slipped free to reveal the soft white—now rosy—skin at her throat. Her hair had escaped from its neat bun, and silken ebony strands curled at the edges of her heart-shaped face.

She quickly clasped her hands together in front of her and bowed her head, hiding her vivid, sapphire-blue eyes, which had been sparkling with laughter when she had first entered the room.

Cruz felt his heart go out to the girl. She made quite a lovely picture in her disarray. It would have been easy to fall in love with her if his heart had not already been taken. She possessed the joy in life, and the innocent belief in happily-ever-after, that had been stolen from Sloan when his brother had betrayed her.

He opened his mouth to reassure the girl there was no harm done but was preempted by his mother.

"Tomasita, such behavior is totally unbecoming to a woman of your age. You will go to your room immediately!"

"*Sí,* Doña Lucia. I am sorry—"

"There is no need to apologize," Cruz found himself

saying, unwilling to see the girl punished simply for behaving as the child she still was in many ways. "There is no harm done. I am sure Cisco was enjoying the game. Were you not, *niño*?" He ruffled his son's sable locks.

"*Sí,* Papa," Cisco replied, grinning back at Cruz.

"Thank you for your kindness, Don Cruz," Tomasita said demurely. Her head came up, but the moment she caught sight of Doña Lucia's reproving stare, she began backing hurriedly out of the room. "I am sorry to have disturbed you."

Cruz spoke quickly before the girl could flee. "We were finished talking, and it is time for supper anyway. There is no need for you to go to your room. You would only have to leave it again to join us."

He had countered his mother's harshness with leniency because it seemed a shame to curb the girl's natural ebullience. To his surprise, his mother seemed satisfied, rather than annoyed, by his gesture.

He stooped down and set Cisco on his toddler's legs. "As for you, Diablito, it is time to wash up for supper. Where is Josefa?"

"I promised Josefa I would take care of Cisco," Tomasita said, her voice timid and still a bit breathless from running. "She was very busy helping Ana set the table for supper."

"Then I give him over to your safekeeping." Cruz gave Cisco a gentle nudge in Tomasita's direction. "Be a good boy and mind Tomasita."

Cisco turned back and said, "*Sí,* Papa. I like Tomasita. She is more fun to play with than Josefa."

Cruz watched as Tomasita's blush became even rosier. His desire to ease her discomfort made him say, "I have some business to take care of with my vaqueros before supper. I will excuse myself and see you later."

Once Cruz had left the room, Doña Lucia approached Tomasita, who by now had captured a wriggling Cisco in her arms. "I defer to the wishes of my son that you be allowed to dine with us. But before you come to the table, be certain you fix your hair, roll down your sleeves, and button your dress properly. After you have eaten, you will go to your room and you will pray on your knees that you learn to behave with more decorum."

With that, she turned her back on the young woman and made a regal exit through the arched doorway of the *sala*.

When she was gone, Tomasita let out a huge sigh of relief. Doña Lucia's stern admonition reminded her so much of Mother María de los Angeles that she could not help feeling homesick for her life in the convent. Yet she knew she would not have been happy staying there.

To be honest, she had welcomed the rescue—yes, *rescue*—by Don Cruz. For lately she had been guilty of precisely the same rowdy behavior at the convent for which Doña Lucia had chastised her.

No matter how hard she tried, no matter how many Ave Marías or Hail Marys Mother María had made her say on her knees on the hard stone floor of her convent cell, she simply could not seem to act as she should.

Now she was to become a wife. Of course she was not supposed to know about her betrothal to Don Cruz. But she had been sitting in the tree outside Mother María's window and so could not help overhearing Mother María discussing the matter with one of the sisters.

So far, Don Cruz had not mentioned their betrothal even once. She supposed he must be waiting to speak to her until she had become more accustomed to him. She could only thank him for his sensitivity to her feelings.

Because she trembled when she thought of what it would mean to marry Don Cruz, as her father had decreed she must. Don Cruz's face was so forbidding. As fierce as a hawk's. And he was so much older, nearly twice her age.

Yet she could not deny he was very handsome. She admired his deep blue eyes crowned by slashing black brows, his proud cheekbones, his blade of nose, his full lips and slightly cleft chin.

However, the thought of touching him, or any man, terrified her.

At least he was kindhearted. For that, she thanked the Good Lord. If only she did not have to marry him. Perhaps if she spoke to Don Cruz of what was in her heart . . .

But it was childish nonsense to think that her feelings mattered. The decision had been made by her father and by his. It was not as if either she or Don Cruz had a choice.

She would do her duty. She owed her father's memory that much.

Tomasita straightened her shoulders and put a cheerful smile on her face. The day of reckoning had not yet come. Until it did, who knew what the Good Lord had planned for her? She would enjoy each day as He had intended and leave tomorrow's worry for tomorrow.

"Come, Cisco," she said. "Let us go wash up for supper."

Sloan lay in the early morning shade of a cypress on the banks of the Brazos River and watched a hawk catch the warm air on an updraft and soar higher into the cloudless blue sky.

It had been five days since Cruz had come for her. Five

days that she had worried and wondered whether he would actually return for her with his vaqueros.

She had no business lying here doing nothing. As overseer for Three Oaks, she had responsibilities. Nonetheless, she had left old Uncle Billy in charge of the field slaves snatching cotton and come here to think.

She had felt a desperate need to discuss her problem with someone, so she had sent a message to Cricket to see if her youngest sister, who was also her best friend, could come and visit. But Cricket had written back in typical Cricket fashion.

Dear Sloan:

You're never going to believe what's happened. I'm pregnant again! It's a relief to be free of the female miseries for nine months, but like a gooseberry clumperton I'm plagued with morning sickness instead. Needless to say, I'd have to be a picklehead (which I'm not) to take a trip on horseback right now.

Anyway, I know you're going to work out your problem with Cruz just fine on your own. You've always been good at solving problems—think how many you've solved for me and Bay over the years. I'll keep in touch. Let me know how things turn out.

Your pregnant sister,
Cricket

P.S. Creed and baby Jesse send their love.

Sloan sighed. She supposed the pattern of her relationship with Cricket had been set too many years ago for her to change it now.

"Howdy there."

Sloan sprang upright and whirled toward the voice, a Colt Patterson appearing in her hand. "Dear God, Luke! I wish you wouldn't sneak up on me like that. I almost shot you!"

Luke had a sheepish grin on his face and an apology written in his hazel eyes. He pulled his flat-brimmed hat off. His hand automatically reached up to brush back the sun-streaked hair that fell across his forehead. "Sorry about that. Guess that, being a Ranger, sneaking around just comes natural. I'll try to give you fair warning next time. So . . . am I forgiven?"

Sloan gestured toward the ground next to her. "Come on and join me. I could use some company." That was an understatement.

The lanky young man slipped cross-legged to the ground along with Sloan. The Texas Rangers didn't have a uniform, and Luke wore an open-throated dark blue linsey-woolsey shirt and fringed buckskin trousers with knee-high moccasins. He looked totally comfortable on the ground. Once they were both seated, an awkward silence fell between them.

Sloan eyeballed the Ranger sideways. She knew Luke for a steady man, but right now his hands were anything but still. He straightened the brim on his hat, smoothed the snug material across his muscular thigh, then played with the fringe on his trousers. Whatever it was he wanted to say wasn't sitting comfortably on his shoulders.

"Spit it out," she suggested. "I doubt it's going to go down any easier even if you keep chewing on it."

He cleared his throat once before he said, "I decided to take you up on your invitation to visit, but I stopped by to visit Cricket and Creed on my way here. Uh . . . Cricket . . . uh . . . said you were in some sort of trouble."

Sloan stiffened. How dare Cricket reveal her personal business to Luke! Not that Luke wasn't the kind of person you confided in. He was. But choosing to confide in Luke was one thing; having the choice taken out of her hands was something else altogether.

"This is none of your business, Luke. Cricket spoke out of turn."

"I just thought—"

"Don't think! Forget anything Cricket said, and mind your own business."

Luke wanted to tell her this was his business. But she would find that out soon enough. "I only wanted to say if there's anything I can do to help, please ask."

Sloan tore at the grass in front of her, mercilessly shredding each helpless blade. "I don't need any help. I can handle my own problems."

She sounded so much like Cricket, it was eerie, Luke thought. But then, Rip had raised his daughters to take care of themselves. Even soft-spoken Bay had a core of iron down her back, though it had taken several years of living among the Comanches to reveal it.

"All right, Sloan, it's forgotten." He pulled out a stem of seed grass and bit down on the end, sucking the sweet juice while he waited for her to calm down. "How's Rip?" he asked offhandedly.

"Mad as a hornet," Sloan replied.

"Oh?"

"This situation with Cruz has him upset."

"What situation is that?"

"Damn it all, Luke! I said I don't want to talk about this." Sloan laughed at herself and shook her head. "Yet here I am spilling the beans. What is it about you that pries at closed lips like a coon at a crayfish?"

Luke shrugged and let a lazy smile tilt his lips up at the corners.

Sloan sighed and muttered, "Hell, I ought to go ahead and tell you. You know the parties involved, but you don't have a stake in the outcome."

Luke kept his mouth shut and waited for Sloan to make up her mind about what she wanted to do. Patience was something he had learned young, right along with disappointment.

Sloan had kept the secret from everyone for so long, it was hard to speak of it aloud. "Four years ago . . ." She cleared her throat and began again. "Four years ago I went to Cruz and asked for his help. I wanted him to take Tonio's child when it was born. As you know, he agreed, and the Guerreros have raised my son. But Cruz demanded something in return, something that's been a secret between the two of us."

When Sloan paused, Luke said, "You don't have to tell me if you don't want to."

Sloan met Luke's sympathetic gaze and suddenly knew why both her sisters had befriended him. She felt an affinity to the young Ranger she simply couldn't explain. Luke's encouraging smile made it easier for her to continue. "I guess I need to talk with someone, and you're here."

She took a deep breath and said, "Cruz asked that I marry him to legitimize Cisco, so he would bear the Guerrero name."

Sloan glanced at Luke to see if she had shocked him, but Luke's expression was more somber than anything else.

"So Cruz took your son . . . but you never married him?"

"Not exactly."

"What exactly?"

Sloan found it hard to meet Luke's inquiring gaze. She fidgeted with her Colt Patterson as she spoke, splitting it into three parts and then putting it back together again.

She continued, "We signed legal papers naming us man and wife. But we didn't say any vows before a priest. And I made him agree that the marriage wouldn't be . . ." Sloan swallowed. ". . . that he wouldn't touch me until Tonio's murder had been avenged.

"You know the rest. I once told Cruz that if he ever wanted out of the marriage, he could have it annulled. But he never did."

"Why not?"

"How should I know?" Sloan answered irritably. She had never questioned Cruz's motives. She had never understood his demand that she marry him. But she would have done anything to get him to take her unborn child.

Now, years later, she was seeing the fruit of her folly.

"So what's the problem with Cruz that has your father upset?" Luke asked.

Sloan took a deep breath and let it out again. "Now that Alejandro is dead, Cruz wants to make the marriage real. He wants me to live with him at Rancho Dolorosa."

"That sounds fair. But I can see how Rip would be a little upset." Luke snorted, then laughed aloud.

Sloan frowned. She hadn't expected Luke to take Cruz's side in the matter, and she certainly hadn't expected him to laugh at her situation. "What's so funny?"

"I'm sorry, Sloan. I didn't mean to suggest your

problem isn't a real one. But it just occurred to me that your father has made all these grandiose plans for his daughters to carry on at Three Oaks after he's gone, and one by one you're all getting married and leaving. What's he going to do once you're gone?"

"I haven't agreed to go with Cruz," Sloan snapped. "And it's doubtful I will—for precisely the reason you've named. I've spent a lifetime learning to manage Three Oaks. It's my birthright. I've been bred to it. Besides, what would I do as the wife of Don Cruz Almicar Guerrero?"

Luke grinned, revealing strong white teeth that overlapped slightly in front. "I can think of a few things, but I'm not sure you want me to mention them."

Sloan flushed. "No, I don't."

"Don't you want to have a husband and children?"

"I have a husband and a child already."

"Not a real husband. And when was the last time you saw your son?"

Sloan paled. "What good is having a husband if I have to give up Three Oaks?"

"The land isn't everything, Sloan."

"To me it is," she replied quietly. "It's the only thing I can count on."

Luke looked into Sloan's chocolate-brown eyes and saw a kindred soul. She knew the bitterness of betrayal as he did. She trusted no one; nor did he. She was alone, as he was.

The big difference was that she now had a chance to move beyond the tragedy that had scarred her life. Cruz Guerrero was nothing like his brother Antonio.

"I think you're making a big mistake if you don't think twice about fulfilling your bargain with Cruz," Luke said.

"I have been thinking. I've done nothing but think for

the past five days, since he showed up at Three Oaks and gave me an ultimatum—come to Dolorosa or he'd be back with his vaqueros to get me." Sloan brushed a wisp of sable hair from her cheekbone.

"How do you feel about Cruz . . . as a man?" Luke asked.

Sloan shivered. She had been carefully avoiding this subject because the truth was that she found Cruz tantalizing in a way his younger brother never had been. But she wasn't about to admit that to Luke.

"What do you want me to say? He's strong and well formed. He has eyes as blue as the Texas sky and crow-wing black hair." She shrugged dismissively. "He's an attractive man. There's no denying it.

"But he's also arrogant and demanding. He's used to giving orders and having them obeyed. And he doesn't know the meaning of the word *compromise!*"

That last accusation wasn't exactly precise, Sloan admitted, but it was true enough to mean problems if she found herself living with Cruz.

"Have you imagined what it would be like to—"

"I don't want to talk about this anymore."

"How can you choose Three Oaks over a flesh-and-blood man when you won't let yourself consider what the man has to offer you?"

"I've had a man between my legs," Sloan said crudely, hoping to end the conversation. "I can't imagine one is much different from another."

Luke didn't contradict her. She would have to find out the truth for herself. "You could give it a try. Things might work out. Did you ever think maybe you could use someone to lean on once in a while, someone to share your troubles and lighten the load?"

"That's the last thing I need." But Sloan knew the

vehemence of her objection was directly related to the immense appeal of Luke's suggestion.

Luke stood up and brushed the grass and dirt from
the seat of his pants. "Sounds like you have your mind
made up."

Sloan rubbed her palms on the knees of her trousers,
then looked up to meet Luke's penetrating gaze. "I guess
I do."

"I'll be going, then." He wasn't going to try to change
Sloan's mind. But he wasn't going to approve of her decision, either. He swung into the saddle and kneed his chestnut gelding away from the river at a walk.

"Luke . . ."

He reined in his horse and looked back at Sloan over his
shoulder, waiting for her to speak.

"You won't tell anyone, will you?"

"Your secret is safe with me."

"Thanks for listening. I . . . needed . . . someone." It
was a hard thing to admit aloud.

"You're welcome, Sloan. Anytime." He nudged his
horse with his heels and soon left her behind him.

Luke felt a well of anger rising inside him and struggled
to subdue it. He shouldn't care what Sloan Stewart did
with her life, but he couldn't seem to distance himself from
any woman in distress. A legacy from his childhood, he
thought with disgust, when his mother had needed someone to rescue her from the mire and he had been too young
to help. He had grown up as fast as he could, but it had still
been too slow to make a difference.

He wanted to help Sloan, but he debated the wisdom of
interfering. Maybe he would only make things worse. He

had no way of predicting how Rip would react to the message he planned to deliver.

Aw, hell! All Rip Stewart had ever wanted was a son. Knowing he had one—even if he was a bastard—was bound to make a difference.

Luke turned his mount toward the plantation house. There was no time like the present for digging up bitter, long-buried secrets.

Chapter 4

SLOAN SQUARED HER SHOULDERS AND LIFTED her chin to confront her father. "I don't care how many of your bastard sons turn up on the doorstep. Three Oaks is mine! And I don't intend to share it!"

Rip quivered with repressed wrath. He had raised his eldest daughter to know her own mind, and he had never been sorry for it. But it was past time she understood that despite the recent stroke that forced him to lean on a cane for support, he was still the master of Three Oaks.

"Until I'm planted six feet underground, Three Oaks is mine," he thundered. "It will be yours when, and if, I say it is."

"You promised—"

"Whatever promises I made to you came before I found out I had a son."

"You'd give Three Oaks to a bastard son you didn't even know about until this morning, when I've worked my fingers to the bone all my life for this land? You wouldn't dare! This plantation belongs to me. I've earned it!"

"Bastard or not, Luke Summers is my son. If I choose to divide Three Oaks between the two of you, I will."

"You can't! You wouldn't! I would never allow—"

"*You* don't allow anything. *I* make the decisions here," he bellowed.

"Not since your stroke, you haven't," Sloan countered, her voice choked with frustration and fury. "For the past nine months, I've made the decisions. I've run Three Oaks and you've leaned back in your rocker and watched me do it. I have no intention of letting you take it away from me now."

"That's enough!"

"No, it's not enough. I haven't begun—"

Rip's hand streaked out to silence Sloan. He could not bear to hear the truth she spoke, and fear—fear that he was growing older, fear that he was no longer in control—had brought the back of his hand across his daughter's proud face.

He saw the growing red mark on her cheek and knew it would soon be a dark bruise. He felt ashamed, but he offered no apology. He'd had no practice at it in the past and now . . .

He could not explain to her the fears that had prompted his violence. His recent close brush with death had created a fierce need in him to ensure the continuity of Three Oaks. He had counted it nothing short of a miracle when Luke Summers had arrived on his doorstep that morning and announced, "I'm your son."

Even knowledge of Luke's bastardy had not forestalled the surge of emotion Rip had experienced at this devil-inspired answer to the fervent prayers of his youth. He could not help his reaction to the knowledge he had a son. He wanted to give Luke a part of himself. And that meant giving Luke a part of Three Oaks.

Rip knew he was being a tomfool, knew he was acting like a ridiculous old man. None of that mattered.

He had a son.

Sloan's eyes never left Rip's face, so she saw the fleeting confusion and remorse, followed by tight-lipped obstinance. His mind was made up. She closed her eyes to shut out the hopelessness she felt. Her cheek burned as the blood rushed to the spot where Rip had backhanded her.

She hadn't expected her father to strike her—not because it hadn't happened in the past, but because it hadn't happened in so long. Rip had learned years ago that he couldn't intimidate her by using force, so he had stopped trying.

She resisted lifting her hand to her cheek to touch the fiery skin. There was no way to soothe the hurt she felt. What he wanted to do was wrong. She opened her eyes again and saw a giant of a man whose hand trembled on his cane. She knew she should feel sorry for him, but her feelings of betrayal trod hard on her sympathy.

She watched as Rip spread his legs for balance and placed the gnarled oak handle of his cane squarely in front of him, leaning heavily upon it.

"I've asked Luke to come for supper tonight," he said. "I told him we had some talking to do. I plan to offer him an interest in Three Oaks."

"The *hell* you will!"

"The hell I *will*!"

As furious as she was with her father, Sloan was even more angry at Luke. How could he have listened to her problems so sympathetically when all the time he had planned to steal Three Oaks right out from under her nose? She placed her balled fists on her hips. "I won't share Three Oaks."

"You don't have any choice."

"Oh, I have a choice, all right." Her lips thinned in determination that equalled Rip's. "If you're so hell-bent on giving Three Oaks to Luke Summers, go right ahead. Just don't expect me to stick around and be grateful for leftovers."

"What is that supposed to mean?"

"It means that if you go through with this absurd plan of yours, I'll leave Three Oaks and never look back."

"Don't threaten me, Sloan. You've already made it clear you'll have nothing to do with Cruz Guerrero. Where else would you go? What else would you do?"

"I'm well trained as an overseer. There's bound to be someone with a cotton plantation along the Brazos River who'll want to hire me."

"There's not a gentleman planter in Texas who'll have anything to do with you," Rip said. "In case you've forgotten, you're a woman. Not one of them would hire a woman to do a man's job."

Sloan was choked silent by the truth of his words. Rip had made her what she was—a woman with a man's dreams and capabilities—and there was nowhere she could be herself except here at Three Oaks.

Which only made what he proposed to do all the more cruel.

"And don't think you can run away and hide with Cricket and Creed at Lion's Dare or with Bay and Long Quiet at Golden Valley," he continued. "Your sisters have their own lives to lead. You belong here at Three Oaks."

"For how long? Until another bastard of yours shows up to take the rest of what's mine?"

Rip had already raised his hand to strike her again when he caught himself. A look bordering on pain etched his blunt features. "Don't provoke me, Sloan. I'm angry enough with you to do something I might regret. There's nowhere you can go. You'd best bite leather and endure."

Sloan stared defiantly at her father. She would have argued further, except it was clear there was nothing more she could say until she found out how Luke Summers felt about Rip's plans. There was a small chance he wasn't any more willing to possess an interest in Three Oaks than she was to have him acquire one. But she wasn't counting on it.

She was still in shock over the revelation that Luke Summers was her half-brother. Although Rip would not tell her exactly what Luke had said, he had convinced her father of the veracity of his claim.

But if Luke was truly Rip's son, why hadn't he spoken up four years ago, when he had first come to Three Oaks? Why had he waited until now to reveal the truth? What exactly had he hoped to accomplish by telling Rip now that he had a son?

Sloan wanted some straight answers and she intended to have them.

"I've made my stand clear," she said. "Right now I have plantation business that needs tending. I'll see you at supper." She turned on her booted heel and marched from her father's study.

Sloan's stomach was knotted in a fist, and the noon meal of salty ham and biscuits she had just eaten with Rip threatened to force its way back up again. She swallowed hard as she left the house. She looked down at her hands and realized they were shaking as badly as Rip's had been. She grabbed the reins tied to a post in front of the house and stepped quickly into her horse's saddle. The animal sensed her tension and sidestepped nervously.

Sloan refused to give the stallion his head, holding him

to a walk. He fought the bit, dancing under her, heading for the road that led away from Three Oaks, which Sloan used when she took him for a hard run at least once a week.

Rip can't do this.

Of course he can. If Rip never taught you another thing, he taught you that nothing's certain in this life.

Sloan shook her head in disgust. She of all people should be aware of that. Hadn't she learned her lesson from Antonio Guerrero? She remembered vividly the night her sister Cricket had told her Tonio was a traitor, that the Texas Rangers had discovered Tonio's plot and had set a trap to catch him. She had ridden hard to reach him, not believing Cricket's tale.

But she had arrived too late. Tonio had already been killed and his body sent home to his family. She had followed as quickly as she could.

Sloan would never forget the pain in Cruz's blue eyes as she had pleaded with him to intercede with his parents to permit her to see Tonio's body. She heard again his mother's voice raised in anguish and remembered Cruz's flushed face as he had returned and said, "Come with me."

The suffocating smell of incense returned to her, and the feel of Tonio's cold lips as she had kissed him one last time in the candlelit shadows of his bier. She had felt the tears form behind her eyes. But she had not cried.

She shivered at the memory of Tonio's mother, Doña Lucia, regal even in her sorrow, dressed in stark black, her eyes red-rimmed as she clutched a wrinkled handkerchief in her hand. Sloan had offered Tonio's mother the only balm she could.

"In the winter I will bear Tonio's child."

"Ah." There had been a wealth of condemnation in the

Spanish woman's voice. "Do you seek someone to take the bastard child off your hands, Señorita Stewart?"

Sloan had been appalled at Doña Lucia's words. But to her shame, she had eventually fulfilled their prophecy.

She had buried her pain in work. She had tried not to think of her son, or his father. She had loved and nurtured Three Oaks instead.

Rip simply could not take Three Oaks from her now. Not when it was all she had left.

Caught up in the turmoil of her thoughts, Sloan had paid no attention to the direction the stallion took. Without her being quite aware of it, they had gone beyond the borders of Three Oaks and she found herself surrounded by wilderness.

Nothing except sagebrush and an occasional pin oak stood between her and *Comancheria,* the vast land to the north claimed by the Comanches. The sudden awareness of her danger brought Sloan from her stupor, and she yanked the stallion to a standstill.

The stallion fought the bit, demanding his head. Instead of quieting him, she turned him toward home and spurred him hard. Startled, the beast bolted away at a gallop.

Sloan let him run until his chest heaved like a bellows and foamy sweat lathered his chest and flanks. Her eyes teared at the whip of the wind, and the smell of leather and sweat stung her nostrils.

The more tired the stallion became, the harder she pushed him. How far could he run? How long could he last? How soon before the pain became too awful for his great heart to bear?

At last she pulled him to a stop. She slipped from the saddle and, finding her knees weak, clung to the animal's thick black mane. His nostrils flared as he sucked air. He stomped a hoof in agitation. She ran a hand down his foam-flecked, sweat-slick shoulder in an attempt to calm him.

Her eyes felt painfully dry. Rip had beaten the tears out of her long ago. Her chest hurt from the pressure inside as she offered soft words of solace to her horse.

"Take it easy, boy." Sloan took a deep breath and slowly let it out again as she regained a measure of calm. Her face was pinched as she admitted, "I've got a bit too much of Rip in me, I guess, taking my pain out on you."

She spoke in a soothing tone of all she had lost and all she feared to lose. How she felt trapped and saw no escape. How she could no more bear the stinging bit of restraint she expected Cruz to apply if she became his wife than the raking spur of sharing Three Oaks with Luke if she stayed with her father. How her helplessness galled her like a wrinkled blanket under the saddle.

There was no way she could have explained her feelings to Rip. He did not expect it; he would not have approved of it. A Stewart never explained, because a Stewart was never wrong. A Stewart never felt pain, or at least never admitted to it. A Stewart wasn't vulnerable like ordinary human beings.

Only Sloan felt awfully, terribly fragile.

The blasphemous thought of sharing her troubles with someone—with Cruz—had tremendous appeal. But could she really expect the arrogant Spaniard to understand her feelings? More important, would he care enough to try?

The stallion's breathing gradually slowed, and he snorted once or twice before his head came up a bit from the ground. Sloan's stiff muscles protested as she stepped into the saddle again. She had indulged in more than enough self-pity, more than enough groaning and gnashing of teeth. Gripping the reins in a white-knuckled fist, she turned her mount back toward the fields, where the slaves were at work.

She spent the rest of the afternoon concentrating on the cotton harvest as though her life depended on it—her tenuous peace of mind certainly did.

For the first time in three years, the cotton hadn't been attacked by either cut worms or army worms, and heavy rain hadn't driven the surviving cotton bolls into the mud to stain and mold. The harvest was bountiful, a reminder of all she stood to lose.

Sloan was grateful for the deep, melodic voices of the field hands singing as they snatched cotton. There could be no more soothing balm for her jumbled emotions than the old familiar hymns.

By suppertime, as the sun set in vivid pinks across an expansive Texas sky, Sloan was exhausted, her face and neck streaked where sweat had turned dust to mud. She had pledged to Rip that the snatching would get done in time to beat the rainy season even if she had to get down off her horse and pick cotton herself. She would leave her father no opening to say she could not handle the responsibility she had been given. But no more could be done today.

Sloan turned the stallion toward the row of cotton where Uncle Billy worked. "It's getting dark, Uncle Billy. Pass the word."

"Shore 'nuff, Miz Sloan."

Sloan waited as men in shades from caramel-brown to coal-black brought their bags of cotton to be emptied in the baskets at the end of each row.

"You looks tuckered out," Uncle Billy remarked. "You needs to rest some, Miz Sloan."

Sloan gave the burly Negro a wan smile as she lifted her flat-brimmed hat and used a kerchief to wipe the sweat from her brow. "When we get the cotton snatched, we'll all take a rest." Sloan turned the stallion and headed for the house.

"Sun be rising early, Miz Sloan. See you gets those eyes closed 'fore the moon be up, hear?"

Sloan didn't answer. Her thoughts had already leaped ahead to the coming confrontation with Luke Summers. If Rip insisted on her sharing Three Oaks with Luke, she would . . . Well, that was putting the harvest before the planting. It remained to be seen what Luke Summers would have to say about Rip's offer.

As she approached the main house, Sloan saw Luke's chestnut gelding tied in the shade of the live oaks. She shrugged her shoulders in an attempt to loosen the sweat-dampened gingham shirt from the places where it stuck to her skin. She wanted a bath. Her lips twisted wryly as the smell of her own sweat rose up to greet her. She also *needed* a bath. Stephen would have already placed the tub in her room and filled it with steaming water. There was no reason why she couldn't take time to rinse off the grime of the day before she fought any more battles.

Sloan heard the murmur of voices in the study on the left as she quietly ascended the stairs in the central hallway that divided the house.

Coward!

The voice shouting inside her head stopped her halfway up the stairs. She was not avoiding a confrontation, merely delaying it, she reasoned in response. She took another step.

Coward! the voice shrieked again.

If there was one thing Rip had instilled in her from the day she was born, it was courage. She was his brave girl. She was his strong one. She must never be afraid. She must face her fears and conquer them. To show vulnerability was to be weak. To show weakness was to lose everything. She knew what she was. And she was no coward. She took another step.

Coward!

Sloan gripped the polished oak banister with a strength that left her hand aching. Then she turned and walked back down to Rip's office, pushed the door open and entered the room. When she did, Luke Summers rose and turned to face her.

He stiffened as soon as he saw her face. "Where'd you get that bruise?"

"None of your business!" she snapped.

Rip flushed as Luke's steely gaze shifted to him. But Sloan offered no further explanation, nor did Luke ask for one.

Somehow Luke looked even taller, Sloan thought, even more intimidating, in Rip's masculine office. This man was her father's son, her half-brother. Yet she noticed Luke and Rip were not much alike, physically.

Luke was whipcord lean, while Rip was a massive, barrel-chested man. She looked for traces of Rip in Luke's features but found little of her father. Only the strong, square jaw was the same. Luke must have taken after his mother. Sloan had to concede she must have been a beautiful woman.

Because she and Luke were of a similar age, Sloan had figured out that her mother must have been pregnant with her at about the same time Luke's mother had been pregnant with him. It appeared Rip had not been a faithful husband. She wasn't sure how she felt about that.

She had never thought about it much, but in all these years she had never seen her father with a woman. Oh, she knew he must have sought out women for his needs, away from the plantation.

But suddenly she wondered why he had never married again—especially if once upon a time there had been another woman besides Amelia in his life.

Sloan nodded briefly to Luke. His eyes seemed to reach out to her, to ask her to take his side. She couldn't afford to do that. She hardened her expression and turned away, afraid she would succumb to whatever it was about her half-brother that had caused her to befriend and confide in him. She paled at the thought that he might not keep her secret as he had promised.

"Sit down and join us," Rip commanded.

Sloan headed for the other vacant chair across from her father. She met Luke's eyes briefly as the two of them sat down and saw a measure of distress that surprised her. She leaned back in the rawhide chair and rested one ankle against the opposite knee, giving a casual appearance at odds with the tension rippling inside her.

Rip took a sip of brandy from the crystal snifter he had been rolling with uncharacteristic nervousness between his palms. "I've been telling Luke that I'd like him to think about staying on at Three Oaks for a while."

"And what did he have to say to that?" Sloan asked.

"I said I'd think about it."

Sloan realized that Luke wasn't about to let her pretend he wasn't there. Yet she directed her next comment to Rip alone. "Just what, exactly, did you have in mind for Luke to do here at Three Oaks?"

"Whatever needs doing. The harvest is backbreaking work for anyone, and you've had more than your share of problems this year."

"I haven't complained," Sloan replied, carefully controlling her voice to keep out the irritation she felt.

Rip flashed a look at Sloan's pale, bruised face and grimaced. "Of course you haven't. That doesn't mean you haven't had problems."

"Nothing I can't handle," she persisted.

"I don't want to take Sloan's place at Three Oaks," Luke said. "I don't have the experience—"

Rip cleared his throat, interrupting Luke's speech. "What you don't know, you'll learn. I'll teach you myself."

"That's a generous offer," Luke said. "But when I came here this morning, it wasn't what I had in mind."

"What did you have in mind?" Sloan asked, her voice sharp with accusation.

Luke met Sloan's stare without wavering. For an instant he let down his guard and she saw confusion and—? Bitterness? Hate?

Luke's voice when he spoke was bare of the volatile emotions she had seen flash in his eyes. "I just wanted Rip to know he's my father."

Luke turned his gaze back on Rip, and for the first time since she had come into the room, Sloan was aware of a treacherous undercurrent between the two of them. Evidently, more words had passed between them than she had been told about.

Did Luke Summers have some hold over Rip that had forced her father into offering a part of Three Oaks to his bastard son? To Sloan's knowledge, Rip had never been coerced into anything. What could the young Texas Ranger possibly have said that would have made her father want to keep him here at Three Oaks?

Then she became aware of something else.

They're both in pain.

It was a startling thought, and an uncomfortable one. Sloan didn't want to feel sorry for either Luke or Rip. Between them, they were turning her life upside-down.

She clenched her fists against the softness welling up inside that urged her to offer comfort. She had to stop behaving like some simpering female. She had to think about her future—about Three Oaks.

"If Luke says he doesn't want anything to do with Three Oaks, then I think you ought to respect his wishes," she said.

"Whether he wants it or not, half of Three Oaks is his," Rip announced.

"I don't want half of this place," Luke replied evenly.

Sloan enjoyed a moment of relief before Rip said, "All right, then, three-quarters."

Sloan gasped.

"I don't want three-quarters, either," Luke said in a steely voice.

Sloan held in the cry of despair that begged for release. Surely Rip could not, would not, offer more.

"All of it, dammit! I'll make you my heir."

"No!"

Sloan and Luke had shouted the word together as they bounded to their feet, but in desperation, Rip kept talking. "I would have offered it all in the first place if you'd just said that was what you wanted."

"Wait!" Sloan cried.

"Wait for what?" Rip slammed down his brandy glass

and grasped his cane. "Luke is my son. He's entitled to Three Oaks."

"You can't do this!"

Rip met Sloan's desperate look with defiant eyes. "Luke will inherit Three Oaks. Of course, you'll always have a place here for as long as you live."

Sloan's heart pounded. Her throat constricted. She blinked to remove the film that kept her eyes from focusing. "*A place here . . .*" The words came out in a raspy whisper. She swallowed hard and tried again. "*A place here as long as I live?*"

"You'll always have a home here," Rip corrected. "I wouldn't take that away from you."

Sloan felt the fury building inside her. "And you think that's enough? You think that will satisfy me?" She laughed, a harsh sound. "How little you know about me! I told you I'd have it all or I'd leave. And I meant it!" She headed for the door in a hurry.

With the aid of his cane, Rip struggled to his feet, needing to stop her, frustrated by his unresponsive body. "Hold it right there! We both know you have nowhere to go."

Sloan whirled and gave her father the full brunt of her wrath. "The hell I don't!"

"Who'll take you in? Think, woman!"

"Cruz Guerrero," Sloan snapped in brash challenge to his will. "Cruz will welcome me with open arms."

Sloan had turned and taken two more steps when Rip said, "Maybe you won't be quite so welcome at the Guerrero hacienda as you think."

Sloan paused, halted by the cat's cream in Rip's voice. "Why is that?"

Rip took his time walking to his desk, riffling through papers until he found the one he wanted. He took a limping step or two toward Sloan and held the paper out in his hand.

Sloan stared at the parchment but made no move to take it. "What is that?"

"It's an invitation to a party. It says that Don Cruz Almicar Guerrero requests the pleasure of your company at a *fandango* to introduce Señorita Refugia Adela María Tomasita Hidalgo of Madrid, Spain, to his friends and neighbors. It seems she'll be living at the Guerrero hacienda." Rip threw the paper back onto the desk.

"When were you planning to tell me about this invitation?" Sloan demanded.

"I only got it yesterday."

Sloan's blood froze at the implications of such an invitation coming after Cruz had given his ultimatum.

Rip continued, "I didn't think you had time in the middle of the harvest to attend a party."

"Well, that's certainly not a problem any longer, is it?" She smiled in a way that revealed her teeth but didn't in the least convey pleasantness. Meanwhile, her mind was racing to determine whether Cruz had changed his mind and decided to take the more respectable Spanish señorita as his bride.

But she had backed herself into a corner. She had no choice now except to seek him out.

It was Luke who broke the vibrating silence that had fallen on the room. "If anyone leaves Three Oaks, it should be me."

Rip tore his eyes from Sloan's white face to meet Luke's troubled eyes. "You're my son. You'll stay here and take care of your birthright."

"What about me?" Sloan whispered. "What about my birthright?"

A flicker of guilt crossed Rip's face before his blunt features hardened. "There's no reason why you can't continue here as before. You're an excellent overseer."

Sloan's incredulous laughter echoed off the high ceiling. It was the first time Rip had admitted she was doing a good job, but somehow this wasn't the way she had expected to hear it. The grating, angry voice sounded nothing like her own. "When you come to your senses, you'll find me at the Guerrero hacienda."

She fled before Rip could say anything more.

Rip's eyes glittered as he stared at the empty doorway. He turned to face his newfound son. "You have no choice except to stay now, Luke. With Sloan gone, I have no one else to oversee the harvest."

"You can do it yourself."

Rip gripped the cane that was keeping him on his feet. "I'm a cripple, son."

Luke flinched at Rip's offhanded claim of paternity. "You're healthy as a bull."

"A crippled bull," Rip agreed. "I can't carry the burden of Three Oaks alone. It's likely to take some time for Sloan to come to terms with my decision . . . and with what she finds waiting for her at Dolorosa." He rubbed his temple as though it pained him. "I need your help, son."

Luke hissed in a breath of air and let it out. "I'll stay, you manipulating son of a bitch. But only until Sloan makes up her mind whether or not she wants to remain with Cruz."

Before Luke could leave, Rip reached out a hand and caught his sleeve. "Wait . . ."

"What for? I think everything's been said."

"Your mother . . . will you tell her . . . I'm sorry?"

Luke sneered. "Little good that will do her now. She's dead."

Rip's face blanched. "I loved your mother, Luke . . . but she wouldn't marry me without her father's approval . . . and he refused to give it."

"You deserted her when she needed you most."

"I never knew she was pregnant!"

"When her family turned away from her, my mother sold her body to support me."

"Why didn't she just ask me for help?" Rip asked in an agonized voice.

"You had already married another woman."

Rip released Luke's sleeve to rub his temple again.

"My mother died a penniless, diseased whore. But you have a son, Rip. You have a goddamn son!"

Luke was gone from the room before Rip had a chance to reply.

Chapter 5

OF ALL THE GREAT MISTAKES SLOAN HAD MADE in her lifetime—loving Antonio, giving up her son, the bargain with Cruz—this was among the worst. She should never have left Three Oaks. After all, possession was nine-tenths of the law.

She had walked out with her pride intact, but she had given up everything she had worked for all her life. If she had stayed at Three Oaks, she would have been in a much better position to defend her claim.

She had no excuse for her flight except that she had been too shocked, too angry, too bruised in heart and soul to behave with her typical rationality. Her hindsight was clear as a spring-fed pool, but in a frontier as merciless as Texas, a body seldom got a second chance.

The hell of it was, she was sitting on her horse in the middle of the Atascosito Road without the vaguest idea which direction she should take. She had told Rip she would be at the Guerrero hacienda, yet she really didn't want to go there. Rancho Dolorosa held too many reminders of the painful past.

But she didn't have many alternatives. She could never

impose on her sister Bay. Her relationship with her middle sister, which had only become something more than tolerance in the past year or so as they had each matured, was too fragile to handle the stress of such close quarters. Besides, the two-room adobe ranch house Bay shared with Long Quiet and their son, Whipp, was too small to house a guest.

She knew Cricket would welcome her with open arms at Lion's Dare, and it was tempting to accept her youngest sister's hospitality. Cricket's sense of humor would no doubt provide a ready salve for her battered feelings.

But Sloan could not bear the thought of admitting to Cricket how badly she had botched things. Running to her youngest sister for sympathy would make her feel like a whipped dog slinking home with its tail between its legs. She would never get over the humiliation of it.

She knew it was lunacy to let mere pride stand in the way of help, but there it was, and she found it an insurmountable barrier.

It was a waste of time to consider seeking work as an overseer for someone else's plantation. Rip was right. No Texan would hire a woman to fill such a role.

There was no other acceptable choice. She would have to go to the Guerrero hacienda.

She told herself it was only a temporary measure while she figured out how to convince Rip he had been a harebrained idiot to disinherit her. All she needed was a place to stay for a while.

Despite her reluctance to confront the ghosts of the past, and her reluctance to spend time near her son, she rode steadily all day and on into the dark toward the one sanctuary that promised solace.

Sloan groaned in dismay when she reached the fortress-like walls that surrounded the Guerrero hacienda and discovered a celebration in progress. She hadn't paid much attention to the parchment Rip had thrust at her, but she had apparently arrived in the middle of the *fandango*.

Gay lanterns strung across the central courtyard reflected off the water sparkling in the tile fountain. Ladies in elaborate satin dresses dotted the courtyard like a colorful flock of birds, but their amiable chatter grated on her ears like the raucous cawing of jays and crows. The aroma of beef roasting over a fire reminded her she hadn't eaten since noon.

She searched for someone she recognized who would allow her access to the hacienda so she wouldn't have to be seen dressed as she was, in her travel-worn planter's garb. Her body went rigid as her eyes lit on the tall, raven-haired Spaniard who wanted her for his wife.

Cruz wore a waist-length sapphire-blue jacket that strained over muscular shoulders and snug black velvet pants that hugged him like a second skin, emphasizing his flat belly, his maleness, and the length of his legs. His ruffled white shirt was the only hint of softness to break the hard, proud lines of his body.

But it wasn't his blatant masculinity that made her pause. It was the way his hawklike features focused on the vision of loveliness dancing in his arms.

They moved slowly, their bodies separated by the appropriate distance but seeming intimate nonetheless. The señorita smiled shyly at Cruz and he smiled warmly back at her, his white teeth flashing in the lantern light.

Sloan could find nothing to fault in the looks of the young woman dancing with Cruz. She was dressed elegantly, her sky-blue silk gown cupping full breasts and showing off a tiny waist before it belled over legs that had to be nearly as long as Cruz's. It had to be the Hidalgo girl. No wonder Cruz had brought her back from Spain. They fit together so well.

The hard, quick stab of jealousy surprised her.

I don't care. I have no right to care.

The only thing binding her to Cruz was an agreement, words on paper to give his nephew the proud Guerrero name. So why did she feel as though she had just been pressed through the baling screw?

Sloan grunted in disgust at her thoughts. She had followed her feelings with one Guerrero brother, and look where they had gotten her—pregnant and widowed before she was a wife. She wouldn't make that mistake again.

She shunted aside the unaccustomed feeling of jealousy. She had told Cruz she did not want him. This was no time to be having second thoughts.

But she couldn't help worrying what Cruz would say when she told him she wanted to stay for a while at Rancho Dolorosa—but not as his wife. Would he turn her away?

"What are you doing here tonight, Señorita Stewart? Your father said you were busy with the harvest and could not come."

Sloan summoned her dignity and turned to face Cruz's mother. Before she could deny that she had come to attend the celebration, Doña Lucia was speaking again.

"I suppose you could not resist coming to meet Cruz's *novia.*"

Sloan stiffened. "Cruz's fiancée?"

"My husband arranged her betrothal to Cruz years ago. Is she not beautiful? Such milk-white skin, not a bit browned by the sun. Such beautiful blue eyes, such a winsome smile. And as tall as my son. See how he does not need to bend at all to speak with her?"

Sloan turned and saw very well that the señorita was a better match for Cruz's height than was her own five feet four inches. She watched as Cruz flashed a smile and lifted the señorita's hand to his lips.

"It will be a most proper match. She is a distant cousin, far removed, but she bears the same royal Castilian blood that flows in my son's veins. Would you like to meet her?"

Sloan was still too much in shock at Doña Lucia's announcement that Cruz had brought back a fiancée from Spain to relish the thought of spouting polite amenities. How could Cruz have demanded she become his wife under such circumstances? She refused to let Doña Lucia believe she was the least bit distressed by her news, which would surely be the case if she begged off. She squared her shoulders and said, "I'd love to meet her."

It took the tap of Doña Lucia's fan on her son's shoulder to draw Cruz's attention away from the young woman. "You have a visitor, my son."

Sloan was grateful for the evening shadows that hid her expression when Cruz turned to see who it was. She fought to control her pulse as he lifted her sun-browned, callused hand to his lips.

"Cebellina! How pleased I am that you decided to come."

Sloan swallowed, suddenly struck dumb by the pleasure she saw in Cruz's blue eyes and heard in his voice. "I . . . I . . . that is . . ."

Cruz kept her hand in his as he drew her forward and said, "Cebellina, I wish to present Señorita Refugia Adela

María Tomasita Hidalgo. Tomasita, this is my . . . my very dear friend, Señorita Sloan Stewart."

The young woman respectfully nodded her head to Sloan and said in beautifully accented English, "Please, call me Tomasita. Don Cruz told me so much about you on our journey from Spain that I think of us already as friends, Señorita Stewart."

"Call me Sloan, please."

Tomasita smiled. "If you wish."

It was a smile of warm welcome and acceptance and therefore completely confusing to Sloan, who had expected this high-bred Spanish woman to be as arrogantly condescending to her as Doña Lucia was.

"I hope your journey to Texas was a pleasant one," Sloan said.

"Don Cruz has been more than kind." Tomasita's lashes lowered to conceal her expressive eyes, even as her hand timidly touched Cruz's sleeve. "I do not know what I would have done if he had not arrived when he did."

Cruz dropped Sloan's hand and covered the slender fingers resting on his sleeve. "You have nothing to fear ever again, little one."

Sloan watched as Tomasita raised her lashes to reveal wide blue eyes that gazed shyly at Cruz. In the next instant, Tomasita turned to Sloan and said, "You are not yet dressed for the party. Shall I take you to a room where you can bathe and change?"

Sloan found herself liking the young woman, who had extended only courtesy and friendliness to a stranger. "I need to speak privately with Cruz for a moment."

"My son is—"

"Excuse me, Mamá," Cruz said. "Will you please take

Tomasita to get a glass of punch while I speak with Sloan?"

He had phrased it as a question, but when Doña Lucia responded with tightly pressed lips, Sloan realized that it had actually been a polite command.

A moment later, Cruz had slipped his hand under Sloan's elbow and was guiding her inside the hacienda, where they could be alone.

They crossed the covered wooden veranda and entered the *sala*, the Spanish version of a Texas parlor. Sloan was struck again by the mixture of delicate Moorish spooled tables from Spain and heavy wooden furniture crafted by the Mexicans to sustain the rigors of the New World. Candlelight reflected off the white walls and made shadows of the numerous recessed arches around the room.

Cruz led her to a heavy rawhide chair near the stone fireplace that took up one whole wall of the room, and bade her sit down.

"I would rather stand."

"As you wish. I am glad you came, Cebellina."

When Cruz reached out to replace a wayward strand of her hair, his knuckles accidentally brushed against Sloan's bruised cheek. She winced at the pain of even that slight pressure on the tender flesh.

"What is this?"

"Nothing." Sloan instinctively covered her cheek with her hand. She realized her mistake and quickly stuck her hand in her pocket. But she saw that she had only increased Cruz's suspicions.

"It's nothing," she repeated.

Cruz reached out and captured her chin, turning her face so her cheek was fully exposed to the candlelight. She watched his eyes narrow and his cheeks pale as his thumb skimmed the dark bruise on her face. "Who would dare to do this?"

She bit her lip and held still in his grip, uncertain what he would do if she tried to escape and unwilling to test his temper right now.

"Who?" he demanded.

"Rip and I had a disagreement. It's nothing to fuss about. The bruise will go away in a few days." She tried a wry grin, but winced when it reached her bruised cheek. "Believe me, I know. It's happened before."

"But it will not happen again. You belong to me now, and I protect what is mine."

His hand circled her nape under her hair and he tilted her face up to his. Sloan shivered at the low animal threat in his voice as he continued, "You will not return to Three Oaks."

"You presume too much!" But her voice came out in a whispered croak that was somewhat less than convincing.

Sloan would have laughed at the absurdity of the situation, except she was afraid she might become hysterical. Cruz's authoritarian announcement rankled, but at the same time, she could hardly defy him and return to Three Oaks under the circumstances. The feeling of being trapped returned.

Sloan freed Cruz's hand from its disturbing caress. When he started to reach for her again, she grabbed both of his hands and held them in front of her. Never having held his hands before, she was surprised at the size and strength of them.

She looked up earnestly at him. "I didn't come here to fulfill our bargain, Cruz." She immediately felt the tension in his hands and quickly continued, "But I do need your help."

"You know you only have to ask, and anything I have is yours."

Completely unnerved by her body's tingling reaction to his touch and the husky sound of his voice, Sloan sought some way to break the growing spell between them. "Won't you need to talk with Tomasita first?"

Cruz frowned. "Why should I want to speak of such things to Tomasita?"

She pulled her hands from his. "There's no need for any more pretense, Cruz. Your mother told me."

"Told you what?"

"That you're betrothed to Tomasita. That you have been for several years."

Cruz's indrawn breath made Sloan feel as though the air had been sucked from her own lungs.

"Mamá speaks of her dreams as reality."

"Did she dream your betrothal?"

Cruz sighed deeply. "That much is true. When your sister Cricket ran away to marry Creed, my father was furious. He still needed the gold your father had promised him as a dowry if she married me . . . and so he sought it elsewhere.

"Meanwhile, I made my vows to you. My father did not tell me until he was on his deathbed that he had arranged my betrothal to the daughter of an old and dear friend."

Cruz reached out again to lift Sloan's chin, so she had no choice except to look into his eyes. "I promised my father only that Tomasita would be well wed, not that I would marry her myself. She is only seventeen. She would have lived her life out among the sisters in the convent if I had not brought her back with me from Spain.

"You must see I had no choice. I could not leave her there." He searched Sloan's face for understanding.

"Does Tomasita know . . . about us?"

"Of course not! And she knows nothing of the betrothal, either. She knows only that I am her guardian," he admitted gruffly. "She will, of course, remain my responsibility until I can find her a suitable husband."

Sloan wasn't sure what to think. She had seen the looks exchanged by Cruz and Tomasita. Maybe he would rather have the younger woman after all. "I've never wanted to hold you to our bargain. I never thought it was fair to you, anyway. If you want to marry Tomasita, I won't stand in your way."

Cruz slanted his thumb across Sloan's mouth to silence her. "I am happy with things as they are. I already have a wife. Just because you have denied me the right to take you to my bed does not make our vows any less sacred."

He bent his head slightly and his lips grazed hers. By the time Sloan tensed, his lips were gone. She avoided Cruz's eyes, afraid of what she would see there, focusing her gaze instead on the frogged braid that trimmed his velvet coat.

The touch of his lips had left her heart pounding. What was it she feared? She could not name it. She only knew there was danger if she stayed near him. Yet she had nowhere else to go. She tried to find words to put the barrier back between them.

"I can never be more to you than a friend. Your brother—"

"—was a fool."

"—was my lover. The father of my child."

Cruz swallowed the urge to shout, "It does not matter what you were to my brother!" It mattered. It wounded him to know she had loved his brother in a way she could never love him. He had fought the vision of Tonio lying next to her, touching her. He'd had honor enough not to try and take her from his brother, but that had not stopped him from wanting her.

"I can wait a little longer to take what is mine," he said quietly. He did not have to say more to know that Sloan understood him.

"Can you tell me what made your father so angry that he struck you?" Cruz asked.

"I told him I wouldn't share Three Oaks."

Cruz frowned.

Sloan sighed and explained, "Rip found out Luke Summers is his bastard son. He's made Luke heir to Three Oaks."

Sloan met Cruz's eyes and couldn't bear the sympathy she saw there. He understood what losing Three Oaks meant to her. She had already chosen Three Oaks once before over a husband and a son. Battling her urge to weep, she forced her chin up another notch and crossed her arms under her breasts.

"My coming here doesn't change things between us. I'll only be here until Rip . . ." Her voice was strained with the effort to talk. "Our bargain was made in the dark of night. It can be ended the same way. I will never . . ."

Cruz did not give her a choice about accepting his comfort. He merely enfolded her in his arms. He laid his face against her cheek and held her until her trembling had eased, and she was once more in control.

"I will have your things brought here and ask Mamá to help you get settled," he said.

"I'll only be here—"

"Do not think of going away. Think only of the pleasure you bring me by staying."

Cruz ignored the desolation he saw in Sloan's eyes. For

years he had lived in the belief that someday she would come to him. She was finally here. And she would never be leaving Dolorosa—or him—again.

"Rest tonight, Cebellina. Tomorrow we will talk. I will send Mamá to you as soon as I can."

Sloan stared after him until he was gone. What had she done? What if he decided not to let her go? He could do it. As her husband, he had absolute power over her. No man would say him nay.

She realized she would have to trust him not to hold her against her will. Sloan shivered. It was a frightening thing, to trust a man.

When Doña Lucia appeared in the doorway, Sloan didn't have to hear words spoken to know she wasn't welcome in the other woman's home. "Follow me, Señorita Stewart."

Sloan's heart began to race when she realized where Doña Lucia was leading her. "I can't sleep here."

Doña Lucia turned, her eyes narrowed in dislike. "I do not want you in Antonio's room either. But Tomasita is staying in the guest room and I have no other bed to offer. It will only be for one night."

Sloan held her tongue. She would leave it to Cruz to explain things to his mother. Anything she said now would only open the floodgates of ill will that existed between them. For the sake of Cruz's generous offer of hospitality, she determined to make an effort to avoid ruffling Doña Lucia's high-flown feathers.

"I will have Josefa bring you some water to bathe."

"*Gracias*," Sloan said.

"Do not thank me, señorita. I do this for the sake of my son. Soon he will be married to a woman worthy of him, and the son you abandoned, my grandson, will have a suitable mother to care for him."

Sloan blanched at Doña Lucia's cruel taunt but, in a supreme effort of will, said nothing. It was clear from the older woman's grim-lipped smile that she knew her barb had found its mark. The gauntlet had been thrown, and Sloan was more than willing to pick it up—but not tonight. Too much had already happened that day.

"Good night, Doña Lucia," Sloan said in a steady voice.

"*Buenos noches,* Señorita Stewart." Having come away triumphant from the first sortie, Doña Lucia was perfectly willing to depart the field of battle. She closed the door quietly behind her.

Sloan was still quivering with indignation when she sank down onto the huge bed. Almost instantly, a servant knocked at the door carrying her carpetbag. He then brought a wooden tub, which the maid Josefa filled with hot water.

Sloan accepted Josefa's help, and within an hour had bathed, dressed in a clean chambray wrapper, eaten a light supper that Josefa had gotten for her from the kitchen, and was in bed with the sheets tucked around her.

She closed her eyes, exhausted, but found she couldn't sleep. A thousand thoughts and not one solution. Was there any chance Luke would disgorge what Rip was forcing down his throat? Meanwhile, how should she act toward Tomasita? Or Cisco? Or Doña Lucia? Not to mention Cruz. Exactly how was she expected to occupy all her empty hours here at Dolorosa?

And where on earth was she going to go from here if Rip didn't change his mind?

•   •   •

Sloan was drifting between wakefulness and sleep but had
the oddest sensation of being watched. When she opened
her eyes, it took a moment to realize where she was. When
she did, she sat up abruptly and discovered she was indeed
being watched.

"*Buenos días,* Mamá."

For an instant, Sloan couldn't breathe. She had not seen
Cisco since January—nearly nine months ago. It was sur-
prising he even recognized her. Then she realized someone
must have told him she was here. She couldn't think of a
thing to say that wouldn't have encouraged the little boy to
come closer, so she said nothing.

"Papa said you have come to live with us."

"Uh . . . for a little while, yes."

Sure enough, as soon as she spoke, it released some sort
of restraint and Cisco headed toward her. The instant he
started to climb up onto the bed, she scrambled off the
other side. "I haven't slept so late for a long time. I guess I
should get dressed," she said.

She turned her eyes away from the confused look on her
son's face when he managed to reach the middle of the bed,
only to find her gone.

He started crawling across the bed toward her again.
"Do you want to see my pony?"

"Uh . . . I don't . . . uh . . . maybe later." Sloan headed
for the dresser on the opposite side of the room, aware that
she was playing an awkward, pitiful game of chase with
her son. But she had no intention of getting caught.

It had nearly killed her to leave him in January. She
wasn't going to let herself get attached to him again in the
brief time she planned to be at Dolorosa. Keeping a distance between them was all she could think to do.

She turned from thrusting her fingers through her tangled hair in time to see that Cisco had managed to climb off the bed and was heading for her as fast as his three-year-old legs could carry him. In a matter of moments he would be reaching out his arms to be picked up. Sloan stared at him in an agony of indecision.

At that instant, the door to the room swung open.

"There you are, Diablito," Tomasita said. "I have been looking for you everywhere."

Realizing he had been caught, Cisco giggled mischievously and turned and ran for the bed, climbing up and scooting under the bedcovers to hide from Tomasita.

Tomasita smiled apologetically to Sloan. "I promised Doña Lucia I would not let him bother you this morning. I will take him away so you can finish dressing."

Before Sloan could protest, Tomasita had retrieved a squirming, laughing Cisco from beneath the covers. The little boy wrapped his legs around Tomasita's waist and cupped her face in his hands to get her attention. "I want to stay and play with Mamá."

"But we promised to help Ana make *buñuelos*. Did you forget?"

Cisco looked over his shoulder at Sloan, who could see he was torn between staying or having a chance to eat some of the crisp, cinnamon-sugar-coated tortillas.

"Go with Tomasita now," Sloan urged. "I can go see your pony another time."

Thus appeased, Cisco was happy to leave with Tomasita.

Alone in the room, Sloan sagged onto the bed. She felt her face contorting and turned to grab a pillow, hugging it against her mouth so no one would hear the sobs she felt building in her chest. She jumped up, still hugging the pillow, and paced the room, fighting the ache in her chest, the constriction in her throat, and the tears burning behind her eyes.

I can't bear it! Please, God, do something! It hurts too much.

She paused at last to stare at herself in the cheval mirror, and froze when she saw another face join hers in the glass.

Chapter 6

"GO AWAY," SHE MUMBLED, HER VOICE MUFFLED by the pillow she had pulled up to cover her face.

"Cebellina?"

"Go away, Cruz."

He grasped her shoulders and turned her around to face him. She pulled the pillow down far enough to see the amused and curious look on his face, crossed her eyes, and then raised the pillow again.

"You're even more beautiful in the morning," he said.

Sloan chuckled at his facetious response to her crossed eyes and lowered the pillow completely from her face. "You're a terrible liar, but thanks."

As his eyes roamed her features and form, she hugged the pillow tighter against her chest, uncomfortably aware that she was dressed only in her chambray wrapper, her waist-length hair in disarray.

God only knew what her face really looked like, with her red-rimmed eyes and her colorfully bruised cheek. She threaded her fingers nervously through her hair in an attempt to remove some of the snarls. She turned away from him to face the mirror but focused on his image in the oval frame rather than her own.

Their eyes met in the mirror and she saw herself reflected in his fathomless blue eyes. "You shouldn't be in here."

"I have waited a long time for this morning," he said.

Sloan tensed as Cruz lowered his head to caress her bare shoulder with his lips. She shivered in pleasure at his touch. She knew she should flee but felt powerless to do so.

If his hands had sought to capture her, to keep her prisoner, she would have pulled away. Yet solely with the touch of his lips upon her skin, he held her in his thrall. Her eyes drifted closed as he bestowed soft kisses along her shoulder and up her neck.

She heard his uneven breathing, felt his body coiled and trembling with need. Her heart pounded in her chest and she drew a sharp breath as his teeth nipped lightly at the lobe of her ear.

When her legs threatened to buckle beneath her, she turned abruptly to face him. "Cruz . . ."

Before she could speak words of denial, his strong arms surrounded her.

They both realized at the same moment that the pillow was stuck ludicrously between them.

Cruz was the first to grin, and Sloan joined him. He grabbed her up in his arms with the pillow between them and swung her in a circle. She heard herself laughing like a carefree young girl.

Abruptly, Cruz set her down and yanked the pillow out from between them, throwing it over his shoulder onto the bed. One of his hands captured her nape while the other grasped her buttocks, forcing their bodies into intimate contact from hips to breast, his male hardness pressing against her belly.

Suddenly the laughing mood was gone, abruptly changed to something much more serious. Sloan looked up at Cruz and saw the determination etched in his features.

"Don't do this . . ." she begged in an agonized whisper.

His eyes were focused on her mouth, and for an instant she didn't think he had heard her. It was only when their lips were a breath apart that he seemed to come to his senses. "Ah, Cebellina, you tempt me to show you how right this would be."

The moan that rose from deep in her throat was torn from her against her will. There was a rightness about the feel of her body aligned with his. But the pure, wanton desire that spiraled through her was a threat she wasn't ready to meet.

She knew what it would mean if she succumbed to his demands. She did not want to be his wife. She did not want to give control of her life to another man. How could her body respond so treacherously to his caress?

"This is wrong," she said, her voice choked with the need she fought.

"How can it be wrong for a husband and wife to desire one another?" he demanded in a voice no louder or less tortured than hers. "I have wanted you for longer than any man should have to wait for his beloved."

Sloan hid her face against his shirt, which smelled of soap and man. "I . . . I don't love you, Cruz. I can't do this. I . . . can't."

He grasped a handful of her hair and pulled her head back to look deep into her liquid brown eyes. He frowned at what he saw. Then his hand tunneled into her hair as he brought her head to rest beneath his chin. His body shuddered as he forced it to his will. He loosened his grip on Sloan's hips, allowing her body to escape the heat of his.

The hand that held her head against his shoulder began to smooth over her silky hair, but it was questionable whether either of them was really soothed by the calming motion.

"All right, Cebellina. We will wait . . . a little longer."

When Sloan sought, at last, to ease from Cruz's embrace, he let her go. She slowly raised her head to meet his gaze. His vivid blue eyes asked questions and demanded answers.

"I have to be honest with you. I don't want to be your wife, Cruz." Her cheeks flushed, then paled. "Your brother would always stand between us. Even if he didn't, we both want our own way too much for us ever to be able to get along. I'll never agree to leave Three Oaks . . . and you're bound to Dolorosa. So you see, there really isn't any hope for this marriage."

"But you *have* left Three Oaks," Cruz reminded her.

"That was a mistake. One I intend to correct. As soon as I can come up with the right plan."

"Then you will accept my hospitality for a while." When Sloan opened her mouth to object, Cruz added, "I insist."

Sloan bristled, but nodded. "All right. But this touching . . . it can't happen again."

"I cannot promise that."

Sloan huffed out a breath of air in frustration. "Don't you see how difficult it will be for both of us if you insist on forcing us together?" Sloan's voice became strained. "Because I won't put my heart . . . or my body . . . in another man's keeping . . . ever."

Cruz thrust a hand through his hair and left it looking wild. "I would never hurt you, Cebellina."

"Tonio said as much."

His jaw tightened in anger. "I am not my brother."

"You're a man. And a man will say or do whatever is necessary to get what he wants from a woman."

"All men are not so treacherous."

Sloan snorted derisively. "Oh no? I'll introduce you to a few of the plantation rakes who came to see me after Tonio's death. They had heard I was pregnant and that Tonio was dead. They only wanted to offer me comfort in my bereavement. Or so they said. It took me a while to realize what they really wanted was—"

Cruz put his fingertips on her lips to silence her. He could easily guess what the young men had wanted. He would have protected her from them if he had known. But being Sloan, of course she had not asked him for his help. "Is there nothing I can do to convince you to trust me?"

"I'll trust your word that you'll keep your distance from me so long as I'm here."

"I will not promise to stay away from you," he said at last. Then he smiled, a warm, heart-stopping smile that revealed even white teeth and made crinkles appear at the corners of his eyes. "But I give you fair warning, Cebellina, that I will do everything in my power to be certain you welcome my touch."

Sloan gasped, then laughed aloud. "You're incorrigible!"

"It appears so." The devilish smile stayed on his face as he continued, "Now, for the reason I came to see you so early. It is Sunday, a day of rest. I have decided we should have a picnic."

In her delight at the whole idea, Sloan ignored the fact

he had already "decided" what they should do. "A picnic sounds wonderful! Is there anything I can do to help get things ready?"

The tension left Cruz's shoulders when he saw she wasn't going to argue with him about going. "I took the liberty of asking Ana to pack a basket for us. I will leave you now to dress. Once we have eaten breakfast, we can go."

Cruz leaned down to kiss her, then remembered his promise. He paused with his lips a hairsbreadth from hers, waiting. When Sloan did not draw away, he tantalizingly brushed her lips with his, then grasped her lower lip with his teeth and nibbled on it, sliding his tongue along its edges before he finally released her.

Sloan was stunned.

"You will find I always keep my promises, Cebellina."

Before she could respond, he was gone from the room.

Sloan found herself humming as she dressed in clean trousers and a shirt and tugged on her Wellingtons. She realized she hadn't been on a picnic since . . . since the previous fall when Bay had used picnics as an excuse to get her together with her son. She and Cruz and Cisco had spent nearly every Sunday picnicking with Bay and Long Quiet under a huge old live oak tree that stood on Dolorosa land. It had been an idyllic time.

She had begun to love her son . . . and to trust Cruz. And then, one day, Cruz had kissed her, and she had realized how much she had grown to care for him, as well as her son. Moments later, Cisco had been attacked by a renegade Comanche.

She stared down at her hands, remembering how they had looked, red with her son's blood.

That was the day she had vowed she would rather not

love at all than face the pain of losing those she loved. Once she was sure Cisco would recover, she had left Dolorosa, determined not to see Cruz or Cisco again.

Sloan forced her memories away. She had always tried to take the best, the most logical, course of action. The day she had decided to keep Cruz and Cisco at arm's length it had made perfect sense. Nothing had altered, really, to make her change her mind. She would just have to avoid Cruz and Cisco as best she could until she left Dolorosa.

She gave her appearance a quick check in the mirror and forced a smile onto her face. Immediately, her spirits lifted. She was looking forward to spending the day relaxing at a picnic.

Her good humor followed her into the dining room, where it was quickly curtailed by the sight of a tight-lipped Doña Lucia staring balefully at an equally tight-lipped Cruz.

Cruz sat at the head of the table, his eyes locked on his mother, who sat on his right. To Cruz's left, Tomasita perched on the edge of her chair, her eyes lowered to the hands folded tightly in her lap, while to Tomasita's left Cisco watched Cruz, his innocent blue eyes wide and wary.

Sloan stood for a moment in the doorway trying to decide where she should sit. The only empty seat, other than the one at the opposite end of the table from Cruz, was next to Doña Lucia. She considered simply skipping breakfast altogether, but she was damnably hungry. She lifted her chin and marched across the room to sit beside the obviously furious woman.

"Good morning," she offered.

Doña Lucia ignored her and hissed to Cruz, "I will not allow it!"

"I have been telling Mamá about our picnic," Cruz said,

his voice firm, his eyes meeting his mother's with an implacable will. "She suggested that Tomasita should join us and that we bring along Josefa to help take care of Cisco."

Sloan didn't know that Cruz had intended to bring Cisco, or she wouldn't have agreed to the picnic. There was nothing she could say now without making a scene at the table, so she responded neutrally, "Oh."

Cruz had not repeated precisely what his mother had suggested, but he was willing to compromise with her by including Tomasita and Josefa in their outing. His mother had been appalled that he intended to take Sloan on a picnic and leave Tomasita home. After all, she had argued, Tomasita would one day be his bride.

Of course Sloan did not need a chaperon, she had added disdainfully, but Tomasita could not go without a woman to watch over her, and thus Josefa had been included.

Cruz looked at Tomasita and saw the young woman was mortified by the battle that had been taking place around her. He knew she must be confused by his mother's attempts to throw them together, especially as she had no notion of their betrothal. The sooner he could find a proper husband for her, he thought, the better.

Two men had seemed particularly attentive to Tomasita at the *fandango*. Both had his approval, and he had noticed that Tomasita did not look at either of them in distaste.

Ambrosio de Arocha was a fine man and a wealthy *ranchero,* as was Joaquín Carvajal. Don Ambrosio had been widowed recently, and Joaquín was looking for a well-bred wife. Cruz made up his mind that if one or both of the men did not approach him in the near future, he would seek them out and invite them to dinner.

Surely a little more time spent in Tomasita's delightful company would convince one of them to offer for her.

"What do you say, Tomasita?" Cruz asked. "Would you like to go on a picnic?"

"I . . ." Tomasita chanced a quick look at Doña Lucia's fulminating expression and finished, "Whatever you decide will be fine with me."

"Then it is settled. You will come with us."

Doña Lucia rose, curtly excused herself and left the room.

It was only after she was gone that anyone dared to speak, and then it was Cisco who said, "I am glad Tomasita can come on our picnic, Papa."

Sloan was startled to hear Cisco call Cruz Papa, and noticed suddenly that anyone who did not know the truth could easily believe they were father and son. Cisco had Cruz's blue eyes, the same noble nose, and a cleft in his chin that was a miniature of Cruz's. Tonio's only legacy to the child appeared to be Cisco's smile—one side of his mouth tilted higher than the other in the same way as Tonio's had.

The fear of succumbing to her son's charm kept Sloan quiet through the breakfast of corn tortillas and scrambled eggs garnished with a spicy tomato sauce. She spoke when spoken to, but didn't participate in the lively conversation carried on between Cisco and Cruz, which was joined occasionally by Tomasita.

She noticed Tomasita seemed more relaxed with Doña Lucia gone from the room, and she didn't appear disturbed by the fact that Cruz had only invited her to come along on the picnic at his mother's insistence.

Perhaps the young woman was not as attracted to Cruz as Sloan had at first suspected. She wondered whether Tomasita would approve Cruz's choice of husband for her with as much docile acceptance. She felt a little sorry for the young woman, whom she had begun to sincerely like.

Once they were on their way in the carriage, Sloan enjoyed the ride across the grassy plains dotted with mesquite trees and patches of catclaw cactus. When she saw the huge ancient live oak appear on the top of a grassy hillock on the horizon, she was very glad she had come.

"Look at all the flowers!" Tomasita exclaimed, jumping from the wagon as Cruz pulled the horses to a stop at the outermost edge of the live oak.

Cisco followed with Josefa in tow, investigating the various fall wildflowers to be found. The tree made an umbrella of shade as large as the entire plantation house at Three Oaks. The live oak branches dipped low in some places and were gnarled and curved with the weight of years. Spanish moss draped the boughs like a shawl, lending majesty to the huge old tree.

"I love this spot," Sloan said softly when she joined them. "It has to be the most beautiful place in Texas."

Sloan felt Cruz step up behind her. His voice, soft in her ear, sent chills down her spine. "It is the memory of the hours I spent here with you in this place that I cherish."

Sloan knew then it had been a good thing that Tomasita and Josefa had been included in the picnic plans. She would never have been able to resist Cruz's entreaties in this magic place.

Sloan silently shared those moments of the past with Cruz—the moment when his lips had first touched hers and the first spark of sexual awareness had passed between them. She felt the invisible bond that stretched between them and shut her eyes against its power.

Cisco's tug on her hand interrupted the tense moment.

"Come and see, Mamá, and you too, Papa. I found a ladybug."

Sloan kept her face blank as Cisco took each of them by a hand and led them to a delicate tulip-shaped flower growing on the banks of a nearby spring. He squatted beside it, pulling the two of them down beside him, and then released their hands to point to the tiny red-and-black-spotted bug crawling on the white petal. "There she is. Do you see her?"

"I see her," Sloan said.

Cisco looked up at Cruz. "Is she not pretty?"

"Yes, she is very pretty," Cruz said. But his eyes sought out Sloan when he spoke.

For a moment Sloan wished things could have been different, that she could have met Cruz first and never given her love to his brother, that Cisco had been Cruz's son.

But he wasn't. The sooner she divorced herself from this make-believe family, the better. She rose abruptly, leaving Cruz on one knee beside Cisco. "I'm going to help Tomasita and Josefa put out all that food we brought along."

"Do not leave, Mamá, I—"

"I have to go," Sloan said brusquely. When she saw the hurt look in her son's eyes and the anger in Cruz's, she whirled and hurried away.

She looked back over her shoulder and saw Cruz and Cisco with their heads bent close together and felt a painful ache in her chest. If only . . . if only . . . If only pigs had wings they could fly, she thought with a rueful shake of her head.

"What can I do to help?" she asked as she joined the other two women.

"We are nearly finished," Tomasita said to Sloan. As Josefa left to retrieve another quilt from the wagon to spread on the ground, Tomasita said, "If you like, you can fill those cups with tea from that jug."

As Sloan poured the tea, she asked, "Do you miss Spain, Tomasita?"

"I miss my friends in the convent," Tomasita replied wistfully. "Although many of the girls my age had already been claimed by their husbands-to-be as—" Tomasita stopped abruptly. She had been about to say, "as I was claimed by Don Cruz," before she realized she was not supposed to know about their betrothal.

"Would you like to be married?" Sloan asked, unable to curb her curiosity. Sloan was surprised by the perplexed expression that appeared on Tomasita's face.

"I do not know." Tomasita was glad for the opportunity to express her doubts to another woman. "I do not think I would like to marry just any man," she said. "But if the man were strong and courageous and handsome, then perhaps it would not be so bad."

Sloan noticed that Tomasita's eyes had unconsciously sought out Cruz while she was speaking.

"You did not mention love," Sloan said.

Tomasita turned shyly to Sloan. "Oh, do you think it is possible I will fall in love? I have read the tales of the knights in armor and their lady loves. I had hoped . . . but I do not think I have ever felt that way. I mean, I have had so little to do with men . . . How will I know when I am in love?"

"When the right man—" Sloan bit her lip to cut herself off. She remembered a story she had told Cricket once, a story about fur boots and how you could have boots made of a lot of different kinds of fur, but one fur would feel better than all the rest. So, too, with a man—one stood out among the others.

Sloan looked at Tomasita's expectant face. Cruz had said he would choose a husband for the girl. It was wrong to put ideas into Tomasita's head that might never be realized. "When the right man comes along, you'll know," Sloan said. "I can't really explain it any better than that."

Fortunately for Sloan, Josefa returned from the carriage, cutting off Tomasita's next question.

After they had eaten a hearty meal, they rested for a while and then followed Cisco's suggestion, seconded by Tomasita over Josefa's frowning objection, that they play tag.

Sloan had been searching for a way to throw off her worries, and the idea of frolicking around like a filly in a field of high grass sounded wonderful. "I think playing tag is a great idea," she had agreed.

Cisco was "it" when they began, and he quickly tagged Cruz, who had been halfhearted in his efforts to escape the toddler. When Cruz began to chase Sloan, thinking how pleasant it would be to touch her, even in so innocent a game, he found her surprisingly fleet of foot.

"You'll never catch me!" She laughed and twirled out of his way.

In her frantic escape, Sloan ran directly across Tomasita's path. Cruz tripped over Tomasita's heel as Sloan fled with a shriek of delight.

Cruz shouted a warning and grabbed Tomasita to protect her from his weight as they tumbled to the ground in a tangle of arms and legs. When they finally stopped rolling, Cruz had come to rest atop Tomasita, their bodies pressed together from breast to hip. For a moment they were both too stunned to react.

Sloan waited for Tomasita's lively laughter to erupt, but heard an indrawn breath instead. Tomasita's head was turned toward her, and Sloan saw the other woman's face was flushed with excitement and . . . awareness.

Cruz appeared mesmerized by the sight of the woman beneath him, and Sloan knew he had to be feeling Tomasita's full breasts and flat belly. Sloan sucked in a breath of air and held it, waiting to see what would happen next.

Josefa's shrill voice collided with the sound of Cisco's childish giggle as the two of them converged on the couple lying on the ground.

"You're 'it,' Tomasita!" Cisco shouted.

"Don Cruz! You must get up," Josefa cried.

Cruz was off Tomasita in an instant. When he would have extended a hand to assist her up off the ground, Josefa stepped between them and put a work-worn hand under Tomasita's elbow to help her rise.

Josefa brushed the dust and grass off Tomasita's wool skirt and straightened the loose cotton *camisa* that had slipped off one shoulder, all the while muttering, "I warned you not to play at children's games. It is not seemly for a young woman to cavort like a child. When Doña Lucia hears—"

"Doña Lucia will not hear of this," Cruz interrupted, his tone commanding obedience. "As you said, we were merely playing a game. No harm has been done."

Sloan wasn't so sure.

There was something more in Tomasita's sapphire eyes when she looked up at Cruz now than had been there before, something that suggested the lively, precocious child had given way to the demure, uncertain woman.

And Cruz's eyes followed Tomasita in a way they hadn't before.

None of the adults were in the mood to play tag any longer, and Cruz only managed to hush Cisco's protesting cries by gathering him up for a piggyback ride down to the nearby spring.

"It is my duty to guard your honor," Josefa said to Tomasita when Cruz had gone. "But you must also do your part."

"But—"

"Listen to me!" Josefa admonished fiercely. "If you continue to act so little the lady, no man will want you for his wife."

Sloan saw from Tomasita's trembling hands as she gathered up the picnic supplies that the young woman was humiliated by Josefa's words. Tomasita's flushed face revealed she was still confused by her reaction to Cruz.

Reluctant as Sloan was to admit it, she thought perhaps Cruz had been as surprised by the womanly form and potential for passion that lay hidden beneath Tomasita's proper facade as Tomasita was herself.

Sloan felt a queer tightness in her chest. She recognized it as jealousy. She had told Cruz she didn't want to be his wife. Only now that she saw him with Tomasita, she realized she didn't want him to be some other woman's husband, either. She was angry with herself for feeling so ambivalent. Either she wanted to be Cruz's wife or she didn't. Which was it?

She had never questioned her attraction to Cruz. But she had done everything in her power not to fall in love with him.

First, she knew the power that would give him: He would not have to command—she would be more than willing to obey. She did not think she could ever learn to trust him enough to give him such a hold on her.

And second, as irrational as she knew it was—and that was what really galled her—she could not help fearing that if she let herself love him, he would die and leave her alone.

So where did that leave her? Unsettled. Unsure. And undecided.

Cruz returned to find the three women had packed away the picnic supplies and were ready to return home. Sloan refused to meet Cruz's eyes, and merely agreed with him when he suggested they should leave.

"We must do this again sometime soon," Cruz said, with forced cheerfulness.

Sloan answered with the ambivalence she had been feeling since the game of tag. "If I'm still at Dolorosa, it might be fun."

Cruz's lips pressed together in disapproval, but Sloan noticed he didn't contradict her. Too bad, she thought. She was itching for a good fight.

Chapter 7

SLOAN NORMALLY ROSE WITH THE COCK'S CROW and was out in the fields by first light. So she felt chagrined when she awoke on her second day at the Guerrero hacienda and realized daybreak had found her abed. She wasn't sure what had finally awakened her until she saw the shadowy form sitting beside her on the bed.

She jerked at the sheets to cover herself as she hurriedly sat up. "What are you doing here?"

"I have duties I must see to, and I did not want to leave without speaking with you."

Sloan had never been more aware of Cruz's claim on her than now, when he made no apology for observing her in her sleep. "You're here now. Talk."

She was startled when he grasped her shoulders and forced her to lie back down. She met his eyes, then let her gaze drop to the long, tanned fingers that touched her skin. Her gaze rose again to meet his, the demand for release there for him to read. He ignored it.

Cruz couldn't believe the seductive picture she made with her glorious sable hair scattered in abandon on the pillow. She had never looked more like his heart's desire.

Sloan tensed when Cruz braced his palms on either side of her head, effectively imprisoning her without even laying a hand on her. Her flesh shimmered in excitement. Her blood went streaking through her veins. She felt as though he had taken ropes and spread-eagled her helplessly before him. Her whole body tautened, struggling against invisible bonds, waiting with delicious urgency for what was to come.

"I have made arrangements for you to rest today," he said, his voice rich and deep.

"I'm not tired."

"The dark circles under your eyes say otherwise."

She turned her face away to escape his piercing gaze.

"Look at me." When she didn't respond, he reached out to cup her chin with his hand and gently turned her face toward him.

"Humor me. Rest today."

"And tomorrow?"

"We will speak of that tomorrow."

"What will you be doing today?" Sloan asked.

"The fall roundup has begun. I ride with my vaqueros."

"I want to come along."

"It is not done." At Sloan's frown, he added, "A lady does not ride with the vaqueros on Dolorosa."

Sloan heard the censure in his voice. It was exactly the kind of rein she had expected him to exert on her behavior, but it distressed her to feel its tug so soon. She had trouble keeping the asperity from her voice. "With whom does a lady ride?"

"With her brother or her father . . . or her husband."

"So you're saying that unless you're my . . . husband . . . I can't ride with you?"

He smiled gently. "That is the way of it."

"That's an old-fashioned attitude that doesn't belong in Texas."

"In Texas, as elsewhere, a woman obeys her man—as she should."

"You're not my man!" Sloan snapped.

"Ah, Cebellina, and whose fault is that?"

The tension crackled between them. She denied his sensual challenge by refusing to acknowledge it. "I need something to keep me busy. I'm used to working. I can't simply lie abed all day and do nothing. I want to come with you on the roundup."

"No."

Sloan looked into Cruz's deep blue eyes and saw that on this, he would not compromise. Her chin jutted mulishly. "You can't stop me."

Before she could react, his fingers had laced with hers above her head, and he had covered her with his body. She stiffened, fighting her body's riotous reaction to his—tender breasts swollen against a hard chest, a concave belly arching to male hips, slender thighs pressed to corded muscles of steel.

Her voice bit like a whip, hard and sharp. "Let me go."

"You will stay at the hacienda?"

Sloan's lip curled derisively. "Is this the way you treat all your guests? Am I a prisoner now?" She watched as chagrin altered his stony countenance, then saw a wry smile forming.

"No one else would dare to provoke me the way you do."

Cruz caressed the calluses on her hands, recognizing them as the signs of a life spent laboring as no woman should have to do. He wanted to cosset her, to treat her like a queen. But she wanted none of it. He could not help admiring her for her spirit, but at the same time he shook his head in dismay at her willfulness. Perhaps it would not be so bad to let her come with him . . . another time.

He released her hands but did not free her completely. He felt her shiver as his hands moved slowly down her upraised arms to her shoulders, until he finally curled one hand around her nape. Absently, his fingers threaded through the dark, silky hair.

"How can I convince you to stay here? Shall I say it would please me if you do? I do not understand what makes you want to do a man's job. Is it not enough simply to be a beautiful woman?"

"No. And I'm not beautiful."

His hands framed her face to prevent her from looking away from him. "Oh, but you are. Very beautiful." His thumb brushed her full lips, then traced the arch of her brow. He caressed her high cheekbone, and admired the softness of her skin.

Sloan fought against the tremors that shook her as Cruz's hands worked their magic. Tonio had never made her feel like this. She was strung tight as a bow with anticipation. She could not move, could not break the contact between them. Her hands were fisted above her head. It was the only way she could resist touching him back.

"You are very tempting, Cebellina," he murmured.

When she opened her mouth to speak, his fingertips stopped her. "Also very stubborn." He smiled at her, his eyes lambent with suppressed desire. "I cannot let you come with me on the roundup, but if you must work, then perhaps Mamá can find something for you to do here at the hacienda. Although you must know, there is no need for you to do anything."

"All right. Fine. I'll stay here and work in the house."

Desperate to escape Cruz's sensual onslaught before she succumbed to it, Sloan would have agreed to anything. The way Cruz made her feel . . . She could not understand or explain it; she could only fight it. Allowing these feelings to grow could only lead to more pain when she returned to Three Oaks . . . as she would. As she must.

When his eyes locked on her mouth, she thought he was going to kiss her. She held her breath as he hesitated, suddenly afraid he would not.

His hooded eyes focused on her lips, his nostrils flared for the scent of her. And then his mouth covered hers, their lips clinging for too brief a moment.

Slowly, as though he were tearing himself away and it was a painful thing, he released his hold on her and stood up.

"I will see you at supper tonight," he said. Then he was gone.

Sloan lay still, waiting for the trembling to stop. She tried not to think about what had happened between her and Cruz, but avoiding the truth wouldn't change it. She had wanted him to kiss her. She had wanted to kiss him back. How traitorous her body was! It refused to acknowledge the danger Cruz represented. She would have to be more careful. She would have to try harder to stay out of his way. And she would have to make it clear he was no longer welcome in her bedroom.

Sloan exhaled as the tension eased from her body and shook her head in disgust. She had actually agreed to do housework! Stephen usually took care of such matters at

Three Oaks. Yet housework would be something to do to pass the time until Cruz returned.

Sloan had no wish to approach Doña Lucia, conscious as she was of the woman's dislike of her, but she knew herself well enough to realize that she would find staying idle all day a worse penance than any chore a vindictive Doña Lucia could find for her.

In deference to where she was, Sloan put on a simple long-sleeved brown calico dress that she had brought with her in her small carpetbag. The dress buttoned all the way to the neck and had a simple white butterfly collar that she adorned with the one piece of jewelry she owned, a cameo brooch that had belonged to her mother.

Sloan so seldom wore a dress that the strangeness of her attire emphasized her predicament. She endured the awkwardness because she had no other choice. She didn't like being in corners, and she was determined to find a way out of this one.

Sloan had just put on her shoes when she heard a knock on the door. Before she could respond, Doña Lucia stepped inside.

"My son tells me you want something to do to keep you busy today, Señorita Stewart."

"I would rather be busy than not," Sloan replied honestly.

"I have servants to do the work in the house."

It was plain to Sloan that Doña Lucia not only didn't want her help, she didn't want her in the house. She bit her tongue on a sharp reply and said, "I'll be glad to do anything."

"Very well. I have asked Josefa to take the rugs outside today and beat them clean. If you would like to help her, you are welcome to do so."

"Thanks." Sloan thought she saw a smile appear on Doña Lucia's face, but if it had been there, it was gone too quickly to comment upon.

Doña Lucia started to leave the room but suddenly stopped and angled her head back toward Sloan. "Stay away from Cisco. Seeing you, talking with you, will only confuse him."

Sloan, who had fostered no intention of seeking out her son, retorted, "I'll see him if I please."

Doña Lucia's face contorted with fury. As suddenly as she had lost control, she regained it and her features resumed their regal mien. The mellifluous voice gave no evidence of anger when the Spanish woman spoke.

"It is respect for my son that makes me hold my tongue when I wish to speak plainly to you. I do not understand why Cruz has invited you to stay in this house. But he has asked me to extend my courtesy to you. As I honored his father's wishes when he was patrón, so do I honor my son's.

"But do not mistake me. I will do what I must to protect Cisco and to see that Señorita Hidalgo is not embarrassed by your presence here."

The woman was gone before Sloan could respond. What could she have said? Doña Lucia's animosity was something she would have to bear for however long she stayed at Dolorosa—which she hoped wouldn't be more than a couple of weeks.

She had been thinking a lot about how she could change Rip's mind, and the solution that seemed simplest was to stay away from Three Oaks and let him try to manage the harvest on his own. Whether Rip realized it or not, for the past few years she had taken a great deal of the responsibility for Three Oaks on her shoulders. Since his stroke, she had carried it all.

Of course, he could hire an overseer to replace her. But Three Oaks had suffered financial losses for two years in a row, and Rip could ill afford the expense. No. If she just stayed away for a couple of weeks, Rip was bound to discover that he needed her far more than he had ever realized.

He wouldn't like admitting he had been wrong, but she would make it easier by resisting whatever urge she felt to say "I told you so" when he asked her to come home.

The only thing wrong with such a plan was that it meant she would have to find a way to survive the scorpions and rattlers at Dolorosa until Rip became suitably enlightened. As Sloan was discovering, that wasn't turning out to be as easy as it might sound.

Sloan convinced Josefa that she wanted to work alone and took advantage of the chore Doña Lucia had given her to beat out her frustration. The job was a dirty one, and before long, her hair and clothing were covered with a fine layer of dust.

Even though it was fall, the sun was warm, and she felt rivulets of sweat trickling between her breasts and down the small of her back. It occurred to her that this work would have been better done in trousers and a shirt. So much for maintaining the facade of femininity.

She was nearly finished when Josefa sought her out. "It is time for the noon meal, señorita."

"Can you bring me something out here?"

"Oh no, señorita. You are a guest. You must eat at the big table."

Sloan sighed and did her best to repair the damages. She

rinsed her hands and face in the cool water of the tile fountain in the courtyard, then brushed off her dress and hair as best she could. There was nothing she could do about the rings of sweat beneath her arms.

"Damn, damn, damn," she muttered.

She bit back an even stronger epithet when she saw Tomasita sitting quietly at the table, her shiny, blue-black hair in a neat bun, her pastel green dress an immaculate confection of layered silk and almond lace that fitted her like a glove through the bodice and then flared in gathers at the waist.

Tomasita smiled brightly at Sloan when she saw her. "I looked for you this morning after breakfast, but Doña Lucia told me you had decided to work outside."

"Uh, yes. I did." Sloan avoided looking at Doña Lucia, knowing she couldn't keep a straight face if she did. Before Sloan got a chance to sit down, there was an interruption.

One of Cruz's vaqueros, a short man with a leathery face that matched the chaparejos he wore to protect his legs from brush, stood with his sombrero in hand at the door to the dining room. He spoke in rapid Spanish to Doña Lucia.

Sloan had spent a great deal of time practicing the language after she had caught Cruz forcing Cisco to learn English so he would be able to communicate with his mother, and she understood the vaquero amazingly well.

"There are three covered wagons camped at the northern border of Dolorosa," he said, "filled with *gringos*. A wheel is off one of their wagons. I do not think they know how to fix it."

"Did you speak with them?" Doña Lucia asked.

"Oh no, señora. I came quickly to tell my patrón what I found." His face filled with disdain for the *gringos*. "They cannot care much for their children. They have no sentry posted to watch for Comanches or—"

"They have children with them?" Sloan interrupted in Spanish.

The vaquero turned to her and Sloan saw in his wrinkled brow the same disdain that must have been accorded the white men with the wagons. "*Sí*, señorita. Two young boys and a little girl."

Sloan turned to Doña Lucia. "We have to help them."

The vaquero looked to Doña Lucia to see whether she agreed.

Doña Lucia bent her head slightly to the vaquero in dismissal. "You may go now. I will tell my son what you have seen."

He never looked at Sloan again, only nodded his head in obeisance and left.

"It will be dark before Cruz comes back. We have to send help now," Sloan said. "Those people are in danger every moment their wagon is disabled."

"This is not your concern. My son will settle the matter when he returns."

"But there are children—"

"My son will take care of the matter," Doña Lucia said, her voice hard.

"If you won't do something, I will." Sloan was up and gone from the table before Doña Lucia could say anything to stop her. She ran outside after the vaquero, who had stepped back into his saddle.

"Wait!"

The vaquero paused at Sloan's command, uncertain whether he should obey, but afraid to disobey.

"Where are the wagons? Can you take me back to them?" she asked in Spanish.

Startled, the vaquero's eyes skipped over the dress she wore, wondering how a woman such as she could hope to be any help. "*Sí,* I can take you to them. But how—"

"Wait here while I change into riding clothes, and I'll come with you. Don't leave. Ask someone to saddle my horse for me." She waited a moment to make sure the vaquero understood before she whirled and ran back into the house.

Sloan stripped quickly to her chemise and pantalets, then yanked on her osnaburg trousers, a long-sleeved gingham shirt, vest, socks, and Wellingtons. She stuck her flat-brimmed hat on her head and strapped on a knife with her belt. Grabbing the two Colt Pattersons in the holsters designed to fit across her saddle, she settled them across her shoulder. Finally, she picked up her Kentucky rifle and checked to make sure she had ammunition.

Sloan had seen the gruesome remains of a Comanche attack in the past and had no desire to be a part of such a tragedy. She would make sure the women and children were taken somewhere safe to wait until the wheel was repaired. A broken-down covered wagon in the Texas wilderness was not a safe place to be.

By the time she reached the dining room again, she felt more like herself. It was amazing what a difference it made to be wearing pants and boots. "I'll be back as quickly as possible. If I'm not here when Cruz returns, tell him where I am."

Sloan had completely forgotten about Tomasita, but the young woman's frightened voice stopped her before she could leave. "Why are you doing this?"

"Those people need help."

"But you do not even know them!"

Sloan smiled at Tomasita's naïveté. "Neither do the Co-manches. That won't stop them from killing and scalping the men, raping the women, or taking the children captive. All I'm offering is simple Texas hospitality. I'm sure Cruz would do the same if he knew they needed help."

"Why do you not wait for Don Cruz?"

"If I wait it may be too late." With that, she turned on her heel and left.

It never occurred to Sloan to wait for Cruz, because she was used to doing things for herself, used to taking action where action was warranted. Nor did she consider what Cruz's reaction would be to her precipitous journey. It simply didn't matter. Delay might mean death to those who were stranded.

It took nearly two hours to reach their destination. By then it was late afternoon. But Sloan knew the fate of the immigrants long before they reached the wagons.

There were vultures circling overhead.

"There is nothing we can do, señorita. We must go back now," the vaquero said when he spied the black cloud of birds.

"Someone may still be alive," Sloan said.

The vaquero shook his head. "Those who may have survived the Comanches are better left to the vultures. It is not safe here. The Comanches may still be near. We must go back."

"You go back if you must. I'm going on."

The vaquero was clearly torn, but he remembered that Doña Lucia had agreed to tell El Patrón what he had found, and surely El Patrón could not blame him if he did not follow this strange, foolish woman to her death. "*Adiós, señorita. Vaya con Dios.*"

Sloan sat for a moment without moving. The vaquero was probably right. About everything. The danger was real. The possibility of finding someone alive was slim. And yet, what if someone had survived? She spurred her horse and headed for the immigrants' wagons.

What she saw when she arrived at the camp sickened her.

A young man lay where he had fallen, an arrow in his throat and another in his chest. He had been partially scalped, and only patches of his red hair remained.

She forced her gaze away from him and found another young man sprawled not far away, an arrow in his leg and several more in his arms and chest.

She saw a woman on her side, with her arm outstretched toward one of the fallen men. She had an arrow in her stomach . . . but her back looked like a pincushion.

The bile rose in Sloan's throat. She quickly searched the barren plains for any sign of the Comanches, but saw nothing. Were the Comanches still out there? She felt the hairs rise on her neck. Maybe they were watching her right now, so rocklike and still that she couldn't discern them.

She steeled herself to walk farther into the pitiful circle of Conestoga wagons. Here she found yet another man and woman. The woman had been shot in the back of the head. The man had put a gun in his mouth and pulled the trigger.

Flies buzzed around their heads, nature's fanfare for two tragic deaths.

Sloan staggered a few steps away and dropped to her

knees to retch. When she was done, she wiped her mouth on her sleeve and turned back to survey the carnage.

The two boys and the little girl the vaquero had mentioned—the children she had come specifically to rescue—were not here. Sloan shuddered to think of their fate as captives of the brutal Comanches.

She wished she had never come here. And she was getting the hell out of here as fast as she could!

Sloan started walking toward her horse, which was tied to one of the high yellow Conestoga wheels. As soon as she turned her back on the dead couple, she heard a noise behind her.

She broke into a run.

The noise followed her.

Sloan was too afraid to look back and identify the danger, afraid of what she would see. She had nearly reached her horse when she heard a child's screech of terror.

Sloan whirled in her tracks and was astonished to see a fragile little girl of five or six racing toward her at breakneck speed. The little girl threw herself into Sloan's arms, which were open to receive her, and clung desperately to Sloan's neck while her legs wrapped themselves in a death grip around Sloan's waist. The child repeated one word over and over, sobbing hysterically.

"Mama, mama, mama, mama, mama . . ."

"It's all right, baby," Sloan crooned as she rocked the child in her arms. "Everything's all right now. I have you now. You're okay. Everything's okay. Easy, baby. It's all right."

Sloan spoke the words without realizing what she said. Nothing in this child's world was all right. Nothing was okay. But she rocked and crooned until the child was quiet, though the little girl continued to shiver in Sloan's arms.

"Do you have a name?" Sloan asked.

The little girl nodded solemnly.

"What is it?"

"Betsy."

"How would you like to take a ride on my horse, Betsy?"

"I'm not allowed to ride. I'm too little."

"How would it be if I hold you in my arms?"

"Okay."

Sloan carried Betsy over to her stallion and reached out to stroke the animal's neck. "He's a very friendly horse. Would you like to pet him, too?"

The little blond girl reached out a hand and tentatively patted the horse. When the animal turned its head toward her, she quickly snatched back her hand.

"He won't bite you," Sloan reassured the child. "He's only curious. All right, now. I'm going to set you up here in the saddle and—"

Sloan froze as she recognized the sound of unshod horses coming at a gallop. She yanked Betsy down out of the saddle and settled the child on her hip. She grabbed her revolvers and a belt of ammunition and threw them under the nearest Conestoga. As the hoofbeats came nearer she crouched low to the ground, cocooning the child in her arms as she slipped under the wagon for the meager protection it provided.

As she did, the sun slipped beyond the horizon. It was the moment between "can see" and "can't." She knew the Comanches never attacked at night, afraid that if they were killed, their spirits would be doomed to wander forever in the darkness. If she could only hold off the savages for a little while, surely Cruz would come looking for her and find them before morning.

She curled her body around the child at the same time she reached for one of the Pattersons. The Comanches would not find her easy prey. She didn't intend to be taken without a fight.

Chapter 8

"I've come to see Sloan Stewart."

Tomasita stared entranced into the gold-flecked hazel eyes of the young man who stood before her. His tall, lean body was slouched deceptively in an easygoing, loose-limbed posture. His thumbs were hooked into the waist of his fringed buckskin trousers, his right hip cocked at a comfortable angle. "She is not here."

"Where is she?"

"I do not know."

The young man flashed her a teasing, confident smile that took her breath away, and Tomasita realized she should not have answered the door. Never having greeted a man without her father or her duenna to chaperon, she had no idea what she should say or do next.

She was horribly conscious of the casual way she was dressed. Her short-sleeved embroidered white *camisa* had a wide yoke that tended to slip off her shoulders and hug the swell of her breasts and her plain black wool skirt didn't come down far enough to conceal the simple leather sandals on her feet. She looked more like one of the *po-*

bres, the peasants who lived in the village, than the future wife of the don.

She couldn't help staring at the stranger, noting the triangle of bare bronze skin at the opening of his navy blue linsey-woolsey shirt, the size and shape of his hands as they splayed across his belly, and the blunt fingertips that drew her gaze to the display of his masculinity in the form-fitting buckskins.

She followed the movement of his hands as he slipped his worn, flat-brimmed felt hat off his head, releasing a tumble of sun-streaked brown hair over his brow. Then he thrust his fingers through the silky stuff to shove it away from his sun-browned face.

Tomasita knew she should speak, but she found her senses occupied with the curious feelings roiling about inside her. Her abdomen pulled tight, as though someone had yanked a drawstring shut. She couldn't seem to catch her breath and brought her hand up to her chest as though that might prod her lungs into action.

She remained silent, unmoving, overwhelmed.

The matter was resolved for her when the tall stranger pushed the door farther open and stepped inside.

"I'm Luke Summers. Sloan's brother."

"Oh." Tomasita searched for something to say besides how relieved she was that he was related to Don Cruz's guest and not some bandido who had come to rob the hacienda and ravish her. She chided herself for her vivid imagination, but with the wild stories she had been told since she had arrived in Texas, surely it was understandable.

"May I come in?" Luke asked.

Since he was already inside, Tomasita said, "But of

course, come in," and stepped back quickly as he closed the door behind him.

Fortunately—or perhaps unfortunately, Tomasita thought with a wistful sigh as she sneaked a glance at the handsome man from beneath lowered lashes—Doña Lucia heard her speaking to someone and came to investigate.

"Who is it, Tomasita?"

"Señor Summers has come to see Señorita Stewart." Tomasita saw the censure in Doña Lucia's eyes, and hurried to add, "I was going to come find you—"

"Go to your room, Tomasita."

Tomasita dropped her chin to her chest and lowered her eyes, humiliated at being ordered about like a child in the presence of the handsome young man. But she did not dare disobey. She knew Doña Lucia was only acting to protect her reputation.

She had been wrong to open the door, wrong to speak to the stranger without a chaperon present. The only dowry she had to offer a husband here in this new land was her purity. Don Cruz would not want a wife who had been sullied by the touch of another.

Yet Luke Summers had not threatened her. She had felt only warmth as he had gazed into her eyes. She stole a peek over her shoulder before she left the room and found his golden eyes admiring her. And then—he winked at her!

Tomasita gasped in disbelief. No man had ever presumed to do such a thing! Was this the result of her wanton boldness in answering the door unchaperoned?

Not watching where she was going, she stumbled over a rough woven rug made of *jerga*. Her blush spread heat from her neck to her cheeks. Her hands flew to her face to hide the rosy marks as she fled the room.

She reached her bedroom and pressed the door closed

behind her, feeling safe in the cool sanctuary. Moving quickly, she kneeled on the prie-dieu, the low padded bench at the base of the recessed arch that held a painted wooden statue of the Virgin Mary.

She crossed herself and folded her hands tightly before her to stop their trembling. Holy Mary! What was wrong with her? Had Luke Summers seen something in her eyes, something in her stance, that had given him permission for what he had done? But how thrilling it had been!

She bit her lip in consternation while wrinkles formed on her smooth brow. She was betrothed to Don Cruz. She had no right to be thrilled by another man's look. She had no business even thinking such thoughts. And, she solemnly vowed, she would not think of the young man . . . Luke . . . of the warm, golden hazel eyes . . . ever again.

Tomasita pressed her hands hard against her thumping heart and began the prayer of forgiveness she had learned from the sisters in the convent she had left behind for a new life in Texas.

Doña Lucia Esmeralda Sandoval de Guerrero raised herself to her full, estimable stature and stared down her aquiline nose at the young Texas Ranger who stood before her in the *sala*.

"She is not for you."

Luke didn't bat an eyelash. The Spanish woman couldn't have spoken words more sure to provoke him if she had planned them for months. Yet he gave no outward indication that he had taken umbrage. "I didn't come to see the girl. I came to see my sister. Where's Sloan?"

Doña Lucia frowned in confusion and for the first time

noticed that the man in front of her had a revolver stuck in his belt. "*That woman* has no brother."

"We share the same father."

Doña Lucia's frown deepened, and she made no effort to hide her scorn. "What business do you have with Señorita Stewart?"

"I want to talk with her."

"That will not be possible."

Luke had kept his tone polite, his manner charming, or at least as charming as the situation allowed. That was his way—preferring honey to vinegar. But the woman was trying even his infinite patience. "Get Sloan."

"She is not here," Doña Lucia explained, suddenly aware of the threat posed by the deceptively relaxed man who stood before her.

"Not here?"

Doña Lucia's lips pursed in a moue of contempt. "She left several hours ago—dressed in men's trousers—with one of my son's vaqueros. I do not know when she will return."

Luke suspected it would be as useless to prod Doña Lucia for more information as it would be to fight quicksand. He reined his temper and said, "Tell Sloan I was here looking for her, and that I'll be back."

Doña Lucia nodded imperiously.

He turned at the door and said, "And say good-bye to Tomasita for me."

"I will say nothing to the girl. Stay away from her."

Luke's eyes narrowed slightly, but his voice was almost pleasant when he tipped his hat and said, "I can find my own way out."

As Doña Lucia watched him leave, a chill of foreboding

shot up her spine. She did not like that one. Trouble seethed inside him.

She rolled the golden wedding band around and around on the third finger of her left hand. It was a nervous habit she had developed after Juan Carlos's death, a tangible reminder of her widowhood and what her destiny might be if her son married a woman whom she could not control.

Cruz must marry Tomasita. She was of noble blood. She was pure. And she was as malleable as butter softened by the sun. Doña Lucia would settle for nothing less in her son's wife.

Doña Lucia was waiting for Cruz in the *sala* when he arrived home that evening, dressed like his vaqueros in a wool shirt overlaid by a striped poncho, with rawhide chaparejos to protect his buckskin britches. His only concession to his status as don were the black Cordovan leather boots to which his large rowled Mexican spurs were attached.

He was covered with trail dust and worn from a day spent chasing Spanish longhorns. He had barely stepped through the front door when Doña Lucia rose and confronted him.

"We must talk about Tomasita."

Cruz slid his flat-brimmed black hat back off his head, letting the tie-string catch it at his throat as it fell. He ran a tired hand through his hair, brushing the damp curls off his brow where they had been flattened by his hat.

His eyes surreptitiously combed the room and the hall beyond, searching for Sloan. When he didn't see her, he turned back to his mother.

"Good evening, Mamá." A weary smile curved his lips. "Have you a brandy to offer me?"

For a moment it seemed Doña Lucia would demand

their discussion come first, but she turned abruptly and sought out the crystal decanter on an ornately carved credenza. She poured out a small measure of brandy into a silver goblet and turned to find that Cruz had removed his hat and settled himself into one of the rawhide chairs situated before the stone fireplace.

"*Gracias,*" he said, accepting the brandy. Doña Lucia paced the room while he took his time sipping the mellow-tasting golden liquid. "So. What is wrong with Tomasita? Is she unhappy? Does she want for anything?"

"She wants only a husband to make her a wife," Doña Lucia said, impatient with her son's attitude toward the young woman. "Your father promised you would wed the girl when she was of age. It is past time you kept that promise."

Cruz hadn't changed his mind about marrying Tomasita, and his mother had to know it. "When the roundup is finished, I will find the girl a husband."

Doña Lucia crossed to Cruz and stared down at him, her black eyes flashing. "*You* are the husband for her. If you do not lay claim now to what is yours, it may be too late for anyone to take her to wife."

Cruz sat forward, suddenly all attention. "What are you saying?"

"Today a man, Luke Summers, came to the door asking for Señorita Stewart."

"Luke is Sloan's half-brother." Cruz refrained from adding that Luke was also now heir to Three Oaks.

"So I learned. Tomasita answered the door to this man. She is an impressionable young woman, and Señor Summers was very charming. If I had not arrived when I did . . ." Doña Lucia let her voice trail off as though Tomasita's ravishment were a foregone conclusion.

"I know Luke. Tomasita was in no danger. He would touch no woman who was not willing," Cruz said certainly.

"Ah, but therein lies the problem," Doña Lucia said. "Tomasita was totally in awe of the young man, no doubt a result of all those years spent among the sisters. Although that is where a young woman of good family should be kept until her husband comes to claim her."

Doña Lucia carefully adjusted the lace ruffle on one of her elbow-length taffeta sleeves before she continued, "You must declare yourself. You must announce your engagement to Tomasita to protect her good name and yours."

Cruz set his brandy on the delicate spool-legged table next to the sturdy rawhide chair, then languidly rose and walked to the fireplace. He pressed his palms hard against the stone mantel, arching his back to stretch out the stiffness that came from a day spent in the saddle. "I do not wish to discuss this any further."

"You must marry Tomasita."

"I cannot."

"Why not?" Doña Lucia pressed, her voice sharp with anxiety. She had begun to have her suspicions, since *that woman* had come to Dolorosa, that her son might have fixed his attentions where he should not.

Cruz looked away toward the smooth Talavera jar, his jaw rigid. "Perhaps I should say instead that I choose not to marry her."

Doña Lucia felt the knot growing inside her. "It is *that woman*. She is the reason you do not choose to make your vows to Tomasita."

Cruz tensed, then turned slowly to confront his mother. "Who told you such a thing?"

"Then it is true?"

"My reasons for taking or not taking a wife are my own."

"I saw you coming from *that woman's* room this morning—"

"Enough!" Cruz interrupted. He asked the question that had been foremost in his mind since he had walked through the door. "Where is Señorita Sloan?"

"Who knows?" Doña Lucia said.

"Send someone to find her. I wish to speak with her," he said, by now equally aggravated.

"She is gone."

Cruz felt his heart skip a beat. "Gone? Gone where? When did she leave?"

Cruz's evident concern for the woman annoyed Doña Lucia even further. "Paco came at mid-meal with a message for you about some *gringo* wagons broken down on Dolorosa land. *That woman* took it into her head to go there by herself."

"You did not think to send word to me of this?"

Doña Lucia saw the anger blazing in her son's eyes and, underlying it, something else very much like fear. "Why should you care—"

He was halfway to the door when he said, "Send someone to Paco's *jacal* to find him and bring him to the stable. I will wait there for him." On his way out the door, he yelled for another servant to send someone to the village for his foreman Miguel and the rest of his vaqueros.

It was clear now to Doña Lucia that her son cared for the *gringa* a great deal more than was proper for a man who was betrothed to someone else. Doña Lucia began planning at that moment to make certain that this impediment was removed.

If Cruz would not send *that woman* away, then she, his

mother, would have to do what must be done. She would be first in her own home, first with her son—no matter what steps she had to take to accomplish it.

Cruz had cinched the high-cantled Spanish saddle on his golden *bayo* when Paco arrived breathless at the stable door.

"Patrón?" he called out anxiously. He had half expected this summons after he had left the woman by herself to find the *gringo* wagons. Had he done wrong? One look at El Patrón's face convinced him that his carefully thought out excuses would not serve.

El Patrón cared for his people, much as a father cared for his children. But likewise, the *pobres* owed obedience and service to their master. The old don had been a fair man. His son had proved himself the same.

Yet there was a steely hardness in the son that had not been present in the father, and a fierceness that Paco had seen aroused in Don Cruz but which had heretofore always been kept under control. The vaquero shuddered to think of that ominous wrath unleashed on any man, but most especially on himself.

Cruz led his horse to the stable door, appearing like an avenging devil out of the darkness. "Today you escorted Señorita Stewart to the *gringo* wagons on my land?"

Paco quickly crossed himself and mumbled, "I only did as the señorita asked. No more. No less."

"Can you take me there?"

"*Sí*, Patrón."

"Let us go, then. *Pronto!*"

Cruz vaulted into the saddle even as his vaquero did the same. Once he had collected the other vaqueros, they rode fast, using the light of the full moon to show them the way.

Cruz knew the Comanches frequently took advantage

of the full moon, often called a Comanche moon, to travel on their raids of the white settlements. He felt a prickle of unease and spurred his *bayo* to greater speed, trusting the stallion to make good use of the day-bright moonlight.

While they rode, Cruz questioned Paco about the *gringos*. How many were there? Were they well armed? How had they greeted Sloan? He jerked his *bayo* to a halt when the vaquero admitted that after seeing the vultures hovering over the *gringo* camp, he had left Señorita Sloan to go on to the wagons alone.

"You saw vultures?"

"*Sí*, Patrón."

"And you left the woman to go on by herself?"

The vaquero sat stoically awaiting El Patrón's judgment as he confessed, "*Sí*, Patrón."

It was only with the greatest effort that Cruz kept himself from felling the man with his fist. Instead, he whirled his mount and brutally spurred the stallion into a gallop.

As he rode, his anger with Sloan grew out of control. She had promised she would stay at the hacienda. He grimaced. No, she had not promised anything. He should have known better than to leave her alone. He should have realized she would do exactly as she pleased.

The fluffy white covers sat like grounded clouds on the immigrants' wagons, yet Cruz breathed no sigh of relief upon seeing them. For there was no cheery fire in the center of the small grouping of tall, swaybacked Conestogas, nor was there the acrid smell of smoke to suggest that a fire had recently been snuffed. There was no movement of any kind. It was too quiet.

Cruz pulled his *bayo* to an abrupt halt and signaled his vaqueros to silence. He searched the nearly flat terrain that surrounded them and noted there was a stand of brush and mesquite trees along the creek a short distance from the wagons. A perfect hideout for Comanches. Cruz felt himself go cold. He had not waited all these years for Sloan Stewart only to lose her to a Comanche lance.

He dismounted and handed his reins to the nearest vaquero. "Wait here while Miguel and I see if there is anyone in the wagons."

Cruz's *segundo* Miguel slid from the saddle, and the two of them moved in opposite directions yet in tandem toward the silent camp.

Paco watched with disbelieving eyes as his patrón and the older vaquero disappeared into the undergrowth. He knew how lucky he was to still be unpunished, but he wondered fearfully what El Patrón would do to him if he did not find the woman he sought.

By the time Cruz reached the wagons, he was certain he would find no one alive. In that he was correct, but he was confused by what he did find. The bodies of two men and women, riddled with arrows, and the bodies of another man and woman killed by bullets, lay inside the circle of wagons. Only one of the dead had been scalped, and the job had been half done, as though something had interrupted the Comanches in their gruesome work. Yet the Conestogas had been completely ransacked, their contents spilling from the wagon beds like beans from a broken jar.

Cruz closed his eyes and swallowed hard. He did not want to believe the Comanches had taken Sloan. In such a way had Sloan's sister Bayleigh disappeared into *Comanchería*. It had taken three years, and a stroke of blind luck, for Long Quiet to find and rescue her.

Cruz met Miguel at the center of the circle of wagons.

"Comanches!" he spat. "Did you see any signs that they have taken the woman I seek?"

He was asking Miguel for a word of hope, but he trusted the vaquero to tell him the truth.

"I cannot tell, Patrón."

"Can we catch them?"

Miguel squatted in the grass next to one of the dead. "The Comanches were here maybe five, maybe six hours ago. They will not stop until they are safe in *Comanchería*. But there is something else here I do not understand."

Cruz followed Miguel's gaze and saw the clothing and tools tossed here and there at random in the circle of wagons. "I know what you mean," Cruz said. "The Comanches would have taken as many of these things with them as they could carry . . . and they would have scalped all of these settlers. Unless . . ."

". . . unless someone else was here and ran them off," Miguel finished. "Bandidos, maybe?"

Cruz pushed his hat off his head and let the tie-string catch it so he could thrust a hand through his hair. "That seems most likely, judging from the condition of the wagons. But who took my—Señorita Stewart? And where are the children Paco mentioned? Do the Comanches have them? Or the bandidos?"

Miguel shook his head. "There is no way of knowing."

"Then we will have to follow both. You take half the vaqueros and go after the Comanches. I will follow the bandidos with the rest."

"The roundup—"

"The roundup will have to wait," Cruz snarled. He left Miguel and stalked back through the circle of Conestogas to where he had left his vaqueros waiting. When he arrived, he simply stood there, his face twisted in a scowl of rage.

"Patrón?" Paco's terrified voice brought Cruz from his nightmarish thoughts.

"Juan, Luis," he said to the two closest vaqueros. "You stay here and bury the dead. Tomorrow, get someone to fix that broken wheel and find mules to haul these wagons back to the hacienda. Also, send a message to the Texas Rangers in San Antonio to see if they can discover whether these people have any family who should be advised of their deaths."

He turned to Paco and said, "Tell Doña Lucia what happened here, and that I will not be returning until I have found Señorita Stewart."

"*Sí*, Patrón."

Cruz's thoughts were bleak as he watched Paco cross himself in fervent relief and spur his mount away.

Miguel had followed Cruz away from the wagons but had stopped to examine the tracks on the ground. "There is something more here, Patrón, that you should see."

Cruz kneed his stallion over to the spot where Miguel knelt next to a jumble of hoofprints.

"These tracks were not made by Indian ponies," the vaquero said.

Cruz read the sign that headed west toward Goliad and San Antonio. Suddenly, he felt the urgency to be gone from this place, a need to know what waited for him at the end of the trail.

"*Vaya con Dios,* Miguel. Till we meet again."

Cruz kicked his fatigued *bayo* into a gallop without thought to the equally tired vaqueros who followed doggedly after him. He was calm. Too calm.

Anyone who knew him well would have realized the signs of danger. Like a feral animal, he hunted his prey. He relished the fight to come. His nostrils flared at the re-membered scent of blood, the feel of flesh against his fist. If his wife had been hurt . . .

He forced his mind away from that thought, but it kept returning. His eyes narrowed, and his jaw tautened. He would kill any man who had harmed a hair on her head.

Chapter 9

SLOAN TIGHTENED HER GRIP ON THE SLEEPING child in her lap and nudged her horse with her spurs to keep him moving at the same steady jog as the mounts of the bandidos who surrounded her. Her left arm and shoulder ached from holding the little girl.

She welcomed the pain because it kept her mind off the paralyzing fear that had gripped her since the bandidos had taken her prisoner at the immigrants' camp. She forced her thoughts away from the ordeal to come. She and Betsy were still alive. For now, that was enough.

The outlaws seemed to be in a hurry to get somewhere and her presence had slowed them down. The leader of the ragtag band, called Ignacio by the other bandidos, had more than once urged her to spur her horse to greater speed.

In a very short time, she had grown to hate the Mexican whose tiny eyes disappeared into the sagging flesh on his cheeks when he grinned and whose bulging stomach was so huge that even his striped serape couldn't disguise it.

When her hiding place beneath the wagons had been discovered, Ignacio had admonished his men, who had openly stared at her with lecherous eyes, to use her if they must but to do it quickly.

Sloan knew she had to act fast, but she wasn't quite sure what she should do. Each of her two younger sisters had faced a similar crisis and come through it alive.

But she was nothing like Cricket or Bay. In the same situation, Cricket would have used her hands and wrestled the bandidos to the ground. Bay would have used her soft heart to turn away their wrath.

Sloan had used her head, blurting a promise of wealth if the bandidos would return her and Betsy—unharmed—to Three Oaks.

Ignacio had laughed cruelly at her offer. They had important business, he had said, and could not be burdened with a woman and a child on their journey. But several of the other bandidos, including an older, rail-thin, leather-faced man called Felipe, had been insistent that they take her along with them and collect the huge ransom she had promised her father would pay for her safe return.

Sloan had tried not to wonder where they were going, tried not to wonder what could be more important to Ignacio than the fortune she had offered for her and Betsy's release. But it was certain Ignacio could be bent on nothing good.

It appeared they were finally nearing their destination and that her curiosity would soon be appeased. In the distance stood a lone live oak. Underneath the tree she saw the silhouette of a rotund man standing next to a closed, single-horse carriage. Her speculation was interrupted by the low rasp of Felipe's guttural voice.

"You should send someone to take a message to the woman's father while we meet with the Englishman."

"*Chingada!* Leave me in peace, Felipe."

Sloan stiffened at the crude profanity spoken by Ignacio. The response she heard from Felipe was equally foul. The sleeping child in her arms stirred restlessly. "It's all right, Betsy. Everything's going to be all right," she crooned.

"*Silencio!* If you cannot control the *niña,* I will get rid of her," Ignacio warned.

Betsy writhed desperately, trying to escape Sloan's grip while fighting demons in her sleep.

"Be still, baby, I don't want to drop you," Sloan cautioned. She felt her pulse speed at the venomous look on Ignacio's corpulent face.

Then the little girl began flailing and kicking in earnest, and Sloan was forced to pull her horse to a stop to try and calm her. "Please, baby, don't fight me. It's all right. You're all right now."

Nothing she did seemed to calm Betsy, whose struggles soon left her panting for breath. Sloan was tempted to wake the little girl, but that seemed cruel since Betsy would likely find the waking world no more pleasant than her nightmare sleep.

The sun crept farther above the horizon, bringing the lone figure in the distance into greater detail. An Englishman, Ignacio had said.

Sloan was aware of the political intrigues surrounding the annexation of Texas, of England's efforts to get Mexico to recognize the Republic as a sovereign state while at the same time encouraging Texas to remain an independent nation. But she had purposely chosen to ignore the whole political situation. Once burned, twice chary.

She knew now why Ignacio hadn't wanted to bring her here. It was entirely likely that political messages were being passed through the outlaws to the Englishman, or the other way around.

She determined that she would stay as far away from the Englishman as possible so as not to hear or see anything she shouldn't. She wasn't about to give the bandidos any excuse to keep her prisoner once Rip had delivered the promised ransom.

She wondered if Cruz was searching for her and whether he was angry with her for leaving the hacienda. He didn't know her very well if he thought she could have stayed at the house once she knew the immigrants were in danger.

She had learned from Betsy as they talked through the night that the little girl was five years old and came from Pennsylvania. Her father's name was Joseph Randolph and her mother's name was Susanna. They had been traveling with her two uncles and her aunt. She had another aunt and uncle who had stayed in Pennsylvania. The nine- and ten-year-old boys who had been stolen by the Comanches were her cousins, Franklin and Jeremiah Randolph. Sloan fought back the tears welling behind her eyes at the memory of the carnage the Comanches had caused.

The Texas frontier was harsh and wild. Annexation meant inviting the civilized world to come and tame it. That couldn't happen soon enough for Sloan.

She blinked her eyes to clear them. There was no time for womanish emotions now. Betsy must be subdued before Ignacio lost patience. The little girl's life depended on it.

"Give me the child," Ignacio said, his beefy arms outstretched to take her.

"She's quiet now. I can handle her," Sloan replied quickly.

At that moment, Betsy awoke abruptly. Terrified, not recognizing where she was or what was happening, her tiny hands turned into claws that raked Sloan's cheeks and chin. She kicked out with her hard-soled shoes and left bruises on Sloan's thighs.

When Betsy gasped a breath and opened her mouth to howl in rage, Sloan covered the child's mouth with her hand.

"Take it easy, Betsy. It's me, Sloan, remember? You're safe with me," Sloan said in a voice made breathless by her efforts. "No matter how hard you fight me, I'm going to hang on to you."

Betsy reached up with her hand and grabbed a hank of Sloan's hair that had come free of its binding and pulled hard enough to bring a muffled cry to Sloan's lips.

Sloan lowered her head, but it wasn't enough to ease the pain. She dropped off her horse on the opposite side from Ignacio, taking Betsy with her.

"*Chingada!*" Ignacio shouted, spurring his horse around Sloan's mount.

Sloan had dropped to her knees in the mesquite grass and altered her grip on Betsy. She turned the child to face her and pulled her into her embrace, capturing Betsy's punishing hands, which still gripped a handful of Sloan's long sable hair.

"It's all right to be angry, sweetheart. But no one's ever going to hurt you again. I'll make sure of that. Nobody's ever going to hurt you again."

Ignacio reached down and grabbed Sloan by the hair. He yanked hard, pulling Sloan to her feet with Betsy in her arms.

"*Puta! Bruja!* We cannot stop. We are late already. If you do not get on your horse right now, I will—"

"You will do nothing," Sloan said, gripping the child tightly. "Or my father will pay you nothing."

Her dark eyes sparkled with fury; her body was rigid with anger. She held her head high, ignoring the pain where he grasped her hair, and dared the leader of the bandidos to do his worst.

Several of the bandidos snickered. One of them, a gaunt youth with a pockmarked face and lank black hair clubbed into a long tail down his back, said, "It would be worth giving up all those *reales* to have such a woman."

"Maybe Alejandro would like to have a piece of this one, eh, Ignacio?" Felipe said. "Too bad her father has so much money."

Sloan froze at the name Alejandro, but realized almost instantly it could not be the same man who had killed Tonio. That man was dead.

"Shut up, Felipe. I will handle this," Ignacio said.

Felipe laughed. "Are you sure she is not too much for you, Ignacio? Perhaps I should give you some help."

The bandidos laughed at the idea of the older man helping the younger one.

"Bah!" Ignacio jerked Sloan's hair one more time. "Get on your horse."

Sloan might have been able to manage such a feat if she were not worn out from supporting Betsy's weight. But her legs were trembling with fatigue and her arms were numb. It wasn't a case of having a choice.

Despite the fact she knew Ignacio was at the limit of his tether, she looked him straight in the eye and said, "You'll have to help me."

"*Chingada!*" Ignacio turned to the boy with the pockmarked face and said, "Ramón, put her on her horse."

Ramón quickly dismounted. His palms dug into Sloan's

ribs, his fingers creeping up to grasp at her breasts as he lifted her enough so she could slip into the saddle and settle Betsy before her. Sloan jerked herself away and glared at the boy, who smiled insolently back at her. As Ramón remounted, Sloan gathered the reins in her hands.

"Now, we ride!" Ignacio said, digging his spurs into his horse's flanks.

Sloan tightened her hold on Betsy as her mount was caught up in the frantic race toward the live oak.

Short minutes later, Ignacio raised his hand to stop his small band of cutthroats and robbers. Sloan watched the frown form on the Englishman's face when he saw her. She frowned, too, with the realization that she could easily identify him if she saw him again.

She quickly turned away from the Englishman's scrutiny. She accepted Felipe's help getting down from her horse but kept Betsy clutched in her arms.

"Felipe, you will guard the woman while I speak to the Englishman." Ignacio didn't wait to see if Felipe followed his order.

Sloan followed the bandido with her eyes as he walked the short distance to the Englishman. The next thing she heard was, "You fool! This meeting was to remain secret. Secret! Do you understand? Your brother's life hangs in the balance. Alejandro will be here tomorrow night, as will the Hawk. You'll ruin everything. Get rid of the woman, and do it now."

"I cannot," Ignacio replied.

"Why not?" the Englishman demanded.

There was silence, and Sloan knew the bandido was looking for a way to explain that the combined will of his band of cutthroats outweighed his own. "The woman says her father will pay a ransom for her safe return."

"Bloody hell! You've jeopardized everything for a handful of *reales*? I'm paying you well for your help. If it's not enough, I'll find someone else to do the job. Get rid of the woman!"

"I will see what I can do," Ignacio said at last.

Sloan had found a spot against a grounded limb of the live oak and settled down in the grass with Betsy in her lap. She had offered no threat to the bandidos since her capture, and she was certain that as far as they were concerned, she was nothing more than a helpless woman. She was sure they did not know she could speak their language—and that it might be just such knowledge that saved her life.

She listened carefully as Ignacio approached Felipe and spoke to him in Spanish.

"You heard the Englishman?"

"Who did not?" He turned and eyed Sloan, who focused her attention on the exhausted child in her arms. "Will the Englishman pay us for the ransom we will lose if we kill the woman?"

"We will be well paid for the work we do for him," Ignacio said. "It is enough."

"It is not enough for me," Felipe replied curtly. "How will he know if we kill the woman or not? We will take her away and tell him we have done the deed. He will never know the difference."

"I do not think—"

"You are an idiot! You never think," Felipe interrupted. "She has not seen Alejandro, only the Englishman. I will take her away from this place. When you have finished your business and the Englishman is gone from here, we will send a message to her father and collect the ransom."

Sloan held in her sigh of relief as Felipe walked away from her toward the other bandidos. It appeared the immediate danger was past. But she would keep her eyes and ears open—just in case things changed. She shifted Betsy into a more comfortable position in her arms. It was bound to be a long, long day.

Sloan didn't see Ignacio's eyes narrow or his nostrils flare in anger as he watched Felipe march away from him. She didn't see him walk over to where Ramón was grooming his horse. Nor did she hear what Ignacio said in low tones to the boy whose features had been left distorted by disease.

"Ramón, you will go with Felipe. When you are well away from here with the woman, you will kill Felipe."

The boy's eyes flickered with the fiendish relish of a wolverine with its blood-rimmed jaws tearing at still-warm flesh. "And the woman?"

"You may use the woman if you wish, but when you are done with her, kill her."

"And the *niña*?"

"Kill them both."

Sloan had no explanation for her lightheartedness. After all, she wasn't safe yet. She and Felipe and the boy called Ramón had left the other bandidos at noon and headed back in the direction from which they had come. Every step took her closer to home. Betsy was sleeping again, her breathing even. Sloan listened absently as Ramón argued with Felipe about the importance of not offending the Englishman.

"If not for the Englishman, Alejandro would be dead," Ramón said.

"We could have rescued Alejandro ourselves," Felipe

retorted. "We had no need of the Englishman to save him from the hangman."

"We would have been caught. *Los Diablos Tejanos* were watching for us. They knew we would come for him. The Englishman's plan was best."

Felipe snorted loudly through his nose. "Of course! If you do not consider that another bandido had to die in Alejandro's place."

"The Englishman did not kill Jorge," Ramón insisted. "It was the Rangers who did the hanging."

Sloan's heart pounded in her chest like a Comanche war drum. She had naturally assumed when the name Alejandro had been mentioned earlier by the bandidos that it could not be the same man who had killed Tonio. But the conversation she had just overheard between Felipe and Ramón left her aghast. Surely it was not possible!

She had not waited in San Antonio to see Alejandro hanged, but Cruz had been there. Surely if Alejandro were still alive, Cruz would have said something to her. Besides, how could the bandidos have duped the Texas Rangers?

Sloan was so involved in her own thoughts that the gunshot at close range was a complete surprise. Her horse leaped sideways at the noise, and she had her hands full to keep Betsy from falling. When she had regained control of her mount, her eyes widened in horror.

Ramón had shot Felipe in the back! The bandido had fallen to the ground and lay in a widening pool of blood.

Ramón turned to Sloan, the gun still in his hand, his boyish face aged years by the lascivious glitter in his eyes. "Now, *chiquita,* we will see how much of a woman you are."

Sloan had no time to indulge her sickened senses. She simply spurred her horse in a quick bid for escape.

Ramón's hand darted quick as a rattlesnake's fangs, catching the reins. Her horse shied at the pull on his mouth, and Sloan made a one-handed grab at Betsy, who started to fall.

It was too little too late. The child's weight pulled Sloan off balance, and the sudden, unexpected scream that issued from Betsy's mouth set the horse to bucking.

Sloan's hands tightened in a death grip around Betsy, and she pulled herself into a tight protective ball around the child as the horse's abrupt change of direction sent them both flying.

The last thing Sloan was aware of was the hard ground reaching up to meet her.

When Cruz saw Sloan riding toward him flanked by two disreputable-looking *tejanos,* his hand clenched into a fist around the reins, causing his *bayo* to sidestep. In the next instant Cruz heard a gunshot, saw the glint of sun off hot iron, and watched in disbelief as one of the two men fell sprawled on the ground.

The terrified scream that followed sent his stomach plummeting. He spurred his horse viciously as Sloan's mount began to buck. By the time she hit the ground, his stallion had closed half the distance between them.

He pulled his rifle from its scabbard, his heart in his throat with fear that the *tejano* who had fired at the other man would turn his gun on Sloan.

Cruz didn't offer the *tejano* mercy; he wouldn't have offered a mad dog mercy. He raised his rifle and fired on the run. The bullet hit the *tejano*'s chest and shoved him backward off his horse, his hands outflung, his dying cry a sound of sheer terror and pain that reminded Cruz he was not a mad dog but a man.

Yet Cruz felt no pity, for at that instant he saw Sloan's twisted body on the ground, curled around the little girl. A bellow of rage and pain erupted from his throat.

He was on the ground beside Sloan in a moment, unaware of his vaqueros, who had followed him down the hill. He gently turned Sloan over and tried to pry her fingers loose from the child, but he met with little success. He contented himself with searching Sloan's body with his hands for signs of injury.

When he found no broken bones, he lifted her into his lap, along with the child in her arms, carefully cradling Sloan's head on his shoulder. He felt savage and could easily have killed the *tejano* again. His lips brushed Sloan's forehead before he laid his cheek next to hers.

She belonged to him. He felt no remorse for killing the man who had threatened her life.

Sloan's first thought when she awoke was how protected she felt. She heard a voice murmuring and recognized it as Cruz's. His rough-whiskered cheek felt good next to hers. Her eyes fluttered open to the sight of the pulse beating heavily at his throat beneath his ear.

She started as she remembered Betsy, but at the feel of the child lying in her arms, she relaxed. She looked down and Betsy met her gaze with solemn eyes.

Sloan smiled down at the little girl and said, "Everything *is* going to be fine now, Betsy."

She looked up at Cruz, and saw that everything was not fine. Instead of the comforting look she had expected, she found the thunderous expression of an angry man.

"I told you to stay at the hacienda," he said, his voice cold with fury. "If I had not arrived when I did—"

"I never asked you to come looking for me," Sloan retorted, stung by his harsh welcome. "I don't have to depend on any man—"

"I am not just any man," Cruz snarled, his eyes blazing. "I am your *husband*!" He saw that Sloan was ready with another argument and cut her off. "Do not argue with me!"

Sloan opened her mouth to do exactly that and caught sight of Cruz's vaqueros heaving Ramón's body onto his horse. Her breath caught in her chest.

She shook her head in disbelief at what had happened. "He was only a boy. How could he have murdered Felipe in cold blood like that? When he turned to me afterward, his eyes . . . his eyes were filled with . . . pleasure."

Cruz's arms tightened suddenly, desperately, around her and the child. "Cebellina, *querida,* I thought I had lost you."

Sloan reached an awkward hand up to his bristly cheek to comfort him. She did not know what to say. Her fingers lightly caressed his face, smoothing his brow and then his lips, where she felt his kiss against the pads of her fingers.

She waited, unmoving, as he lowered his head and found her mouth with his. His tongue came searching . . . And she gave freely what he sought.

Pressed uncomfortably between them, Betsy stretched restlessly, finally pushing them apart.

Sloan couldn't meet Cruz's eyes, even though she felt his gaze upon her. Instead, she concentrated on brushing the fine blond hair back from Betsy's forehead. She knew she should get up, get away from Cruz, but she had no will to leave his comforting embrace.

At last, some buried shred of her independent spirit finally asserted itself.

"Let me up," she said. She struggled to sit upright, but

immediately felt dizzy and disoriented. She closed her eyes in an attempt to stop the whirling landscape. "Cruz . . . I think I'm going to . . ."

Sloan fainted.

"Cebellina!"

Cruz caught her head against his shoulder and searched her again with a frightened hand at this newest sign that she had suffered some injury in her fall. Again, he found nothing.

He met Betsy's wide-eyed, fearful gaze but could think of no words to reassure the child. So he pulled them both tight against his breast and simply held them there.

"Cebellina, *mi vida,*" he whispered in her ear. "You must be all right. I cannot live without you."

"You don't seem to be able to live with me, either," came the muffled response.

Cruz turned Sloan so her face was no longer hidden against his shirt and saw a wry smile form on her dust-streaked face.

"Where are you hurt?" he asked.

"I . . . I think I'm more tired than hurt," Sloan admitted. "And maybe a little dizzy from the fall."

"Then rest, Cebellina, *adorada, querida.*"

As he murmured love words, Sloan felt a blush rising from her throat to tint her cheeks a rosy pink. She cleared her throat and interrupted, "Uh . . . how did you find me?"

"Paco led me to the wagons. Can you tell me more about what happened there?"

"I don't really know. I got there after the Comanches . . . Betsy's cousins, Franklin and Jeremiah, were taken captive. We have to go after them, Cruz. We have to—"

"I have already sent my vaqueros to look for them,"

Cruz said in a soothing voice. "If they can be found, my men will find them."

He left unsaid that if the Comanches had escaped to the northern plains, there was little or no chance of the two boys ever being seen again—except as Comanche raiders themselves.

"Once the *niña* has had a chance to rest," he said, "I will have my vaqueros take her to San Antonio so that she can be returned to her family."

"No! I mean, her parents are dead."

"Perhaps there is yet some family living who will want to claim her."

"She has an aunt and uncle in Pennsylvania," Sloan conceded. "But until they can be contacted, I'll take care of her. She needs me."

Cruz felt his neck hairs bristling. "You have a child of your own to care for at Dolorosa—whom you ignore. Will you give more time to a stranger's child than you give to your own son?"

"Cisco doesn't need—" She bit her lip on the denial of her son's need for a mother's love. She saw how neatly she had been trapped. "If that's the price you ask for my keeping Betsy, then I'll pay it. I agree to spend time equally with both children."

"I did not mean to put a price—"

"There's a price for everything," she said. "I'm not so heartless as you think, Cruz. I have not denied my son a mother's love and felt nothing."

He looked down into her deep brown eyes and saw the suffering in their depths. "Tonio is dead. The past is past."

"The past is always with us," she countered. "But I promise to spend more time with Cisco. So long as you understand I will not open my heart to him, knowing that I won't be staying long."

Cruz's features hardened at the same time as his grasp on her tightened. "You are mine now, Cebellina. I do not intend to let you leave Dolorosa."

"You won't dare to hold me there against my will!"

"Try running off again and see what I am willing to do," he retorted. "Leaving the hacienda as you did was dangerous."

"What I did I've done a thousand times before. If you want a wife who's docile and obedient, one who'll sit at home and wait for you to return and handle every little problem that comes up, you'd be better off with Tomasita."

"I do not want Tomasita. I want you!"

Betsy's whimper caused them both to stop and take stock of where they were. Although Sloan didn't want to drop the subject, in deference to the child, she didn't raise it again. Words wouldn't change his mind.

"Will you help me to stand, please?" she asked.

It was a small step for her to ask him for his help, but in such ways were long journeys traveled. Cruz nodded before he set her down on the grass and stood up himself. Then he reached out his arms and said, "Hand the child to me."

"I can carry her," Sloan protested.

"She is too heavy for you. I will take her."

Sloan sighed. "All right."

Cruz caught himself before he smiled. Yes, just so were long journeys begun.

Sloan had expected the child to protest being shifted to Cruz's arms, but Betsy just looked up at him and was silent.

"Can you mount by yourself?" Cruz asked Sloan.

"Of course," she replied, although she wasn't at all sure she had the strength. One of the vaqueros brought her horse to her and held it while she pulled herself into the saddle. As Sloan watched, Cruz easily bore Betsy's weight with one arm as he mounted his *bayo*.

As they rode, Sloan was aware of Cruz's piercing gaze on her and turned away from him to escape it. The sight of the two bandidos slung over their horses reminded her of something important she had forgotten to mention to Cruz.

She turned back to him and was startled by the longing she found in his eyes. It took her a moment to regain her train of thought.

"There's something I forgot to tell you," she said. "After the bandidos captured me, they took me with them to a meeting they had with an Englishman. I overheard the Englishman say that he planned to rendezvous with a man named Alejandro and someone called the Hawk tomorrow night. This man called Alejandro they were talking about . . . I think it's the same Alejandro who murdered Tonio."

"That is not possible," Cruz said. "I saw Alejandro Sanchez hang with my own eyes."

"They said something about it being someone else who was hanged—not Alejandro. Is that possible?"

She watched Cruz and thought for a moment she saw doubt flicker in his eyes.

"Alejandro is dead."

"But we should contact the Rangers, don't you think, and tell them about all this."

He said only, "Perhaps."

"Aren't you even a little bit curious about what's going on?" she persisted.

"I am not my brother. I do not concern myself with political intrigue."

He watched the pain come and go on her face, and it tore away at something inside him to speak so harshly—and falsely—to her. But he had no choice. He called to one of his vaqueros.

"Patrón?"

"Take those two bodies to the pueblo and see if anyone can identify them. Tell Doña Lucia that the señorita and I will not return until tomorrow."

"*Sí,* Patrón."

A moment later, he and the other vaqueros were gone in a cloud of dust.

"We aren't going back to Dolorosa?"

"Not right away."

Sloan waited for Cruz to explain himself, but when he didn't, she asked, "Where are we going?"

"We are going to Gonzales to be married by a priest."

Chapter 10

"You're crazy if you think I'm going to agree to bind myself more closely to you," Sloan said.

"I was not asking for your permission."

Cruz spurred his horse into a trot, and Sloan quickly kneed her mount to catch up to him.

"Why are you doing this?" she demanded.

"We made a bargain. Tonio has been avenged. It is time you kept the promise you made to me four years ago."

"There's no need to say vows before a priest," Sloan argued.

"I want no question in your mind that we are truly man and wife—that we belong to one another body and soul."

Sloan was desperate to avoid saying marriage vows before a priest, because once Cruz married her in a church, he would never let her out of their bargain. "What if Alejandro isn't dead?"

"He is."

"What about Three Oaks?"

"What about it? Our agreement never depended on your inheriting Three Oaks. Even if it did, have you had word that Rip has changed his mind?"

Sloan was silent. Over the past four years, she had denied to herself that she was Cruz's wife. He was forcing her to remove the blinders she had worn and accept the fact she was the wife of a Spanish *hacendado*.

She wasn't sure which distressed her more, the fear of dealing with Cruz woman to man or the fear that she would be ceding him control of her life. At last she said, "I don't understand why you want me for your wife."

"It is enough that I do."

She met his eyes and saw they blazed hot with desire. But was desire enough on which to base a marriage? She was afraid he would make her feel . . . things . . . she didn't want to feel ever again.

There was always, lingering at the back of her mind, the thought that he was Tonio's brother. She had given herself fully, freely to Tonio. She doubted she could ever do so with another man.

Cruz pulled his horse to a stop next to Sloan and reached over with his free hand to gently brush back an errant strand of sable hair from her face. "Do not look so troubled, Cebellina. You have been mine for four years. The words of the priest will only bless our union."

"Cruz, this marriage was a bad idea. It was conceived in desperation and born in haste. I . . . I've changed my mind. I want an annulment."

"No."

"No? Just like that? No?"

"Just like that. No."

"Can't you see this isn't going to work? I can't be what you want in a wife."

"You are exactly what I want. I admire your courage, your strength of will, your intelligence." He paused and grinned. "And, of course, your beauty."

"I'm a terrible mother," she said.

"No, Cebellina, you are not. You gave up your child because of a great hurt. Your heart is full of love for—"

"I don't love you!"

His eyes met hers and he said simply, "But I love you."

Cruz would have said more except Betsy began wriggling in his arms. "Easy, *niña*."

Betsy reached out for Sloan, speaking with her eyes and her hands rather than her voice.

Sloan angled her horse closer to Cruz's and opened her arms for the little girl. Betsy launched herself from Cruz's lap, and Sloan caught her in mid-air, pulling her close. "I've got you, sweetheart. Rest now." Betsy quickly settled in Sloan's lap.

"If she gets too heavy for you, I will take her again," Cruz said. "A child looks good in your arms, Cebellina. I look forward to seeing you growing round with a child of ours."

"I don't know whether I want more children."

Cruz said nothing, but Sloan watched his hands tighten on the reins until his knuckles were white. She hadn't even come to terms with the possibility of lying beneath him as his wife, let alone bearing his child.

"Could we discuss this marriage business?" Sloan asked.

"What did you have in mind?"

"We could forget about the priest and—"

"I won't compromise on that," Cruz said flatly. "If you want to suggest ways we can be happier married to one another, then I am willing to listen."

"Very well," Sloan said. "To start with, I'm used to doing as I please."

"Your days are yours to fill," Cruz said. "The nights belong to me."

Sloan felt her cheeks pinken. She cleared her throat and said, "And exactly how am I to fill my days? All I know is cotton. Dolorosa caters to cattle."

"That is entirely up to you. There are many things that must be done on a ranch the size of Dolorosa. Of course, you will have the house—"

"Your mother takes care of the house," Sloan interrupted.

"You can spend time with your son."

"At Three Oaks I was responsible for managing an entire plantation. While the needs of one small boy must surely be great, they can't begin to compare with what I'm used to doing."

"Then you can spend some time with me learning to run Dolorosa."

Cruz was surprised at the words he had spoken. Yet he was not sorry he had said them. His friends would have found the idea of including their wives in their ranching business repugnant.

Yet because of the way Sloan had been raised, she would be able to understand and share both his worries and his triumphs in a way no ordinary woman could.

Sloan was appalled at how enticing she found Cruz's suggestion. To spend the days with him, to share his burdens and his successes . . . It almost sounded too good to be true.

Yet even if it were, she had ties to Three Oaks that couldn't be so easily dismissed. Would she feel the same sense of satisfaction from watching Dolorosa grow and prosper?

"I admit your idea sounds good," Sloan conceded. "And I'm willing to give it a try. But I have another suggestion."

"I am listening."

"I will be your wife." Sloan licked her lips nervously and continued, "But I want your promise that after, say, six months or so, if it doesn't look like it's working out, I can leave."

Cruz was silent for so long Sloan wondered if he had heard what she'd said. Then she noticed the furrows on his brow and the rigidity of his body. He had heard, all right. He just didn't like what he'd heard.

Cruz knew that Sloan fully expected to be unhappy at Dolorosa. In essense, she was offering him six months of marriage in exchange for the favor he had done for her four years ago. He could refuse. After all, it was not part of the bargain they had made.

But he was willing to gamble that her feelings for him, and for her son, ran deeper than she thought. He was willing to gamble that in six months she would not want to leave.

"I will agree to your suggestion," Cruz said, "with one condition."

"Which is?"

"That you will give yourself to me as openly and honestly as you gave yourself to my brother."

Sloan gasped. "I can't! I won't take the risk—"

"The risk of what? That you might fall in love again?" Cruz challenged. "I want the same chance my brother had. If you will not give it to me, I will have to take what I can get. And that means marriage on my terms."

Sloan was upset and didn't try to hide it. "You're asking me to do something I swore I would never do again. I can't promise you I'll be totally open and honest with you because

I'm not sure I can be. You can't wipe the slate clean, Cruz.
You can't be first. I can't give my innocence twice!"

"Then promise to give me what you can, Cebellina.
That will have to be enough."

Sloan was silent for a long time. At last she said, "All
right. I'll give you what I can."

He had already gotten more from her than she knew. He
pulled his horse to a stop. "In six months, the choice is
yours—to go or to stay. You have my word on it."

He held out his hand to her, and Sloan solemnly shook
it. Then he turned her hand palm upward and kissed it. An
arrow of pleasure darted up her arm.

"You don't play fair," she said.

He smiled roguishly. "I play to win."

As they rode onward, Sloan realized she no longer felt
trapped. Of course, the relief she felt hinged entirely on
Cruz's word that he would only hold her to the new bargain.

The strange thing was, she believed him. She frowned.
Despite her protestations that she could trust no man, it
seemed she had trusted Cruz. And so far he had not betrayed that trust.

She looked sideways at him from under lowered lashes.
That would bear thinking about.

Cruz took her to the primarily Spanish-speaking Texas
town of Gonzales, northeast of San Antonio along the
Guadalupe River, where one of the few priests to be found
in the Republic, Father Vicente Delgado, was known to be.

They found the priest in a one-room adobe house at the
far edge of town, giving last rites to an old Mexican
woman who had her loved ones gathered round her. When
Father Delgado at last made the sign of the cross, someone
whispered in his ear, and he looked beyond the crowd to

the tall man at the rear. Slowly, he made his way toward Cruz.

"We have come to seek your services, *Padre*," Cruz said.

"Let us go where we can talk in comfort," Father Delgado replied.

He led Sloan and Cruz, who was once again carrying Betsy, down the dusty street to a small adobe structure and gestured them inside. The house had two rooms, one in front and one in back, separated by a striped blanket that had been hung between the two. It reminded Sloan of the house where her sister Bay lived.

It was almost dusk, and Father Delgado lit a candle on the table in the front room. He pointed to a narrow cot to one side. "You may lay the child down there if you like," he said to Cruz.

Cruz started to set Betsy down, but she grasped his neck and wouldn't let go. "I will hold her," he said with a rueful smile.

"Then sit here." Father Delgado gestured Sloan and Cruz to a bench on one side of the simple wooden table, then sat down on the opposite bench.

"How may I help you?" he asked.

"We want you to marry us," Cruz said.

"Certainly. I will arrange to read the banns—"

"Tonight."

"But, señor, I cannot—"

Cruz handed a small pouch full of coins to the priest. "Surely, Father, it is possible to get a dispensation in special circumstances."

Father Delgado looked from Cruz to Sloan to the child in Cruz's arms and asked, "Are there special circumstances?"

"Only that we wish to be together as man and wife,"
Cruz admitted solemnly. "Will you marry us?"

The priest weighed the small rawhide bag in his hand.
The people of his church needed money, but that was not
the only, or even the most important, reason he decided to
grant the *hacendado*'s wishes. He knew from the look in
the man's eyes that he would not wait the weeks until the
banns had been read before he sought out the woman. Perhaps he could do them both a service, and serve God as
well, if he removed the reason to sin from their paths.

"Yes, I will marry you, my children."

Father Delgado watched the faces of the two young
souls before him and saw that his announcement had
brought neither of them great joy. The *hacendado* looked
grimly satisfied. The woman looked grimly resigned. They
both looked grimly determined.

Father Delgado sighed inwardly. He was tempted to
withdraw his offer to marry them, but one look at the *hacendado* convinced him that trouble lay that way. He
sighed aloud. He would join them in the eyes of God, and
pray to the Good Lord to guide them to earthly happiness.

"Do you have a place to stay in Gonzales?" the priest
asked.

"We will find something," Cruz said.

"May I offer my humble dwelling for your comfort?"

"We would not want to intrude—"

"It is no intrusion," Father Delgado assured Cruz. "I
promised to sit with the family of Señora Santiago for a
while, so you are welcome to use my home to refresh yourselves before the wedding. And I will be perfectly comfortable on the small cot I keep at the mission. I will have no
need of my bed here tonight."

"Then, yes, we would be glad to stay," Cruz said.

"Are you hungry?" the priest asked.

Cruz looked to Sloan, who admitted, "A little."

"I'm hungry," Betsy volunteered loudly.

Sloan smiled and reached over to embrace the little girl, which meant putting her arms around Cruz as well. She felt the muscles of his arms bunch under his wool shirt, and she turned her face up to find his eyes hooded with need.

She forced her gaze back to Betsy's face. "We'll have to get you something to eat," she murmured to the child.

Sloan's thoughts weren't on food, however, but on hunger of a different sort altogether.

The sound of Father Delgado clearing his throat brought Sloan upright. She shook her head slightly as though to clear it.

"I am afraid the fare I have is simple, but it is nourishing," Father Delgado said. "You will find pinto beans cooking out back on the fire and corn tortillas and a bit of *cabrito* in the cupboard over there." He gestured across the table.

"*Cabrito?*" Sloan whispered to Cruz.

"Roasted goat," Cruz whispered back.

Sloan just had time to straighten the wrinkle of disgust on her nose before the priest turned back and said, "Eat, take time to prepare yourselves, and meet me in the church when it comes full dark."

Shortly after the priest left, a young Mexican girl arrived with some clothing for Sloan.

"Father Delgado's wedding gift to you," the girl said.

Sloan could not imagine how or where the priest had so quickly obtained the garments, but she was grateful she would not have to be married wearing pants and boots.

She went into the back bedroom and, with Betsy's help,

dressed herself for her wedding. She first put on the white embroidered *camisa,* with its lace trim along the square neck and the short, gathered sleeves. Then she added the matching white cotton skirt with its colorful embroidered border of tiny pink roses and trailing green vines along the bottom hem. A set of ivory combs held her hair back from her face, which was then framed by a delicate white lace mantilla. Simple leather sandals adorned her feet.

Since the night was cool, Father Delgado had also provided a triangular shawl with the same beautiful pattern of pink roses and vines embroidered on it. The long fringe on the shawl felt silky against her arms when she wrapped herself in it.

Sloan stayed as long as she could in the bedroom, but the hour until dark passed with all the speed and raging turmoil of a prairie fire. At last she stepped past the striped curtain into the front room to greet Cruz.

"Isn't she bee-you-ti-ful?" Betsy said from her hiding place behind Sloan's skirt.

"Very beautiful," Cruz agreed with a smile. Sloan's eyes were the warmest brown he had ever seen, her lips soft and berry-red. The simple peasant wedding blouse framed her smooth shoulders, leaving her throat bare and exposing the racing pulse beneath her ear. The skirt emphasized her narrow waist and womanly hips and exposed her slim ankles. He wanted to hold her in his arms, to smooth the blouse off her shoulders and skim the skirt down her supple legs. He forced himself to patience. Soon she would be his wife in fact as well as name and he could do with her as he wished.

He brought his hand out from behind his back and handed Sloan a small bouquet of wildflowers. "I thought you might like to carry these."

As their fingers touched, a bolt of desire streaked

through Sloan. She quickly accepted the flowers and brought them up to her face to hide her growing blush of pleasure. She inhaled the pungent sweetness, meeting Cruz's gaze over the top of the bouquet.

His eyes were hooded with desire, his nostrils flared, as if to catch the scent of the wild blossoms—or the scent of her.

Betsy broke the thread of tension growing between them when she demanded, "Is it time to go yet?"

Cruz reached out and lifted the little girl into his arms. "*Sí, niña.*" He turned to Sloan and asked, "Shall we go?"

"I suppose so," she replied, unable to keep the nervousness from her voice.

Now that the moment of truth was upon her, Sloan realized the enormity of the step she was about to take. When she entered the candlelit Spanish adobe mission with Cruz at her side, her heart was in her throat. She had been baptized Catholic at her mother's insistence, then raised Protestant by Rip after her mother's death.

She knew little of the Latin ritual that was to come, only that its very strangeness lent it potency in her mind. She followed Cruz's lead, dipping into the font of holy water after him, crossing herself when he did, even bending her knee in a mirror of his genuflection.

They walked slowly down the aisle of the church to the altar, where an imposing wooden cross bearing the carved figure of an agonizingly crucified Jesus drew her eye. As he had promised, Father Delgado was waiting for them.

Attempts to seat Betsy elsewhere were met with quite vocal resistance, and so the three of them, Cruz, Sloan, and Betsy, knelt on the velvet padded bench before the altar.

Sloan folded her hands with the flowers between them

and rested them along the wooden rail, then bowed her head as the priest began to drone his Latin refrain.

She dipped her nose into the flowers to counter the overwhelming odor of incense that reminded her of the painful confrontation she'd had with Doña Lucia at Tonio's bier.

She heard Cruz murmuring a response in Latin, but let her eyes drift to the flickering candles along either side of the altar.

The candles mesmerized her, sending her back to a night long ago, when she and Cricket and Bay were children. There had been a bad thunderstorm, and Cricket and Bay had come racing to her room to huddle under the covers with her until the worst of it had passed. She had lit a candle and with that single bit of illumination they had waited out the storm together. They had talked of their dreams for the future.

"I'm going to spend my whole life doing exactly what I want," Cricket had said.

"What's that?" Sloan asked.

"Having fun!" Cricket replied with a laugh.

"I'm going to meet a handsome man who'll carry me away on his magnificent black stallion," Bay said, her violet eyes dreamy.

"Who would want a tall, skinny thing like you?" Cricket teased.

"The man I love will simply die for a woman with violet eyes and flaming red hair," Bay said with great dignity. "The rest of me won't matter."

Cricket broke into hysterical guffaws, and Sloan smiled.

"It's your turn, Sloan," Bay said.

"I'm going to make Three Oaks the biggest and best cotton plantation there ever was."

"That's not a dream, Sloan," Cricket objected. "A dream

is supposed to be what you would do if you could have anything you want. Tell us something that doesn't have to do with Three Oaks."

Sloan had remained silent for a moment and then said, "I would be married in a beautiful white gown in a church where every planter from up and down the Brazos had gathered to watch and admire me."

"What does your husband look like?" Cricket asked.

"Let's see. He has blue eyes—"

"—filled with love for you," Bay interrupted, violet eyes still dreamy.

"How did you know?" Sloan said with a grin. "And a mouth so kissable I'll be tempted to—"

When Cruz touched her hand, Sloan jumped, torn abruptly from her daze. She looked up and found a well of wanting in his deep blue eyes. His lips were full and inviting. She slowly leaned toward him and then caught herself.

The dreams of a child were only that, she told herself firmly. Dreams. This was a very different reality.

Cruz gestured with his head toward the priest, and she looked up into the benevolent bearded face that was all of the elderly man that showed, shrouded as he was in his robes. The priest spoke to her in Latin, but the words meant nothing. She turned back to Cruz, her eyes questioning.

"You must make your vows now," he said. "Father Delgado is asking if you will consent to take me as your husband."

For a moment it was all Sloan could do not to rise and flee the church. She gripped her hands more tightly together around the bouquet of vivid wildflowers and asked, "What do I have to say?"

"He will tell you the words. Repeat them after him."

And so, in a language she didn't understand, Sloan repeated the words that bound her to Cruz, body and soul.

After he stopped speaking, Father Delgado made the sign of the cross and Cruz leaned over to brush his lips against Sloan's.

"Are we done yet?" Betsy asked.

"We are done," Father Delgado said with a smile. "And I must say you were a very good girl through it all."

"Sloan promised she would give me some *buñuelos* if I was good," Betsy said.

"It's almost bedtime for you," Sloan said.

"I'm not tired," Betsy chirruped. "I want to eat my *buñuelos* now. I can go to bed anytime."

Cruz laughed ruefully. Bed was exactly where he wanted to be right now, and not because he was tired, either. Betsy's presence complicated matters. But in Texas one learned to adapt.

Father Delgado walked back to his adobe house with them to join in a celebratory cup of wine and to make sure Betsy got her *buñuelos*. The priest seemed totally unaware of Cruz's impatience to bid him farewell. Having found a new ear, the priest readily told several of his favorite stories.

The evening passed quickly and eventually Sloan laid Betsy down in the big bed in the back room to sleep.

She and Cruz visited a little longer with Father Delgado before a yawn from Sloan caused the priest to say, "You are tired, señorita—no, no. Now it is Señora Guerrero. Forgive me. I was selfishly enjoying the conversation without any thought for—"

"I was enjoying it too, Father, but it has been a long day." Sloan rose from the hard bench at the table and surreptitiously rubbed her bottom to bring some feeling back into it. She caught Cruz's amused gaze.

They shared a secret smile before Cruz turned to Father Delgado and said, "I am ready to ask that favor of which we spoke earlier."

"Certainly, my son. I will watch the child for you. Do not worry about her. Not at all. I will have everything well in hand."

"*Gracias, Padre.*" Cruz slipped his arm around Sloan's waist and headed her toward the door without giving her a chance to object.

"What do you think you're doing?" Sloan hissed as they reached the darkness beyond the doorway. "I don't want to go anywhere. I'm tired. I want to go to bed."

"There is already someone in your bed."

"So I'll join her."

"On our wedding night?" Cruz asked, his brows raised.

"It's just one night."

"A very special night, Cebellina. One night above all others."

"I don't see what makes it so special."

"This."

Sloan felt Cruz's hand curve possessively around her waist, drawing her to a halt, while his fingertips tipped her chin up for the briefest brush of his lips against hers.

"And this."

His lips came down again, this time with fierce possession, branding her as his own. Sloan didn't know what to do with her hands. She had the urge to touch him, yet his only contact with her was the hand at her waist and the urgent press of his lips against hers. He turned his head, and his mouth left hers to caress her cheeks, her eyelids, her nose, and then her lips again.

Cruz heard the moan in his wife's throat and slanted his mouth onto hers, his tongue teasing her lips apart. Her mouth was warm and sweet . . . and willing. But no more than that.

It wasn't enough.

He wanted her to feel the same wild, insatiable need he felt. When the time came that they joined their bodies at last as man and wife, he wanted her to desire him as she had never desired another man . . . as she had never desired his brother.

Sloan felt a sense of desolation as Cruz eased his mouth away. She shivered as he traced her damp lower lip with his thumb.

"Come with me, Cebellina."

"Where are we going?"

"Where we can be alone."

He reached his hand out to her, and she took it. He led her to the edge of town and beyond, to a grassy valley. It was clear this was where he had come for the wildflowers, for they abounded here, their faces folded to the moonlight.

She realized now that he had planned to bring her here all along, for he quickly retrieved a rolled-up blanket that had been tucked in the hollow of a gnarled live oak and spread it across the dewy ground. He took her hand and helped her sit down on the square of striped wool, and then he joined her.

They faced one another, filling their senses with each other.

"You are even more beautiful in the moonlight." Cruz gently cupped her face with his hand.

Sloan leaned into his palm, wanting his gentleness. It was a light touch, the touch of a man dealing with innocence rather than experience. For that, Sloan thanked him from the bottom of her heart.

"Four years is a long time," she murmured. "A lifetime."

"Take all the time you need," he said, his voice warm and a little husky.

"Father Delgado—"

"Father Delgado does not expect us back before dawn."

She smiled, and he let his fingers trace the line of her curving lips. His branding touch made Sloan ache with need. With every caress, every kiss, he claimed her for his own. She learned the texture of his lips—hard and then so, so soft—and savored the flavor of his mouth—tobacco and wine and something distinctly Cruz.

She was hardly aware that Cruz had coaxed her down so she was lying beneath him. His hand found her collarbone and traced it, then slipped down to the swell of her breast above her *camisa*. He untied the bow that held the gathered blouse and loosened the cloth. She could see it surprised him to find she was wearing nothing underneath.

He eased the cloth down and away, exposing her to his gaze. "What a wonder you are, *querida*." When he captured her naked breast with his hand, Sloan froze.

He stayed exactly as he was, waiting for her to accept his claim. "*Te adoro,* Cebellina," he murmured in her ear.

It felt too good. How could it feel so good? She had thought Tonio had given her all the pleasure a woman could feel. He had said so, had he not?

But it was as nothing compared to what she felt now. Sloan bit her lower lip to stifle her cry of dismay. She almost could not bear the comparison, because it made her realize what a very gullible young woman she had been.

She sought out Cruz's hand on her breast and traced the heavy knuckles, the slender fingers, all of them making up a hand that possessed incredible strength but touched her with tenderness.

Why was she fighting this? She wanted him to touch her. He was her husband. It was his right to touch her in any way he pleased. And that he chose to please her, well, she would be a fool indeed not to recognize the difference between what Tonio had given her and what Cruz was offering.

She ignored her pounding heart and pressed gently on the back of Cruz's hand, hoping he would realize she liked what he was doing and wished him to continue.

She felt her body tensing with anticipation as his fingers began to move slowly, gently finding the rosy tip of her breast and teasing it until she groaned deep in her throat from the pleasure. She writhed upward under him, wanting his mouth on her breast, wondering how it would feel, but too shy to ask for it.

As if sensing her need, he lowered his head to possess her.

His tongue came searching first, barely touching her nipple. She hissed out a breath of air. He teased her, licking, then withdrawing, until at last she grasped his hair in both hands and wouldn't let him go.

When she heard him chuckle, she stiffened.

He immediately lifted his head to look at her. "What is wrong, Cebellina?"

"Are you laughing at me?" she whispered. "At my . . . at my need . . ."

"It is *joy* I am feeling, Cebellina, that is all," he said urgently.

She stared into his hooded eyes, silvery-blue in the moonlight and saw no sign of the ridicule she had feared was the source of his laughter. She found only wonder and delight . . . and desire.

"I . . . I want to touch you," she said. "Will you take off your shirt?"

He sat up and slipped off the plain wool shirt he had worn to their wedding. She stared at his chest, liking the whorls of thick black hair that covered his bronzed skin. She reached out without thinking and threaded her fingers into the wiry mass.

"It's so soft!" she exclaimed. "I'd forgotten how—"

He stiffened against her hand and she realized her mistake. She had reminded them both that this was not her first time with a man. Cruz was second. His brother had come first.

She awkwardly withdrew her hand.

Cruz was the one who reached out again. He took her hand and placed it back on his chest. His voice was commanding. "Touch me, *querida*. Feel that I am different. Feel that I am not my brother."

She looked up into his sapphire eyes and found a gleam of savage possession. He demanded her acquiescence, and she discovered she had no choice except to obey him. Her lips followed where her hands led.

"Your skin is so warm. And salty," she murmured. She brushed her cheek against his chest, liking the feel of his rough hair and the hard muscle beneath it. She heard the pounding of his heart, racing at least as fast as her own.

Her hands roved over his sinewy shoulders, down his strong, heavily veined forearms. Then she placed them on his chest and ran them tauntingly through the whorls of crisp black hair, following the triangle down his stomach to its apex at the line of his trousers.

"Take them off," she ordered, her voice teasing.

"Take off your skirt," he replied.

She looked up into his face only to find all playfulness gone. His lambent gaze held hers as he slowly stripped off her skirt and pantalets. A moment later he had bared his powerful body. From beneath lowered lashes, Sloan surveyed his broad chest, his narrow waist, his lean flanks, and that other masculine part of him that demanded attention.

"You are so . . ." Sloan didn't want to, but she couldn't help comparing him to Tonio.

Tonio had been a boy. Cruz was a man.

"Come, Cebellina. It is time we became man and wife."

He played her body like a harp, finding the sweetest notes, plucking the strings, fanning them, then plucking them again. Holding her, stroking there, strumming high and low, he orchestrated their love song, until the music had caught them both in a crescendo of excitement.

With every touch, he branded her as his own, demanding that she be his, and his alone.

Their sweat-damp bodies clung, and Sloan shivered as Cruz moved over her, pressing her down on the blanket, raising her hands over her head and capturing her wrists with one hand. He quickly spread her thighs with his knee and lowered himself onto her. She felt the press of his engorged shaft seeking entrance, and panicked.

"Cruz, no! I—"

With a single thrust he was inside her. She was slick and wet, and it was impossible to deny that she had wanted him, that she had been more than ready for him.

"It is done. You are mine."

The look on his face was fiercely possessive as he tilted her hips and seated himself deeper inside her, laying claim to her. He stroked slowly, drawing out the pleasure.

Sloan felt herself rising higher and higher, driven by the frenzied music of love.

Cruz's body clamored for satisfaction; he denied it. She must know she belonged only to him; she must accept his possession. His mouth found Sloan's and he mimed the action of his hips.

He heard the grating, almost animal cries of satisfaction that ground from Sloan's throat as she arched upward. He felt her body squeezing tight around him, strains of sweet satisfaction rolling over her, and spilled his seed inside her with a cry of exultation.

Cruz lay atop Sloan, their chests moving in tandem as they labored to bring enough air to ease breathlessness.

"That was . . . incredible," Sloan said.

"*Querida, mi amor, mi vida*," he whispered in her ear. "*Te quiero.*"

Sloan didn't know what to say in response to his fervent declaration of love. He must know she couldn't say the words in return. Because she didn't love him. Sloan shivered, suddenly aware of the cool night air.

Cruz slipped off her and pulled the blanket around them both. He turned her into his arms, his breath moist against her temple. "Do not worry, Cebellina. The feelings will come."

"And if they don't?"

Cruz settled her head on his shoulder, his arm firmly surrounding her, as they gazed up at the moon and stars together. He kissed her temple, and then her mouth. "Let us leave tomorrow's worries for tomorrow. Tonight is ours to enjoy."

Chapter 11

SLOAN HAD WONDERED ALOUD ON THE RIDE back to Dolorosa whether the fact she was now a *really* married woman would show on her face the first time she came eye to eye with Cruz's mother.

Cruz had laughed and said, "Of course not!"

Sloan wasn't so sure.

"You will be able to keep your secret for a few more days, Cebellina," he had said with a smile. "For I must leave you when we return to Dolorosa and finish the roundup. When I return, we will both sit down with my mother and give her the happy news."

They arrived back at Dolorosa late that afternoon. Doña Lucia welcomed Sloan and Cruz with a forbidding stare, while Tomasita cooed over blue-eyed Betsy, who was once again in Cruz's arms, her head against his shoulder.

"I'll take Betsy," Sloan said as she stepped up onto the veranda. She tenderly brushed the damp bangs away from Betsy's forehead. "I'll put her down for a nap in Tonio's room."

Cruz watched Sloan turn and enter the hacienda. It was clear she had allowed the little girl to pierce the shell around her heart that she had used to keep Cisco away. He worried that when Betsy returned to her family—and surely her aunt and uncle would want her—Sloan would be forced to face yet another loss.

Sloan had laid Betsy down and covered her with a quilt when she heard a silk skirt rustling behind her. "One of my son's vaqueros can take the girl to the mission orphanage in San Antonio in the morning."

"She'll be staying here until her uncle can be contacted." In response to any objections Doña Lucia might make, Sloan added, "I've already spoken to Cruz. It's all settled."

"I see. What if her uncle does not want her?"

"Then I'll keep her myself."

Doña Lucia's brows rose in speculation. "You would not keep your own son, yet you will raise the orphaned child of another? What kind of woman are you?"

Sloan bunched her fists at her sides. "That isn't really any concern of yours, is it?"

Doña Lucia opened and shut her fan in agitation, but said nothing, simply turned and left the room.

Sloan stared after her. Cruz's mother had prodded an old wound and found still-proud flesh. She shouldn't have been so surprised that she could feel ashamed of the fact she had abandoned her son. It had not been one of her better decisions. But she wasn't going to let Doña Lucia's words keep her from taking the very best care of Betsy.

She sought Cruz out in the *sala* and found him riffling through papers on his rolltop desk. "Your mother is . . . upset . . . about Betsy's presence here," she said.

Cruz rose and took Sloan's hands in his. "My mother is not master here. I am. Does that settle the matter?"

"Well . . . yes, I guess so."

He turned back to his desk.

Sloan noticed he seemed distracted and in a hurry. When he had collected a number of papers in a leather satchel, he turned and found her still standing there.

"Was there anything else you wanted to speak with me about?" he asked.

"No."

"Then I will say *adiós*. I must join the roundup. I have already been gone too long."

"I thought you were going to teach me how to run Dolorosa," Sloan said, realizing that once again she was being left behind. "I thought we were going to be partners, riding side by side."

"The roundup is no place for a woman."

"Not even for your wife?"

"Especially not for my wife."

Sloan saw the banked desire that darkened Cruz's blue eyes until they were the color of a stormy day. His free hand grasped hers, and his thumb caressed her callused palm.

She felt her skin heating and jerked her hand away, appalled to see how quickly she had succumbed to his mesmerizing touch. "All right, I'll stay here . . . at least until I can contact Luke and see what's going on at Three Oaks. Perhaps Rip is ready to have me come home."

Cruz's protest was cut off by a shriek of terror from Tonio's bedroom. Sloan's horrified eyes met Cruz's before they both raced toward the room where she had left Betsy.

When they reached the doorway, they found Betsy crouched on top of the pillows at the head of the bed, whimpering. Cisco was on his knees beside her, his small hand patting her shoulder in an attempt to calm her.

"Do not cry, *niña,*" Cisco said.

Sloan hurried to the bed and sat down beside Cisco. "What happened?"

"I did not mean to make her cry, Mamá. I only wanted to play with her."

Tears had begun to fill Cisco's eyes. Sloan felt the urge to pull him into her arms and soothe his tears away, as she had done for Betsy, but she caught herself just in time. That way lay disaster.

Because she could not follow her natural inclination, her voice was more harsh than she had intended. "Never mind. I'm sure Betsy will want to play with you later. Right now, though, she's resting. Why don't you find Tomasita and see if she wants to play?"

Sloan had told herself that Cisco was too young to recognize her rejection for what it was. The lost, miserable look on his face made it plain she was wrong.

But he only said, "Sí, Mamá," and ran from the room.

Sloan suddenly realized that she hadn't thought twice about sending her son to seek out Tomasita while she stayed to comfort a child who was not even her own flesh and blood. Maybe Doña Lucia was right. Maybe there was something unnatural about her.

Sloan looked up and found Cruz watching her intently. She dropped her eyes from his. He did not have to speak for her to feel his censure. She had promised him she would treat the children equally. She was somehow going to have to get over the reserve she enforced around her son.

The child on the bed moaned. Sloan settled herself comfortably on the feather mattress, with her back leaning against the ornately carved headboard, before picking Betsy up and cradling her in her arms. She was totally absorbed in the child until she felt Cruz's touch on her arm.

She looked up, startled, and said, "I thought you had left."

"We never finished our discussion."

"Our discussion?"

"Of what you will do to fill your days at Dolorosa while I am gone."

Sloan absently rubbed her hand against Betsy's rosy cheek.

"But I see there will be much to occupy your time," Cruz said brusquely. "I must go, Cebellina."

"You're leaving right now?" Sloan didn't like the bereft sound of her voice. She cleared her throat and said, "How soon will you be back?"

"Not for a week at least, perhaps longer. I want your promise that you will not leave Dolorosa—for any reason—until I return."

Sloan's lips flattened in the mulish expression Cruz had learned to recognize.

"I can't promise anything."

"If you are not here when I get back, I will come after you."

Betsy whimpered at the tone of Cruz's voice.

"You're frightening her."

"Be here. *Adiós,* Cebellina." His hand curved around her nape as he gave her a quick, claiming kiss.

Sloan stared after him as he walked out the bedroom door, his satchel under his arm. He hadn't even given her a chance to say good-bye.

A moment later she wondered what possible use he could have for a satchel of business papers on the roundup.

.   .   .

Cruz walked quickly through the house, frustrated with the series of events that had made it necessary for him to attend to affairs of state at a time when he would much rather attend to affairs at home.

He had meant what he said about including Sloan in his work at Dolorosa—even the roundup. However, that was impossible right now, because he wasn't headed directly for the roundup. First, he had a rendezvous with the Englishman, and he had no choice except to be there.

He rode like a man possessed, certain he would never arrive in time. He pulled up his *bayo* as he reached the camp of Mexican bandidos under the lone oak tree. He searched the gathering for the dapper Englishman and found him by the fire. Cruz froze as he recognized the man sitting beside Sir Giles.

However incredible it seemed, Alejandro Sanchez was alive.

Cruz saw from the startled expression on Alejandro's face that he was equally surprised to see Cruz.

Alejandro turned to Sir Giles and demanded angrily, "What is he doing here?"

"Didn't you know? My dear man, this is the Hawk. From now on, you two will be working together."

"I think not," Cruz said in a cold voice. "This bastard murdered my brother."

"I executed a traitor and a fool," Alejandro retorted. "One in whose footsteps you follow—Hawk. Or were you also involved in Tonio's plot? For shame, Don Cruz, letting the Rangers capture your brother. If not for that—"

"You have said enough, Alejandro," Cruz said curtly, interrupting the bandido's speculation. "Whatever I was . . . whatever I am . . . you will pay for taking my brother's life."

Sir Giles looked from one man to the other, and saw them bristling, hands fisted, ready to fight. "Bloody hell!" he exclaimed. "I don't give a damn what your personal differences are. I have work that has to get done."

"Have you tasted the delights to be offered by Tonio's *puta*?" Alejandro taunted Cruz.

"Shut your mouth, Alejandro, or this time I *will* cut out your tongue."

"Where is she now?" Alejandro asked. "Have you tired of her so soon? I would not have thought she was much in bed myself, but Tonio bragged—"

Cruz's hand shot out to grip Alejandro's throat. In an instant the civilized man was gone, replaced by a ferocious beast. Alejandro was helpless in his grasp. The cold point of a sharp blade was pressed to the flesh beneath Alejandro's jaw. "If you say another word about my wife, I will kill you."

The two men measured one another, a mad dog and a ferocious hawk, both deadly, both capable of dealing swift and sure death.

"Gentlemen, gentlemen." Sir Giles stepped toward the two men, but stopped short, suddenly aware how little he could do to stop them.

Cruz regained control by reminding himself of the importance of his mission. As suddenly as the beast had come, it was gone. He released Alejandro and sheathed his knife.

There was more at stake here than seeking revenge for his brother's death and the insults to his wife. Tonio would be avenged—when the time was right. And for all his threats, Alejandro could not reach beyond the fortressed walls of Cruz's hacienda to harm Sloan.

"I don't care what your personal grievance is against

this man," Sir Giles said to Cruz. He turned back to Alejandro. "What is important to me is that the two of you
manage to deal with one another. Now, what is it to be?"

Alejandro shrugged. "So long as you pay me well, I will
work with the devil himself."

Sir Giles looked at Cruz and thought maybe Alejandro
was going to get his wish. "And you, Hawk? What say
you?"

"I am willing to put my personal feelings aside. Until
my mission is finished."

Cruz's gaze clashed with Alejandro's. They both knew
the day would come when they would fight to the death.
Until then, they would watch and wait.

Because neither man intended to be the one to die.

Two days after Cruz had left, Sloan received a letter from
Cricket.

Dear Sloan,

   *Luke wrote and told me what happened. I can
hardly believe we have a brother! But then, I've
always known there was something special about
Luke. Can you believe what a noodleheaded
lumpkin we have for a father? Imagine giving
everything to a* son!
   *Luke said you had gone to Dolorosa. I would say
my feelings were hurt because you didn't come here,
but I suspect you had your reasons.*
   *Is there any truth to the romance Bay suggested
might be sprouting between you and Cruz? I hope
so. I saw how Cruz watched you at Jesse's
christening last year. His eyes fairly glowed!*
   I expect you to write me all about everything. I

*wish I could be there, but this muffin growing inside
me (we're probably going to end up naming the poor
thing Muffin), isn't cooperating lately.*

> *Your worried sister,*
> *Cricket*

It took Sloan hours to compose a reply, but time was
something she had a great deal of lately.

Several days after Cruz had left, Miguel returned with
the rest of Cruz's vaqueros, empty-handed from their
search for the two Randolph boys.

Sloan was glad she hadn't offered any hope to Betsy
that her cousins were alive. In a few years, they would be
very much Comanches in thought and deed. They were as
lost to Betsy as though they had died.

Besides writing to Cricket, Sloan had spent a great deal
of time sending out letters in hopes of reaching Betsy's
aunt and uncle. She had also sent a note to Luke telling
him about the mysterious Englishman, and Alejandro and
the Hawk. She had urged him to come visit Dolorosa again
so they could talk.

The rest of her time was spent playing with Betsy,
avoiding Cisco, and missing Cruz.

It was devastating to admit that she was thinking about
Cruz, because it meant she cared. And if there was one
thing she had been determined to do, it was to avoid caring. Loving meant becoming vulnerable to hurt. And she
had already been hurt enough for one lifetime.

She didn't understand her feelings for the proud
Spaniard, but she could hardly deny they existed. The
question was what she should do about them. She had married Cruz because she had owed him that much. But that
didn't mean she had to open her heart to him.

She stayed close to the hacienda for two weeks after she had sent her letter to Luke, expecting him to arrive any day. When she received neither a letter of response nor a visit from Luke, and Cruz still hadn't returned, she decided to put an end to the waiting—and escape for a while the golden cage in which Cruz had imprisoned her.

Early the next morning, she packed a few of her belongings in her carpetbag before going in search of Tomasita. She found her still abed.

Sloan leaned over Tomasita and whispered, "Tomasita, wake up."

Tomasita woke abruptly and sat bolt upright. Sloan had to put a hand out to keep the young woman from jumping out of bed.

"Oh, Sloan, it is you. I thought it was Mother María and that I was late for morning vespers again."

Sloan chuckled. "You can go back to sleep in a minute. I wanted to ask a favor of you."

"Anything."

"I'm riding to Three Oaks today. I don't expect I'll be back tonight. I left Betsy sleeping in my bed. Will you keep an eye on her for me while I'm gone?"

"But of course," Tomasita said, and then added, "Are you not afraid to go riding so far by yourself?"

Sloan shrugged. "Not especially."

"It must be wonderful to be so brave, not to fear the Comanches or bandidos or wild animals or snakes or scorpions or—"

"If you keep that up, I may begin to wonder whether you think I'm brave or just plain crazy," Sloan said with a grin.

"I often wished for the courage to leave the convent and go in search of . . . I do not know what. But I suppose courage is something one is born with. And I was not."

"I'm sure if you had really wanted to leave the convent, you would have found a way to do it," Sloan said. "I don't think any of us really knows what we're capable of doing until the need arises. Then I think we sometimes surprise ourselves.

"I have no choice about making this journey. I have to find out what's going on at Three Oaks. Give Betsy a hug for me."

"I will." Tomasita's voice was slightly accusatory as she added, "And I shall hug Cisco, too."

Sloan turned her head so Tomasita wouldn't see that the jibe hurt. "Of course." She whirled on her heel and headed for the door.

"Sloan?"

Sloan paused at the sound of Tomasita's anxious voice.

"Be careful."

"I will."

The ride to Three Oaks was hours long, the flat, grassy terrain becoming rolling hills studded with an occasional pin or live oak the closer she came to Three Oaks. As far as Sloan was concerned, the journey gave her far too much time to think.

When the plantation house finally came into sight, she had long since planned arguments to use on both Rip and Luke in order to reclaim her lost heritage. She stepped down off her horse and hitched the reins to the post in front of the house.

She left her carpetbag tied behind the saddle. There was no sense announcing she planned to visit for a few days before she was sure she would get the answers she wanted from Rip.

She opened the door and walked inside—to utter silence. "Hello? Is anybody home? Rip? Luke? Stephen?"

No answer.

She walked into Rip's office to see if there was anything on his desk that might tell her where he had gone. She found the notice of Wilkerson's regular sale of slaves, livestock, and a variety of wares in Houston, but couldn't believe Rip would have traveled that far in his weakened condition.

In fact, she couldn't believe he had left the house at all. He had only done so rarely since his stroke in January, unwilling to expose the weakness in his right hand and leg to his neighbors and business associates.

So where was he now? Where was everybody?

Luke was furious with Rip, furious enough to spit nails. Their relationship had deteriorated over the past few days to barely veiled animosity.

Each day since Sloan had left for the Guerrero hacienda had been harder than the one before. He had about made up his mind to have it out with Rip when the letter had come from Sloan. Then Rip had discovered a problem with the cotton gin that he had sworn he couldn't handle alone, and what with one thing and another it had been weeks, instead of days, before Luke could get away.

He sighed with relief as he spotted the whitewashed adobe hacienda where it sat on a hill, its broad veranda overlooking the Brazos River. He would get an answer from Sloan today. Whether she planned to stay with Cruz or go home to Three Oaks, he was giving her fair warning that he would be saying his *adiós* to Rip and riding back to San Antonio before the month was out.

Luke rode slowly through the small village where Cruz's vaqueros lived in a combination of mesquite *jacals* and adobe homes. Chickens roamed freely in the streets, and were occasionally forced to abandon some tasty morsel in indignant haste in order to stay beyond the threat of his horse's hooves.

He passed a mercantile store that reminded him he hadn't had a cherry stick in a long time, and a cantina with swinging doors that reminded him he hadn't had a whiskey in a long time, either. Time enough for that later, he decided.

The last and largest building he encountered before reaching the walls that surrounded Cruz's hacienda was an obviously abandoned mission with a high bell tower. Luke might have sought out a priest, if there had been one, to rid himself of the guilt and hate that sat upon his shoulders like a hair shirt.

But perhaps it was just as well there was no holy man here. He was not yet ready to give up his lifelong animosity for his father.

He almost didn't see Tomasita.

She was standing by the mission, her hand running delicately over the pockmarks left by musketballs and cannon over the past years of strife. Nearby, a heavyset Mexican woman played with two children, one of whom he recognized as Cisco.

He had forgotten how beautiful Tomasita Hidalgo was . . . but not how far beyond his reach she was. He was a bastard, a Texas Ranger who had to feed his horse, buy his ammunition, and provide himself with room and board on thirty-seven fifty a month. Doña Lucia had made it clear he was totally unsuitable for the high-born, well-bred Spanish woman whose loveliness now caught his eye.

As he approached her, he slowed his gelding. He really

shouldn't stop. It could only cause problems. But at that moment his horse's shoe struck a stone and she turned.

When she recognized him, a shy, fleeting smile crossed her face, before she quickly turned away again to face the crumbling wall. Her hand brushed its surface as though by doing so she could read the story it had to tell.

He pulled his chestnut to a stop behind her. "Howdy."

Tomasita pivoted slowly, her eyes lowered so that lush black lashes lay in crescents along the milky white skin of her cheeks. Her hands were clasped together in front of her, and her voice was breathless when she responded, "*Buenos días,* Señor Summers."

Luke dismounted in a single graceful movement that left him standing a foot in front of her. "Call me Luke."

Tomasita glanced quickly at Josefa only to discover that the old woman had followed the children around the corner to the back of the mission. She was alone.

Flustered, she could only think to say, "All right . . . Luke."

Her eyelids flew open when she felt the knuckles of his hand brush her face. His hand cupped her cheek, and he lifted her chin. She felt herself begin to tremble even before he spoke.

"I like the way you say my name."

Tomasita cleared her throat but couldn't seem to form any words. She kept her eyes lowered so all she could see was his strong, masculine forearm, covered in a light dusting of sun-bleached hair. She wanted to reach up and touch it to see how it felt. Appalled at her thoughts, her eyes flew to his face to see if he had realized what she was thinking.

"You're a very beautiful woman, Tomasita. Your skin is as soft as a wild rose petal." He smiled and added, "And,

right now, just as pink." He lowered his hand. "Am I embarrassing you?"

She stared back at him, seeing eyes that were warm and
alive with innuendo. Frightened by his intent gaze, not
quite understanding what she saw in his eyes, she lowered
her head again. "Yes. No. I do not know. Holy Mary . . ."

Luke's gentle laugh brought her blue eyes up to meet his
golden hazel ones. There was something in his eyes, something that called to her, asking her to trust him.

"I am not used to a gentleman speaking his mind so
honestly," she admitted with a tremulous smile. "I thank
you for the compliment."

"No thanks are necessary. Unless you'd like to thank me
by going for a walk along the river with me this Saturday."

"Oh, but I could not!"

"Why not?" he asked, a lazy grin on his face. "I'm sure
we'd have a good time."

Tomasita felt her heart beating nearly out of her skin. "I
mean, maybe I could, but I cannot accept such an invitation."

"Why not?" he persisted.

"Don Cruz would never allow it." She saw that Luke
was ready to continue his persuasion, so she explained, "I
have only my good name to offer a husband. If I met you at
the river . . ."

Tomasita's blush, which had almost receded, rose again
when her tongue tied at the thought of the discussion they
were having.

Luke bit his tongue. He could not say that if she joined
him, she would leave the river no different than she had
come. It was more than likely he would take at least a
kiss . . . and maybe more.

He wanted her—in a way he had never wanted another

woman. There was something about her that shook him up inside. It might have been her innocence.

In all the years Luke Summers had taken what he wanted from women, he had never taken a woman's virginity. This woman was obviously untouched.

Yet he wanted her. He didn't understand it. He was a little awed by it. But not enough to leave her be and go about his business.

"So, has Cruz already picked out a rich *ranchero* to be your husband?"

Unable to tell Luke of her betrothal to Don Cruz, Tomasita hedged, "I do not know."

"And don't care?"

Luke seemed upset, but Tomasita didn't know why. "Of course I care! But it would not be proper for a woman to choose her own husband. There are things which must be considered."

"Such as?"

"A man's family, for one thing."

As soon as she had spoken, she knew she had said something dreadfully wrong, for Luke's eyes turned from gold to green and his full lips flattened into a thin line.

"What else?" he demanded.

"His ability to provide a home for his wife and their children."

"Anything else?"

Tomasita licked her lips nervously before adding, "I . . . I suppose there are other things. I cannot think of them right now." She couldn't think because Luke's whole body radiated anger.

"What about love? What about a man who would care for you?" Luke asked, his voice soft, his tone taunting.

"Love will come with time. And surely my husband will learn to care for me. I will be obedient—"

Luke's cynical laugh cut her off. "Obedient. Yes, I'm sure you'd be that. If I ask something of you, Tomasita, will you obey me?"

"It . . . it would depend on what you asked," she said, her voice a mere whisper. What had happened to the charming young man who had first greeted her?

Luke leaned toward her until she could feel his breath against her ear. His intense voice was low and husky and sent shivers down her spine. "Tell me what *you* want, Tomasita. That's all. Just tell me what you want from the man you marry."

"I . . . I . . ."

"Do you want a man who'll make fire race in your veins?"

Tomasita held her breath as Luke's lips caressed her temple, then followed the shell of her ear and trailed down to her neck. She shivered from feelings that were new and breathtakingly exciting. She closed her eyes and tilted her head slightly to offer her neck for further adoration.

His fingers thrust into her silky black hair and captured her head between his hands. "Look at me," he commanded.

Tomasita raised her eyes to his face and found all the desire a woman could want blazing in his eyes. "What do *you* want, Tomasita?"

"Aiii! Señor! What are you doing? Take your hands off her. *Pobrecita! Mi niña!*"

Tomasita whirled to find Josefa barreling toward her on the run, her apron waving like a sheet on laundry day. Tomasita tried to step back from Luke, only belatedly realizing that he had kept his hold on her.

He pulled her into his arms and gave her a quick hard

kiss. Then he whispered in her ear, "I'll meet you on Saturday at dusk, by the river." He treated her to another of his roguish grins before he lithely mounted his horse and escaped.

"You had better run away, señor," Josefa shouted after him, her breath coming in outraged spurts. "You do not belong here. When Don Cruz hears what you have done—"

"That is enough, Josefa," Tomasita said, attempting to calm the heavyset woman, whose face was streaming with sweat from her exertion. "No harm has been done. I see no reason to say anything of this to Don Cruz or Doña Lucia."

"But that man—"

"Did nothing!"

"I saw him—"

"You saw him do what? Kiss me? And where will you tell Doña Lucia you were when this man kissed me? How will you explain that you were acting as my duenna yet could not forestall the señor?"

Tomasita saw the exact moment when it dawned on Josefa that if she told Don Cruz and Doña Lucia what Luke had done, she would also have to admit that she had let Tomasita out of her sight. She would be as much at fault as Tomasita, and they would likely both be punished.

"I will say nothing of this," Josefa agreed at last. "But I will be watching you from now on, like the cat watches a mouse, waiting to pounce."

Her tirade was interrupted by Cisco and Betsy, who had run up to show off a musketball they had found.

Tomasita's mind was only half on their excited child-talk. The other half was on Luke Summers. His lips had caressed her temple, her ear, her throat. He had even kissed her on the mouth! And she had enjoyed it. Holy Mary, she had wanted more of it! What kind of woman was she to let him take such liberties?

But it had seemed so right at the moment. She touched her lips. They were still wet, and a little swollen. Did she dare try to sneak away to see him on Saturday, knowing that if he tried to kiss her again she would let him do it? How could she even think such a thing when she was betrothed to Don Cruz?

"Tomasita, do you like it?"

She looked down to see Cisco holding up the rusty musketball.

"*Sí,* we shall take this back to the hacienda with us. Your papa will be home soon, and he will surely want to see it."

And if Cruz did not return before Saturday, what then? Tomasita closed her eyes and prayed to the Blessed Virgin to give her strength to resist the awful temptation that had been laid in her path.

Chapter 12

SLOAN SENSED SOMEONE IN HER BEDROOM WITH her and rolled over in the large feather bed. As she slowly sat up she saw Rip standing at the foot of her bed, silhouetted against the last rays of the sun.

She had only meant to rest for a moment, but she must have fallen asleep. She realized that the bed was no place from which to conduct the arguments she had formulated, but Rip didn't give her a chance to get up before he began speaking.

"Well, well, well. The prodigal daughter has returned."

Sloan bristled at his smug tone. She rose from the bed and stood beside it, tucking her gingham shirt into her trousers.

"It's about time someone showed some common sense around here," he said.

She leaned down and tugged on a Wellington, then had to search before she found the other boot under the bed. While she was pulling it on she asked, "Where's Luke?"

"Don't know. Don't care."

Sloan's eyes narrowed in speculation. "That's a new

tune you're singing. I must say I like the sound of it, though."

Rip chuckled. "Don't get your hopes up. He'll be back."

"What makes you so sure?"

"That boy hates my guts." Rip took his time getting to the ladder-back chair in the corner of Sloan's room. After he had settled himself in it, he leaned his hands on the handle of his cane and said, "Don't look so surprised. Surely you guessed everything wasn't honey and roses between me and my son."

"No. No, I hadn't . . . exactly." Sloan hopped up on the foot of the bed and let her heels dangle over the bedstead. "Why does he hate you?"

"It's a long story, and not a very pleasant one. I'd as soon not repeat it. Suffice it to say, there are things that happened that I'm not proud of. Things that hurt Luke's mother."

"Is there anything you can do to mend fences?"

"No. Luke's mother Charity died a few years ago."

A look of such great longing, mixed with pain, came across Rip's face that Sloan nearly got up to go to him. In another instant, the strained look was gone and he was in control again.

"There's nothing I can do to help her now," he said with a sigh of regret. "And Luke isn't going to let me forget it."

"But there's something you can do to help him. Is that it?" Sloan said. "Is that why you want to give him Three Oaks?"

"Something like that," Rip admitted. "It isn't that I wouldn't have wanted to help him anyway. After all, he is my son."

"How do you know he's actually your son?"

To her surprise Rip grinned. "Charity made sure he knew about my birthmark. Luke has the same one."

"I never knew—"

"It isn't in a place that shows."

Sloan had never thought of her father as an ordinary person with ordinary flaws. He had always been someone larger than life, the bedrock of Three Oaks, the stubborn, opinionated head of the household.

Now she realized he was only a man, one who had made a terrible mistake once upon a time. It was a mistake he clearly regretted and one that would likely haunt him the rest of his life.

It was also a mistake for which she was being forced to pay the consequences.

Sloan scooted off the bed and walked the few steps necessary to lay a hand on Rip's shoulder, offering the comfort she hadn't dared to offer before.

Rip's head came up with a jerk, and his gray eyes turned dark as he perused her face. "I assume you've come back to be my overseer."

"I've come back to claim what's mine."

Rip chuffed out a breath of air. "What about Cruz?"

"What about him?"

"The man seemed pretty certain he wanted you for his wife. Do you mean to tell me he's changed his mind?"

"Not exactly."

Rip cocked a brow and waited.

"No, dammit, he hasn't changed his mind," Sloan admitted in a rush.

"Seems to me your marrying Cruz would be the perfect answer to all our problems," Rip said. "You would be mistress of Dolorosa, and I could leave Three Oaks to Luke. Everything would be even all around."

"Except I don't want Dolorosa. I want Three Oaks," Sloan retorted.

"We don't always get everything we want."

A silence descended between them as they both digested the bitter truth of Rip's statement.

"Why are you so determined to disinherit me?" Sloan asked.

"Maybe I'm just trying to do what's best for you," Rip said, his brow furrowed.

"I'll be the judge of what's best for me."

Rip took a good look at his eldest daughter, who defied him with shoulders back, chin up, and arms crossed aggressively under her breasts. He had trained her well, molded her in his image. Perhaps he had done too good a job. Perhaps she was going to plow bullheadedly forward in the wrong direction just to get her own way.

He had learned a few hard lessons over the past few years. The hardest of them was that he wasn't as smart as he had thought he was. He had dreamed of having three sons, of creating an empire that would begin with Three Oaks.

Now he realized that he hadn't counted on the vast opportunities Texas would offer his children. He hadn't counted on their wanting to take off, like eaglets leaving their aerie, in search of their own domain.

He hadn't counted on the choices being taken out of his hands.

Rip had watched his two younger daughters leave Three Oaks and start fulfilling new lives with their husbands. He couldn't help wanting that same kind of happiness for Sloan, the child with whom he had shared so much of the burden of Three Oaks, the one on whom he had been hardest because she must be best.

She had always been independent, and determined to do everything her own way. Now she was going to throw away the chance of a life with Cruz in order to possess Three Oaks.

For the first time in his life, he didn't know what to do. So he said, "I guess I'll let you and Luke fight it out."

Sloan could hardly believe her ears. "You have no objection to my claiming Three Oaks?"

"You'll have to settle the matter with Luke. He makes the decisions about Three Oaks now." Rip rose from the chair and walked across the room, not stopping until he reached the door. "If you want to wait, Luke said he would be back along about sundown. It's good to see you, Sloan."

It was all the welcome she was going to get, Sloan knew, and yet it was more of a statement of caring than he had ever made in the past. Still, her sense of betrayal ran deep. Luke hated Rip; she loved her father; yet Rip had given control of Three Oaks to his son.

Damn right she planned to wait and talk to Luke!

She was sitting in Rip's office when she heard footsteps in the central hallway. She waited for Luke to come in, belatedly realizing that she had heard the steps of two men.

"Howdy, Sloan," Luke said.

She turned her head to greet him and was stunned by the sight of Cruz standing next to him. "What are you doing here?"

"I was about to ask you the same thing. I came home and found you gone. I thought we had an understanding."

Sloan rose to confront Cruz. "I understood what you wanted. But I don't think you have an inkling of what I want." She turned to Luke. "Rip told me he's given control of Three Oaks to you."

"If that's what he said, it must be so," Luke said.

"I want it back."

"Why?" Luke asked. "You're married to Cruz. Or so he just told me. You'll be living at Dolorosa."

"I . . . we . . ." She looked into Cruz's eyes and saw him dare her to deny it. "This has nothing to do with whether I'm married to Cruz or not."

"I'm afraid I have to differ with you," Luke said. "A woman belongs with her husband.",

Sloan didn't know what argument to use against that reasoning.

"But that's not why I went to Dolorosa looking for you today," Luke said.

"You went to Dolorosa?"

"I've just come from there. That's where Cruz and I hooked up. What I wanted to tell you is that I'm sorry about the way things turned out. I never wanted to be a cotton farmer. I never wanted Three Oaks. I just wanted . . . Aw, hell."

He stuck his thumbs in the front of his pants and said, "The bulk of the harvest is finished, so I'm going to take care of some Ranger business in San Antonio that needs tending."

"Is it something to do with Alejandro and the Hawk?" Sloan watched as Cruz and Luke exchanged guilty glances. "It is, isn't it?"

Sloan felt a frisson of excitement when Luke's frown seemed to confirm her speculation. "Alejandro's alive, isn't he? And working with a spy called the Hawk?"

"Stay out of this, Sloan," Luke said.

"Do not worry, *amigo,*" Cruz said. "I will keep her out of trouble."

"The *hell* you will!" Sloan said.

"Listen, Sloan," Luke cajoled. "Those bandido spies mean business. They—"

"Spies?"

All eyes turned to find Rip silhouetted in the doorway to his office. Luke groaned in disgust.

"What's all this talk about bandido spies?" Rip demanded.

"It's nothing," Luke said.

"Don't give me that bullshit, son. It's something, all right, and I want to hear what!"

Luke had stiffened when Rip called him son, and Sloan was certain he wasn't about to explain anything to Rip.

Luke proved her wrong when he said, "You know how it is. There's plenty of intrigue where politics and money are concerned. The English aren't too happy about Texas becoming the next state. Seems there's a bunch of British investors who'll lose money if Texas joins the Union, so there's some manipulation going on to try and stall annexation. That's all there is to it. Nothing the Rangers can't handle."

"So that's why you had to leave Three Oaks?"

Luke pursed his lips. "Part of it."

"And the rest of it?"

"I explained that once. I don't see any need to go over it again."

"I do."

"I've done all the talking I plan to do."

Sloan felt the animosity flash between the two men like heat lightning. She should have been glad to have them at odds, but it distressed her to see father and son bristling at one another like two wildcats. And she didn't see any easy solutions to the problems that plagued them.

But Luke's declaration had offered her the first hope

she'd had since he had shown up at her father's doorstep that she would regain possession of Three Oaks.

That possibility created its own set of problems. Suppose she did become heir to Three Oaks again. How was she going to manage the plantation until the six months she had promised Cruz were up?

She decided she could figure that out later. Right now, she needed to make sure that Rip understood she wanted Three Oaks no matter what.

"Why waste your time trying to convince Luke to take Three Oaks?" she said, breaking the silence that had descended. "If he doesn't want the responsibility, I'll take it."

This time, all three men turned to stare at her. She found them in various states of discomfort. Luke was flushed with embarrassment; Rip's face was a picture of frustration; and Cruz's features were taut with fury.

"That is an offer you are not free to make," Cruz said, his voice menacingly soft.

Rip's brow furrowed as he looked from his stiff-backed daughter to the towering Spaniard. "Something *else* going on here I don't know about?"

"Sloan is my wife."

"That true, Sloan?" Rip asked, his bushy brows lowering even more.

Sloan swallowed the pool of saliva that had gathered in her mouth. "I might have promised—"

"You are mine!" Cruz said in a hard voice.

Sloan took two steps to put them toe to toe. "Like hell I am! I don't—I won't—belong to anyone. Least of all some arrogant—"

Cruz grabbed her shoulders and jerked her forward against his broad chest. He gathered a handful of her hair in his fist and tilted her face up to his. His lips claimed ownership as surely as if she had been branded. His mouth slanted across hers, his tongue thrusting beyond her lips and ravishing her mouth, seeking the honey she had guarded so closely, and compelling her to share it with him.

Sloan was lost. She wasn't conscious of her hands tunneling into his silky hair to pull his head down and keep his mouth where it was. She wasn't aware of her lithe body arching into his male hardness, of her hips seeking a haven between his outspread legs, or of her tongue dueling with his and demanding equal sway.

The sound of Rip clearing his throat brought Sloan abruptly back to her senses. She opened her eyes to find Cruz's hooded gaze intent on her face. She was shocked to see her hands threaded through his hair, her body aligned with his. She stepped back with a kind of half sob, the back of her hand covering her mouth.

Sloan couldn't speak. She simply stared at Cruz, unable to believe how easily he had made her forget who and where she was.

"That tells me all I need to know," Rip said.

Sloan whirled on her father. "That tells you *nothing!*"

Rip chuckled. "Loving your husband is nothing to be ashamed of."

"But I don't love him." Sloan stiffened as she felt Cruz step up behind her.

"Enough words have been spoken, Cebellina. They change nothing. You will come back to Dolorosa with me."

"But—"

"You are my wife."

He didn't say any more, but then he didn't need to. Sloan had never been so frustrated in her life. To protest further would be useless. How could she deny the way she had melted in his arms? But it wasn't love. It couldn't be love!

Sloan stalked away from Cruz to the desk from which she had run Three Oaks for the past nine months and ran her hands along its grainy surface. Nothing in her life was going the way she had thought it would.

After she had given her child to the Guerrero family, she had thought that would be the end of it, that she would be able to forget what had happened with Tonio and get on with her life. She had never expected a brother to show up on her doorstep. She had never expected Cruz to hold her to her promise. She had never expected to feel the things that Cruz made her feel.

Cruz might want her. He might desire her. But what kind of life would she have married to him? He had already forbidden her to leave Dolorosa once and come after her when she had disobeyed him. What would happen if she stayed with him? She had to make him understand before it was too late how important it was to her to make her own decisions.

"We must leave if we are to reach Dolorosa before nightfall," Cruz said, interrupting her thoughts.

"I don't want to go."

"You can go on your own two feet or over my shoulder," Cruz said. "But you are going."

Sloan had always been a rational being. Faced with those two choices, she chose her own two feet. She was still in a daze as Rip escorted her, Luke, and Cruz to the front porch. She turned to her father, wondering what he would do now that he was left without either his eldest daughter or his bastard son to manage Three Oaks.

"Good-bye, Sloan," Rip said.

Her father didn't reach out to her. Sloan told herself it

didn't matter. She had never received the outward signs of affection from her father that Cruz now showered upon her.

She felt her throat constrict when Rip laid a hand on Luke's shoulder—which Luke stepped away from—and said, "There's work to be done, son."

"I'm leaving, too," Luke said.

"What's that?"

"I said I'm leaving."

"What's this? Three Oaks needs you, son. With Sloan married and gone—"

"Three Oaks will manage fine without me," Luke interrupted. "I've done what I came here to do. There's no reason for me to come back here again."

Rip leaned heavily on his cane, his face impassive as Luke stepped into the saddle.

Luke turned to Sloan and Cruz. "So long. I'll visit when I can."

"*Adiós, amigo,*" Cruz replied.

Cruz had kept his hand at Sloan's back as he stepped off the porch, moving her toward their horses. They had mounted up before Rip spoke again.

"You'll see this will all work out fine," he said. "Luke will be back. He won't give up everything I've offered him."

And what about me, Father? Sloan thought bitterly. *What about all the promises you made to me?*

But she knew the futility of arguing. Rip was stubborn, and there was no changing his mind. By now she should be used to it—betrayal from those she loved most. She glanced sideways at Cruz.

Was it any wonder she didn't want to put her life in his hands? Someday he would betray her too.

•　　•　　•

Doña Lucia stared at her son in disbelief. "That is not possible!"

"I assure you Sloan is my wife."

"But . . ." Doña Lucia paused as she saw the implacable look on Cruz's face. *That woman* had done it—insinuated herself in Cruz's life until he was bewitched—just as that witch had put Tonio under her spell.

Well, she would not have it! She would find a way to quickly and permanently remove Sloan Stewart from her son's life. "What about Tomasita?"

"My marriage to Sloan does not concern Tomasita."

Doña Lucia's lips pursed. "How could you let your lust for *that woman*—"

Cruz slammed his fist down on the table with such force it collapsed, sending a leg spinning wildly across the floor. "Enough! You will speak of my wife with respect, or you will leave my house."

"But *that woman*—"

Cruz rose up from his chair like an avenging God. "Enough!"

Doña Lucia's jaw snapped shut like a steel trap, and she dropped warily into a nearby chair.

Cruz rolled his eyes to the ceiling in exasperation before he strode angrily from the room.

He found Sloan standing beyond the doorway, white-faced. He grabbed her elbow and ushered her out the back door to the arbored patio. The night hid her face, but he could feel her shivering beneath his touch.

"She's right, you know," Sloan said. "It is lust."

"She is wrong."

"What else could it be?" Sloan challenged.

He met her gaze in the starlit shadows and said, "I love you. I have loved you from the first moment I saw you."

"When I was your brother's woman? You loved me then?" she demanded.

"Even then." The heat rose in his face, and he was grateful for the darkness. "I hated my brother for what he did to you." He brushed his knuckles against her cheek. "We will put the past behind us and start—"

"Even if I agreed to such a thing, there's no guarantee I could ever come to love you. Are you willing to take that kind of chance with your future, Cruz?"

"I can envision no future that does not include you," he said, his jaw taut. He stepped closer, until their bodies were facing one another, bare inches apart.

Sloan could feel the heat of him, smell the tobacco and tangy male scent that she had come to associate with him.

"Everything will come in time, Cebellina. We have a lifetime to learn to live together."

"I only promised you six months," Sloan contradicted.

"I need you in my life."

"I can't promise you anything. I may not be able to give you what you want."

"I will take my chances." He gathered her into his embrace, bringing them together from breast to thigh. His hands stroked down her back until they reached her buttocks, and he gently coaxed her against him.

She sucked in a breath of air when she felt his arousal hard and hot against her.

"Relax, *querida.*"

"I can't!"

One of his hands kept their hips pressed together while the other tangled in her hair, drawing her head back. He closed her eyes with soft kisses, grazed her cheekbone with his mouth, teased the edges of her lips with his teeth, and finally bit down gently on her lower lip, tugging on it until Sloan opened her mouth to him.

"This is madness," she whispered.

"Then we are both mad."

He took her mouth with passion, his tongue claiming her, ravaging, demanding. Sloan's hands balled into fists as she fought the urge to return in full measure what Cruz gave to her.

A sharp gasp from the nearby darkness broke them abruptly apart.

Sloan's eyes slowly focused on the confused, wide-eyed gaze of Tomasita Hidalgo. Sloan turned equally stricken eyes on Cruz, who swore vociferously under his breath as he stared back at Tomasita.

Nobody spoke for a moment, and Sloan looked back to Cruz to see how he planned to explain their behavior to the impressionable young woman.

"I intended to speak with you, Tomasita, to tell you that Sloan and I . . ."

"You do not owe me an explanation," Tomasita said, her voice brittle. "I have eyes. I can see for myself what has happened here."

"There is nothing wrong with what you saw, Tomasita. Sloan and I are married. We have been married for four years," he said.

That statement prompted a gasp of horror from Tomasita. "But my father . . . your father . . . they promised. . . . We are betrothed!"

"How can you know of that?" Cruz exclaimed. "If Mamá has said anything to you—"

"Doña Lucia said nothing. I overheard Mother María speaking of it at the convent."

"All this time you thought . . ." Cruz thrust a hand through his hair. "I had hoped you need never know," he said.

He ground his teeth at the tragic expression on Tomasita's face. "I did not mean . . . it is nothing to do with you," he said, groping for words to lessen the hurt he could see in her pain-filled eyes.

"You are a lovely young woman," he said. "But my father made the promise to your father without my knowledge. By the time I found out about it, I had long since committed myself to Sloan."

"Then you never intended to marry me?"

"No."

"Why did you not just leave me in the convent?"

"I promised my father I would see that you were well wed."

"That is not necessary," she said, her spine stiffened by pride. "I do not choose to marry at all."

"That choice is not yours to make," Cruz said. "You are under my protection. I will decide what is best for you."

Tomasita looked from Sloan to Cruz and then backed away. "I think I will go to my room now."

Sloan watched in dismay as the young girl made what, under the circumstances, was a surprisingly graceful exit. "She would have made you a much better wife than I," Sloan murmured sadly.

"I do not love her."

Sloan turned, and her heart rose to her throat at the fierce look of possession she found in Cruz's deep blue eyes. "I'm not like Tomasita, Cruz. I could never let you make my choices for me. I make my own decisions. I always will."

"Perhaps, Cebellina. We will see."

Sloan's eyes narrowed. "There is no *perhaps* about it, Cruz."

"We will see how you feel in the spring, shall we?" he said. "Maybe you will change your mind."

Sloan frowned. He could wait all he wanted. She wasn't going to change her mind.

Until the incident in the courtyard, Tomasita had not intended to meet Luke Summers. But when Saturday came, she still had not stopped feeling angry with Don Cruz.

It had been embarrassing, of course, to find her supposed fiancé in another woman's arms. But it had been humiliating to discover that she had been kept ignorant of the truth about their betrothal, like a spoiled child who might cry if she cannot have her candy.

Meeting Luke Summers alone seemed a dangerous enough adventure to prove she was a grown woman and not the green girl that Don Cruz had apparently considered her.

After supper, Tomasita told everyone she was going to her room to bed. Instead, she sneaked out beyond the walls that surrounded the hacienda and made her way to the river in the failing light. Her heart was beating crazily in her breast, and her breath was coming in short spurts because she ran practically the whole way. When she finally got where she was going, she realized what an unbelievably childish thing she had done.

The only sounds she heard were the water burbling lazily over stones and the wind rustling through the cypress trees along the banks. Otherwise it was deathly quiet.

She had worn a dark wool skirt and a white *camisa,* but had covered her head and shoulders with a dark crepe de chine shawl with fringe so long it reached her ankles. She stood shivering in the darkness, waiting for a man to arrive whom she had met only twice and who had taken liberties with her both times.

The total idiocy of her actions dawned on her at about the same time she heard the hooves of a horse plodding directly toward her.

"Holy Mary," she whispered. "Protect this foolish woman!" She turned and ran as fast as she could back toward the hacienda, not caring who it was on the horse, praying to the Father above that it wasn't someone bent on harming her.

She was still running when she felt a muscled arm snake around her waist and haul her from the ground. She tried to scream, but a callused hand covered her mouth, shutting off the sound.

She struggled like a wildcat, scratching, frenzied, frantic . . . until she heard the male voice in her ear crooning sweet, soft love words.

It was Luke Summers. He had come as he had promised.

Tomasita slumped in his arms, her head falling back against his muscled chest, her breathing becoming less tortured as her brain acknowledged that the danger was past.

She felt his moist breath on her ear as he said, "All through bucking, little mustang girl? I'm going to take my hand off your mouth now. Easy, girl. Everything's all right now. Easy."

Tomasita found herself gentled much as he might have gentled a wild mustang, with soft strokes and gentle words. She didn't fight him when he lifted her farther into his lap.

She was not so naïve that she did not recognize his

heightened state of excitement. It was both thrilling and a little awe-inspiring to know he found her desirable as a woman.

His arms looped around her, holding her snugly against him. She could feel her breast pressing against his chest. It felt wonderful . . . natural . . .

"Let's go over here a ways and see if we can find a comfortable spot," Luke said. "I'm glad you came, Tomasita. I'm real glad you came."

Tomasita didn't say anything. She was too busy feeling things. Warmth. Excitement. Tension. Need.

He stepped down from the saddle in a lithe movement and lifted her down with him. He settled her in the grass along the banks of the river and sat down next to her. "I need you, mustang girl. I've been needin' you for days."

She felt his hands at her waist. They began to roam across her ribs and then upward toward her breasts. She quickly covered his hands with her own. "This is not right," she protested.

While she was talking, his hands kept moving under hers. His fingertips skimmed her nipples, bringing them erect and sending shivers of sensation racing to her core. "You must stop. That feels . . ."

She moaned as he gently pressed her down into the grass. "What are you doing?"

"Loving you. Come on and touch me, mustang girl. I need to feel your hands on me."

Before she could say anything, he had taken her hands and put them against his bare chest. When or how he had rid himself of his linsey-woolsey shirt, she had no idea. His skin felt hard and smooth under her fingertips.

He moved her hands where he wanted them—across his flat nipples, down the center of his chest to the crisp hair that grew in a line down to his navel, and down even farther, across the front of his trousers, where he was hard and heavy.

"Ah, mustang girl, you make me feel so good. Let me touch you. Let me make you feel as good as I do."

Tomasita's breath was coming in short spurts. Her whole body seemed alive with feeling. "Luke, Luke, I feel too much. I cannot breathe. I cannot—"

His hands gently palmed her breasts through the soft *camisa* and the sensation was so exquisite that she simply held her breath, hoping to prolong it. Then his mouth touched her through the cloth, wet and hot.

"Ahhh." Tomasita grabbed handfuls of Luke's hair as though to pull his mouth away, but instead she arched her back and held him there, her teeth gritted in an agony of pleasure. She moaned deep in her throat.

Luke nuzzled her bare skin above the cloth, then trailed wet kisses along her throat to her ear, and finally found her mouth.

At first he just teased her, touching her and backing off. "You ever been kissed before, mustang girl?" he asked, his voice tender.

Tomasita shook her head.

He laughed, a low, husky sound. "You wanta be kissed some more?"

Tomasita smiled. "*Sí,* vaquero. I want to be kissed."

His lips barely touched hers, skimming one side of her mouth and then the other. He teased and taunted, his tongue dipping out occasionally to taste, to wet her lips, to probe, and then to retreat.

At the same time, his hands roamed her body. He palmed a breast and the nipple budded beneath his fingertips. His hands danced across the heart of her desire, too quickly gone for her to offer a protest. He chased a shiver down to the small of her back with his fingertips.

Working in tandem, his mouth and his hands played with her like a wolf with a lamb. There was never any question he would have his quarry.

Tomasita met Luke's lambent green eyes through a haze of pleasure. Every nerve was sensitized. Her whole body felt weak. There was no chance to flee—her legs would not have supported her.

But she had no desire to flee. Right or wrong, good or bad, nothing seemed to matter. Only the man and the moment.

"That's it, mustang girl. Open your mouth for me now. Open up and let me come in."

The feel of his tongue in her mouth was not so foreign as she might have imagined. He thrust and withdrew, thrust and withdrew, and she found herself wanting to keep him there. So the next time he thrust she caught his tongue and sucked on it to hold him there and heard him groan.

Her hips arched into his hardness. She tried to slip her fingertips beneath the cloth at his waist, to reach his buttocks, but the buckskin pants he wore fit too well.

He slipped her skirt and underdrawers off, and soon she felt the grass beneath her back, cold and slightly wet with dew. Just as quickly, he undid the ties on his own pants and shinnied out of them.

She was immediately aware of the feel of his warm hardness against her, probing, prodding.

His hand teased its way down across her naked belly into the curls below, until he reached the petals he sought. His knee nudged its way between her legs, separating her thighs, opening her, making her vulnerable.

She whimpered, frightened.

"Easy, now. It's okay to buck a little now. Don't want to tame you, mustang girl. Just want us to take an easy ride together. You and me, girl. Just a crazy, wild, man and woman ride."

She could feel his fingers touching—soft, careful, wonderful. His mouth teased hers. His fingers taunted her nether lips. Then his hands were on her hips, tilting them, and he was probing, pushing.

She met his eyes, his gaze heavy-lidded as he slowly pressed inside her, filling her full of him.

She cried out with the pain as he took her innocence, bucking wildly, wanting free. His lips caught the sound, soothed it, made the pain his own, until he had slipped deep inside her, possessing her, making them one.

"It's all right now. The worst is over. Only pleasure now. Just the two of us. Together for the ride."

He kissed her tears away. Then, slowly, gently, he began to move. The sensations were overwhelming. She felt suspended. Her hips arched up to him, her hands grabbed hold of him, determined to stay with him.

Luke groaned with pleasure.

Tomasita groaned, too.

She felt a rushing pleasure, a fleeting sensation that threatened to leave her in the dust if she did not reach out for it. She found his mouth with hers, grasped his shoulders with both hands, and let the feelings roll over her. Overwhelming. Unbelievable. Undeniable.

When she was herself again, she felt the weight of his body shift off hers, felt him pull her snug against his warmth. Between gasps of air, he chuckled to himself. She chuckled too.

She felt wonderful. She had found her life mate, her

heart's desire. She had found the man who would be her husband. She would gladly stay in Texas now.

"When will you speak to Don Cruz?" she said, her voice soft, shy.

"Speak to him? About what?"

"About our marriage."

She felt him stiffen beside her. She met his solemn gaze with eyes that had seen too little of the world.

"Sorry, mustang girl. I'm a bronc that can't be lassoed. Guess I should have realized you wouldn't know that."

"I do not understand."

He huffed out a breath of air. "I'm not the marrying kind, Tomasita. I'm a Texas Ranger. That makes me a traveling man. I'm on my way to San Antonio right now. Don't know when I'll get back."

Something curled up tight inside her. She had made a terrible mistake, made assumptions she should not have made. No other man would have her now.

She felt her throat constricting, felt her chest tightening until she was afraid she might suffocate. She rose awkwardly and searched desperately for her clothing, dressing herself as quickly as possible.

Nearby, Luke clothed himself slowly, methodically.

When she was dressed, Tomasita turned to face the man who had taken her virginity. "I . . . I did not know . . . I should not have presumed . . ." She swallowed over the lump in her throat.

Luke felt bad. He felt awful, in fact. He had only intended to steal a few kisses. Or maybe just caress her soft skin a little. Somehow things had gotten out of hand.

He had always been able to stop himself in the past. But he had wanted Tomasita like he had never wanted another woman. Needed her like water in the desert. And he had known he might never have another chance to possess her.

So he hadn't stopped.

Luke reached out to touch Tomasita, but she jerked away. "Will you be all right?" he asked.

"I will be fine. Do not concern yourself."

Tomasita turned and walked away from him back toward the hacienda. She heard him swear under his breath, heard him kick his mount, heard the muffled hoofbeats as the horse galloped away.

Suddenly, the night sounds were deafening. Crickets and frogs. The water. The wind. The scream that rose in her throat and could not find escape.

Chapter 13

CRUZ TURNED TO FILL HIS SENSES WITH THE woman lying across from him in the huge Spanish bed they shared as man and wife. The linens smelled of the lavender soap she used, and the musky odor of sex.

She looked like a woman who had been well loved. Her sable hair billowed around her face on the pillow, her lush sable lashes fanned her cheeks, which were scattered with a light dusting of freckles. Her mouth was parted and her lips were full and swollen from the passionate kisses they had shared during the night past.

Her fiery responses had enflamed him. Over the past two months they had spent together, the loving had only gotten more intense, more fulfilling. He knew he would never get his fill of her.

But though he had possessed Sloan's body, she had kept her heart and soul apart. He was hardly in a position to cast blame, however, since he also had been selfish with parts of himself.

His clandestine work for the British had forced him to exclude Sloan on more occasions than he wanted to consider. It had taken a lot of time to gather the information

Sir Giles wanted, and he could hardly tell his wife the real reason he had not wanted her to come along with him on his journeys.

He had also been unable to share with her his fury that Alejandro Sanchez had escaped justice. Cruz had chafed at the fact that until the Republic no longer had any need for his services—that is, until the annexation of Texas had been approved by the American Congress—he could not take any action against his brother's murderer.

He had bitten his tongue and bided his time through November and December. Three encouraging political events occurred during this period that led him to believe annexation might finally be at hand.

In Mexico, a revolution drove Santa Anna from the presidency and the new president, General José Joaquin Herrera, was a man disposed to peace with Texas.

In Texas, Dr. Anson Jones, a man pledged to support Sam Houston's policies favoring annexation, was elected to replace Houston as the next president of the Republic.

In America, a virtual unknown, James Knox Polk, of Tennessee, a friend of Sam Houston's and a man in favor of westward expansion, was elected to replace President John Tyler.

Lately, Cruz had read accounts in American newspapers that said the annexation of Texas was "inevitable." In fact, it was considered a foregone conclusion that when the American Congress reconvened in February, 1845, it would immediately ask Texas to become the twenty-sixth state.

Cruz had not been surprised to receive word that Sir Giles wanted to see him. He suspected the British had come up with some final, desperate plan to thwart annexation. Because once Texas was annexed, the British citizens

who had invested millions of pounds in Mexican bonds secured only by land in Texas would have to admit, at last,
that their investments were not worth the paper they were
printed on.

Cruz was not looking forward to the trip because it
meant leaving Sloan—again.

She had seemed content at times over the past two
months, but was agitated and impatient at others. He was
no more certain now that she would still be with him at the
end of April—when the six months she had agreed to give
him were up—than he had been the night the priest had
married them.

As he gazed at her in the pale gray light of dawn, her
lids slowly lifted. For an instant he thought he saw pleasure
in her deep brown eyes, but whatever her feelings for him,
they were quickly masked.

"Good morning," she said, her voice rough from disuse.

He reached to brush a stray curl from her cheek, noting
the softness of her skin, the silkiness of the hair beneath his
fingertips. "Good morning." He leaned over and pressed
his lips against hers.

He felt the tremor go through her as they touched, and
was hard-pressed to control his desire for her. He had to
speak now or he would never be able to leave her.

"I must leave for San Antonio today."

"Meeting another *ranchero*?" she asked, her brows rising skeptically.

"*Sí.*"

She kept her lids lowered so he couldn't see her eyes,
and her hands toyed with the cotton sheet that barely covered her full breasts. He saw the shadow of a dusky nipple
through the cloth and his loins responded by tightening
with pleasure.

"I want to go with you," she said.

"No."

"Why not? It isn't as though I would intrude on your business. I have acquaintances of my own in San Antonio I could visit, and I could check to see whether there's any news about Betsy's uncle while I'm there."

Cruz could hardly explain that she would be in his way when he made contact with Sir Giles, but neither could he come up with a satisfactory reason to keep her at Dolorosa. "I will not have time to keep an eye on you—"

"Why would you need to do that?" she said with asperity. "I'll keep an eye on myself."

Cruz ignored her statement and rose from the bed to dress.

Sloan forced her gaze away from the lithe muscles that bunched in her husband's shoulders as he stretched, the strong arch of his back, the taut, hard buttocks which, she noticed with chagrin, were decorated with fingernail-shaped crescents she had put there last night in a moment of mindless passion. She could find no fault with his body, but she was more than a little perturbed by his attitude toward including her in his business.

She had been an obedient—almost docile—wife, allowing Cruz to come and go as he pleased, leaving her behind at Dolorosa, failing to include her more times than not. But she was beginning to feel the constraints of being a dutiful wife. Taking care of Betsy and playing with Cisco weren't enough to keep her occupied. The nearly complete absence of responsibility, after so many years of being responsible for so much, left her feeling restless.

Not only that, but the constant strain of her relationship with Doña Lucia, and the lingering uncertainty of whether

her marriage with Cruz would last, were starting to wear on her. She needed to get away.

So she said, "If you don't take me with you, I'll simply go on my own as soon as you're gone."

Cruz frowned. "You agreed—"

"I have to get away from here for a while, Cruz." Her voice was calm, but inside she was wired as tautly as a bowstring. "Either I go with you or I go alone, but I'm going."

Sloan had sat up abruptly to state her ultimatum, unmindful of the sheet that had covered her nakedness. Once her tirade was over, she realized the cloth had fallen to her waist and Cruz was staring at her. Her nipples puckered under his intent gaze, and she grabbed at the sheet to cover the signs of her vulnerability to him.

Cruz knew he couldn't keep her here if she made up her mind to go. He realized he would have more success keeping her ignorant of his reasons for traveling to San Antonio if she came along with him. When necessary, he could make his excuses and leave her safely in their room at the hotel while he met with the Englishman.

Besides, he found the thought of having Sloan to himself, of being alone with her away from Dolorosa, exciting.

When Cruz sat down beside her on the bed, he had donned his trousers and boots, but his chest, with its mat of thick black hair, was still bare. Sloan struggled to keep from staring, but it was a battle she was happy to lose.

"All right, Cebellina, you may come with me," he said. "I plan to leave right after breakfast."

In her happiness, Sloan leaned over to kiss him on the mouth. "I'll be ready." When she would have withdrawn, she found herself captured in Cruz's embrace.

"You are so beautiful, *querida*." Cruz tantalized her with his lips. "I am the most fortunate of men."

Sloan found herself loath to leave his arms, dizzy with pleasure. She moaned as his hands caressed the curve of her hip. "I should get up." She reached out a hand and laid it on his bare chest.

He shuddered with the pleasure of her touch. "As you wish, Cebellina. We can continue this in San Antonio."

It was spoken as a promise, but Sloan couldn't help hearing the threat to the high walls she had built around her heart. She was afraid to love him; she was afraid she already did.

At the breakfast table, Cruz broke the news that Sloan would be coming with him to San Antonio and heard the same refrain from nearly everyone seated at the table.

"Can Cisco and I come, too?" Betsy asked.

Sloan reached over to catch a spoonful of *chorizo*, a mixture of scrambled eggs and sausage, that was about to fall into Betsy's lap. "Not this time, sweetheart," she said, dropping the bit of *chorizo* into the girl's open mouth.

"I could ride my pony. I would not be any trouble," Cisco promised.

Sloan turned to her other side, where Cisco had stuffed the last bit of a generously buttered tortilla into his mouth and was licking his fingers clean. She took the napkin from his lap and began wiping his fingers. "No, you're always an angel," she said with a grin. "That's why your nickname is Diablito."

Cruz watched with something akin to awe as Sloan and Cisco grinned at one another. Cruz's eyes never left Sloan's hands as she carefully wiped her son's face with his napkin, then brushed a wayward curl back from his brow. She straightened Cisco's shirt on his shoulders and tugged one of his ears playfully before settling his napkin back in his lap.

Such moments were rare, and therefore all the more to be treasured. More often than not, Sloan would stop herself from actually touching her son. He had watched her fight a battle with herself every time she came in contact with Cisco, in order to keep from loving the child. There were chinks in her fortress walls, but they were far from being demolished.

"I wish I were going, too," Tomasita said. "San Antonio sounds like such an exciting place."

Cruz heard the wistful note in Tomasita's voice. He had been remiss in finding a husband for her, but he had been distracted by the roundup and then by this business with the British government. He decided to write a letter to both Don Ambrosio and Señor Carvajal the day he returned from his trip to San Antonio.

To Cruz's surprise, his mother said nothing about Sloan's accompanying him except, "I will see about preparing a meal for you to take along on your journey."

"Ana can take care of it," Cruz replied. He had not been ignorant of the cold shoulder his mother had turned to his wife, but at Sloan's behest, he had not confronted her for her behavior.

Too late he realized that perhaps he should not have so casually dismissed what he now perceived as a tentative olive branch from his mother. Because instead of insisting, Doña Lucia merely agreed, "As you wish."

Sloan hadn't realized how hard it was going to be to leave Betsy and Cisco behind. When it was time for her to mount up, the little girl threw her arms around Sloan's neck and wouldn't let go. Cruz pried Betsy loose and handed her to Josefa.

As they rode away, Sloan looked back over her shoulder and saw that Betsy was sobbing out her misery in Josefa's arms. Cisco stood apart from them, his face equally unhappy, but aware, even at his age, that a man did not cry out his sorrows.

Despite what Sloan knew were good reasons for keeping herself aloof from her son, at that moment she felt like turning her horse around and hugging Cisco good-bye. Cruz's next words saved her from such folly.

"Come, Cebellina. We have a lot of riding to do before dark."

Sloan was exhausted by the time they arrived in San Antonio. Actually, she was feeling more than a little sick. Her stomach was upset, and she had been so dizzy the last few miles before they reached San Antonio that she'd had trouble staying in the saddle.

She had drunk most of the water in her canteen but still had an unquenchable thirst. Nor did the water settle her stomach. Her nausea only seemed to get worse.

If it had been hotter she might have suspected sunstroke. But it was January, and besides, she had worn her hat all day. She couldn't imagine why she felt so bad—unless it was something she had eaten. She hid the way she was feeling from Cruz, because it would only prove to him that she should have stayed at home.

Whether it was a mild case of sunstroke or something she had eaten, she felt certain that if she could get some rest she would feel better in the morning. She dropped like an adobe brick onto the four-poster bed when they finally reached their room at Ferguson's Hotel.

"Are you sure you do not want a bath first?" Cruz asked with a chuckle when a cloud of dust shot up from her clothes.

"I'll get one in the morning. It's late," Sloan mumbled. "Would you help me with my boots?"

Cruz tugged her Wellingtons off and watched her curl up around one of the pillows. She was asleep moments later. He wanted to stay with her. He wanted to curve his body around hers and feel her warm flesh against his own. But he reluctantly admitted that Sloan's fatigue had provided him the perfect opportunity to meet with Sir Giles.

He stayed in the same hotel as Sir Giles because it made it less likely he would be watched coming and going. Cruz knocked three times at a door just down the hall from where his wife slept peacefully. When it opened a crack, Cruz said, "It is the Hawk."

"It's about time you got here," Sir Giles said, gesturing Cruz inside. "You're late."

"I brought my wife with me. The ride took longer than I expected."

"I will never understand why you bothered to marry your brother's whore. Tonio proved she was free for the taking."

Cruz stiffened. The hackles on the back of his neck told him Alejandro was sitting in the rawhide chair in the far corner of the room.

Alejandro continued, "I am sure it was worth the delay to have that *bruja* in your bed while you are here, eh, Don Cruz? Perhaps while she is here I will see if she is ready to welcome yet another into her bed."

Cruz turned to confront Alejandro, and found the bandido's face half in and half out of the shadows. A row of crooked teeth flashed in a taunting smile beneath the bandido's bushy moustache.

Cruz realized he had been arrogant to assume he could protect his wife from a man without a conscience. Alejan-

dro wouldn't fight fair. He wouldn't fight clean. And if he
ever got his hands on Sloan, he would take what he wanted
and throw away whatever was left. Cruz's hands balled into
fists, but he managed to curb his desire to wipe the smile
off Alejandro's face.

"Damn and blast, man! You know better than to bring
your wife along at a time like this," Sir Giles complained.

Cruz turned cold blue eyes on the Englishman. "It is
done. What do you want from me? Why did you ask me to
come?"

Recognizing the peril of harassing Cruz, the stout Englishman got directly to the point. "Mexico is on the verge
of giving Texas its independence. I need you to find out exactly what the Texas government is willing to concede to
get Mexico to sign over sovereignty."

"I do not have the political connections—"

"Ah, but you don't need to be present at the negotia-
tions," Sir Giles said. "You need only briefly intercept the
letters between the parties involved."

"I am not a thief."

"Only a traitor," Sir Giles said, his lips curled cynically.

When Cruz remained adamant in his stand, Sir Giles
said, "Oh, very well. Perhaps Alejandro is better suited to
that task. I have another, more important, job for you anyway.

"The former American chargé to Texas, Beaufort
LeFevre, is coming here to work with the current chargé
toward annexation. While LeFevre is in Texas, I want you
to keep an eye on him. I want to know everyone he sees,
everything he says."

"How do you propose I accomplish that?"

Sir Giles smiled, exposing the gums above his teeth.
"It's quite simple, my boy. LeFevre will be staying with

Rip Stewart. You will merely take your wife home for an extended visit with her father."

Cruz couldn't stop the sardonic twist of his lips. "I suppose I have no choice about this."

"No, you don't."

"When is LeFevre coming?"

"We don't know. When he does come, I'll expect you to join him at Three Oaks."

"Anything else?" Cruz asked.

"That is quite enough, don't you think?"

Cruz didn't bother to answer, just turned his back on Sir Giles and headed for the door. The Englishman's voice stopped him before he could leave.

"Hawk . . ."

Cruz paused but didn't turn around.

"You aren't considering changing your allegiance at this late date, I hope. Because if you do, Alejandro has made it plain he would be willing to solve any unpleasant . . . complications that arise from such an unfortunate decision."

Cruz angled his head briefly toward the shadows where Alejandro Sanchez sat. Then he left the Englishman's room as quietly as he had entered. He had not mistaken the warning he had been given. From now on, he would watch his back.

When Cruz returned to his room he found Sloan in a considerably different state from the one in which he had left her.

In no way could the woman lying tangled in the sweat-soaked sheets of the four-poster be described as resting peacefully. She was curled in a fetal ball and gripping her belly. The groans coming from her throat seemed wrenched from deep within her.

Something was desperately wrong with his wife.

He lifted Sloan into his arms. "Cebellina, your skin is on fire. What is wrong? What has happened?"

"I hurt."

"Where?"

"My stomach . . . my head . . . everywhere . . . all over," Sloan gasped out.

Cruz felt fear such as he had never felt before. His heart pounded erratically; his palms were wet. He did not trust the Anglo doctors who healed through bloodletting and purge. Yet where else could he turn?

"I'm so thirsty," she said.

He laid Sloan back down on the bed so he could get her some water. The pitcher that sat on the dry sink across from the bed was empty. He picked up the canteens they had brought with them from Dolorosa and realized that while his was nearly half full, hers was almost empty.

He brought both canteens with him to the bed. "How long have you felt sick?"

"I don't know."

"Did it start after we arrived?"

"No, earlier in the day. Sometime after we ate," she confessed. "I thought it might be sunstroke."

Cruz held up her nearly empty canteen. "If you've drunk this much water, how could it be sunstroke?" he demanded.

"I don't know," Sloan mumbled. "I don't know."

"Maybe it was something you ate."

"We ate the same things," she said with a moan. "You would be sick, too."

"Maybe the water in your canteen is tainted," he suggested.

"If so, why aren't you sick? We filled our canteens from the same well. It couldn't be the water. Except . . . I did refill my canteen at the small pond where we stopped to eat. But I could have sworn it wasn't brackish."

Cruz poured a small amount of the water from her canteen into his hand. He sniffed at it, then touched the tip of his tongue to his palm. It tasted all right, but that was no guarantee it wasn't bad. He stared at his wife, feeling the panic begin to rise. "I do not know, Cebellina. It might be anything. I just do not know!"

"Help me, Cruz," Sloan cried. "It hurts!"

He stood helpless in the face of her pain. Suddenly, he realized he knew someone in San Antonio who might know where he could find a good doctor.

"Hang on, Cebellina," he urged, kissing her feverish brow. "I'll be back as quickly as I can."

Chapter 14

CRUZ RETURNED A SHORT TIME LATER WITH A distraught and concerned Luke. They had dragged along a thin, white-haired physician, who had obviously been rousted from his bed.

Cruz suffered along with Sloan through the agonies of the purging applied by the doctor as "the most efficacious remedy for any malady of the stomach." But the white-haired doctor warned Cruz that if Sloan's illness had been caused by something she had eaten or drunk, "It's probably already worked its way well into her system." He could only tell Cruz that her pain seemed to be in her stomach, and, "If she doesn't die tonight, she'll probably recover."

Luke escorted the doctor out the door before Cruz had a chance to vent his frustration on the hapless man for such an unpromising prognosis.

As the evening wore on, Cruz was grateful that Luke had decided to stay. The night that followed was long and, in many ways, horrifying. He had to face the very real possibility that the woman he loved might die.

For hours, Sloan was delirious. Cruz began to get an

inkling from the disjointed babble she spouted just how many demons she lived with.

"... Where's my baby? ... I can never love you ... *Yes,* dammit! I'll marry you! ... fit like fur boots ... Traitor? ... No! He can't be dead.

"... Three Oaks is mine! ... Worms in the cotton? Plow it under and plant again ... I need a bath ... never invited ... too many calluses ... betrayed again ... Luke ... Luke ... a bastard son ..."

Cruz had never felt so helpless. He tenderly sponged Sloan's forehead and dabbed at the perspiration on her upper lip, willing her pain away. But there was more.

"... blood ... so much blood ... Cisco is dead! I can't bear the pain ... not again ... Doña Lucia is a witch ... Tonio's lips are so cold ... no more ... please, no more ...

"... stupid bargain ... beautiful Tomasita ... please don't touch me ... It feels so good ... It hurts, Cruz ... Why does it hurt?"

Cruz covered his face with his hands to hide his red-rimmed eyes. Her pain unmanned him. Her revelations devastated him. It was like looking behind the walls she had erected to keep him out and seeing all the old wounds—hurt upon hurt upon hurt—that had caused her to build that wall in the first place. He could not bear to watch her suffering.

At long last, she slipped into an uneasy slumber.

Cruz rolled his head on his neck to ease the tension, then turned to Luke and said, "I feel so helpless. Is there nothing we can do?"

"We just have to wait." Luke put a hand on Cruz's shoulder and felt the other man flinch. "It isn't long now until dawn. Remember, the doctor promised that if Sloan made it through the night, she'll live."

"She's in so much pain!" Cruz said, the words wrenched from him.

Luke simply nodded. He had heard Sloan's feverish murmurs and knew it wasn't only Sloan's physical pain that was worrying Cruz.

Cruz thrust both hands through his hair in agitation. "Oh God, she has to live!"

"What do you suppose made her so sick in the first place?" Luke asked, hoping to distract Cruz from his distressing thoughts.

"Maybe the water in her canteen—she filled it up when we stopped to eat. We will probably never know for sure."

Luke rose from the chair beside Cruz and crossed to the foot of Sloan's bed. He leaned against the bedstead of the four-poster and crossed his legs at the ankles. "Damn scary to think you could just get sick and die without ever knowing what hit you," Luke mused. "Makes you think twice about all the things you've left undone . . . like maybe you should tie up all those loose strings before you lose your chance. You got any loose strings out there, Cruz?"

Cruz sighed and leaned forward in the chair beside Sloan's bed, crossing his arms on top of the mattress. "One in particular."

"What's that?"

"You have met Tomasita Hidalgo, I believe."

Luke was silent for a moment, and when Cruz turned to see why Luke hadn't answered, he saw the Ranger's cheeks were flushed. He watched Luke's Adam's apple bob as he swallowed uncomfortably.

"I've talked to her some," Luke admitted at last.

Cruz smiled. "I think perhaps you find her attractive," he teased gently.

"She'll make someone a beautiful wife."

Cruz rested his chin against his hands. "My father had plans that she would become *my* wife, plans that went astray because I married Sloan. I think Mamá still believes that if it were not for Sloan, I would take Tomasita for my wife."

"Is she right?" Luke asked, an inexplicable tension in, his shoulders.

Cruz shook his head. "There is only one woman for me. If I cannot have Sloan, I do not want another. But as for what I have left undone—I must find a husband for Tomasita. I have delayed too long already."

Luke feigned disinterest, but his voice was rough when he asked, "Do you have anyone particular in mind?"

"Don Ambrosio, for one. He was known to dote on his first wife, and I trust him to be kind to Tomasita. Of course, he is a little older than I would like."

"How old?"

"Forty-six, I think."

"He's old enough to be her father!"

"An older man would be able to teach her the way she should go."

Luke made a disgusted face. "Who else do you have in mind?"

"Joaquín Carvajal is very wealthy, but he is almost too young, only twenty-two."

"I'm twenty-three," Luke said with asperity. "Are you saying I'd be too young a husband for her?"

"Are you asking my permission to court her?"

"And if I were?"

Cruz turned to face Luke, suddenly aware that the

Ranger hadn't asked the question idly. He frowned, unsure what to say. For any number of reasons, Luke Summers was not the sort of man he would have chosen as a husband for Tomasita Hidalgo. He liked Luke and he respected his abilities as a Ranger, but Luke had a rogue's reputation.

"Do you think you could be satisfied with only one woman?" Cruz asked.

"What the hell kind of question is that?" Luke retorted.

"I would be lying if I said no Spanish gentleman ever had a mistress," Cruz said. "But still, no Spanish gentlemen has ever had quite so many ladies as your reputation imputes to you. I would like to know whether you would be able to put Tomasita first, before the others."

"There would be no others!"

Cruz raised a brow at the vehemence of Luke's reply.

Realizing that he had nearly given himself away, Luke added, "That is, I'd surely devote myself to the woman I picked for my wife."

"I see," Cruz said. "And I would ask your plans for taking care of her."

Luke grimaced. "A Texas Ranger doesn't make the kind of money that can support a woman like Tomasita."

"You are Rip Stewart's son," Cruz countered, "and heir to Three Oaks if you want it."

"I don't want anything from Rip."

"Not even if it means you could marry Tomasita Hidalgo?"

Luke pursed his lips in thought. Finally, he said, "I'm not looking for a wife, Cruz. Not even one as beautiful as Tomasita Hidalgo."

Cruz saw the distress in Luke's eyes and wanted to ask what it was that had soured so young a man on marriage. But in this land, one man did not ask another about his past. He watched as Luke walked around to the other side of the bed and reached out to gently brush a lock of hair from Sloan's face.

Cruz stared at the Ranger, wondering why a man who obviously loved women seemed so determined to deny himself a woman's love.

"Guess there's not much more I can do here," Luke said, crossing to the door. "I'll check back early tomorrow morning to see how Sloan's doing."

"I will see you then. *Vaya con Dios, mi amigo.*"

Cruz kept a vigil that lasted until dawn. He sponged Sloan's brow to keep her cool and rearranged the covers when she kicked them off. He recognized the signs that told him the danger was finally past, but he was impatient for her to wake up and tell him she was all right. As the sun came up, he lowered his eyelids to protect his bloodshot eyes from the light. His head fell forward to rest on his arms on the bed and in the next instant he was asleep.

When Sloan awoke, her mouth felt like it was full of cotton. Her muscles ached, and she groaned as she turned from her back to her side. She slowly opened her eyes, trying to orient herself.

She saw a head of tousled black curls and a beard-stubbled face lying on a large sun-browned hand covered in a dusting of black hair. Cruz was sound asleep, his mouth open slightly. She smiled over the secret knowledge that Don Cruz Guerrero snored.

Everything came back to her. The dizziness, the nausea, and Cruz's return with that odious doctor. She lifted her hand, surprised when it obeyed her command, and laid it gently on the crown of Cruz's head, tunneling her fingers into his silky hair in what was undeniably a caress.

Why hadn't she met him first, before Tonio, before

everything had happened that made her afraid to love him back?

Her hand trailed down from his hair to his nape, and then around to his bristly jaw. The feel of a man's jaw in the morning was an intimate thing she had only come to know since living with Cruz. She loved the feel of her smooth cheek against his rough one, and wished she felt well enough to lift her head from the pillow and lie next to him.

Her forefinger tracked the cleft in his chin, and she thought how distinctive it made him look. She marveled at the softness of his lips as she lightly traced them, while the feel of his breath on her fingertips caused a quiver of expectation deep inside her.

Cruz came awake to the languorous touch of his wife's hands on his face. He held himself still, as though she were a curious kitten and he might frighten her away if he moved.

It was the first time she had made an overture to touch him on her own, and he was both delighted and confused. Surely this must mean she cared for him.

He groaned with pleasure as her fingertips soothed his brow, and she instantly removed her hand.

Cruz slowly lifted his head and stared at Sloan. Her eyes were wide with trepidation. He wanted to take her in his arms and tell her she was safe with him, that he would never hurt her. He had said as much before, but she hadn't believed him. Only time would convince her of the truth.

Unfortunately, he only had four months left before she decided whether to stay with him or go.

"Good morning, Cebellina," he said in a sleep-raspy voice. "It is good to see you feeling so well."

So, he was going to ignore the fact she had been touching him, Sloan thought. All right. Fine. "I'm feeling much better. But you're looking a little the worse for wear," she replied, unable to keep the smile from her face.

He rubbed his jaw with his hand and then thrust all ten fingers through his hair in a futile attempt to tame it. "I could use a bath and a shave. How about you?"

"I'd like a bath. I think I'll skip the shave."

Cruz stared at her dumbfounded. When he saw the mischievous sparkle in her eye, he chuckled and then laughed.

Sloan joined in his laughter, realizing as she did that it was the first time she could remember laughing in a long, long time. She grasped her ribs and said, "Please, I'm too sore for this."

"I will go see about getting some water for your bath. Are you sure you feel well enough to get up?"

As Sloan shifted in an attempt to sit up, Cruz slipped an arm around her shoulders to help her rise, grabbing the pillows to fluff them up behind her. "Comfortable?"

She felt wonderfully tense. Pampered. Loved. Anything but comfortable. "I'm fine. But I'm thirsty. And starving."

"I'm hungry, too."

It was plain to Sloan that it wasn't food that interested him. His arm was still around her shoulders and she saw the teasing glint in his eye as his finger traced her lower lip. "I was thinking more in terms of coffee, sausage, and eggs," she murmured.

It took Cruz another second to realize she had teased him again. The edges of his mouth curved in pleasure. "*Sí*, Cebellina. I will feed your hunger—with breakfast."

He turned abruptly and was gone.

The world suddenly seemed a brighter place, and Sloan had no explanation for it. What had changed?

While Cruz was gone, breakfast arrived. She ate and felt strong enough afterward to try out her wobbly legs, venturing all the way to the door. She was on her way back to the bed when she heard vaguely familiar voices outside in the hall. She stepped back to the door and leaned her ear against the wood in an effort to hear better. The argument was short and vicious. An English voice and a response in Spanish. Sloan inched the door open and peeked outside.

She stifled a gasp. Alejandro! And the Englishman! They were arguing about the Hawk . . . who was apparently right here in this hotel!

As they walked toward her, she quickly shut the door and leaned back against it. She couldn't let Alejandro escape again. Yet what could she do in her weakened condition to stop him? Only moments later she heard a knock on the door. She froze.

"Who is it?"

"It's Luke. Open up."

Sloan flung the door open and dragged Luke inside. "Come in! Quick!"

"What's going on?"

"I just saw Alejandro Sanchez in the hall."

Luke frowned. "Are you sure? I didn't see anyone."

"I tell you I saw him in the hall arguing with an Englishman. You've got to do something!"

Luke took Sloan by the shoulders and backed her up to the bed. "I think you'd better lie down."

"I am *not* having delusions, Luke. I didn't imagine seeing Alejandro. He was there. He's alive, and you can bet he's plotting something with that Englishman. Surely you can find out who the Englishman is and—"

"I already know who he is."

"You do?"

"His name is Sir Giles Chapman. He's here in San Antonio as a cotton agent for a British textile mill."

"He's here as a spy."

Luke shook his head. "You've got quite an imagination, Sloan, if that's what you think. Have you seen that man before?"

"I certainly have. He's the Englishman I wrote you about, the one who met with the Mexican bandidos. They were arguing about the Hawk—he's staying in this very hotel."

"Hmmmm. Have you got a description of this Hawk fellow? Any clue as to who he might be?"

"None at all," Sloan admitted.

"Look, Sloan. If Alejandro is in San Antonio, I can have him arrested. But I'll need more proof to do something about the Englishman. After all, it would be a diplomatic nightmare to accuse him of spying without more evidence than just your word against his. What I can do is keep my eyes and ears open for any suspicious activities."

Sloan frowned. "You can't do anything more than that?"

"Nothing."

"I guess that's it then. I want to see Cruz's face when he hears Alejandro is alive. You will let me tell him, won't you, Luke? You won't spill the beans?"

"Not if you don't want me to."

Luke was glad Sloan had accepted his reassurances that there was nothing he could do about the Englishman. He only hoped there weren't any more surprises in store before he and Cruz got this whole mess straightened out. "I better go see if I can find Alejandro. I'll be seeing you, Sloan."

Sloan had much too much time to think after Luke left the room. She wondered what could be keeping Cruz. Surely it didn't take this long to arrange for breakfast and a tub of hot water.

The hot water came a few minutes later, along with a young Mexican woman who offered to help Sloan with her bath. Sloan declined the help and, as soon as the young woman was gone, quickly stripped and slipped into the hot water. She laid her neck back against the metal rim, stretched out as much as the round wooden tub would allow, and luxuriated in the relaxing effects of the hot water on her aching muscles.

Cruz had entered the room quietly, thinking that Sloan must surely have taken her bath by now and gone back to bed. To his delight, he found his wife still sitting naked in the tub. She had gathered her thick sable hair into a knot at the top of her head, but numerous tendrils had escaped and lay along her neck and shoulders. The crests of her breasts rose barely out of the water.

His approach went undetected, and he was on one knee beside her when she realized his presence and opened her eyes.

In the several hours he had been gone, the look in those brown orbs had changed. They were wary now, and demanded answers he couldn't give.

"I saw Luke downstairs. He said he came visiting and you were feeling much better."

When Sloan followed Cruz's gaze, she realized that her nipples had come out of the water when she sat up. She crossed her arms protectively around herself. Realizing the strangeness of hiding herself from Cruz when they were man and wife, she scooted back down under the soapy water to make it less obvious what she was doing.

Cruz's hand made little circles in the soap-clouded water along the edge of the tub, and Sloan felt the ripples as intimately as though he had touched her flesh.

She shivered and asked, "What took you so long coming back?"

"I checked to see if there was any word from Betsy's family. There was a letter from her uncle."

"What did he say? Do they want her?" She forgot about her nakedness and gripped the edges of the tub with her hands. She held her breath, already knowing from the look on Cruz's face that she was going to lose the little girl. "Read it to me."

As Cruz got to the end of the letter, Sloan's heart began to pound.

> . . . *I'm right glad you were at least able to save Betsy. She was named after my wife, Elizabeth, and Lizzie and I are plumb anxious to have her with us. I'll take passage as soon as can be downriver to New Orleans, and from there by ship to Galveston, then overland to Rancho Dolorosa. I expect you'll take good care of our Betsy 'til I can get there to bring her home.*
>
> *Your servant,*
> *Louis Randolph*

"That's wonderful for Betsy," Sloan said in a choked voice.

"But not so wonderful for you," Cruz answered gently. "I am sorry, Cebellina. I know you wanted to keep the child."

"Of course I didn't want to keep her. I'm happy . . . oh, Cruz!" Sloan threw her arms around his neck. "Hold me. Please, hold me. I don't think I can bear it!"

Cruz leaned over and grasped Sloan under her arms, helping her stand, then wrapped her in a towel as she stepped out of the tub. Then he slipped his hand under her thighs and lifted her into his arms. He carried her over to the bed and tried to lay her down, but she wouldn't let go of him.

"Stay with me. Lie down with me. I don't want to be alone right now."

"Let me pull off my boots."

She clung to his neck, not even releasing him for that chore. He grunted as the second boot came off and a moment later joined her on the bed, hugging her with all his might.

Sloan welcomed the safe cocoon, but even that wasn't enough to make her forget.

"I want to feel your skin next to mine."

She shoved the towel aside and worked frantically on the buttons of his shirt, stripping it off his shoulders. Her hands and mouth were already busy on his skin, tasting the flavor of him, testing the texture of skin and sinew and bone. Her tongue laved a male nipple and drew it to a peak, which she nipped with her teeth.

She heard Cruz's groan of pleasure, felt the tension in his body as her mouth laid a line of kisses across his collarbone. His breathing was shallow, his body taut with need.

"I want you," she rasped. "I need you."

Cruz wanted the words to mean more than he feared they did. "I am yours, Cebellina. Only yours."

She went wild in his arms, her mouth on him everywhere, and he responded in kind. A euphoric battle of the senses followed, their bodies twisting and turning, hands and mouths seeking flesh and finding it.

Sloan pressed her hand intimately on the front of his trousers, stroking him, feeling him harden and grow.

"I want you inside me. Now."

She went to work on the buttons of his trousers and laughed when his hands got in the way. "I can do it," she said breathlessly. "Let me."

He lay still beneath her hands, and she played with him, teasing and taunting as each button gave way.

"Lift up," she said in a sultry voice. When he did, she reached inside the back of his trousers and skimmed them off his buttocks and down his legs.

Once he was free of the garment, he pulled her back up to lie full-length on top of him and let her legs slide down on either side of his thighs.

His hands skimmed down her back to her naked buttocks and he heard her moan as he pulled her snug against him. He nuzzled her neck with his lips and kissed his way up to the shell of her ear where he whispered, "I am yours, Cebellina. Now. Forever. Do with me what you will."

Sloan rubbed herself against him, feeling the silky softness, the steel hardness. She reached down and guided him inside her, feeling him push against her flesh, spreading her, and then she surrounded him, taking him inside.

The feeling of oneness was exquisite. Sloan smiled. "You feel wonderful."

Cruz chuckled. "I must return the compliment." His thumb pressed against her at the point where their bodies met. The slight friction made her groan.

She set her hips in motion and his thumb kept pace, so the pleasure came from both inside and out. She leaned toward him and his mouth captured her breast.

Sloan was bombarded by sensation. She leaned back, but he rose with her until she was sitting straddled across his lap. His hands slipped around to clutch her hips to remain seated deep inside her.

She sought his mouth and thrust her tongue inside, mimicking the dance below. She was hungry, ravenous for him.

They slipped onto their sides, and he rolled with her until she was beneath him. She arched up to meet his thrusts, her senses spiraling higher, reaching for the promise of pleasure, and finally with a hoarse cry, finding it.

With her shuddering climax, Cruz thrust deep, wanting his seed to find fertile ground, wanting to give her a child to fill the emptiness in her heart.

They lay exhausted, clutched to one another, their sweat mingling with the scent of their sex.

"I love you, Cebellina." Cruz didn't expect an answer, and he didn't get one.

Sloan slipped her arms around him, and burrowed her face into his shoulder, a hazy smile on her face. It had never been like this before. Never.

She knew then that she could not ask Cruz whether he had known Alejandro was still alive when he had come for her. It was better not to know the truth.

She did not think she could bear it if she found out Cruz was a liar, just like his brother.

Chapter 15

TWO WEEKS LATER DOÑA LUCIA WATCHED FROM the veranda as her son arrived back at Dolorosa, his laughing, smiling wife by his side, more in charity with one another now than they had been before they left.

"How was your journey?" she asked as her son climbed the few steps to greet her.

"It went well," Cruz said, "except Sloan was ill the day we arrived in San Antonio."

"Oh? That is too bad."

"A stomach ailment. But it quickly passed, and as you can see, she is fine now."

"So I see."

Cruz and Sloan quickly excused themselves and hurried inside to search for Cisco and Betsy.

Her back stiff, her black eyes inscrutable, Doña Lucia turned and walked into the *sala* to be alone. She seated herself imposingly in one of the heavy Mediterranean chairs, spread her ruffled burgundy satin skirt around her, and carefully straightened the lace at her elbows. This was how she had planned to meet her son when he told her of his grief at the tragic death of his wife.

Doña Lucia tightened her grip on the thick arms of the chair. She was greatly disappointed with the failure of her bold plan. What had gone wrong? Perhaps *that woman* had not drunk enough of the water in her canteen. Perhaps the tasteless poison had not been as strong as the old gypsy woman had promised.

Or perhaps Cruz's tender care had saved his wife's life.

Apparently, it had not occurred to her son that his wife might have been poisoned. Which meant that she would have another chance to accomplish what she had failed on the first try. She would have to wait until the gypsies came again to get more poison from the old woman.

Next time, she would make sure she had enough. Next time, when *that woman* became ill, she would not recover.

In the six weeks following her return to Dolorosa, Sloan spent a great deal of time with Betsy, knowing that her days with the child were numbered. She waited anxiously for the arrival of Betsy's Uncle Louis. She knew if she were smart she would be drawing back from her involvement with the little girl. But there was something about Betsy that precluded that possibility.

On the other hand, since her return from San Antonio, Sloan had consciously backed away from Cisco, as though it were only a matter of time before something happened to take him from her, too. It wasn't rational, but there was nothing reasonable about her deep-seated fear that those she cared for most were destined to be torn from her.

Sloan opened the letter she had just received from Bay. The missive turned out to be softly worded and steel-laced, very like Bay herself.

Dear Sloan,

   You know I'm not much good with horses (except for petting their noses) or I would have come sooner to see how you are.
   I'm sorry Cruz was away when I came to visit, but at least that gave us more time to talk. I agree with you that Betsy is adorable, but honestly, I don't know how you can resist Cisco. He looks more like Cruz every day.
   Tomasita is absolutely charming. Did you notice she spent the whole afternoon holding Whipp? She said she has always dreamed of having a baby of her own. Do you think her husband should be chosen by Cruz? That doesn't seem fair. How do you think she and Luke would get along?
   Oh my! This is turning into a book, so I had better close. I wish you happiness. Please let me know if Long Quiet and I can ever be of help.

All my love,
Bay

Sloan was gazing out the bedroom window at the many flowers blooming in the courtyard, musing about the hidden messages in Bay's letter, when she saw Tomasita grab onto a rose trellis to steady herself, close her eyes, and take several deep breaths, all the while holding a hand to her belly.

Sloan picked up Bay's letter and reread the paragraph about Tomasita. When she looked up again, Tomasita had sunk onto one of the stone benches in the courtyard. When had Tomasita's waist thickened? Where had she gotten the dark circles that shadowed her eyes?

Sloan could hardly credit what she was thinking, yet the

signs were there. It was true Tomasita had seen several young men over the past few weeks, as Cruz had brought a parade of suitors to supper. But how could Tomasita possibly be pregnant when she had been so carefully guarded, so closely watched?

Sloan rose from her desk and walked out into the courtyard.

When Tomasita heard footsteps, she quickly opened her eyes and stood up, nervously smoothing her wool skirt.

"You look tired, Tomasita. Are you all right?"

Tomasita blanched. "I am fine. Why do you ask?"

Sloan noticed the girl's hands had gone reflexively to her womb before she had clasped them together at her waist. "Is there anything you would like to talk about, Tomasita?"

"Like what?" Tomasita asked, brazening it out.

"If you are in any trouble—"

"What makes you think I am in trouble?" Tomasita interrupted.

Sloan's heart went out to the other woman. "I can help," she said softly.

"No one can help me," Tomasita said, her eyes bleak. "I am lost."

"I will speak to Cruz—"

"No! Say nothing. Please, if you care for me at all, say nothing." Tomasita turned and fled the courtyard.

Sloan knew Tomasita couldn't hide her problem for long, but for so long as she could, Tomasita's secret was safe with her. Yet Sloan could not help wondering—who was the father of Tomasita's child?

The day of Tomasita's reckoning came sooner than either of them had expected, for the moment they sat down to supper, Cruz said, "I have found a husband for you, Tomasita."

All eyes turned to Tomasita, who kept her gaze riveted on her plate of enchiladas, beans, and rice.

Cruz continued, "Do you remember Don Ambrosio de Arocha, the gentleman who came to dinner the first Sunday after I returned from San Antonio?"

"*Sí,* Don Cruz. I remember him," Tomasita answered.

Sloan remembered the prospective bridegroom, too. Don Ambrosio was a thin, erect, very stern-looking man. Distinctive, dark-eyed, he had a pointed beard and a thin moustache. But he was gray-haired and, frankly, old.

Cruz continued, "Don Ambrosio has asked me for your hand in marriage. I have arranged for a dowry, and we have signed a betrothal contract. The wedding will take place as soon as the banns are read."

Sloan wondered if Don Ambrosio could be the one who had gotten Tomasita pregnant and if that was the reason for such haste. That hardly seemed possible, though, since she herself had acted as duenna to the mismatched couple and they had spent only a few moments together in the courtyard.

Sloan watched Tomasita to see whether the news of her betrothal pleased her. The young woman said nothing, did nothing. In fact, her face remained impassive. Sloan knew Cruz had noticed Tomasita's lack of eagerness or excitement, because she saw him frown.

Doña Lucia was livid.

After they had finished eating, Sloan followed Tomasita, planning to offer whatever solace she could. To her surprise, the young woman did not go directly to her room. Instead, she walked out of the hacienda, through the fortress gates, and down toward the river.

Sloan traced the younger woman's steps to a spot along the river bank where the grass grew tall and thick cypress trees allowed only scattered rays of late-evening sun to reach the ground.

When Tomasita realized she was being followed she froze and demanded, "Who is there?"

"It's me. Sloan."

Tomasita slowly turned to face her. "Oh. I thought . . . I wished . . . never mind."

"Did you think it might be the baby's father?"

Tomasita gasped.

Sloan took another step closer to Tomasita. "I know you're pregnant, Tomasita."

"How could you? I only found out . . . Holy Mary. Who else knows?" she said as she grabbed Sloan's forearms, her voice frantic.

Sloan turned her hands and grasped Tomasita's arms, wanting to comfort the other woman. "It appears no one else knows. Although all the signs are there for anyone to see."

When Sloan heard the first sob, she opened her arms and the young woman threw herself into her consoling embrace. For a few minutes Sloan did nothing but hold Tomasita while she cried. She had been in this position herself, and hearing Tomasita's hopeless sobs brought back memories.

"Oh, Sloan, what am I going to do?" Tomasita wailed through her tears. "I cannot marry Don Ambrosio. I cannot! I am in love with another man."

"The father of your child?"

"Yes."

Sloan grasped Tomasita by the shoulders, looked into the other woman's tear-streaked face and demanded, "Who is he, Tomasita? What bastard got you pregnant and then disappeared?"

Tomasita stared at Sloan wide-eyed but remained silent.

Sloan's heart began to race and her stomach turned over as she had a horrifying thought. "Please . . . not Cruz . . ."

"No! Oh no. It is Luke. Luke Summers!"

"Luke?" Sloan asked, her voice sharp with relief, her mind not fully grasping what had been said.

"*Sí*. Your brother, Luke."

Sloan was stunned. "He couldn't do such a thing!" But she realized that of course he could.

Luke was adept at seducing women. A rake. A rogue. A bastard in name, and now in deed. But she had never believed he would stoop so low as to steal an innocent's virtue. "When? How?"

"Do you remember the day you went home to Three Oaks? Luke came here to find you, but you were gone. He asked me to meet him later, here at the river. I was not going to do it . . ."

"But you did," Sloan said flatly.

Tomasita covered her face with her hands. "Holy Mary. What a mess I have made of everything."

"Don't worry. It's not too late to straighten things out," Sloan said soothingly, her arms once again surrounding Tomasita in comfort. "We'll simply go to Cruz and explain what's happened. He'll talk with Luke and arrange for Luke to marry you instead of Don Ambrosio."

Tomasita jerked out of Sloan's embrace. "No! Don Cruz must not speak to Luke. I do not want Luke to know about the baby. Promise me you will not say anything to Don Cruz!"

Sloan realized that Tomasita was on the verge of hysteria and calmed her by agreeing to keep her secret. "This isn't something you can keep hidden for long," she warned. "And you certainly can't marry Don Ambrosio without telling him about the baby."

"I know."

"Tomasita, why don't you want Luke to know about the child? I can't believe he wouldn't want to know you'll bear his son or daughter."

"Luke has already made his wishes known. He does not want to marry me."

"But if Cruz spoke to him—"

Tomasita cut Sloan off with a bark of bitter laughter. "*Sí*, Don Cruz may very well be able to convince Luke to marry me. But do you think I want him for my husband on those terms? At least if I marry Don Ambrosio, there is hope that someday he will learn to love me."

"Are you so sure Luke doesn't have any feelings for you?"

Tomasita turned to face Sloan, her mouth drawn in harsh lines. "Would he have left me as he did and stayed away this long if he cared?"

Sloan's voice was soft when she asked, "Why did you make love with him, Tomasita, if you weren't sure he loved you?"

Tomasita dropped her chin to her chest and twined her hands together in front of her. "Because I love him. I think I have loved him from the first moment I saw him. Even before I discovered you had married Don Cruz, I wanted to meet Luke at the river. Finding you with Don Cruz only gave me the excuse I needed to do what I had wanted to do all along.

"If that was all I could ever have, I was willing to take the risk to have it. When I gave myself to him, I thought he wanted to marry me. I did not understand that he did not feel the same way about me as I did about him."

"What about the child? Will you keep it?"

Sloan watched as serenity bathed Tomasita's features. "Oh yes, I will keep the child. And I will love it with all my heart."

Sloan desperately hoped that Tomasita's feelings didn't change. For so, too, had she begun her pregnancy, with vows of everlasting love for her unborn child. "Let's go back to the hacienda. It isn't safe to be out here alone."

The two women made the trip back to the hacienda arm in arm, separating at the rear of the house to quietly make their way to their respective rooms.

"Where have you been?"

Sloan hadn't been expecting Cruz to confront her the instant she walked into their bedroom. She settled for the truth. "I went for a walk."

"Alone?"

"Am I not allowed to be alone?" she asked to avoid the need to lie.

She felt Cruz's arms surround her, felt him almost crush her with his strength as he pulled her close and nuzzled her ear. "I was worried about you, Cebellina."

"I can watch out for myself, Cruz."

"Do this for me, *querida,*" he coaxed. "You have your hands full with so many other things. Let me worry about you."

He kissed her ear, slipping the tip of his tongue along the shell-shaped rim, heating her skin with his breath. She felt herself melting against him, defenseless against his onslaught.

"Say you will."

"I will," she said as she sought out his throat with her mouth. She loved the salty taste of his skin, the man-smell of him. When her hands curved around to grip his buttocks, she heard him laugh.

"What's so funny?" she asked.

"I am hoping I will be one of the things that keeps your hands full."

She laughed and playfully squeezed his buttocks. "Me too."

Sloan awoke in the middle of the night with a lazy stretch, feeling loved, sated, and satisfied. She turned over and reached for Cruz, only to discover his side of the bed was empty.

At that moment a streak of lightning slashed across the sky, followed by a horrendous blast of thunder. She supposed Cruz must have been awakened earlier by the storm. She slipped a robe on over her nakedness and set out in search of him, lantern in hand.

She stopped by the room now shared by Cisco and Betsy to see whether the storm had woken either of them. Cisco was sound asleep, but she found Betsy whimpering in her bed.

She set the lantern down on the bedside table, then sat down next to Betsy and lifted the little girl into her lap. "Are you afraid of the storm, sweetheart?"

Betsy trembled in her arms. "Yes."

"There's nothing to be afraid of," Sloan crooned. "It's just a lot of light and noise."

"The lightning killed Jenny," Betsy said.

"Who was Jenny?"

"My sister. She didn't come in the house when Mama called her. The lightning hit Jenny, and I saw her catch fire.

Mama said God came and struck Jenny dead for disobeying her. I've been good, haven't I, Sloan? God won't strike me dead, too, will he?"

"Oh, sweetheart, you've been very, very good." Inside, Sloan raged at the mother who had been so heartless as to suggest that God punished disobedient little girls by striking them dead with lightning bolts.

How could she possibly assuage the little girl's fear? She started by saying, "You know, if you stay inside during a storm, the lightning can't reach you."

"Are you sure?"

"Very sure." She felt Betsy relax slightly in her arms.

"Mama said—"

"I know what your mama said," Sloan interrupted. "But it wasn't true. Your mama was feeling bad because your sister died and she put those unhappy feelings into words. God isn't going to strike you dead with lightning if you misbehave, Betsy. If that was the case," she said with a reassuring smile, "think of all the thunderstorms we should have had here at Dolorosa by now."

Betsy smiled back tremulously. "I guess you're right."

Sloan brushed the bangs back from Betsy's forehead, never more aware that Betsy was going to live with her aunt and uncle—strangers who might tell her equally terrifying stories.

She hugged Betsy hard, then forced herself to lay the child back in her bed. "You should try to go back to sleep. Any day now your Uncle Louis will be coming to get you, and you want to be well rested when he arrives."

"I like Uncle Louis," Betsy volunteered. "He lets me ride on Ben."

"I trust Ben is a horse," Sloan said, dropping a smacking kiss on Betsy's nose.

"Oh no, Ben is a mule. He pulls Uncle Louis's plow."

"Riding Ben sounds like fun." She tucked the quilt snugly around Betsy. "Do you think you can sleep now, sweetheart?"

Another bolt of lightning flashed, followed brief seconds later by a deafening rumble of thunder.

Sloan felt Betsy trembling, but the little girl gave her a brave smile.

"That's my girl. Remember, you're safe as can be, snug in your bed."

She kissed Betsy once more on the forehead before she rose to leave the room. She had reached the door when Betsy called, "Sloan?"

Sloan stopped and turned back to her. "Yes, Betsy?"

"Could you tuck Cisco in real snug, too? Just in case."

Sloan stood stunned for a moment before she followed the little girl's bidding. She set the lantern back down on the bedside table and sat down beside her son.

Bay had been right in her letter. How much like Cruz he looked! She ran her fingertips across his baby cheek, then leaned over and kissed him on the brow. So soft. So sweet. Her child and not her child.

His hands were thrown above his head in abandon, and one leg lay crooked outside the covers. She made no effort to rearrange him, simply tucked the covers in at shoulders, waist, and hips, knowing she was being watched from across the room.

"I want to love you, sweetheart," she whispered to her sleeping son. "I do want to love you. But I'm so afraid. I know it's as foolish for me to fear that you'll be taken away from me as it is for Betsy to fear the lightning. But oh, my son, how real the fear feels!"

She kissed her son again, picked up the lantern, and

crossed to the door. Without looking back she said, "Good night, Betsy. Sleep tight."

Sloan desperately wanted to be held by Cruz. She hurried to the *sala* and almost wept when she found it empty. She went back to their room, but the bed was still empty. Where was he? Had he been called out into the storm by one of his vaqueros?

What she had told Betsy hadn't been a lie—the little girl was safe inside the house. But outside in the storm, there was great danger. As flat as the surrounding terrain was, a man on horseback provided a tantalizing target for lightning.

Sloan had already dressed herself in pants, shirt, and boots to go in search of Cruz when she admitted the folly of such a gesture. It would be far better if she went back to bed and tried to sleep. However, she wasn't the least bit tired, and she knew she would never be able to sleep so long as the storm was lashing the adobe house with its fury.

She was having a glass of brandy in the *sala* when she heard voices at the front door. She rose from her chair before the fireplace, a smile widening on her face because she knew it had to be Cruz, home safe at last. She had only taken two steps toward the front door, however, when she heard another voice—a voice she recognized all too well.

"I expect you to do your part, Hawk."

"I always have, have I not?" Cruz answered.

"Well, good-bye then. Damn and blast this storm!"

"Never come here again, Englishman."

Sloan sagged back against the adobe wall as she heard the front door close and the sound of Cruz's boots on the tile floor as he walked toward the *sala*.

For an instant she thought of hiding. But what purpose would that serve? She already knew more than she wanted to know. Hiding wouldn't change the facts.

Cruz Guerrero was as much of a liar and a traitor to Texas as his brother had been.

Chapter 16

Sloan started to run without having any clear idea where she was going. She shoved Cruz to move him out of her way, but he backed up quickly to keep himself between her and the front door.

"Sloan, stop! Where are you going?"

"I heard you with the Englishman, Cruz. Or should I call you *Hawk*?"

Cruz's face turned ashen. "Wait. I can explain."

"Oh, I'm sure you can," she said with open sarcasm. She paled as a thought came to her. "Am I supposed to die for having seen the Englishman?"

"No. Christ, no! Let me explain—"

"I don't want to hear anything you have to say, *Hawk*." She tried to brush past him again, but his hands came up to frame either side of her face. He forced her to look up into his eyes.

She didn't believe what she saw. He couldn't be hurting. He couldn't be in pain. She was the one who had just had her heart torn out.

"I love you. I have always loved you," he said. "This other business has nothing to do with us."

Her eyes flashed with disdain. "I'm sure Tonio would have told me the same thing—if he had lived long enough to explain himself."

"Dear God. Please, Sloan, listen to me."

She jerked herself from his grasp and backed away from him. "I see I'm *Sloan* now. What happened to your precious *Cebellina*? I guess pretty love words aren't necessary any more to keep the blinders on my eyes. Don't follow me, *Hawk*. I never want to see your face again!"

While he stood watching her in stunned disbelief, she fled past him out the front door. His *bayo* was still tethered to the rail out front and she grabbed the reins, leaped into the saddle, and kicked him into a gallop.

An instant later Cruz came out of his stupor and realized that not only was Sloan leaving him, she was doing so in the worst spring storm they'd had in years. Lightning flashed, reminding him of the danger.

He raced outside in time to see her gallop through the fortress gates. He ran to the stable, taking time only to slip a bridle on the fastest horse he had, a half-broken buckskin stallion, before he slipped onto its bare back and headed after Sloan.

He yanked the buckskin to an abrupt halt outside the fortress walls. Lightning flashed again and he saw hoofprints in the mud, already filling with rainwater. He heaved a sigh of relief when he realized she wasn't headed in the direction of Three Oaks. It looked as though she had decided to go to Golden Valley, where her sister Bay lived.

He grasped a handful of black mane and tightened his legs on the buckskin's ocher sides before spurring the half-wild stallion. The animal responded by rearing in protest, neighing its refusal to be dominated by either man or nature, before it bolted away from the fortress into the black abyss created by the storm.

Sloan hadn't planned a particular destination when she had fled the hacienda. She was merely running and had given the stallion his head. It was only when the *bayo* began to tire that she realized she was headed toward the huge live oak where she and Cruz had first kissed. If there was a more dangerous place to be during a thunderstorm, Sloan didn't know where it was. Yet she was so overwhelmed by Cruz's betrayal she truly didn't care right now whether she lived or died.

It was only now that he had betrayed her that she realized she loved Cruz Guerrero with a depth of soul and spirit she had never imagined possible when his brother had broken her heart. Though that wound had somehow healed, she was certain this one never would.

When she reached the ancient live oak, she was awed by its majesty in the face of the elements. Its gnarled branches took on grotesque proportions in the flashes of white light, refusing to bow to the wind's demand, while its leaves rustled a furious defiance. She pulled the exhausted *bayo* to a halt beneath the glorious oak and sat there, shoulders back, chin high, recklessly waiting for lightning to strike.

There was something exhilarating about flaunting the fates, daring them to end her life. She raised her face to the drops of rain that fell like tears from the giant tree and let them mingle with her own. Suddenly, her face contorted and her jaws opened wide for the inhuman howl of pain that wrenched its way out of her mouth.

Cruz heard the ululating wail of human agony carried on the wind and spurred the stallion to even greater speed. A moment later, a flash of lightning revealed Sloan's silhouette on horseback beneath the towering oak. Cruz wanted to howl himself. How dare she take such a chance with her life! She belonged to him!

He knew she must have seen him in the same bolt of lightning, yet she remained beneath the natural lightning rod she had chosen for her resting place.

Cruz cupped his hands around his mouth and shouted, "Cebellina! Get away from the tree!" But the wind captured his warning and carried it away.

She did not move.

And so he had no choice except to join her in her death-defying venture.

When he reached her, he yanked the buckskin to a sitting stop and shouted over the wind, "You are gambling with your life. Come away from here, and we will talk."

"Don't like the odds, *Hawk*? Maybe you had better leave, then. You see, my luck hasn't been too good lately and—"

He grabbed the *bayo's* reins to lead him away from the danger, but Sloan saw what Cruz was attempting to do and simply slid out of the saddle. Cruz had only gone a few steps before he realized what she had done.

Once the stallion no longer had a rider to control him, he attacked the half-wild buckskin Cruz was riding. Cruz's mount half-reared and kicked at the *bayo* with its hind legs. The *bayo* danced skittishly away, pulling at the reins and forcing Cruz around so the two stallions faced one another.

In an instant the air was charged with expectancy, the storm forgotten as the two great beasts arched their necks, nostrils flaring, ears flattened against their heads as they tested one another in an instinctive effort to establish supremacy.

The *bayo* reared, stripping the reins from Cruz's hand,

and pawed the air, trumpeting a challenge that was quickly answered by the half-wild buckskin.

Sloan saw the danger to Cruz and, acting without thought to her own safety, rushed forward to try and catch her horse's reins and bring him back under control. As she reached out a hand for the trailing leather, the *bayo* reared again and its hooves struck her on the hip, sending her tumbling to the ground.

The pain was excruciating. Sloan barely had time to acknowledge it, however, before she was blinded by a piercing white light. She felt her eyebrows being singed as she threw up her hand to cover her face. For an instant the hairs stood up all over her body. A deafening crack of thunder followed.

When the sound had at last shuddered to a stop after a series of rumbling echoes, Sloan's face wrenched in an agonized expression of remorse and relief. By some miracle she had survived the bolt of lightning that had struck the magnificent oak.

Then she heard the sharp crack of splitting wood.

The live oak had been cleaved by the lightning, but the ancient tree had only been strong enough to withstand for a short time the pull of gravity that began to take its toll.

Sloan watched in horror as a fissure opened down the length of the tree and fully a quarter of the giant oak started its plunge downward to crush her. She tried to escape, but found it hard to move quickly with her injured hip.

She saw Cruz shaking his head to clear it. He was on the outer edge of the area where the branches would fall.

"Cruz! Look out!"

Cruz had been thrown from his horse by the repercussion from the lightning bolt. At the same moment he heard Sloan's warning, he identified the awful sound of wood splintering and sensed, rather than saw, the heavy branches of the shattered oak on their downward arc.

It only took one frightening look to see Sloan wasn't going to make it out on her own. It never occurred to him to save himself. He headed for his wife on the run.

He had mere seconds to reach Sloan, mere seconds to get them both to safety. He didn't have time for grace. He simply snatched Sloan up in his arms like a rag doll, and ran.

He had nearly reached the limits of the tree's vast umbrella when the outer limbs caught his shoulders and shoved him downward. He barely had time to drop Sloan into a narrow ravine and cover her body protectively with his own before the weight of the gnarled limbs crashed down on him.

Sloan woke to bright daylight but couldn't figure out where she was. Her hip ached abominably, and something heavy was weighing her down, making it hard to breathe.

Then it all came back to her. The weight, of course, must be Cruz's body.

"Cruz?" she whispered tentatively. "Are you awake? Are you all right?"

When she received no reply, she closed her eyes and prayed, reaching out searchingly with the hand she could move easily. Cruz's hand lay beside her on the ground, but it was cold and limp. She felt for a pulse at his wrist but couldn't find one.

She shuddered at the thought that he might be dead, and fought against panic. A small tremor sped through his body and she realized he must be alive.

"Cruz," she murmured from a throat swollen closed by guilt. "Please don't die. Please, for me, try to stay alive."

Surely someone would have noticed this morning that they were gone from the hacienda. Cruz's vaqueros would already be searching for them. But how would they know where to look? The storm would have washed out all signs of their journey. It could be hours before they were found—if they were found at all.

Sloan uttered several colorful curses before she managed to control her tongue. She had gotten herself and Cruz into this mess. It appeared she was also going to have to get them both out.

Sloan first tried to slide sideways out from under Cruz, but soon realized that was impossible because a limb had pinned them in place. However, the ravine into which they had fallen continued along for several feet beyond where they were lying. She began to work her body forward and out from under Cruz. It was slow going because a sharp pain ran down her leg each time she moved her hip.

It took much longer than she had thought it would to finally free herself, and when she did, it was frightening to realize that Cruz still hadn't regained consciousness. She forced her way upward through the layers of branches until she was standing upright.

The surrounding tree limbs only reached as high as her hips. Cruz had nearly managed to carry her to safety. Ten feet beyond where they were lying, the tree's branches ended, and several yards beyond that, the *bayo* stood munching grass. She wondered why he hadn't bolted for home until she realized that the dragging reins had gotten caught in a scrubby mesquite tree and tethered the horse as neatly as if she had done it herself.

She worked her way to clear ground and limped painfully to the *bayo*, praying that the saddlebags contained the necessities to help them survive. She could have cried for joy when she found a small ax for chopping firewood, matches, a blanket, some beef jerky, a bandanna, a small knife, and a canteen of water. She hugged the ax to her bosom while she drank some of the water.

"Cebellina! Where are you?"

"Cruz! I'm here! Wait, I'm coming." Sloan experienced a searing joy at the sound of Cruz's voice, which dimmed as she realized all that stood between them now. She hissed in pain as she jarred her hip. Soon she was straddling a tree limb beside him.

"I have tried to roll over, but my legs are caught," he told her.

"Are you hurt anywhere else?"

"I have a devil of a headache," he said through clenched teeth. "What about you?"

"I'm fine." There would be time enough later to mention her hip. "Lie still. I found an ax in your saddlebags and—"

"The horses did not head for home?"

"The *bayo*'s reins got caught on a mesquite. We can ride home as soon as I get you free."

Cruz wondered if Sloan realized what she had said. *We can ride home.* Did she consider Dolorosa home? Did this mean she was coming back to stay with him despite what she now believed about him? He could not bring himself to ask, so instead he said, "What can I do to help?"

"Just lie still. I can handle this."

It turned out that Sloan had been slightly optimistic when she had spoken. The ax was small and the limbs were thick. Also, her hip bothered her, and she had to rest frequently to take her weight off it. That soon became apparent to Cruz, who exclaimed, "You *are* hurt!"

"My hip got bruised when the *bayo* struck me with his hooves," she said, dismissing his concern. "It's nothing to worry about."

Neither of them spoke as Sloan continued hacking away at the branches of the live oak, but a conversation was taking place, nevertheless, in both their minds.

Why did he agree to work with the Englishman?

I should never have agreed to do it. I knew the chance I was taking that she would find out.

I don't understand how this could have happened to me twice in one lifetime.

Do I dare tell her the rest of it?

Oh God! I can't turn him in to the Rangers. But how can I stay silent about what I know?

I will tell Sir Giles I am out of it. I will quit.

And I can never trust him again.

I love her, but I cannot explain all of this to her yet. She will simply have to trust me.

"I've about hacked through this branch," Sloan said at last. "I should have you free in a minute."

She had been lifting away branches as she chopped them off and had cleared an area around Cruz's head and shoulders. As soon as there was space, he had tried to sit up, but had felt a searing pain in his head when he tried to lift it.

Sloan had finally threatened she would make it hurt a lot worse if he didn't lie still until she was finished. She had seen the dried blood on his temple, and that, coupled with his pain, made her worry that he was more seriously injured than he was letting on.

The sheer size and weight of the limb pinning Cruz's legs made it difficult for Sloan to move it, even though she had freed it from the rest of the tree. At last she managed to drag the branch out of the way. She stooped down and laid her hand on Cruz's shoulder. "Can you turn over by yourself?"

He moaned. "I thought you said you never wanted to see my ugly face again."

Sloan drew in a sharp breath. "This is no time for jokes."

"No, I guess it is not." He hissed with the pain as he hugged his arms to his body and slowly rolled over. Once he was flat on his back, he groaned again.

"How do you feel?"

"I do not think anything is broken, but I have one hell of a headache."

Sloan knelt beside him and ran her hand impersonally over his rain-damp clothes, checking to make sure he was telling the truth. She felt the muscle and sinew that lay beneath the cloth and wondered if she would ever be able to give herself freely to him again.

She forced her thoughts away from the future to the here and now. When she was done with her examination, she confirmed, "Nothing's broken as far as I can tell, unless you've cracked your skull."

"I do not think it is that bad," he said with a wry grin.

She had to accept his word. She expressed her tremendous relief by easing her aching body down onto the grass, crossing her arms, and raising them to cover her face as she leaned her head back against a fallen branch.

Cruz dragged himself up onto one elbow and reached out a hand to comfort her by softly stroking her hair. "Please do not cry. I could not bear it."

Sloan sat up, eyes dry, and said, "I wasn't crying. I was thinking."

"Oh? What have you decided?"

"If we can get ourselves up on that big palomino stallion, we can be home by dinnertime."

There it was again. The reference to Dolorosa as home. Cruz let himself hope. It was all he had left.

Sloan struggled upright, then leaned over so Cruz could hook his arm around her shoulder.

Cruz's head spun once he was upright, and he had to stand still for a minute before he regained enough balance to move. "That was some bump on the head," he muttered.

Together, they made their way to the *bayo*. Sloan helped Cruz drink a sip of water from the canteen, then drank some herself. She dampened the bandanna with some water and washed the blood from his face as best she could. She tied the bandanna around his forehead to keep the dust out of the cut until they could get home and stitch it up.

She bit back a moan when he gave her a push to help her into the saddle. He moaned when he stepped up onto the stallion behind her.

They traveled at a walk, since anything more than that would have been painful. Cruz slipped his arm around Sloan's waist and pulled her back against him. "We must talk, Cebellina."

Sloan sighed.

"I am sorry you found out the way you did that I have been working with the Englishman."

Sloan closed her eyes and bit her lower lip to keep from crying. Until now, there had been some faint hope she might have been mistaken. But Cruz had just confirmed her worst suspicions.

"I can only tell you I have my reasons for what I am doing."

Sloan searched Cruz's face for the answers he hadn't offered and found only the aristocratic pride that demanded her trust. She wanted so much to be able to give it. But too much had happened in the past for her to remain silent.

"Did you know Alejandro Sanchez was still alive when you married me?" she asked.

"No, not until later. A bandit named Jorge Gutierrez was hanged in Alejandro's place. His face was covered with a black bag. I saw Alejandro's turquoise and silver bracelet and assumed it was him."

Sloan grunted. So he hadn't lied about that, at least.

"Are you all right?"

"I jostled my hip. I'll be fine."

"Where do we go from here?"

"I'm not sure I can ever trust you again, Cruz. And I don't think I could bear a lifetime of doubt and suspicion. Maybe it's time I went home to Three Oaks."

Sloan felt Cruz's arm tighten around her and the swift exhalation of his warm breath on the back of her neck.

"Dolorosa is your home," he said fiercely. "You cannot go back to Three Oaks now. You still owe me two more months—"

"Surely you can't expect me to abide by that agreement after everything that's happened."

"Oh, but I do. I have told you this other business has nothing to do with us."

"It does if it means you have to lie to me."

Cruz swore under his breath. "I cannot explain myself now. You will have to trust me."

"You ask the impossible," she whispered.

Cruz's hacienda should have been a welcome sight, but there was too much left unsaid that they knew would never be spoken once they reached their destination. Yet neither of them slowed the *bayo* when he picked up his pace as they neared the fortress gates.

Sloan didn't mention leaving again, but she had made up her mind to return to Three Oaks as soon as her hip was mended enough that she could sit a horse comfortably.

They rode through the fortress gates to exclamations of relief from the *pobres,* who had been told to be on the lookout for Señora Sloan. Tomasita had discovered her missing early that morning, and Cruz's vaqueros were out even now searching for her. Runners were quickly sent to carry word that Don Cruz's wife was safe.

"Patrón! Patrón! You have found the señora. *Gracias a Dios!*" Josefa cried, running out of the house to greet them with Cisco and Betsy clinging to her skirt.

Tomasita followed close behind her exclaiming, "You are hurt, Don Cruz. What happened?"

Doña Lucia remained on the veranda, her lips twisted in disgust as she realized that once more an opportunity had come and gone to be rid of her son's *gringa* wife. "Come inside, Josefa, and bring the children. Tomasita, your presence is not needed here. Go to your room."

Once satisfied that Josefa and Tomasita had responded to her commands, Doña Lucia turned to the *mestizo* servant beside her and ordered, "Sancho, send for the *curandera,* María. We have need of her."

Cruz carefully eased his aching body off the stallion, then reached up to help Sloan down. He put his arm around her and pulled her close, walking with her up the steps of the veranda to greet his mother.

"Good morning, Mamá."

"I will not ask why you thought it necessary to go riding in a thunderstorm," Doña Lucia said to Sloan with icy hauteur, "but when you risk my son's life with your childish games—"

"That is enough, Mamá. Please excuse us. We are both hungry and tired and need to avail ourselves of María's healing hands."

Cruz tightened his grip on Sloan and stepped around his mother, unaware of Doña Lucia's whitened knuckles fisted in the folds of her satin skirt or her eyes that stabbed Sloan's back.

"Thank you," Sloan said once they were inside the adobe hacienda.

"For what?"

"For defending me."

"I apologize for the fact that I should need to defend you. Mamá is set in her ways. It is not easy for her to accept the fact that I have chosen my own wife."

Sloan's limp was worse because her bruised muscles had stiffened in the saddle. Cruz simply picked her up, his eyes daring her to protest, and carried her to the bedroom, where he laid her on their bed. He removed her boots and sat down beside her while they waited for the *curandera* to arrive.

Doña Lucia arrived in the doorway moments later with a tray containing two silver goblets and a bottle of brandy. "I thought you might need something to fortify yourselves until María arrives."

Cruz had to admit a brandy sounded good. His mother turned slightly away to fill one goblet with the golden liquid and offered it to Sloan, who had inched herself upright with the pillow supporting her back. Then she filled a second goblet for Cruz.

Doña Lucia waited to see Cruz take a sip of brandy from the goblet she had handed to him—she wanted no chance of a deadly mistake. This time she would be rid of *that woman* for good, and her death could be blamed on some injury she had acquired in the storm.

Satisfied that she had accomplished what she had come to do, Doña Lucia left the room, saying, "I will go see what is keeping María."

Cruz sat back down on the bed beside Sloan and touched his goblet to hers, offering a toast, "To long life. To happiness. To love." He lifted the goblet and took another sip of the fine brandy.

Sloan lifted the goblet to her lips and held it there for a moment, as she contemplated whether she could honestly drink to such a toast. But in her mind's eyes she saw nothing of happiness and love, and despaired of a long life spent without them. Distraught by the shattered images his words had conjured, she felt the goblet slip from her hand, soaking the sheets in brandy.

"Oh no!" She stared at the brown stain, thinking how quickly what had once been pure was now unclean. "I don't know what happened. I thought I could handle—oh, Cruz!"

All the pain she had held in abeyance during the crisis just past came flooding across her. "I can't bear it. How could you do it? How could you lie to me just like Tonio?"

Her head fell back against the pillow, and she turned her face away from him, squeezing her eyes shut to hold back the tears, gritting her teeth to contain the sobs.

Cruz slipped farther onto the bed next to her and laid his head on the pillow beside her. He gently eased his arm across her waist and felt her flinch beneath his touch. "I am sorry for your pain, Cebellina. You will never know how sorry."

He lay beside Sloan, holding her, until he felt the tension ease from her body. She was asleep when Cruz realized how drowsy he felt himself. He closed his eyes, just to rest a moment until María arrived.

The *curandera,* María, was a wizened old woman, who wore ragged clothes and generally smelled of the poultices she devised. When she entered the room, she found Sloan and Cruz both asleep on the bed.

She checked Cruz first, clucking her tongue and shaking her head as she pried open his eyelids and peered into his eyes. She rinsed the blood from the wound at his temple and decided that it would not need stitching if she pulled it together and bound it that way. With quick, sure hands she checked to make sure he was otherwise uninjured before turning her attention to the woman.

She remembered Señora Sloan well. She had first met the señora a year ago when Cisco had been knifed by a Comanche, and Don Cruz had defended the señora's right to stay with her son when the *curandera* had demanded that the room must be cleared of those who had no need to be there. Doña Lucia had left. Señora Sloan had remained and efficiently assisted María as she had stitched the wound closed.

The *curandera* had seen the adoration for this woman in Don Cruz's eyes when he had thought no one was looking, and she had thought then that Señora Sloan would make a worthy wife for her patrón. She wondered, as she gently woke the señora, whether the young woman had learned to return Don Cruz's affections. If so, she would need all her courage to face the news that María had to impart.

"Señora, wake up," the *curandera* said, gently slapping Sloan's cheeks.

Sloan blinked her eyes open. "Is Cruz—"

"I have done what I can for El Patrón. Now it is time to take care of you."

"I'm only a little bruised—"

María shook her head and clucked her tongue as though chiding a small child as she helped Sloan strip off her clothes and put on a chambray wrapper. "That is a bad bruise on your thigh, señora, and needs something to reduce the swelling."

"What *is* that?" Sloan demanded, her nose wrinkling in disgust as María applied a strong-smelling poultice.

"Something that will have you feeling much better soon," the *curandera* assured her. "But I am afraid I must bring you more pain, señora," María said as she covered Sloan with the sheet.

"What do you mean—more pain?"

"Don Cruz—"

"What's wrong!" Sloan turned frantically to look at the man who, until now, she thought had been peacefully sleeping. "He's not dead, is he?"

"No, señora. He sleeps."

Sloan turned back just as quickly and frowned at the *curandera*. "If he's just sleeping, then what's wrong with him?"

"It is not only his body that sleeps," María explained, "but his soul as well."

Sloan all too quickly realized what the *curandera* was trying to say. "Oh my God. You mean he's in a coma? He's not going to wake up?"

"Be calm, señora," the *curandera* said. "I do not know how long he will sleep. It may be he will wake in the morning, his body and soul rested. But it may also be that he will take longer to wake."

Sloan stared at Cruz in horror. "He might die?"

They were interrupted when Doña Lucia appeared at the door and announced, "There is someone here to see you, Sloan."

"Who is it?" she asked.

"He says his name is Louis Randolph. He says he has come for Betsy."

Chapter 17

SLOAN FELT THE DISBELIEF GROW, SPINNING HER insides like a tumbleweed in the wind. "It can't be. He can't take her right now. I mean . . . it's too much . . ."

She directed all her senses inward in an effort to calm the furor there, so she didn't notice the astonished look on Doña Lucia's face when the older woman realized Sloan was not the least bit sick. Nor did she see the look of horror when Cruz's mother realized that her son lay unmoving on the bed.

"Did he—Did you—?" Doña Lucia gasped.

Sloan stared down at Doña Lucia's hand, which had curled, like a bird's claw, around her forearm. Sloan pulled her hand free and said, "Did he what? Did I what?"

Doña Lucia crossed to the mahogany bedstead in a haze and reached out a hand to touch her son's pale whiskered cheek, fearing the worst. He simply could not have drunk from the poisoned goblet. She had watched carefully to make sure—and then she saw the wet brown stain on the sheets. *That woman* must have spilled the poisoned brandy, rather than drinking it. Doña Lucia ground her teeth in fury. She had failed again. And she had barely kept herself from blurting out what she had tried to do.

"Will he recover?" Doña Lucia asked the *curandera*.

"Only time will tell," María said.

Sloan followed Doña Lucia and now stood beside her looking down at Cruz.

Doña Lucia stepped back as though Sloan was filth that would soil her gown. "You should be lying there, not my son. The blood of kings runs in his veins. He should never have married his brother's *puta*!"

Sloan was in shock. Too much had happened in too brief a time. "I want you to leave this room now," she said. "I have to dress to greet my guest."

Doña Lucia didn't know what to make of Sloan's calm but firm request. Left without an enemy with whom to do battle, she looked one last time at her unconscious son, turned, and left.

Sloan pulled on a clean shirt and vest, but needed the *curandera*'s help getting her pants and boots on.

"You should be in bed, señora," María said.

"I can't sleep now. I'll rest later."

In the *sala,* Sloan found Betsy perched on one of her Uncle Louis's knees and Cisco straddling the other. Louis Randolph was a big man. He was dressed like a farmer, in a dark gray homespun shirt, baggy denim overalls, and short, heavy black boots, all of which had seen a great deal of wear. He had shaggy light brown hair and ears that stuck out from his head like handles on a sugar bowl.

"Hello. I'm Sloan Guerrero."

Louis smiled, his brown eyes sparkling with good humor. "I'd get up, ma'am, but I seem to have two bronc riders here holdin' me down."

He briefly released Betsy to reach out his hand, and

Sloan bent forward to shake it. His hand was heavily callused, and though Sloan was sure he was quite strong, his
grip was gentle.

"I'm obliged to you for puttin' yourself in danger to
help my kin," he said, his voice a deep, sincere bass that
rumbled in his broad chest. "And for takin' care of Betsy. It
near broke my Lizzie's heart when my brother and his wife
took off for Texas. My Lizzie and me, we love this child
like she was our own."

"I'm glad she'll have a home where she'll be welcome
and can grow up happy," Sloan said.

When Louis met her eyes, she realized he was trying to
make this as easy for her as he could. She was grateful to
him and looked for a way to thank him for his kindness.
"Can you stay and have a meal with us?"

"I'd like to, but I've got to get back on the trail if I want
to catch the packet from Galveston back to New Orleans.
I'd welcome the chance to thank your man for his hospitality, though," Louis said.

"I'm sorry, but Don Cruz was in an accident and he's
not well enough to . . ." Sloan's throat closed and she
couldn't continue.

"I'm sorry to hear that, ma'am. I truly am. Betsy, why
don't you say good-bye to Miz Sloan now." Louis lifted
Betsy off his knee and stood her in front of him.

Sloan went down on one knee and opened her arms to
Betsy, who flew into them. "I'm going to miss you, Betsy."
Sloan levered Betsy away from her embrace and forced
herself to smile at the little girl.

"I'm going to miss you, too," Betsy said. "I'll remember
what you told me, and I won't be afraid."

Sloan hugged Betsy again, fighting tears.

"I've made arrangements to have all my kin's things

shipped back to Pennsylvania," Louis said. "Is there anything of Betsy's here that has to be packed for her?"

"A few things. I can get them for you now." Sloan was grateful for the excuse to leave the room. She released Betsy and said, "You're going to have a wonderful life, Betsy. Maybe someday you can come back to Texas and visit me."

Sloan looked over Betsy's head and met Louis's eyes. She knew then that Betsy would never be coming back. It had probably taken Louis and Lizzie's life savings for him to make this trip. There would be no money for anyone to make such a trip again. Sloan rose and it was all she could do not to run from the room.

She was in Cisco's bedroom putting the last of Betsy's clothes and toys into a traveling bag when Cisco tugged on her pants leg. She turned and sat down on his bed. "What is it, Cisco? Do you need something?"

"I don't want Betsy to go away. I want her to stay."

He stared up at her, and Sloan heard his unspoken request for comfort. She abruptly brushed at his sable curls, then pulled her hand back when she realized what she was doing.

"I don't want her to go, either. But Betsy's Uncle Louis and her Aunt Lizzie love her and want her to come live with them in Pennsylvania."

"But I will miss her."

"So will I, darling. I'll miss her very, very much." Sloan clasped her hands tightly together to keep from lifting Cisco into her lap. Unable to hold back the tears that had begged shedding for the multitude of things that had happened today, she let them fall.

Cisco's lip quivered when he saw the wetness that scoured her face. "Mamá?"

Sloan looked down and saw that her son's brow was furrowed worriedly, his chin trembling. She swiped at her tears with the heels of her hands, realizing she was upsetting him. "Yes, sweetheart, what is it?"

"Maybe I could play with you. Then you wouldn't be so lonely when Betsy is gone."

Sloan felt the tears welling again as she stared down at her son, with his blue eyes and his curly brown hair, his high cheekbones and his cleft chin—the innocent face of a child who had borne the brunt of all her anger at his dead father . . . and her fears of being hurt again. Yet despite it all, he had offered love where love had been withheld.

"Oh, Cisco . . ."

She reached out and suddenly scooped him up into her arms, hugging him tightly to her breast. "Oh, Cisco . . . my baby . . . my darling son . . . I do love you so!"

She rocked him in her arms, crooning love words. She told him all the things they would do together while Cruz was getting well and all the things they would do together once Cruz was back on his feet.

"But first," she said, swiping at her nose and eyes with her sleeve, "we had better get Betsy's things packed so her Uncle Louis doesn't miss his ship in Galveston."

Betsy's leave-taking was not nearly so bitter for Sloan with Cisco's warm body snuggled sleepily in her arms. She was able to wave good-bye with a smile on her face before turning back to the adobe house and all that waited there, good and bad, frightening and infuriating.

An hour later, after she had been admonished by María that she must keep up her own strength if she was to be any help to Don Cruz, Sloan was sitting at the dinner table with a subdued Doña Lucia and an equally quiet Tomasita when they were approached by Paco, the vaquero who had brought word of the *gringo* wagons on Dolorosa land.

"What is it, Paco?" Doña Lucia asked irritably.

"The storm damaged many of the *jacals* in the pueblo. I came to ask Don Cruz's permission to have his vaqueros help fix them."

"Don Cruz is ill," Doña Lucia said.

Paco stood waiting for further instructions.

Doña Lucia frowned in exasperation and said, "The *jacals* will have to wait."

"But, señora—"

"Do not dare to question me!"

Paco had started to back away when Sloan interceded. "Go out to the veranda, Paco, and wait for me there." When Paco had left the room, she turned to Doña Lucia and said, "Perhaps whoever Cruz usually leaves in charge of the vaqueros when he is away from Dolorosa on business could take care of the problem."

Doña Lucia sat sullen and silent for a moment until it became clear that Sloan was willing to wait her out. "Miguel Padilla is Cruz's foreman, but he would not presume to act without orders from his patrón."

"Can't someone else give orders?"

When Doña Lucia once again remained silent, Sloan demanded in exasperation, "Who's going to manage Dolorosa until Cruz recovers?"

"I . . . I do not know."

"Unless you have a better suggestion, I will give the orders that need to be given."

Doña Lucia rose imperiously from her chair. "How dare you—"

Sloan rose to her feet with equal dignity at the opposite end of the table. "Shut up and sit down."

Doña Lucia was so shocked at Sloan's order that she sank back into her chair, mouth agape.

"We don't know how long it will be before Cruz is back on his feet, but I don't intend to have him recover only to find that Dolorosa has been neglected in his absence. I'm giving you fair warning that I intend to make sure that doesn't happen. If you think you can do a better job, you'd better say so now."

"Why would you do this for us?" Doña Lucia asked, eyes narrowed speculatively.

"I'm not doing it for you. I'm doing it for Cruz."

"The vaqueros will not listen to you, *gringa*."

"I assume, then, that you won't interfere if I give it a try." Without further ado, Sloan pivoted on her good heel and limped out to joined Paco on the veranda. "Take me to Miguel Padilla."

Paco's face did not hint at what he was thinking, but he had seen how El Patrón cared for this woman. He would not dare take a chance of offending her. He simply said, "Follow me, Señora Guerrero."

Sloan's nervousness built during the short, uncomfortable ride to the village. She stepped inside Miguel's *jacal* with great trepidation. She had to convince Cruz's foreman to take her seriously. Otherwise her efforts to help Cruz would come to naught.

"*Buenos días,* Miguel."

"*Buenos días,* Señora Guerrero."

"Doña Lucia told me you're in charge of Don Cruz's vaqueros."

The rangy vaquero nodded. His face was as ageless as a mountain peak, eroded by wind and weather. He wore the spurred wing boots and rawhide chaparejos of the vaquero.

Sloan's mouth was bone-dry. She licked her lips to

dampen them and continued, "You've probably heard that Don Cruz was injured in the storm last night. Until he's well, I'll be giving the orders on Dolorosa."

"Please pardon me for asking, señora, but what do you know of ranching?"

"To tell the truth, cotton's really what I understand best," she said with a self-effacing smile. "But I learn fast. For instance, I know that vaqueros will work harder and with better tempers if they have a dry, warm bed to come home to—which means the first thing we must do is repair the *jacals* that were damaged in the storm."

"What you say makes sense." Miguel's lips quirked at the corners, creating deep crevices in his granite face.

"So my first order is to repair the *jacals*." Sloan's body tensed in anticipation of his refusal to obey her.

Miguel stole a glance at Paco, who had been the source of several colorful stories around the campfire about the patrón's *gringa* wife, none of which had been believed.

Miguel assessed the petite woman who stood before him dressed as a man. It appeared Paco's stories of a beautiful young woman with fire in her eyes and steel in her backbone had not all been the fanciful imaginings of a storyteller.

"It shall be done," Miguel said at last.

Sloan exhaled a breath of air she didn't realize she had been holding. "Good. When can we start?"

Miguel cocked a questioning brow at Sloan's inclusion of herself in the work detail. "The work begins now."

Sloan threw herself into the effort to chop more mesquite posts to replace those that had been broken, sank her elbows deep in the mud and straw mixture that was packed between the cracks left once the posts had been stood upright to form a wall, and restored thatching on ruined roofs.

She wasn't the only woman who joined in the effort to repair the *jacals*. But her seemingly inexhaustible supply of energy despite her injury earned her the awe and respect of the vaqueros, their wives, sisters, and mothers.

As the day ended in a gorgeous sunset of pinks and purples striping the horizon, Sloan sought out Miguel once more. "Are there other matters that require immediate attention?"

By now Miguel was ready to do anything Sloan demanded, so it surprised him to hear her asking for his opinion of what should be done next. Her earnest expression convinced him that she was sincere in her desire to do what was best for Dolorosa in her husband's absence. And what was good for Dolorosa was good for the vaqueros who lived there. Any lingering resentment he might have had about taking orders from a woman were quelled. "*Sí, señora.* Don Cruz wanted a brush corral built to hold the mustangs we will capture in the spring hunt."

"Then we must begin with that tomorrow." Sloan rubbed her hand gently along her bruised hip, then arched her back and rubbed her balled fists into the aching muscles just above her buttocks. "I'll meet you at dawn at the fortress gates."

She was rolling her head in slow circles when Miguel replied, "As you wish, Doña Sloan."

Sloan's head snapped up at the title of respect and met the wily vaquero's dark brown eyes with gratefulness. Miguel nodded his obeisance before he turned and left her.

For the next week, Sloan worked with the vaqueros during the day and spent the nights sitting beside Cruz, holding his limp hand in hers and recounting everything she had said and done, as though he could really hear her.

The double duty took its toll on her. Shadows formed beneath her eyes, and her face became gaunt with the signs of fatigue. Yet she couldn't rest. She was determined that when Cruz awoke he would find Dolorosa had not suffered in his absence.

Paco's stories around the campfire about the devoted and spirited wife of El Patrón were no longer greeted with chuckles of disbelief. In fact, other vaqueros offered their own stories of how Doña Sloan had thrown her lasso over the head of a bawling calf and pulled it from a boghole, how Doña Sloan had ridden her horse like the wind in pursuit of an especially fast mustang, and how Doña Sloan had taken the time to sit with Esteban's wife as she labored to deliver their first child.

They did not understand how she could do the work of a man and yet have the soft heart of a woman, but she had proved it time and again. They would have walked through fire for her.

But it had been whispered on more than one set of lips that when Don Cruz was well, he would never allow Doña Sloan such freedom to come and go. For, after all, a man's wife belonged at home.

Sloan was oblivious to their speculation. Anyway, she was too exhausted and sick at heart to care.

She was sitting in a chair beside Cruz's bed, her cheek lying on Cruz's hand where it lay on the bed, when she heard the door open. It was a sign of how tired she was that she didn't even raise her head to see who had entered the room.

She heard voices murmuring behind her and the sound

of something heavy being settled on the tile floor. Finally, her curiosity roused her.

She turned to find that Tomasita was directing the servants to set up a bath for her. She sat, unmoving, while the wooden tub was filled with hot water. Finally, Tomasita sent the servants from the room and closed the door.

"I thought a bath might relax you so you can sleep," Tomasita said.

"Thank you. I don't know what to say."

Tomasita helped Sloan undress, then wrapped her in a towel.

"You must rest more," Tomasita chided, "or you will soon be sick yourself."

"I know you're right," Sloan readily agreed. "And I wish I could but—"

"Come, step into the bath." Tomasita led Sloan over to the steaming water like a helpless child and then held on to the towel as Sloan settled her sore muscles into the hot water.

Sloan sighed in ecstasy. "Ahhhh. This is wonderful. Thank you, Tomasita."

"It is the least I can do."

Sloan looked at Tomasita and realized she wasn't the only one with dark circles under her eyes. "How are you, Tomasita? Have you been feeling well?"

"As well as can be expected under the circumstances."

"Have you decided what you're going to do about Don Ambrosio?"

"I am going back to Spain."

"What?"

"To the sisters at El Convento del Sagrado Corazón in Madrid."

Sloan watched Tomasita slowly lower herself into a

nearby rawhide chair. "Are you sure that's what you want to do?"

Tomasita met Sloan's eyes and said, "What other choice do I have?"

"You can tell Luke about the baby."

Sloan watched the pain darken Tomasita's sapphire eyes before the Spanish woman replied, "He would never forgive me for forcing him to marry me. I could not live with him knowing that he did not want me."

"Perhaps he cares for you a great deal more than you think."

"Please do not offer me hope where there is none."

Sloan leaned her head back against the cool metal rim of the wooden tub and closed her eyes. "You can run away if you want. But I thought you had more gumption."

"I did . . . I do . . ."

"Do you really want your son or daughter to grow up without knowing his father, the way Luke did?"

They were both silent while Sloan soaked in the tub. At last, Sloan stood and Tomasita quickly wrapped the towel around her.

"Promise me you'll think about it," Sloan said.

"All right. Now I will leave you to get some rest," Tomasita said. "It has been a long day."

"Yes, it has," Sloan agreed with a wan smile. "A very long day."

Sloan was too tired even to put on a nightgown. She simply crossed to the opposite side of the bed and slipped under the covers beside Cruz. She only meant to doze, but it had been too long since she had given her body a rest, and as soon as she closed her eyes, she was sound asleep.

Sloan was having a wonderful dream. Cruz was making love to her, his hands gently roaming the naked curve of

her hip, spanning her belly, cupping her swollen breasts.
She felt his lips follow where his hands had been, until his
thumb caressed her jaw. His lips touched hers and it felt so
real. It felt—

"*Te adoro,* Cebellina."

Sloan stiffened. That voice was no dream. Her eyes flew
open to the sight of Cruz lying beside her, his eyes open
and—seeing her.

"You're awake!" She embraced him, their bodies warm
against each other as tears of relief welled in her eyes. A
brilliant smile broke across her face and she leaned back to
look up at him.

"You're a sight for sore eyes," she said.

"Have I been ill long?"

"You've been unconscious for eight days."

"Eight days! I have to—" Cruz tried to sit up, but he got
so dizzy Sloan had to help him lie back down again.

"Don't worry. Everything's been taken care of while
you've been ill."

"How could that be? Miguel only takes orders from me.
There must have been damage from the storm and—"

"It has all been taken care of," Sloan repeated, soothing
his troubled brow with her hand. "I handled everything."

Cruz was very still for a moment, and Sloan looked to
make sure he was still all right.

"You handled everything?"

"Someone had to take charge. So I did."

"My vaqueros followed your orders?"

"Yes."

"I see."

"You do?" Sloan said, surprised at his apparent acquiescence to her activities.

"Yes, and I thank you. Now that I am well, though, I can take over and leave you free to—"

"Not so fast," Sloan said, sitting up and using the sheet to cover her nakedness. "I don't want to be free."

"No?"

"No. Besides, you're not getting out of this bed until I'm sure you're completely well. And that means not until María says so. There's no sense in your vaqueros tramping in here to disturb you, either. If you want to give orders, fine. You can do it through me. I won't have you getting up too soon and winding up dead. Do you understand me?"

When her tirade was over, Sloan saw that Cruz was trying very hard not to smile.

"This isn't a laughing matter!" she spat.

At that, Cruz did smile. "No, it is not. When a wife protects her husband from his own stupidity, it is very serious business. All right, Cebellina, I will give my orders through you. But I want to talk with Miguel about what has been done while I have been ill."

"I guess that wouldn't hurt," Sloan said grudgingly. "But not for long. If you have any questions after that, you can ask me."

"*Sí*, Cebellina. We will work together, you and I, as a husband and wife should."

Sloan stared at him. "I'm only helping until you get well," she said. "This isn't going to be a permanent thing."

"Of course, Cebellina," he said. "Whatever you say."

Chapter 18

EARLY THE NEXT MORNING, WHEN CRUZ MET with Miguel and heard what Sloan had accomplished on Dolorosa while he was in a coma, he realized how badly he had misunderstood and underestimated the woman he had made his wife.

Cruz had always known that Sloan was overseer for Three Oaks, but he had never seen her acting in a position of authority. When he had first regained consciousness, he had been willing to indulge his wife and allow his orders to be funneled through her to Miguel. He had never expected Miguel to treat her as though she were actually in charge. Seeing them deep in conversation at his bedside, he realized that was exactly what had happened.

"So you see, Miguel," Sloan was explaining, "if the crops growing in each vaquero's garden are thinned and then layered with manure, the plants will grow taller and bear larger vegetables."

"*Sí*, Doña Sloan," Miguel replied. "I understand. I will tell my vaqueros what you have suggested."

Sloan turned to Cruz and asked, "Is there anything more

you wanted to know from Miguel regarding what was done in your absence?"

"No. I have heard enough."

Miguel rose from the rawhide chair beside Cruz's bed and said, "May your good health return quickly, Patrón."

"*Gracias,* Miguel. I expect to be rejoining you soon. Until then, you will continue as before, taking orders from Doña Sloan."

A flicker of surprise flashed in Miguel's dark eyes at Cruz's command. When he had learned that Don Cruz had recovered, he had thought he had seen the last of Doña Sloan among the vaqueros.

But it would be a foolish man who did not take advantage of such a talented wife. And Don Cruz was no fool. Miguel nodded his obeisance to Cruz, then shifted his stance and did the same to Sloan before he turned and left the room.

"I see you have made a conquest," Cruz said as Sloan closed the door behind Miguel.

She turned and walked back to stand beside the bed. "What do you mean?"

"The man who just left this room would gladly lay down his life for you."

"Only because I am your wife."

"No, it is more than that. How did you garner his approval so quickly? It took weeks after my father died before I had earned his acceptance and respect. You have done it in eight days."

"I didn't do anything special that I know of," Sloan said. "Just dug in and went to work like I would have at Three Oaks."

Cruz heard in her description of her actions what she hadn't known how to explain. What other woman would have worked side by side with his vaqueros? None that Cruz knew.

He had never before comprehended how much this woman needed a position *beside* him—in more places than at the dining table and in bed. No wonder she had dreaded leaving Three Oaks and coming to live at Dolorosa. No wonder she had not been as truly happy living with him as he had hoped.

For the past four months, he had—no matter that it had been by necessity—kept her separate from the work on Dolorosa that was so much of his life. He saw now the mistake he had made. He only hoped it was not too late to make amends, and to offer her a life she would willingly share with him.

"You have done very well, Cebellina. There are some things I will need your help to get accomplished in time for the spring roundup."

Sloan relaxed, realizing she had been braced for criticism and received praise. Not only that, but Cruz seemed both eager and willing to have her help. "I'll do anything I can," she offered. "Before we get started, there is someone else who has been waiting to see you."

Sloan went to the door and called for Josefa, who arrived moments later with Cisco in tow. As soon as he saw Sloan, the little boy came running and leaped into her arms. Sloan picked him up, and chattering happily together, they walked across the room to Cruz's bedside.

Cruz was astounded—and pleased—at this sudden change in Sloan's behavior toward her son. It was another miracle for which he saw no clear explanation. "You two look happy."

"Cisco and I have something we have to tell you."

"Good news, I hope."

"Good for Betsy," Sloan replied.

"Betsy's Uncle Louis came to get her," Cisco explained as Sloan set him down on the bed next to Cruz. "She is going to live on his farm."

"It must have been sad to say good-bye to her."

"*Sí,*" Cisco said. "Mamá cried."

Sloan sat down on the bed beside Cisco. "But Cisco said he would play with me and keep me from being so lonely. And you know . . . I'm not." She smiled at Cisco and gave him a big hug.

Cruz felt a queer tug in his chest. They would be a family now, he and Sloan and Cisco. Somehow she had put the past behind her and offered them all a chance at a future together.

Then he remembered the reason she had fled into the storm. He had brought the past once more into the present, apparently consorting with the Mexicans—just like his brother, Tonio—against the interests of the Republic. Did Sloan think she had married a dishonorable man, a traitor to Texas?

She had said nothing this morning about his activities as the Hawk, had asked no questions about why the Englishman had visited Dolorosa. It appeared that she did not intend to do so. Why? he wondered. Had she forgiven him?

He did not think so, not when his crime had been such a clear echo of Tonio's. But if she had not forgiven him, why was she being so helpful? Why hadn't she run home to Three Oaks when he had been unable to stop her?

He had learned long ago to let sleeping dogs lie. There would be time in the weeks ahead to find out how Sloan felt, to explain what he could, and to excuse what he couldn't. For now he had to learn to share with her, to include her in the parts of his life that he had hitherto kept separate.

After Cisco had visited with Cruz for a while, Josefa came to get him. Sloan once more closed the door, shutting out everyone else, but this time, instead of coming to sit beside Cruz, she leaned back against the door, her eyes on the polished toes of her boots.

"There is one more thing we need to discuss." She looked up and met his inquiring gaze.

Cruz sat up slowly. "What is that?"

"Tomasita has changed her mind about marrying Don Ambrosio."

He frowned. Did she think to make this decision for him also? However much he realized the necessity of sharing responsibility with her, he still bridled at the newness of it. Here was something that need not be her concern. "Tomasita will do as she is told," he said. "I have already signed the contracts with Don Ambrosio. It is done."

Sloan didn't miss the irritation in his voice. His face was pale and dotted with perspiration. She crossed to him and put a hand on his shoulder to force him back flat on the bed. "Rest now. We can speak again later."

"I have nothing more to say on the subject."

"Very well. Then say nothing more," she said with asperity.

Sloan brushed the sweat-damp hair from his brow as though it were the most natural gesture in the world. "Go to sleep now. Rest and get well."

The feelings of love that welled inside her made her uncomfortable. How could she love him and distrust him at the same time? Could she ever forgive him for masquerading as the Hawk?

She had promised him six months. She had six weeks left until the end of April. She need not think about leaving him now. That could come later.

Sloan stayed with Cruz until she was sure he was asleep and then went hunting for Tomasita. She found her kneeling at the prie-dieu in her room. Sloan entered the room silently and stood inside the door, listening to the quiet, comforting murmur of the young woman's voice.

"Tomasita?"

Tomasita stood immediately and crossed to Sloan. "Is something wrong? Has something happened to Don Cruz?"

"No, he's fine. I wanted to talk with you. Shall we go for a walk?"

Tomasita followed Sloan out to the courtyard among the blooming jonquils. She took a seat on one of the stone benches and patted the place beside her. Once Sloan had joined her, she said, "Something is wrong. What is it?"

"Cruz is determined that you will marry Don Ambrosio. Which means if you plan to tell Luke about the baby before you make your decision whether to return to Madrid, it must be soon."

"Holy Mary." Tomasita put a hand to her pounding heart. "I cannot speak to Luke. I cannot."

"You must. You owe it to your child. You owe it to yourself."

"I will think about it."

"Think hard. And think fast. You haven't much time. Once Cruz recovers, he is sure to press for your marriage to Don Ambrosio. You'll find Luke at Three Oaks," Sloan said. "He's gone there to oversee the spring planting of cotton."

Sloan felt a tightening in her belly at the recognition that this year, for the first time in her life, she hadn't been on hand to set the cotton seeds in the fertile soil to sprout and grow. She had been busy with an entirely different kind of birth—thousands and thousands of longhorn cattle dropping their spring calves. She had found the experience equally miraculous and equally demanding.

Over the next few days, as Cruz regained his strength, the March weather remained fractious, and Sloan was kept busy with the calving that went on despite the wind and the rain. However, each day she found time to ask Tomasita whether she had done anything about approaching Luke.

For her part, Tomasita found herself unable either to seek out Luke or approach Don Cruz, terrified of the responses she would get.

What if Luke would not marry her?

Her heart would break.

What if Don Cruz refused to allow her to return to Spain?

She would be forced to marry Don Ambrosio and live her life with one man when she loved another.

What if he did send her back to the convent?

After living in the world, such a lonely, quiet life would be too terrible to endure.

And so she did not do anything.

With Tomasita's wedding day rapidly approaching, Sloan took matters into her own hands. She sent a message to Luke telling him that she needed to speak with him and to please come to Dolorosa as soon as he could, and left the rest up to fate.

To Sloan's surprise, she received a prompt message back from Luke.

Dear Sloan,

Beaufort LeFevre and his daughter, Angelique, have arrived at Three Oaks, where they're staying

*while Beaufort waits for his audience with President
Jones. Beaufort is part of the contingent of
American politicians sent to convince the Texas
government that annexation is the best way to go.
Personally, I have to agree.*

*Anyway, the gist of the situation is that I wish I
could get away, but I can't. Whatever time I don't
spend out in the fields is taken up by Angelique.*

*She is even more beautiful now than she was four
years ago, when she and Beaufort came to visit at
Three Oaks. The scars she got from the time
Cricket's pet wolf attacked her hardly show at all.*

*Why don't you come to Three Oaks and bring Cruz
and Cisco? Oh, and bring Tomasita, too.*

> *Too busy to spit,*
> *Luke*

If she had been the only one involved, Sloan might have
refused the offer to come visit Three Oaks. It was bound to
be a painful venture for her. Besides, she didn't want Cruz
anywhere near Beaufort LeFevre.

But for Tomasita's sake, she knew she had to accept.
Because as far as Tomasita's situation was concerned,
Luke's letter was alarming. If Sloan remembered correctly,
Angelique LeFevre had set her claws in Luke four years
ago, if only briefly. It wouldn't have surprised her if An-
gelique and Luke became lovers again.

On the other hand, maybe seeing Luke with Angelique
was just the kick in the pants Tomasita needed to make her
stake her claim on the Ranger.

That evening, Sloan planned how best to approach Cruz
to be sure he would agree to what she asked. When he excused himself after dinner, saying he wanted to check on

his *bayo*, she nodded, planning to give him a few minutes alone before she joined him.

When she reached the stable, she heard voices. In moments she recognized them and froze in the darkness. Cruz! And the Englishman!

"I warned you not to come here again," Cruz snarled.

"I had no choice. Time is running short. The American Congress has passed a resolution offering statehood to Texas under very favorable terms. Your President Jones has agreed to wait at least ninety days before acting on the American proposal. Jones is, at this very moment, preparing an ultimatum to present to the Mexican government. He is demanding an immediate acknowledgment of independence from Mexico in exchange for his pledge that the Republic of Texas will never allow itself to be annexed by the United States.

"I want you to detain Beaufort LeFevre at Three Oaks until Jones has had time to finish his ultimatum and dispatch it to the Mexican authorities."

"How long do you think that might take?"

"Bloody hell! How should I know?"

"And if I refuse?"

"You wouldn't like the consequences of failing me, Hawk."

"I am not afraid of Alejandro Sanchez, Englishman."

"I thought not. That's why I made sure I have a little extra insurance?"

"What insurance?"

"Some letters your brother left with the Mexican government. They implicate your wife in a pretty nasty little plot to overthrow the government of Texas."

"Those letters must be over four years old."

"A traitor is still a traitor, no matter how much time passes. I will leave you now, Hawk. Don't disappoint me."

Sloan waited in the shadows until the Englishman had settled his rotund body in his carriage and driven away. She remained there while Cruz lit and smoked a cheroot, the sweet tobacco smell floating to her on the slight breeze.

She closed her eyes and held her breath when he finally left the stable and headed back toward the house. Then she slid down along the side of the adobe structure until she was sitting on the ground, her forehead resting on her knees.

Cruz had actually tried to quit his work for the British government. But it was clear the Englishman had no intention of allowing that to happen. She could hardly believe the incredible source of the whip wielded by the Englishman to keep Cruz in line.

The question now was what she should do with the information she had acquired.

Her first thought was to confront Cruz with what she had heard. However, it was unlikely he would agree to change his plans, and if he knew she was privy to them, he might take steps to make sure she wasn't around to interfere with them.

Or she could tell Luke what she had heard. But he might feel compelled to report Cruz to some higher authority. Texas and Mexico were still at war—although all the battles were being fought on paper.

Cruz's actions could easily be construed as treachery by those Texans who had lobbied so hard for annexation. She didn't presume to understand why President Jones was presenting such an ultimatum to Mexico. No matter what the Mexican government did now, most Texans would vote for annexation when the issue was presented.

She would simply have to do something herself to thwart the Englishman's plans. It seemed they would be playing right into the Englishman's hands if they accepted Luke's invitation to Three Oaks, but it was important for Tomasita's sake that they go.

Perhaps she could delay their departure a few days, or maybe even a week. With luck, Beaufort LeFevre would have already made contact with President Jones by the time they arrived.

Now, she just needed to find some reason to keep Cruz involved at Dolorosa.

Sloan pushed herself up onto her feet, brushed herself off, and headed back to the house. For the first time in months, her step was light. Things weren't settled by a long shot, but she had never felt so much in control of her life.

That night in bed, Cruz said casually, "We have not been able to get much work done in this weather, and it has been a long time since you have seen your father. It has been even longer since he has seen his grandson. How would you like to visit Three Oaks?"

"I guess that would be all right," Sloan said. "But there are a few things I have to get done here before we can leave."

"What sort of things?"

"I promised Miguel I would—"

"Anything that Miguel must do, he can do without your help."

Sloan played idly with the dark hair on Cruz's chest. "But these are projects I suggested. I would like to see them through to the finish. You don't mind, do you?"

She smiled secretly as she felt Cruz fidgeting. Of course he minded, she thought, but what could he say?

Cruz was thinking about the promise he had made to himself to include Sloan more in his life. He only wished he didn't have this intrigue with Sir Giles hanging over his head. "Very well, Cebellina. But I will come and help, that you may be done the sooner."

"Of course," she agreed with a pleased grin. "I would like that very much."

Each morning for the next week, Sloan kept Cruz occupied with one project after another. The weather helped by being absolutely awful. It rained, the wind blew, and the storms left more damage that had to be taken care of before they could think about leaving.

She could see Cruz was getting anxious about the delay. But she was as determined to keep him at Dolorosa as he was to leave.

"Miguel promised that today he would put up the *corrale* in the village," Sloan said as she dressed in the predawn light.

She could hear the control in Cruz's voice as he asked, "What *corrale*?"

"The one for orphaned newborn calves." Sloan crossed to Cruz and put her arms around his waist, resting her cheek against his broad chest. "It's a perfect solution to a cruel problem. Your vaqueros don't have the time or patience to bother with calves that have been orphaned before they can survive on their own. If we build a *corrale* in the village, the vaqueros could leave the newborns there and the women and children could raise them and have their own source of beef."

"You are giving my longhorns to the *pobres*?"

"Only the calves that would die if they were left on the range."

"Those longhorns are wild. What makes you think their calves will accept nourishment from a human hand?"

"Because we've already tried it, and it works."

Cruz shook his head in resignation. "I should have known you would have your arguments well planned. All right. When do we start?"

Sloan hugged him tightly and felt a fierce spiral of need well inside her.

Sensing her tension, Cruz tipped her chin up with his hand and touched his lips to hers.

Her response was instant and powerful. She sought his lips with hers, feeling a hunger that grew even as she fed it. She felt her nipples budding against his hair-rough chest and rubbed against him. She heard him groan and tugged at his ears, pulling his head down to kiss her again.

"We have work to do," Cruz said, his breath shallow.

"It can get done later," she whispered. "I . . . I want you."

Sloan was almost as surprised as Cruz was by her admission. She had little time to think about what she had said before Cruz swept her into his arms and carried her back to bed.

Their lovemaking had a different tenor, less restrained, a joining of not just bodies but spirits. Demands were made and answered. Prayers were offered and fulfilled. Touching one another became a matter of necessity. Ravenous with hunger, Sloan took what she needed; thirsting, she drank from the cup of love. There was nothing gentle about their mating; it was wild, tumultuous, consuming.

Cruz tried to be gentle, but Sloan would not allow it. Her hands were all over him, touching, embracing, scratching, pressing. Her mouth and tongue and teeth tantalized him, seeking pleasure in the giving of it.

The need to be inside her was excruciating, but she would not let him in. She kissed her way down his belly, laughing deep in her throat as he groaned in pleasure. He grabbed a hank of silky sable hair and pulled her away before she drove him mad.

Then his mouth was on hers, his tongue thrusting deep inside.

Sloan felt everything, heard everything, smelled everything with senses that were heightened beyond bearing. She tried to keep Cruz's tongue in her mouth, but failing that, followed his tongue when he retreated and tasted the roof of his mouth and his tongue and the silky cavern beyond.

His mouth moved to her throat, biting, then soothing. She arched her hips up into his, sheathing him, and felt him harden and swell inside her.

Then his mouth was on her breasts, gentle licks and strong sucks, the contrast exciting beyond belief. She was forced to release her grasp on him as he kissed his way down her stomach to the nest of curls that hid her femininity.

His tongue was gentle and slow, and she had trouble catching her breath.

Sloan writhed helplessly beneath Cruz as he held her up to his mouth and took what he wanted. Her body quivered as his tongue dipped and retreated, teasing and taunting. She gripped the sheets with her fists as she welcomed the waves of satisfaction.

The coarse, grating noise in her throat was bestial, primal, a harsh evocative sound that was echoed by Cruz. Her hips arched upward one last time, all her muscles tensed, her body concentrated on the ecstasy that rolled across her.

Sloan lay enervated after the last spasm had passed, her body trembling as Cruz's silky hair lay against her belly.

Their loving had been so much more than she had bargained for. She lay still as her body quivered with feeling.

She felt his tender kiss on her belly and lifted a limp hand to lay it on his head and tunnel it through his hair. She turned her head away to hide the tears that welled. "I . . . this was . . . wonderful."

Sloan wanted to give back to Cruz what he had given her. "Come here," she said.

"Where?"

She smiled. "Here." She urged him up over her, spreading her thighs to make a cradle for him between them.

In moments he was hard and ready, and she reached down with her hand and slowly guided him inside her. Her smile broadened as she heard his hissing sigh of satisfaction.

Then they lay still.

Sloan felt full. She welcomed the swelling in her breasts, the achy feeling of need, the urge to arch upward, to take him deeper inside her, to keep him there and take his seed.

She arched her hips slightly, but it was enough. He grasped her buttocks and angled her for his thrust. His mouth sought hers gently, and his tongue mimed the slow, steady movements below.

She was on fire. Her pulse raced, and she felt her heart beating crazily. Her breath came in short spurts. He kept his thrusts slow, building the tension, building the pressure.

"Cruz, I need . . . more."

He thrust deeper, harder, faster. She arched up to take more of him, her hands and mouth desperately tasting and touching whatever part of him she could reach. The tension was unbearable. She clutched his back and bit his shoulder hard as she climaxed in wave after wave of unbearable pleasure.

Cruz felt her body tightening around him and released his seed deep inside her with a sigh of utter satisfaction.

They lay together for a long time—until their bodies had stopped shuddering, until their breathing had returned to normal, until the sweat had dried on their skin.

Cruz was the first to move. He rolled onto his side and pulled Sloan into his embrace. "There is work to be done, Cebellina."

"I don't want to get up."

He chuckled. "Neither do I."

"Cruz, what just happened between us . . . It doesn't mean I've made up my mind to stay." She felt Cruz stiffen beside her. "I care for you a great deal. More than I thought I could care." She took a deep breath and said, "More than I cared for Tonio."

She felt him shudder beneath her fingertips.

"But I'm not sure whether I can ever love you fully, whether I can completely let go of the past . . . or ever trust you again. And I care enough for you to want you to have more than I fear I can give to you."

His arms tightened around her. "We have time on our side, Cebellina. There is no rush to decide anything now."

"I just wanted you to know," she said in a quiet voice.

"I thank you for that," he replied solemnly. "And now we have important work to do."

She lowered her brow quizzically. "Important work?"

He smiled. "Think of all those orphaned calves that will not get any breakfast if we do not get moving."

She smiled back at him and rose to dress. She felt wonderful. In fact, she couldn't keep the smile off her face. She greeted Doña Lucia at the breakfast table unaware that she radiated happiness.

Doña Lucia had watched with growing frustration as Sloan insinuated herself into every facet of life at Dolorosa. Her hopes of having a daughter-in-law who would defer to her wishes, one who would be meek and obedient to her will, had remained woefully unfulfilled.

She had tried twice to be permanently rid of her nemesis, and failed both times. The near catastrophe of her second attempt had convinced her that perhaps she should change her tactics.

So Doña Lucia had looked around for another way to control her new daughter-in-law. She had found what she considered the one soft spot in *that woman's* underbelly: her son. Through Cisco, Doña Lucia hoped to bring Sloan to heel.

Sloan was on her way out the door with Cruz when Doña Lucia said, "Do you want me to send for the *curandera* to come see Cisco?"

Sloan halted in her tracks. "Is he ill?"

"He did not feel well this morning. I had Josefa put him back to bed."

Sloan turned to Cruz, worry plain in her eyes, and said, "I think I had better stay—"

"You do not need to stay," Doña Lucia interrupted. "Tomasita and I can take care of your son."

At that well-aimed prod, Sloan turned to Cruz and said, "Why don't you go ahead? I'll join you as soon as I'm sure Cisco is feeling better."

Cruz leaned down to kiss Sloan quickly on the mouth and murmured, "You are a good mother, Cebellina," before he left.

When Sloan entered Cisco's bedroom, she saw him playing quietly on his bed with a wooden horse. That by itself was a good indication something was amiss. Cisco was seldom quiet. He looked flushed, and his eyes were overly bright. She sat down beside him and put a hand on his forehead. It was more than warm.

"How do you feel, *mi hijo?*"

"Not so good, Mamá."

"Where does it hurt, sweetheart?"

"Right here." Cisco covered his stomach with a small hand.

"Would you like for me to hold you for a while until you feel better?"

"*Sí*, Mamá."

Sloan settled onto the bed, then lifted her son into her arms. He snuggled against her, laying his head on her breast. The newborn calves would have to wait, she thought. She had a child of her own that needed her attention.

She held Cisco most of the morning while he slept. Toward noon, Doña Lucia came to check on her grandson. She sat down in the ladder-back chair beside the bed and asked, "How is he?"

"Fine," Sloan said. "It seems to have been a simple stomachache. He's better, I think. But now that he's asleep, I think I'd like to get some fresh air."

"As you wish," Doña Lucia said agreeably, as she watched Sloan square her shoulders and march from the room.

It had all been so easy she could hardly believe it. Easy

to give Cisco a potion that would upset his stomach. Easy to separate Sloan from Cruz at the front door. And she would find other ways to keep *that woman* and her son apart.

Doña Lucia smiled with satisfaction. Not a bad day's work, and the day was only half done.

Once outside, Sloan was appalled to see how bruised the sky looked. It was only midday, yet angry black, purple and gray clouds spilled over one another, digesting one another. They hung low, protruding from the sky like swollen udders, completely blocking the sun.

The breeze felt cool after the warmer weather of the past week, and it didn't take much guessing to know they were in for a bad thunderstorm. She almost turned back around, but the thought of confronting Doña Lucia again kept her moving toward the river.

Sloan had just found a comfortable spot in the shade of a cypress and sat down when she heard a distinctive yet indescribable hissing sound. Her eyes widened in terror when she turned and saw a grayish white funnel snake down from the clouds, just beyond the hacienda. Twisting and bending with deadly grace, the vortex began to suck up the surrounding countryside. Dragging its writhing tail along the ground, it quickly became clothed in a shaggy sleeve of dust and debris.

Sloan's scream of terror and fear was lost in the deafening roar of the tornado as it mauled the face of the earth. The hacienda was in the direct path of the twisting nightmare, but its freakish behavior made it impossible to tell whether it would actually strike the house.

Sloan jumped up and started to run. There was a root cellar beside the adobe house to which they could all escape to safety, if only she could reach the house in time.

"Tornadooooooo!" she screamed at the top of her lungs.

She had barely taken five steps when the tornado enveloped the hacienda with its insensate fury. Terror held her paralyzed as she watched nature's bedlam—a black cage full of screaming lunatics—beating at the house, clawing at it, trying to crush it.

Even at this distance, the menacing wind ripped at her, sending her hair whirling in a mock dance of death. She felt her skin pierced with flying splinters and looked down to discover it was only straw, borne with tremendous force by the screaming, hissing dervish.

As swiftly as it had come, the tornado turned and headed away, leaving the village beyond the hacienda untouched.

A cacophony of wailing and crying erupted from the village. The women and children who had taken what refuge they could from the storm now ran for the hacienda, in hopes of rescuing those who might have survived the tornado's onslaught.

Sloan stood frozen for another instant before she joined the throng.

The first thing she saw as she approached the carnage left by the tornado was a rooster that had been stripped of its tail and back feathers—plucked alive! The sight of its naked pink skin made her shiver. Her heart was in her throat as she forced herself to gaze upon the devastation nature had wrought.

The hacienda had been flattened. The stable had been picked up and moved a hundred yards away. The fountain in the central courtyard remained untouched. It made no sense!

All Sloan's thoughts were focused on the house. Cisco

was inside. And Tomasita. And Doña Lucia. And Josefa and Ana. No one could have survived such a disaster.

She tore at the broken adobe bricks, along with the *pobres* from the village, hoping against hope that someone was alive inside the house or that they had seen or heard the tornado coming and had taken refuge in the root cellar.

Sloan's fingers were soon raw and bleeding, but she kept on digging. She fought the strong hands that tried to drag her away from her work until she realized that Cruz had come with his vaqueros.

She burrowed into his arms and held him tight for an instant, before she pushed him away again. "I can't find Cisco. And I haven't seen Tomasita or your mother, either. We have to keep digging!"

With the help of Cruz's vaqueros, the work went much faster. What they found as the debris was cleared away was not encouraging. Ana was dead, and Josefa, both crushed to death by the kitchen wall and ceiling, which had collapsed. Where were the rest who had been inside the hacienda? Could they possibly be alive?

"They might have gotten to the root cellar," Sloan said, panting with fatigue as she threw adobe bricks behind her.

Cruz remained silent, his lips pressed together in a thin line. He was less willing to be optimistic, but neither did he wish to take away what hope Sloan still had that her son might be alive.

Two hours later, they found Tomasita alive and unhurt. The two women embraced each other, and Sloan fought tears of relief as Tomasita explained she had found refuge under her mahogany bedframe, which had kept the weight of the adobe from crushing her. She was fine.

"You should go rest," Sloan urged.

"I want to help," Tomasita said. "Please. Let me do this."

Sloan didn't take time to argue, but returned to the unpleasant task at hand. It was Miguel who uncovered Doña Lucia's hand under a large chunk of adobe. There was no pulse.

Sloan met Cruz's eyes and shared with him the painful knowledge that his mother was dead. He said nothing, but his face paled and Sloan saw that he had his jaw clamped tightly to prevent the quiver that threatened.

"Get her out of there," he said at last, his voice hard and flat.

They worked carefully, revealing, at odd moments, a thick strand of her black hair that had worked loose from her bun, the layered ruffles of her skirt and a black shoe.

She was curled protectively around something. It only became apparent what that something was in the last moments as her body was uncovered.

"It's Cisco," Sloan said in a disbelieving whisper. "Cruz, it's Cisco!" she shouted. She fell to her knees beside Cruz, who was gently loosening his mother's grasp on her grandson.

"Oh, Cruz, please, I want to hold him."

"Be patient, Cebellina. He may not be—"

"I know he's alive!" Sloan said fiercely.

At that moment, Cisco whimpered and blinked open his eyes. He rubbed them, trying to clear away the dust. When he saw Sloan and Cruz, he cried, "Papa! Mamá!" and reached out his arms to them.

A crushing embrace followed as they clutched one another. Sloan saw through blurred eyes the tears that scoured Cruz's cheeks, and heard him swallow over a sob, in the way a man will do.

She closed her eyes and held on, feeling she had been given another chance to be a wife and mother. Another chance to start over with this man and this boy. Another chance for happiness.

She intended to reach out and grab it.

Chapter 19

SLOAN POUNDED TWICE ON THE FRONT DOOR TO
Three Oaks and had lifted her fist to pound again when the
door opened.

Luke took one look at her torn and dusty clothes, at the
tear-streaked face of the child in her arms, and at the disha-
bille of the young Spanish woman who stood, eyes down-
cast, behind her and said, "What the hell happened to you?
Where's Cruz?"

"A tornado hit Dolorosa. Cruz will be here in a minute.
He's taking care of the horses."

Luke encircled Sloan with one arm and led her into the
house. "Are you all right? And Tomasita—" His anxious
glance skipped past Sloan to the young woman behind her.

At that moment, Tomasita lifted her eyes to meet Luke's
gaze. Sloan saw that Luke wanted to take Tomasita in his
arms, but he made no move toward her. Then the moment
was gone.

Sloan closed her eyes and swayed with fatigue. Everything was such a mess. Here she was at Three Oaks, and
while it was fortunate that Tomasita now had a chance to
work out her differences with Luke, Sloan had to face the

fact that circumstances had put Cruz exactly where the Englishman wanted him.

And yet, where else could they have gone?

"What happened?" Luke asked again.

"There's nothing left of the hacienda but a pile of rubble. Cruz's mother was killed, and Ana and Josepha."

"I'm sorry to hear that," Luke said.

"We need a place to stay until the house can be rebuilt." Sloan swallowed and said, "There wasn't anywhere else to go."

Luke swore under his breath. "This is your home, Sloan. This is where you should have come."

At that moment Angelique LeFevre appeared from the parlor and joined Luke. The former chargé's daughter was a petite, blue-eyed blonde whose golden hair was styled in lovely sausage curls that framed her face and bounced when she moved her head. She wore a long-sleeved lavender day dress of muslin de laine trimmed with purple ribbon.

Angelique laid a proprietary hand on Luke's arm and said, "Won't you introduce me to your guests?"

"They're hardly *guests*, Angel," Luke said. "You might remember Rip's eldest daughter Sloan. I believe you met her four years ago, when you first came to Texas with your father."

"Yes, I believe I did." Angelique smiled broadly. "How are you? This must be your son. You were expecting a child at the time I met you, as I recall. What an adorable little boy. What's his name?"

"Cisco." Sloan stepped away so Angelique's hand missed connecting with the curls on Cisco's head.

"The child's father was . . ." Angelique tapped a slender finger against her chin, thinking.

"Tonio was killed," Sloan said bluntly. "I married his brother, Cruz."

"Ohhhh. Really?"

Sloan's lids shuttered her flashing eyes and her hands fisted in the folds of the blanket covering Cisco. If Angelique LeFevre said one more word about Tonio . . .

"Uh . . . this is Refugia Adela Maria Tomasita Hidalgo," Luke said, shifting Angelique's fascinated attention from Sloan. "Tomasita is Señor Guerrero's ward."

"How interesting." Angelique eyed Sloan as she shook hands with Tomasita, and Sloan saw the speculation in the petite woman's eyes.

"Tomasita is betrothed to Don Ambrosio de Arocha. Their marriage was supposed to have taken place next week," Sloan said. "But of course there will be a delay now because of the damage caused by the tornado at Dolorosa."

Sloan saw from the tension in Luke's body and the way his eyes flew to Tomasita that he was surprised and disconcerted by this news. Thank goodness. She hoped he realized he was going to have to act quickly if he wanted Tomasita for himself.

"You must be devastated by the delay," Angelique said to Tomasita, eyeing her thickened waist speculatively. "Perhaps Luke and I might come to the wedding?"

Sloan watched Tomasita stiffen at the way Angelique had invited herself to the wedding and also laid claim to Luke's company.

"I won't be going to Tomasita's wedding," Luke said.

Tomasita flushed, and Sloan wanted to grab Luke by the ears and shake him. Couldn't he see the young Spanish woman was in love with him?

Cruz arrived at the door to a welcome greeting from Luke. Cruz took Angelique's hand and said, "I am charmed, señorita. You are every bit as lovely as I had heard you were."

Where had Cruz heard such a thing? Sloan wondered. She caught Angelique's eye and flashed the message, *This one's mine!* Only belatedly did she realize what she was admitting by making such a claim.

"Where's Rip?" Sloan asked.

"He's in bed," Luke replied.

Sloan felt a sudden tension in her shoulders. "It's barely suppertime. What's he doing in bed?"

"He hasn't been feeling well the past couple of days. He picked up a spring cold and can't seem to shake it. You can check and see if he's awake. It's about the time he usually comes downstairs," Luke said.

Sloan was already halfway up the stairs when she said, "I think I will. I'll just put Cisco down for a nap first in the crib in Cricket's old bedroom."

Cruz watched Sloan go with a sinking feeling in the pit of his stomach. He hoped Rip wasn't seriously ill. Rip's death would force to a head the issue of who was to inherit Three Oaks.

Even if Rip willed the plantation to Luke, there was the distinct possibility Luke might deed it back to Sloan. If she ever got title to Three Oaks, she would have to make a choice.

And Cruz still was not sure she would choose him.

He turned to Luke and asked, "Is it only a cold that has Rip laid up?"

Luke shrugged. "So far as I can tell. I'm damn sorry to hear what happened, Cruz. I'll send word to Lion's Dare and Golden Valley. I know Sloan's family will want to do everything they can to help."

"Thanks, Luke. I appreciate the offer. When I turned the

horses over to the man at the barn, he said Beaufort LeFevre is here."

"I wrote Sloan a week ago about it. Didn't she give you the message?"

Cruz frowned. "No. She did not." He looked up the stairs. He would give Sloan a chance to get settled and then they were going to have a talk.

"Would you like to meet my father?" Angelique asked. "I'll be glad to take you to see him. He's staying in the bachelors' quarters out behind the main house."

Cruz smiled and extended his arm to Angelique, who placed her palm daintily upon it. "I would appreciate that." He turned to Luke. "Will you see that Tomasita gets settled?"

"Yes, of course."

With that assurance, and with another exchange of glances that said volumes and issued admonitions, Cruz turned with Angelique and walked out the front door.

Luke and Tomasita were left alone. Luke gestured to a rocker bench along one wall of the central hallway. "You look tired. Would you like to sit down?"

Tomasita laced her fingers together and gripped them hard in front of her. "I . . . No thank you."

They stood there awkwardly for another moment before Luke said, "Are you all right? You weren't hurt by the tornado?"

"No." She looked up into his hazel eyes, but if he cared at all for her, his feelings were carefully hidden in their golden depths. She took a deep breath and said, "Your child and I are both fine."

Luke completely lost his composure. Tomasita watched a myriad of emotions pass through his eyes, beginning with elation and ending with anger, before he regained control.

"I won't ask if it's mine. I guess there's little doubt of that, as closely as Cruz has you watched." His voice hardened as he asked, "Have you told the man you're planning to marry that you're carrying my child?"

"I do not plan to marry Don Ambrosio."

"Sloan said—"

"I am going back to Spain."

Luke felt as though he'd just been kicked in the gut. "You're leaving Texas?"

"As soon as I can. I am going back to live in the convent."

Luke grasped her arms in desperation. "You don't belong in any damn convent!"

"Where else can I go? No gentleman of class will have me now that I am . . . And I cannot impose on Don Cruz forever."

Luke frowned. "Does Cruz know about the baby?"

"I have not told him yet. When I do, I am sure he will understand my decision."

Luke snorted. "Like hell. After he beats the pulp out of me, he'll have us standing in front of a preacher so fast it'll make your head spin."

In a small voice, Tomasita asked, "Would that be so bad?"

Luke couldn't meet her eyes. "Aw, hell."

"I guess it would," she said, sounding defeated. She turned to go back out the front door. "I should not have come here."

Luke grabbed her arm and spun her back around. "Wait a minute. Where are you going?"

Her eyes flashed with anger. "None of your business!"

"I'm making it my business."

"Like you made the blond woman—*Angel,* I heard you call her—your business?" she hissed. "Do you think I have no pride? I saw the way you let that woman put her hands on you! If you do not care enough to marry me, at least do not expect me to stay and watch you with your lover."

"*Angel* and I aren't lovers," he ground out, equally furious. "I might have bedded her once upon a time, but that's all over and—"

Tomasita's palm whipped around and slapped Luke hard. "I do not want to hear any more! I suppose you will be describing me the same way to your next conquest."

Tomasita tried to pull herself from Luke's grasp, but he held on and backed her up against the wall, holding her there with his body.

"What the hell did you do that for? I just got through telling you Angel and I aren't lovers—"

"Anymore!" Tomasita interrupted. "Just like I am not your lover anymore." She couldn't stop the tears that started to spill. "I feel so . . ." She took a deep breath in an attempt to forestall the sob that sought release. "I feel so . . . dirty."

Tomasita couldn't look at Luke. She felt his hand on her chin forcing her face up, but she kept her gaze on the floor.

"Look at me, Tomasita."

"No."

"Then listen to me, mustang girl."

"Pretty words will not help now, Luke," she said, her heart pounding painfully after hearing his endearment. "What is done is done."

"You don't have to go back to Spain," he said, his voice hoarse with emotion. "I'll take care of you."

She allowed herself to hope. She lifted her gaze and met

his eyes, that were now more green than gold. "You will marry me?"

His eyes darkened. "No. I didn't say that."

"I cannot accept less than that, Luke. Let me go."

"Goddammit, you can't leave me!"

"Why not? What are you offering me that has more honor than returning to the convent?"

"I'm telling you I want you to stay with me. I'm telling you I need you."

Tomasita heard the agony in his voice. But what he was offering was not enough. "I could not bear the shame."

Sloan was halfway down the stairs when she saw that Luke had Tomasita backed up against the wall. "What's going on?"

"Stay out of this, Sloan," Luke warned.

Sloan continued down the stairs until she was standing across from Luke and Tomasita. "You can't get what you want with force, Luke."

"How the hell do you know what I want?"

"If you care for her, Luke, you'll let her go."

Luke turned his attention back to Tomasita. "We aren't done talking about this." Then he stepped back, and she was free.

"Come with me, Tomasita," Sloan said. "I'll get you settled in your room."

Tomasita didn't look at Luke as she walked past him and followed Sloan upstairs.

"Are you all right?" Sloan asked as she made Tomasita comfortable in Bay's old bedroom.

"I am fine. But I have my answer from Luke. I will tell Don Cruz tonight that I have decided to go back to Spain."

"Oh no you won't," Sloan said, taking Tomasita's shoulders and giving her a shake. "This isn't over yet. Not by a long shot. If you want Luke, you're going to have to fight for him."

"How? He has said he does not want to marry me. He is furious—"

"Of course he's furious. He's in love with you, and you're forcing him to admit he cares for you."

"But what can I do?"

Sloan put her arm around Tomasita and said, "The first thing you're going to do is get some rest. Then just be sure you wear your prettiest smile to dinner, and leave everything else up to me."

Sloan took a quick look in on Rip but discovered he was sleeping. She told herself rest was the best remedy for a bad cold and left him undisturbed as she headed downstairs to find Cruz.

When Sloan found out that Cruz had been shown to the bachelors' quarters by Angelique LeFevre, she was ready to rip the other woman's hair out by the roots. When she followed after Cruz, she wasn't thinking of his connection to the British or the importance of keeping track of his conversations with Beaufort LeFevre. She was thinking of her husband in the clutches of that blond, curly-headed hussy Angelique. Especially when Cruz didn't know yet that she had made up her mind to devote herself wholeheartedly to making their marriage work.

Sloan stepped across the threshold of the bachelors' quarters ready to do battle with Angelique, only to discover a full-fledged political discussion in progress between Cruz and Beaufort LeFevre. She was assailed by the familiar aroma of Cruz's cheroot and the smell of a stronger, less pleasant cigar. As she stood in the doorway, all eyes turned to focus on her and the discussion ceased.

"Why, hello, little lady," Beaufort said in his charming Louisiana drawl. He rose and took her hand in his, making contact, pressing the flesh. "You look dearly familiar. Sloan . . . is that right?"

"Yes, sir. Don't let me interrupt you. I'll just sit over here."

The parlor was intended to be cozy. With the four of them sitting there, it was almost crowded. She sat in the wing chair next to the one Beaufort occupied and eyed Cruz, who shared the tiny brocade-covered settee with Angelique. If looks could kill, Sloan would already have planted Angelique six feet under.

"As I was saying," Beaufort continued once he was settled again in his chair. "I've heard public opinion here in Texas is leaning toward annexation."

"Whether it is independence and the Republic or annexation and statehood, I think Texans just want the promise of peace with Mexico and an end to the uncertainty," Cruz replied.

"Well, it seems to me you can blame Sam Houston and Anson Jones for the uncertainty," Beaufort said.

"What do you mean?" Sloan asked.

Cruz answered, "I think Beaufort is referring to the fact that Texas is negotiating both with Mexico for independence and the United States for annexation at the same time."

"What's wrong with that?" Angelique asked, her blue eyes wide and innocent.

"Nothing's wrong with it, my dear," Beaufort said, "so long as the politicians choose the correct alternative in the end."

"Which is?" Sloan asked.

"Why, annexation, of course," Beaufort said with a smile.

"This has all been very interesting," Angelique said, "but I must admit I would rather take a pleasant walk along the river before the sun sets. Would you care to join me, Don Cruz?"

"I must regretfully decline," Cruz said. "I have only just arrived with my wife and my ward, and I need to be certain they are settled comfortably before I can do anything else."

Which left him open to accept an invitation later, Sloan thought dourly.

"If you will excuse us, Beaufort, I will take my wife back to the house."

"Certainly, Don Cruz. I'll look forward to talking more with you later."

"And I with you."

"I think I'll walk back to the house with you," Angelique said, "if you don't mind."

Sloan noticed that this time Angelique didn't give Cruz a chance to decline. She claimed Cruz's arm the moment he stood up, and there was no way he could gracefully get out of the situation.

When Cruz offered his other arm to Sloan, she wasn't so stupid as to refuse it. But she wondered if he was making a comparison between the sweet-smelling, blue-eyed blonde, in her lavender muslin de laine dress, on his left arm, and his wife, with her dusty pants and shirt and flyaway hair, on his right.

As soon as they entered the house, Sloan turned to Angelique and said, "I know you'll excuse us. Cruz and I have some private business to discuss." She grasped Cruz's hand and started up the stairs to her old bedroom.

Halfway up the stairs, Sloan turned and smiled smugly back over her shoulder at Angelique, who had been left tapping her toe at the foot of the stairs.

"That was neatly done," Cruz said as Sloan closed the door behind them in her bedroom.

She pulled her boots off and jumped onto her bed, lying back with her hands crossed behind her head. "I thought so," she said with a smirk. She sat up, cross-legged. "That witch can find herself another man. You're taken!"

The smile on Cruz's face as he crossed to Sloan gave ample evidence of his pleasure at her possessiveness.

He pulled off his own boots and joined her on the bed. He playfully pushed her backward, untangling her crossed legs as he lay down beside her. "I like being taken by you," he teased. "How would you like me? With or without clothes?"

Sloan laughed. "You're crazy, you know that?"

"Crazy with love for you." He had her vest off and his hands were busy unbuttoning her blouse.

"Cruz, don't. Everyone will know what we're doing if we don't go back downstairs soon."

"Is that not exactly what you wanted? For Angelique to know I belong to you?"

She couldn't deny there was a certain pleasure in that thought. But the feel of his mouth on her throat made it hard for her to think at all.

He pulled off his shirt and her chemise and they were suddenly flesh to flesh. She arched her back and rubbed her breasts against the crisp black hair on his chest. Cruz grabbed her buttocks and pressed her into the cradle of his thighs.

"*Querida,*" he murmured. "*Alma de mi vida.*"

His mouth was hot on her, his tongue claiming the softness of her mouth in a rhythmic accompaniment to the dance of his hips. She parried his thrust with her tongue and claimed what was hers.

His callused hands deftly unbuttoned her trousers, and he slipped his hand beneath her pantalettes, cupping the heart of her. She followed his lead and slipped her hand into the front of his trousers, cupping the heat of him. He was iron-hard, filling her hand, and she teased him mercilessly even as he returned the favor.

His mouth set out on a journey over her face and shoulders, laving her skin, nipping, and then kissing the hurt. Meanwhile, his fingers spread her silken petals and slipped inside as she flowered for him.

"I want you inside me," she gasped, shoving his trousers down over his hips.

He freed her from his loving grasp long enough to strip her as well, and when they were both naked, he pushed her gently back into the feathered mattress, spread her legs wider with his knees, and mounted her.

She captured him with her thighs and arched upward, urging him deeper inside, taking the fullness of him and demanding more.

He rolled them both over so she was on top of him and growled "You are mine, Cebellina."

She looked down into his blue eyes, dark with avidity, at his nostrils flared to bring air to his heaving chest, at his raven black curls, wild where her hands had thrust through them. She smiled. "And you are mine."

The sense of power was immense. She lifted herself nearly off his shaft and then, ever so slowly, settled back down again. She watched his teeth clench as the air hissed from his chest.

"You are playing with fire, Cebellina," he warned.

"I know." She grinned, fully aware of the danger in taunting him. He grasped her thighs in an attempt to keep her down on him. She allowed him his small victory but rocked her hips against his, increasing the friction until they were both aflame with pleasure. One of his hands left her hip and slipped between them, fanning the flames.

She was lost in her own deep well of pleasure when he at last turned her once again so she was beneath him. He tilted her hips and thrust before withdrawing, teasing, taunting, and thrusting again.

She was beyond being rational. She wanted. She needed. She demanded.

And he gave . . . and took.

Sloan felt the rising crest of pleasure and at the last instant fought against being overwhelmed by it. But it was too late. She cried out as her body shuddered against his, and heard his cry of triumph as their bodies and souls became one.

Gradually, she became aware of his heavy weight on top of her, of their chests heaving with equal effort to bring air to tortured lungs, and of the musky smell of their sex.

Cruz started to move off her, and she tightened her arms around his sweat-slick body. "Don't go yet. Stay where you are."

"I am too heavy."

"It feels good."

And so he stayed with her.

She closed her eyes, feeling for the first time truly content. This was what she needed. This was what she wanted. Dear God, she loved this man. Despite everything, she loved him.

And she would stick by him, no matter what. If that was unwise, if that was making the same mistake twice in one lifetime, so be it. She was committed. She would follow him through fire, race with him through hell, and never look back.

It was dark when Sloan awoke, and Cruz was gone. It took her a few moments to realize it was still daytime. A storm had darkened the sky until it was almost black. For a moment she feared another tornado, but realized the air didn't feel the same—it was less oppressive.

She heard the limbs of the live oaks slapping against the house as the rising wind whipped through them. Then came the slight whistling sound the wind made as it forced its way through the nooks and crannies of the house.

The eerie whisper of the wind had always made her shiver, even when it wasn't cold. She smiled as she felt herself shiver right on cue. She reached out and pulled the covers up more snugly over her shoulders.

The sudden spring storms were wild and fierce in Texas. This wasn't anything she hadn't experienced dozens of times before. In the past, seeing the sky darken so forbiddingly had always left her with a feeling of high anticipation for the powerful raging of the elements. After the tornado she had just experienced, she had a new respect for its power.

Sloan shivered again and wished Cruz were still in bed with her and that she could turn and snuggle into his strong arms for comfort. There had been little opportunity in her life to seek comfort outside herself. She had always taken care of herself, had even wanted it that way. Now she wanted to reach out and grasp the hand Cruz had outstretched to her.

There were muffled sounds of movement downstairs, and Sloan realized that if she wanted to touch Cruz, wanted to hold him, she only had to seek him out. She quickly rose and washed and dressed herself.

She passed Tomasita's room on the way downstairs, but the young woman wasn't inside. Her father's door was still closed so she made the slight detour to the end of the hall to check on him again.

She knocked on his door and heard a gruff, "Come in." She opened the door and found Rip still abed. "How are you?"

"What are you doing here?" he demanded.

"Dolorosa was destroyed by a tornado this afternoon. It made sense for us to come here."

"Well, of course, you should all come here. Did everybody come through okay?"

"Almost everybody. Cruz's mother was killed."

"That's too bad," Rip said.

"I thought you'd be heading downstairs for supper tonight," Sloan said, unwilling to speak further of the tragedy.

"That was my plan, but I'm still feeling poorly, so I decided to eat up here."

Sloan walked over and stood beside the bed. He looked tired, his gray eyes dull, without the sparkle that had once lit them. He coughed, and Sloan noticed it hurt him to breathe. "Are you sure you don't want me to send for a doctor?"

"Won't hear of it. Now, get on downstairs and take care of our company."

Sloan left him with a feeling of foreboding. She had never known Rip to stay in bed if he could be out of it. Even the time a mule had stepped on his foot and broken it, he hadn't been down long.

If he wasn't up tomorrow, she would arrange for a doctor to come and see him whether he wanted one or not. She determined not to bring up the subject of Three Oaks until he was in fine enough fettle to fight back.

Sloan descended the staircase slowly, not sure what she would find below. She followed the voices to the dining room, located beyond the parlor at the back of the house. There she found Angelique holding court at the supper table like a queen with three very attentive male subjects, and one very irritated lady-in-waiting.

When Cruz saw Sloan, he rose from the table and came to greet her. He took her in his arms and whispered in her ear, "I did not want to wake you. I thought you would need your rest for later tonight."

Sloan blushed at the implication of his words, but they made her feel warm inside. After she filled her plate from the array of dishes set out on the sideboard, she sat down in the chair Cruz had saved for her next to him. It didn't take long to realize she had arrived just in time to see the sparks fly.

Apparently, after having no success with Cruz, Angelique had turned her attentions to Luke. Sloan saw that Tomasita was highly agitated by the situation. It was equally obvious that the young woman could hardly act jealous of Luke without revealing to Cruz that she and the Ranger knew more about each other than their names.

Luke wasn't helping matters. He was paying close attention to Angelique, leaning toward her and hanging on every word.

"Sounds like you had a pretty good time, Angel," Luke said. "Wish I'd been there."

"I wish you had been there, too," Angelique said, laying her hand on Luke's arm. "I know you would have been able to help me with my gown."

"I'm sure I'd have figured out something," Luke said with a grin.

Perhaps if Sloan had gotten downstairs a few minutes sooner, she could have steered the conversation away from danger, but it was too late now to do anything but watch helplessly as Tomasita rose from her seat, picked up her glass of wine, and dumped it on Luke's head.

He bolted out of his chair, shouting, "What the hell did you do that for?"

"You know why I did it," she shouted back. "*Cabron! Bribon!* I love you, you insufferable idiot! I cannot stand to watch that blond *bruja* bat her eyes at you anymore."

She turned and raced out of the room and up the stairs, leaving Luke standing stunned behind her.

"Aren't you going after her?" Sloan demanded.

Luke wiped his face with his napkin and threw it down on the table. "You're damn right I am!"

He sprinted after Tomasita, and Sloan had to grab Cruz's arm to keep him from following him.

"I cannot leave them alone," Cruz said.

"He won't hurt her," Sloan replied. "She's carrying his child."

She heard Angelique's gasp and watched as Cruz's face darkened with anger.

"How could he dare to dishonor her? How could she dare to act the whore for him?"

Sloan's face lost all color as the greater implications of Cruz's tirade became clear. Any woman who bedded a man without benefit of marriage was a whore. By virtue of her actions with his brother, she must also be a whore.

Cruz caught sight of Sloan's shocked face and said "Cebellina, I did not mean—"

"Excuse me. I think I'll go take a walk."

Cruz quickly followed her, leaving a stunned Angelique alone at the table.

Cruz caught Sloan in the central hallway and grasped her by the arms to keep her from escaping. "You will listen—"

"There is no need to explain, Cruz," she said. "You only said what you honestly believe."

"I spoke in anger," he said. "And I spoke in haste. I never meant to suggest that your relationship with Tonio was the same thing as—"

"But it was. Exactly the same. If Tomasita is a whore, then so am I."

Cruz flushed. He met Sloan's eyes, his gaze serious and steady. "I do not care. It does not matter. I have only one name I want to call you, and that is *wife*. I love you."

Her love for him was still a fragile thing. Should she take the chance that he might change his mind? Should she take the chance that someday, in a fit of anger, he might call up the past in equally ugly words and put it between them?

They were distracted by a shout and the sound of Tomasita racing down the stairs with Luke running full tilt behind her.

Sloan and Cruz turned in time to see Tomasita lose her footing and tumble down the last few steps. When she reached the oak floor at the bottom, she lay still, her right foot twisted at an odd angle.

Everyone stood frozen for a moment, the only sound Luke's harsh, "Oh God, no!"

Then they were all running to reach her. Luke got there first and gently cradled her face in his hands. "Tomasita?"

Her eyes fluttered open and she moaned. "The baby . . ." Her hands grasped her womb and she curled into herself.

Sloan quickly checked Tomasita's ankle for broken bones. Discovering none, she said to Luke, "Nothing's broken, but her ankle is badly sprained. I . . . I don't know about the baby. Take her upstairs and I'll send for the doctor."

"Do not touch me," Tomasita hissed at Luke.

He ignored her, lifting her into his arms and moving as quickly as he could without harming her further.

Sloan sent Stephen for the doctor, and then followed Luke upstairs to Tomasita's room.

"You should leave, Luke, so I can undress her for the doctor," Sloan said.

"I'll do it."

"Luke, she doesn't want—"

"I'll do it!"

Sloan stepped back from the bed and watched as he gently began undressing Tomasita.

Tomasita watched Luke with pain-filled eyes, but she said nothing as he bared her body to his suffering gaze. Her teeth bit into her lower lip as she held her womb tight against the twinges she felt inside.

"I'm sorry," Luke said, his voice broken.

Tomasita did not answer, just turned her face away from him.

Luke found a chambray wrapper in a nearby chest and slipped it over Tomasita's head.

"The doctor will be a while coming," Sloan said. She met Luke's eyes and saw the agony there. If she'd had any doubts that he loved Tomasita, they were answered.

"Isn't there something I can do?" he pleaded.

"Hold her. Love her," Sloan said softly.

Luke sat beside Tomasita and took her unresisting hand

in his. "Tomasita, I'm sorry. Please say you forgive me. Say you'll marry me."

Sloan held her breath to see how Tomasita would respond to Luke's plea. When she turned to face Luke, she only shook her head sadly.

"You do not have to marry me, Luke. Our baby . . . My baby . . ." She couldn't finish the sentence. "Go away. Please, go away. I cannot bear to look at you."

Luke avoided Sloan's eyes as he stood up and left the room.

As soon as he was gone, Tomasita burst into tears.

Sloan sat down beside the young woman and awkwardly patted her shoulder. She couldn't bring herself to say, "Everything will be all right," because this was all wrong. So very wrong.

She had been so sure that Luke and Tomasita belonged together. So what had thwarted their happily-ever-after ending?

Sloan's eyes widened in shock as she identified the thieves that had robbed Luke and Tomasita of their happiness. She recognized them because she knew them so intimately: the fear of loving, the fear of losing, and an unwillingness to trust.

Chapter 20

WHEN THE DOCTOR FINALLY ARRIVED, SLOAN kept vigil with him until they were certain the baby was all right and there was no danger Tomasita would miscarry.

Luke asked to see Tomasita again, but was refused with the explanation that Tomasita was very tired and anything that might upset her, including a visit from him, wasn't good for her right now.

When the worst of the danger was past, Sloan walked downstairs to the parlor and found Luke and Cruz sitting on opposite sides of the room. She could have cut the tension in the room with a knife.

Cruz clenched a burning cheroot between his bared teeth. Luke gripped a glass of Rip's Irish whiskey in his white-knuckled hands. It looked as though they had been fighting. A vivid bruise marred Luke's cheekbone, and Cruz had a cut lip.

"Tomasita and the baby are going to be fine," she announced from the doorway.

"Thank God." Luke bowed his head over his hands, which clutched the whiskey glass beneath his widespread knees.

She walked over to Cruz and touched his lip where it bled. He flinched away. "What happened?"

"Nothing."

"Are you coming to bed now?"

"Not right away. Luke and I have some more talking to do."

"Are you sure it's talking and not fighting you have in mind?" Sloan demanded, her voice sharp. "It's not going to help Tomasita if the two of you kill each other."

Cruz sighed. "You are right. Come here, Cebellina. I need to feel you in my arms."

Sloan went to him and allowed herself to be pulled down onto his lap and comforted. He whispered in her ear, "I promise Luke's handsome face will look as good tomorrow as it does tonight. Go to bed, *querida*. I will join you when I can."

Sloan kissed him on the mouth gently in deference to his split lip. "Good night, Cruz. Good night, Luke."

She left the parlor and started up the stairs, but changed her mind and silently walked back down and out the front door. A lot had happened in the past few weeks, and she needed to be alone to think.

Sloan had always considered herself brave, but she thought maybe she was about to make the most courageous decision of her life. The decision not only to love Cruz, but to trust his love to be constant no matter what challenges they faced over the years to come.

Once outside, she headed for the stables, where she lit a lantern and began saddling a horse.

"Who's that?"

Sloan realized she must have woken August, who had a room at the back of the stable. "It's me, Sloan."

"Miz Sloan? What you be doin' up this time o' the night?"

"It won't be long before the sun is up. I thought I'd take a ride. I'll be back before morning light."

"Weather don't look so good."

"At least the rain is done. There's nothing left of the storm but a little wind."

"That Texas wind ain't nothin'. It's somethin', all right. You be careful."

Sloan led her horse outside and held tight to the reins when it skittered nervously away from a leaf blowing in the wind. "Hold still, you critter," she said. She stepped into the saddle and kicked her mount into an easy lope. There were traces of light, enough to create shadows that made her horse hard to handle.

"Easy, boy," she murmured. "Easy. Nothing but shadows, boy. Nothing to be afraid of."

Just like her fears. Only shadows. Nothing to be afraid of. She felt stronger, surer of her choice. There were no guarantees. You took what life gave you and you made the best of it. And life with Cruz could be the very best. She knew it.

Sloan had kept her horse at a lope for half an hour when she saw a campfire in the distance. She was curious because the fire was so close to the house. Anyone crossing Three Oaks could have asked for, and received, the hospitality of the house. Whoever it was must have spent a hard night between the wind and the rain. She kicked her horse, thinking the least she could do was offer the travelers a hot breakfast.

It was also possible that whoever sat by that campfire hadn't sought shelter at the house because he had known he wouldn't be welcome. And so, before Sloan got much closer, she stopped to check that the twin Patterson Colts in her saddle holsters were loaded and angled her horse around so she approached the camp from behind.

Sloan could hardly believe her eyes when she saw the rotund figure sitting on a rock before the campfire. The Englishman! He must have planned a rendezvous with Cruz.

She had already turned her horse to flee when someone grabbed the reins and pulled her down out of the saddle. Her scream was cut off by a rough, hard hand across her mouth.

"The effort is wasted, *chiquita*," Alejandro said. "There is no one to hear you but me."

Cruz stared unseeing into the scattered coals in the fireplace. He had finally given Luke permission to court Tomasita, but not before he had vented his anger at the Ranger. Luke had left a few moments ago to sit at Tomasita's bedside. It was nearly dawn and long past time he joined his wife in bed.

Moments later, Cruz frowned as he stared at a bed that hadn't been slept in. He turned and walked down the hall to Tomasita's room, knocked, and when Luke answered the door, asked, "Is Sloan in there?"

"No. Isn't she in bed?"

"No."

"Did you check the other bedrooms?"

"Not yet." Cruz checked what had been Cricket's bedroom and found Cisco sleeping soundly. He walked down the hall and hesitated before knocking on Rip's door. When there was no answer, he carefully opened the door and found Rip asleep—and alone.

Cruz hurried back downstairs. Sloan wouldn't be in the downstairs bedroom with Angelique, but he quickly checked the other rooms without finding any sign of her.

He left the house and headed for the barn. There, August gave him news that made his heart skip a beat.

"She come to get her horse 'fore daybreak. Said she'd be back by mornin'."

Cruz heard a robin singing cheerfully outside the barn as he saddled his *bayo*. The storm had spent its fury overnight, and the sun was shining brightly. He and Sloan should be starting the new day together. Where was she? Why wasn't she back yet?

Her trail was easy to follow, and he felt a cold chill when he saw which way she had headed. His stomach was knotted by the time he reached the campfire, where the Englishman waited for him.

"Where is she?" Cruz demanded.

"Where is who?"

Cruz was off his horse and had the Englishman by his fancy neckcloth in two seconds flat. "My wife!"

"Easy, man, easy," Sir Giles soothed. "She's being well taken care of."

"Where is she?"

"Alejandro has her," Sir Giles gasped through a half-crushed windpipe. "You're choking me."

Cruz released his hold enough so that Sir Giles could talk. "Where is Alejandro?"

"He's gone to his hideout. I don't know where it is."

Cruz tightened his hold again, nearly cutting off the Englishman's air.

"I'm telling the truth. I don't know where he is," Sir Giles croaked.

Cruz let go of his hold on the man, and the Englishman dropped into an untidy heap on the ground.

"You had better pray that I find her soon, and that I find her untouched. Because if I do not, I will be back for you. I suggest you get out of Texas. It is not a healthy place for you anymore."

"You're forgetting something," Sir Giles said as Cruz remounted his *bayo*.

"Oh?"

"What about the evidence I have against your wife?"

"Do whatever you want with it. It was never any good anyway." With that enigmatic statement, Cruz spurred his stallion in the direction of the tracks that led away from the Englishman's camp.

As soon as Cruz was gone, Sir Giles Chapman picked himself up, scowling at the irreparable damage done by the mud that now stained his bright yellow trousers.

Things were not working out exactly as he had figured. He didn't trust Alejandro, and he believed Cruz's threat. He had better get to Alejandro's hideout as quickly as possible and make sure that nothing happened to that crazy Spaniard's wife.

Sloan was frightened. She was tied hand and foot, and that sense of helplessness alone was enough to curdle her blood. To make things worse, ever since they had arrived, Alejandro had been drinking steadily.

The small adobe house to which Alejandro had brought her was the same one in which he had murdered Tonio. Four years later, the door still hung on one leather hinge, the open windows lay bare, and flies buzzed around them. She sat on the dirt floor in a corner of the room and watched as Alejandro leaned back in a rickety chair and stuck his feet up on the wind-and-weather-scarred table. He tipped a bottle of beer up and drained another swallow. He smiled beneath his bushy moustache and his eyes narrowed as his cheeks rounded.

Sloan shivered at the gruesomeness of his drunken features.

From the lascivious glances being thrown her way, it was plain he was thinking about fulfilling the promise he had made in the stinking San Antonio jail cell so many months before. She reminded herself she was Rip's daughter. She was brave; she was strong; she was no coward. But that didn't stop her stomach from churning.

"Tell me, *puta*, does your blood run hot every time Tonio's brother touches you?"

She heard the chair legs hit the floor and Alejandro's spurs scrape off the table. A moment later, he stuck a dirty hand under her chin and shoved her head upward. His breath smelled of sour chili and Mexican beer.

Her dark brown eyes flashed with hate and contempt. "*Pendejo!*"

He hit her with his fist and knocked her into a sideways sprawl. Then he grabbed the front of her shirt with both hands and yanked, sending buttons popping in all directions as he tore the shredded garment off her shoulders.

His hands grabbed her breasts through her chemise and kneaded them roughly as his weight came down on top of her. He tried to shove her legs apart with his knee and realized, through his drunken stupor, that her ankles were tied together.

"*Chingada!*" He rolled off her clumsily and onto his knees. He pulled a knife from the sheath at his waist and slipped it through the knots that held her feet.

The instant she was free, Sloan kicked Alejandro in the groin as hard as she could.

He hissed in breathless agony and pitched over in a heap on the floor.

She had trouble getting to her feet because she had been tied up for so long, but she knew that she didn't have much time before the bandido recovered. She grabbed the knife from the floor and cut her hands free. When she finally managed to stand up, she slipped the knife into her belt, feeling hope rise in her breast that she would actually escape.

She spared one more glance at Alejandro, then turned to the door—only to find her way to freedom blocked.

"Going somewhere?" Sir Giles waved Sloan backward from the door with the pistol in his hand.

He looked from the growing bruise on Sloan's cheekbone to the Mexican bandido writhing on the floor and said, "I told you to leave the woman alone. Now, get up off the floor. Don Cruz has already come looking for her. I want her kept in a safe place where he won't be able to find her."

"It is too late for that." Cruz snaked an arm around Sir Giles's throat and put his Colt revolver to the Englishman's temple.

"Cruz!" Sloan cried in relief.

"Move over here, Sloan."

Sloan had started toward Cruz when Alejandro reached out and tripped her. As she fell, he caught her in front of him and rolled so there was no way Cruz could shoot at him without taking the chance of hitting Sloan.

Alejandro made it to his feet in a surprisingly agile move, rising with Sloan as a shield, her arms bound by his grasp around her waist. He had grabbed his pistol and held it at Sloan's temple in a mirror image of Cruz's hold on the Englishman.

Alejandro grinned slyly. "So, Don Cruz, it is a standoff, no? Except, I do not care if you kill the Englishman."

Sloan watched the whites appear in Sir Giles's eyes as the Englishman said, "I am worth a lot more money to you alive, Alejandro, than dead. Don't forget that."

"What is money compared to revenge?" Alejandro said. "This man put me in a stinking jail cell. This man would have hanged me." As he tightened his grip on Sloan, his hold on her hair pulled her head back at an awkward angle. "And this woman would have unmanned me. No, I think I will have my revenge now. There will be time enough later to think of money."

Alejandro turned his head and shouted out the window, "Ignacio! Tomás!"

"They are indisposed," Cruz said, his lips twisting sardonically.

"*Chingada!*" Alejandro quickly regained his composure. "That makes no difference. Move out of the doorway and let me pass, or I will kill your woman now."

Sloan watched a transformation occur as Cruz's eyes darkened. His hackles rose and his body tensed like a wolf ready to spring. She felt Alejandro's arm tensing and knew that in a moment he would shoot the Englishman—and then kill Cruz.

She lifted her hand far enough to reach Alejandro's knife where she had put it in her belt, and in the same motion stabbed him in the thigh as hard as she could.

When Alejandro shrieked, she threw herself onto the ground and was met there by the Englishman, whom Cruz had also shoved out of his way. There was the deafening roar of two gunshots occurring almost simultaneously, a grunt of pain, a bitter laugh, and then silence.

Sloan lifted her head to search for Cruz and saw him slumped against the wall, his eyes closed, the side of his shirt covered with blood. She whirled to find Alejandro slumped against the opposite wall—his eyes glassy with pain, and then vacant, the life gone.

She was too stunned to move.

"Nooooooo." The wail of pain and grief wrenched itself from deep inside her. She beat her fisted hands futilely upon the dirt floor. "Not again . . . not again . . ."

She was inconsolable, and so she fought the consoling hands on her shoulders—until the sound of the reassuring voice found its way through to her consciousness.

". . . it is all right, Cebellina. I am fine. It is only a small wound."

Her head came up off the ground and she scrambled to her feet, her hands pulling at his shirt where he had been shot. "How badly are you hurt? I have to do something to stop the bleeding. Sit down. Sit down!" She shoved him into the rickety chair at the table and he pulled her down into his lap, capturing her hands to keep them still and cutting off her protests with his mouth on hers.

Sloan couldn't get enough of him, the taste of him, the smell of him, the feel of him. She tore her mouth away to say, "I love you, Cruz. I love you. I love you."

Then he was kissing her again, his heart as full of her as his body was starved for her.

The sound of the Englishman clearing his throat brutally interrupted them. "This is all quite fascinating," he said, "but haven't you forgotten something?"

They both turned to find Sir Giles standing with a pistol aimed at them.

Cruz held Sloan still in his lap when she tried to jump up. "I have not forgotten anything, Sir Giles. You are free to return to England at any time. But I would suggest you make it soon."

Sir Giles narrowed his eyes in confusion. "I'm the one holding the gun, Hawk. I will give the orders."

Cruz raised his voice only slightly and called, "Luke! Creed! Long Quiet!"

Instantly, three tall, forbidding men bearing Colt revolvers appeared to stand guard at the windows and door to the adobe house. Beside Luke stood Beaufort LeFevre.

"My friends promised to leave Alejandro to me," Cruz said. "But I will be happy to accept their assistance in dealing with you. I suggest you drop your gun, Sir Giles."

"I still have the papers your brother left—"

"I'm an agent for the Texas government, Sir Giles. Of course my wife is not a traitor."

Sloan gasped and stiffened in Cruz's arms.

Luke grinned as he met Sloan's astonished look.

Sir Giles sputtered, "But you gave me information—"

"—that the Texas government wanted you to have. Matters have reached the point now where there is no more need for me to play the Hawk. Now that Texas will soon be annexed, we do not need to worry about the threat of war with Mexico anymore."

"I am sure President Jones will explain everything to your government," Beaufort added from his position beside Luke. "You should be receiving orders to return home directly."

"Mexico will fight annexation. There will be war," Sir Giles warned. "And Britain—"

Cruz raised a hand to cut off the Englishman. "Britain had better think twice before getting involved. You can tell your superiors that Texas will have the entire might of the American nation behind her in any hostilities that might arise. Mexico will not just be fighting Texans next time— she will be fighting the entire United States Army.

"You are not welcome here any longer, Sir Giles. You had best go back to England."

Sir Giles Chapman was, after all, a diplomat and not a soldier. He turned his pistol butt-first and handed it to Cruz. He bowed slightly to Creed and Long Quiet where they stood at the windows, in graceful acknowledgment of his defeat, before he turned and walked out the door past Luke and Beaufort LeFevre.

"I guess I'll be taking my leave of Texas, too," Beaufort said. "My work here is done." He turned to Luke and added, "I'll be taking Angelique with me. I can see there's nothing here for her."

"Good-bye, sir," Luke said, shaking Beaufort's hand. "Your daughter is a beautiful woman. I'm sure she'll find the right man for her someday."

Beaufort arched a disbelieving brow, but in true diplomatic fashion agreed, "I'm sure you're right. You can count us gone within the week."

Sloan tried again to leave Cruz's lap, and this time, after he had covered her with his shirt, he let her go. Shoulders back, she stalked away from him and out the door of the adobe house past her two grinning brothers-in-law and her smiling half brother without looking back.

She had not gotten far when Cruz caught up to her and turned her around to face him. "Do not run away from me, Cebellina. Not now. There is no reason for it."

"You don't call deceiving me a good reason?" Sloan said.

"I had no choice," he said, his voice low and insistent. "I

wanted to tell you a hundred times, but I was under strict orders of secrecy."

"Oh, Cruz . . ." Sloan's stoic facade crumpled and she threw herself into his arms. "I'm so sorry I doubted you. I'm so sorry I believed the worst of you. I'm so sorry I compared you to Tonio!"

"I am not my brother, Cebellina. I will never betray you. I love you more than my own life."

He pulled her into his arms, but grunted in pain when she squeezed the place where he had been nicked by Alejandro's bullet.

"We have to get you home," she said. "We have to take care of your wound."

Cruz sighed. "And where is home? Will you help me rebuild Dolorosa?"

"Of course I'll—"

Sloan was cut off by Luke's appearance at her elbow. He was shifting from foot to foot, and he wouldn't meet her eyes. "What is it?" she asked. "Did something happen to Tomasita while I was gone?"

"No, no, she's fine," Luke said. "But I'm afraid I have bad news for you."

Sloan held her breath waiting for the ax to fall.

"It's Rip. The doctor checked him after he looked at Tomasita. Rip's cold is more than a cold. It's pneumonia. And it doesn't look good."

Sloan was worried by Luke's news and filled the ride back from Alejandro's hideout with talk to help keep her mind off what she would find when she arrived at Three Oaks.

"Did Cricket come with you?" she asked Creed.

Cricket's handsome husband, who had been Luke's boss before he left the Texas Rangers to take his place at Lion's

Dare, flashed her a grin and met her gaze with chagrined amusement in his topaz eyes. "I couldn't keep her home."

"But she must be—"

"—ready to deliver any second. I know. She wanted to be here to help," Creed said. "We brought Jesse along so you could see how much she's grown. She's nearly two now."

"Did Bay come, too?" Sloan asked Long Quiet.

"I could not keep her home," he said with a grin that matched Creed's.

"Did you bring Whipp? It must be getting close to his first birthday."

Long Quiet's gray eyes softened, and there was nothing of the fierce savage in the half-breed's voice as he said, "He will be a year old when the moon is next full."

Sloan dropped back to ride beside Luke. She slowed her horse until they were far enough behind the other riders that they would not be overheard. "Did you know Cruz was working for the Texas government as the Hawk?"

"Sure did."

"And you didn't tell me?"

"Brothers can't tell their sisters everything," he said with a grin.

"I guess not." Her expression sobered as she asked, "How is Tomasita? Is she feeling any better?"

"A little."

Sloan saw the guilt in Luke's face. "It was an accident, Luke. Tomasita and the baby are both fine."

"If I'd just taken no for an answer, neither Tomasita nor the baby would have been in any danger in the first place. But the ladies don't say no to Luke Summers. They never have. Not until now, when it really matters."

He turned bleak eyes to Sloan. "I love her. I think I've

loved her all along. I just couldn't admit it to myself. When I think of spending my life without her, it's a cold, lonely future I see."

"So ask her to marry you."

"I've already done that. She said no."

"Did you tell her you love her?"

There was a long pause before Luke answered, "No."

Sloan snorted in exasperation. "No wonder she said no! The woman's crazy in love with you, Luke, but she has her pride, too. She isn't about to let you marry her out of pity, and until you declare your real feelings, that's all your offer can mean to her."

"She might have loved me once. But after everything that's happened—"

"That's enough of that! When we get back to Three Oaks, we're going directly to Tomasita's room, and I'm not leaving until I hear those three words come out of your mouth. Then if Tomasita says no, you can moan and groan and I'll be more than glad to hold your hand in sympathy."

Sloan spurred her horse to catch up to Cruz at the head of the column of riders. "I just realized I haven't thanked you for saving my life," she said.

Cruz smiled. "My pleasure, Cebellina. But tell me, why did you go riding off in the middle of the night in the first place?"

Sloan ducked her head so he couldn't see her eyes. "I wanted to be alone to think."

He arched a brow but didn't ask the obvious question. Perhaps it was because he didn't ask that she offered to share her thoughts.

"I wanted to think about us. About our marriage. About our future together."

"I can see why those thoughts might keep you awake,"

he said with a teasing grin. "They have kept me up many a night, I must admit."

It was the easy grin of a man who knows his love is returned, who knows that whatever doubts existed in the past no longer exist.

"Did you always believe we would end up together?" she asked suddenly.

"Life with you is never a certain thing, Cebellina. That is why I am so looking forward to it."

"Stop your horse," she said.

He pulled his *bayo* to a halt.

Sloan grasped his neck with her hand and pulled his head down so she could kiss him on the mouth. His lips were hard at first, then gradually softened as the kiss deepened. The feeling she was being watched eventually caused Sloan to break the kiss. She opened her eyes to discover four grinning faces surrounding her and Cruz.

"Can't we get a little privacy here?" she asked.

"Sure, Sloan," Creed said, kneeing his mount past her.

"You bet," Long Quiet answered.

"Far be it from me to interrupt the course of true love," Luke said.

"Pardon me, madam," Beaufort LeFevre said, tipping his hat as he rode past.

When they were alone again, Cruz said, "May I ask what inspired you to kiss me here in the middle of the trail?"

"Do I need a reason to show you how much I love you?"

"Do you love me? The forever, enduring kind of love?"

"I think so," she said, her expression troubled. "That's what I thought about on my ride—whether love is forever, and enduring. I think that no matter what tried to tear us apart now, my love for you would endure. But I can't see the future."

This time it was Cruz's mouth that captured Sloan's. It was a kiss of possession, a kiss that said, *I will love you forever—no matter what.*

"Nothing can tear us apart," he said, his voice hoarse with feeling, "so long as we are determined to be together."

Chapter 21

"YOU CRACKBRAIN JOBBERNOLL! WHAT WERE you thinking to ride out in the middle of the night like that. You had us all worried sick," Cricket greeted her eldest sister.

"Oh, my," Bay said, hugging Sloan, a gesture becoming less awkward for them as they grew older. "You're a mess. What happened to you?"

Sloan suddenly realized how she must look—bruised, disheveled, and wearing the shirt Cruz had given her off his back to replace the one Alejandro had torn away. "Despite the way I look, I'm fine," Sloan said. "Really."

Her protestations didn't save her from her sisters. Cricket ordered up a tub, and Bay raced to see what she could find to doctor Sloan's bruised face. Sloan was reminded of the homecoming she and Cricket had given Bay when she had returned from her life among the Comanches.

Sloan's absence from Three Oaks hadn't been nearly so long as Bay's, but she had still found her family's welcome cup of love full to overflowing.

It was pleasant to be coddled, to have her sisters worry

over her and pamper her. In the past, she had been the one
to worry. She had been the one to coddle—although she
hadn't been much for coddling.

As with everything else, that was changing too. She no
longer needed to be mother to her sisters. They were mothers in their own right. They had grown up and changed. As
she had changed.

Allowing herself to love Cisco and Cruz had meant un-
folding the softer side of her nature. It had taken her by
surprise, like fluffy cotton bursting from a sharp, prickly
boll. It had left her able to accept her sisters' pampering
and coddling and to enjoy it wholeheartedly.

"Have you seen Rip?" Sloan asked Cricket as she dried
herself off with a towel.

"Yes."

"How is he?"

"He's been sleeping most of the time since I arrived.
The way he sounds . . . it *hurts* to listen to him breathe.
When he coughs, you can see how much pain he's in. It's
awful."

Despite Cricket's warning, Sloan was unprepared for
the sight of her father fighting pneumonia. Even in sleep,
he struggled to breathe. She couldn't stand to watch his
pain.

She quickly left the room to go in search of Luke. She
found him downstairs in Rip's office, working on the
books for Three Oaks. He looked comfortable sitting behind Rip's desk.

If she was destined never to have Three Oaks herself,
she begrudged it least to Luke. But that issue hadn't yet
been decided, and she hoped it wouldn't be for years to
come. Rip wasn't about to let a little thing like pneumonia
put him down.

"Are you ready to talk to Tomasita now?" she asked.

Luke wiped his hands nervously on his trousers and then stood. "Are you sure she loves me?"

Instead of reassuring him, she grabbed him by the wrist and hauled him upstairs after her. He pulled free at the door to Tomasita's room.

"I can handle this alone," he said.

"Of course you can," Sloan agreed. "But I'm not sure Tomasita can. Come on, let's go inside."

Sloan could tell that Bay had been here to visit. The curtains were drawn wide to let in the sunshine, a vase of spring flowers sat on the table beside the bed, and Tomasita was sitting up in bed with at least a half dozen pillows fluffed up behind her.

"Hello, Tomasita," Sloan said.

Tomasita turned from gazing out the window at the fields. The smile that had been on her face faded when she saw Luke standing beside Sloan.

"What are you doing here?" she demanded, her eyes flashing angrily. "I told you I did not want to see you again."

"Luke has something he wants to tell you," Sloan said, sensing that Luke was going to bolt rather than take the chance of being rejected again.

Luke looked desperately at Sloan, then back at Tomasita. "I love you," he blurted.

"What did you say?"

Luke crossed to the bed and stood facing Tomasita. Determined to see this through, he cleared his throat and repeated, "I love you."

Sloan slipped out the door. She had done her part. They could handle the rest themselves.

"May I sit beside you?" Luke asked.

Tomasita eyed him warily. "All right." She inched over a little in the four-poster to give him room to sit.

Luke gently laid a hand on Tomasita's belly. "Don't pull away," he said, to stop her from doing just that. "I want to feel our baby inside you. I want a chance to prove how good we'd be together, a chance to be a father to this baby. I want you to marry me."

"You do not have to marry me to be a father, Luke. Babies come whether marriage vows have been said or not."

"I want you for my wife. I want to spend my life with you," Luke said, his hazel eyes earnest.

Tomasita closed her eyes and then opened them again. This wasn't a dream. Luke was really here, saying he loved her, saying he wanted to marry her.

Luke was starting to doubt Sloan's word. So far, Tomasita hadn't exactly jumped at the chance to marry him. Fear forced him to confront her. "Sloan said you loved me. Was she right?"

"Yes."

"Does that mean you'll marry me?"

"Yes."

"And we'll live happily ever after?"

Tomasita was silent for a moment and Luke held his breath.

"Oh yes," she answered. "Most definitely yes."

"Come here, little mustang girl," Luke murmured as he reached over and lifted her into his lap. "Come here and give me a kiss."

Sloan hesitated with her hand on the doorknob to Rip's room. The past few days had been hell. Rip's condition had worsened, then gotten better, then worsened again. She had barely had the chance to say a few words to him since Cruz had rescued her from Alejandro's clutches.

She had just returned from riding the boundaries of Three Oaks, only to discover that her father's illness had reached the critical stage. The family had gathered at his bedside. Either he would live through the day . . . or he would not.

Rip had already conquered one life-threatening bout with illness in the past year. She closed her eyes against that memory—slurred voice, sagging flesh, grayish skin, lumplike hands of clay. She tried telling herself pneumonia was different. It only made it hard to breathe; it would not take the life from his skin and bone.

But deep down, she knew she was only deceiving herself. Pneumonia was just as capable of killing Rip as the stroke he had conquered a year ago. She dreaded watching her father have to fight for his life again.

Surely she could find the courage to endure this tragic moment, as she had endured all the other challenges in a lifetime filled with adversity. Her personality had been molded by Rip long ago—by example, by instruction, by force, when necessary.

She had become indomitable, a fighter, the strong, brave heir to Three Oaks. She had never once given up or given in. She had to believe that Rip would follow his own teachings and that if it was humanly possible, he would overcome this second ravaging of his body by the forces of nature.

Sloan felt Cruz's comforting hand on her shoulder and turned her head to meet his concerned gaze.

"Are you all right, Cebellina?"

She smiled at him. "I'm fine. More than fine."

Her shoulders straightened; her heart lightened. This time, things were different. She did not have to face this calamity alone. She turned the knob and entered Rip's bedroom with her husband by her side.

Sloan had only rarely come into Rip's room. It was a spartan place. A giant four-poster bed, a tall cedar chest bearing a framed miniature painting of her mother on a stand, a copper-topped dry sink with a flowered pitcher and bowl for water sitting on top, and a worn rawhide chair comprised all the furniture and decoration in the room. It was good there wasn't more or all those who had come to observe the bedside vigil wouldn't have fit.

A very pregnant Cricket sat in a chair beside Rip's bed while Bay perched on the edge of the mattress holding his hand. Their husbands, Creed and Long Quiet, stood on the opposite side of the room while Luke leaned against the bedpost at the foot of the bed. Only Tomasita was missing from the family that surrounded Rip, and Sloan knew that was only because she was still recuperating from her fall.

"How is he?" Sloan whispered to Cricket.

"I'm not dead yet," Rip replied irritably. "Speak up so I can hear you."

The strength of Rip's voice startled Sloan, yet she could see it was a struggle for him to talk.

"You don't have to talk," she said. "I can see for myself you're still ornery enough to complain."

"Come closer, girl. Bay, get out of her way so she can sit down."

Sloan and Bay exchanged brief, chagrined smiles of understanding for Rip's brusque dismissal of his middle daughter.

Sloan reached out a hand and brushed a stray lock of

gray hair from Rip's forehead. It was a gesture of love he would not have tolerated had he been standing on two feet.

"I'm glad to see that husband of yours has managed to keep you safe here at home since your latest escapade."

"I'm safe, all right, but—" Sloan stopped, unwilling to bring up the antagonism over Three Oaks.

"But what?" Rip prodded.

"I don't want to argue—"

"Then speak up, girl."

Exasperated, Sloan said, "I was going to say that this isn't my home anymore. You saw to that."

Rip grunted as he exhaled. It was plain he intended to have his say and the pain be damned. "Hell, girl, what did you expect me to do when that Spaniard came hunting for his wife? Let you sit at Three Oaks and wallow in regret for the rest of your life?"

"What?"

"You heard me. I had to find some way to make you sit up and take another look at that hombre, didn't I?"

"Don't you dare say you disinherited me for my own good," Sloan bit out.

"That was the gist of it."

"Don't try to tell me you didn't want a living, breathing *son* to carry on at Three Oaks!"

Sloan held her breath as Rip grimaced in pain.

"Oh glory, girl, what I wouldn't have given to have three sons!"

There was utter silence in the room as Rip's three daughters absorbed that devastating statement.

Sloan watched a lone tear slip down the side of her father's face and felt her stomach knot. She couldn't help being born female, and she wasn't about to apologize at this point for being a daughter instead of a son. "I wish—"

Rip cut her off with a bitter epithet, then began coughing. His face was a deathly gray by the time he managed to stop.

"Stop talking, you old fool!" Sloan cried. "Can't you see it's killing you?"

"If I don't talk, I may never get a chance to say this," he rasped. "I didn't get the sons I wanted, but Lord knows I did the best I knew how with you three girls. Nothing turned out like I had it planned. Not for Cricket. Not for Bay. And not for you, Sloan, my eldest, my heir."

"I am not your heir. Not anymore."

"Oh yes. My heir."

Sloan frowned in confusion, thinking maybe the fever from his illness had caused him to forget what he had done. "You disinherited me. You gave everything to Luke."

Rip glared at her and said, "I'm not saying I didn't think about it, but—"

"*Think about it?* I heard you myself! You offered Three Oaks to Luke."

"Only so you'd have a chance to find out whether you wanted to stay with the Spaniard."

Sloan stared at him in disbelief. "You're not joking, are you? How could you—"

"Shut up a minute, girl, and listen to me!" It took him a moment to catch his breath and to come up with the energy to talk, but talk he did. "You always were hard to rein when you got the bit in your teeth. I'm telling you I never for a minute planned to take Three Oaks away from you. I wanted Luke to stay around, and I figured if he thought—"

"You lied to him, too? You never intended to give him anything—your own son?"

Rip snorted in disgust, which started another coughing fit that left Sloan so frightened she was furious with him for speaking at all. And yet what if he was right? What if he never got another chance to say the things he needed to say?

"Dear Lord, girl," Rip said when he had recovered. "If you could hear yourself talk. Are you ranting at me because you thought I gave Three Oaks away or because I didn't do what I threatened?"

"I'm riled because you manipulated my life. Because you didn't respect me enough to speak plainly about what you were thinking. And because I love you, you stubborn old man, and it was tearing me apart to hate you for what you had done."

There was a tense silence. No one moved. No one breathed. At last Rip hissed in a painful breath of air and said, "Three Oaks is yours. Always was. Always will be."

He had not, of course, apologized. It was a tremendous concession, Sloan knew, that he had even bothered to explain himself to her. She clenched her teeth to hide the betraying quiver of her chin.

Rip's eyes moved slowly around the room, meeting the fierce, protective gazes of his daughters' husbands; sharing the understanding of his son, Luke; adoring Cricket, his pride and joy; approving Bay, his not-so-disappointing daughter; and respecting Sloan, his eldest, his right hand, his other self. "I've said my piece. Are you all going to get out of here and let me die in peace, or are you going to stand there and worry me to death?"

Sloan wasn't conscious of Cruz's touch at her elbow leading her from the room, wasn't conscious of being ushered into her bedroom or of being picked up in Cruz's arms and held in his lap in the rawhide chair beside the window. Too many thoughts held her prisoner.

She heard Cruz's deep voice crooning to her, offering a

haven, a surcease from suffering. She slid into the comforting niche he provided and hid from the anguish that threatened to overwhelm her.

It was dark by the time her thoughts released her to the world of the present. Cruz still held her in his arms, his chin resting at her temple. His fingers moved gently on her skin, caressing, reassuring. He felt solid, a rock to steady her and keep her from foundering.

"I'm hungry," she said.

He smiled. "I am not surprised. You missed dinner and supper both. Would you like to go downstairs and see what we can find?"

He had started to help her stand when she said, "After everything that's happened, I can hardly believe I'm heir to Three Oaks."

She felt his whole body tense. He sat down again and pulled her back into his arms, holding her close. She could tell he was struggling with something. She reached up to smooth the lines of worry from his brow, but he jerked away from her touch. Hurt, she laced her hands tightly in her lap and waited.

He chose his words carefully when he finally spoke. "I am leaving Three Oaks tomorrow to begin rebuilding Dolorosa. I want you to come with me."

"How can I?" she protested. "Rip is so sick! Who'll take care of Three Oaks until he's back on his feet? He needs me here."

"I need you, too. Dolorosa needs you."

Sloan tried to get up, but Cruz held her where she was. His voice was low, intense, urgent. "I love you, Cebellina. I want to make a life with you. Earlier, you spoke of love lasting forever, of nothing ever coming between us. But it seems there is something that can come between us.

"You must choose between a life at Three Oaks and a life at Dolorosa with me. I wish there were a way you could have both, but it simply is not possible."

He paused long enough to trace the rigid line of her jaw with the pad of his thumb. "If you do not come to Dolorosa with me tomorrow, I will know you have chosen Three Oaks."

"I'm needed here now!"

"I need you with me."

"Don't force me to choose now, Cruz," she warned, "or you may not like my decision."

He stood up so suddenly she had to grab at his shoulders to keep from falling. His hand automatically circled her waist. Standing body to body, lightning flashed between them. Cruz reached up a hand and twined it in her hair. His blue eyes were hooded with need, his nostrils flared for the scent of her.

His head angled downward, and he took his time, daring her to run, daring her to stay. His mouth, when it settled on hers, was gentle, with a sweetness that made Sloan ache.

He slowly unbuttoned her shirt and slipped it off her shoulders, leaving her in her cotton chemise. Sloan shivered as his lips found the pulse beneath her ear. It was as though he had never touched her before, as though this were the first time . . . or the last.

"Touch me," he said, his voice a deep rumble in her ear. "Put your hands on me."

She pulled his shirt off and threaded her fingers through the hair on his chest, traced the hollows below his collarbone, and admired the washboard of muscle across his belly. The more she touched, the more she wanted to touch.

He returned the favor, mirroring her touches, murmuring love words as his hands caressed her through the soft cloth of her chemise. He wanted to give her pleasure; he wanted her to remember this night.

He lifted her into his arms and carried her to the soft feather mattress on the bed. He undressed her slowly, enjoying the feel of her skin beneath his fingertips.

Soft, he thought.

She mimicked him, running her hands down the front of his trousers, then feeling the texture of smooth buttocks and hair-roughened hips as she stripped him bare.

Hard, she thought.

Their loving was no less gentle than the touching had been. He entered her slowly, taking his time, testing her patience. When he was seated deep inside her, he said, "I want you to have my baby."

He expected her to resist the idea, and she didn't disappoint him.

"I can't—"

"Oh, but you can, Cebellina." He grasped her wrists and stretched her hands out above her on the pillows. His smile was feral. "I want to watch your belly grow round. I want to hold your hand while you labor, and bring our child into the new, civilized world that Texas will surely become. I want to be at your side while we watch our son or daughter grow."

He withdrew slightly and then pressed slowly, steadily back into her, thrusts that reached to the heart of her.

He spilled his seed inside her with a joyous cry of exultation.

The seed might not take root. It might be rejected by the woman, as she might reject him. But he had given her the one gift he could leave with her if this was their last night together.

He didn't mention his ultimatum.

She didn't mention her warning.

They slept in one another's arms and woke to the sound of children laughing and a baby crying. Still dressed in her chambray wrapper, Sloan left Cruz to investigate all the noise.

Cricket's daughter Jesse was playing with Cisco, while Bay's son Whipp was demanding to be nursed. Sloan felt an ache deep inside, an inexplicable yearning for the happiness she saw in her sisters' faces, and touched her womb where Cruz had planted his seed.

If there was no child there now, there never would be. She loved Cruz, but there was only the promise from him to guarantee that their love would last. Who knew what might pull them apart? Look what had already happened. Within days of his declaration, he was allowing this situation to come between them.

It was too dangerous to love Cruz. Three Oaks would always be there. It was the reasonable choice.

Cruz took one look at Sloan's face when she returned to the bedroom and knew she had made up her mind. Still, he had to hear the words. "Will you come with me to Dolorosa?"

She met his gaze with a courage she drew from somewhere deep inside and said, "I can't leave Three Oaks right now."

She said nothing more as she finished dressing in planter's garb, ready to do a man's job with a woman's hands and heart.

Cruz's face was grim as he finished dressing. When he spoke his voice was hard, his blue eyes cold. "*Adiós*, Cebellina. I will make arrangements to visit Cisco. A young boy should be with his mother."

Before she had time to protest, he was gone. She heard

his booted step on the stairs, then the murmur of voices, before the front door to Three Oaks slammed shut. Closing her inside. Closing him out.

She ran after him but got no farther than the portal to her room before she stopped. Cruz was being totally unreasonable! Didn't that arrogant Spaniard know better than to give her an ultimatum at a time like this? She didn't even know whether Rip was going to live or die. And she wasn't about to follow after him like a distressed puppy.

Her chin jutted obstinately as she left her room and headed down the stairs. She found Luke waiting for her at the bottom.

"Aren't you going after him?"

"No."

"I thought you were smarter than you're acting. And more forgiving."

Sloan snorted. "Forgiving? Who am I supposed to forgive?"

"Cruz."

"For what?"

"For being Antonio's brother."

"I don't know what you're talking about," Sloan said.

"I'm talking about blaming Cruz for the fact his brother broke your heart. He isn't going to betray you, Sloan. He isn't going to die and leave you—"

"Stop it!"

"Three Oaks is going to be slim comfort on a cold night, Sloan. Texas is going to blossom like a flower in spring once it becomes a state. You can spend your life with a man who loves you, helping him grow the sweetest smelling, prettiest garden on earth, or you can spend it alone. What's it to be?"

Sloan bit back her retort. If having Three Oaks was what

she really wanted, why didn't she feel happier right now? Why did she have the urge to go running out the front door after a tall, arrogant Spaniard? Because the truth was, *Three Oaks wasn't enough.*

"All right, Luke. Say I admit that you're right. Say I agree that I need Cruz. That means I'll be living at Dolorosa. Who's going to take care of Three Oaks?"

Luke frowned. "You can work something out with—"

"You're going to have to do it, Luke."

"What?"

"You deserve it. I don't need it, and it would make Rip as happy as a wolf at a lambing. Say you'll do it."

"I—"

"Hurry up! I want to go after Cruz, but I'm not leaving until I'm sure there's someone here to take my place."

Luke grinned and stuck out his hand. "You drive a hard bargain, Sis."

Sloan grabbed Luke's outstretched hand and pumped it twice before she turned and ran for the front door.

Cruz was coming out of the stable with his *bayo* when Sloan caught up to him. She ran full force into him and threw her arms around his neck.

"I love you. I'm going with you. You're never getting rid of me," she said between planting frantic kisses on his face. "When do we leave?"

Cruz claimed her mouth in a devastating kiss. When they finally came up for air, he found the presence of mind to ask, "What about Three Oaks?"

"Ask Luke. Three Oaks is his responsibility now."

Cruz swung her in a circle, laughing aloud in relief. "I love you, Cebellina. I will do my best to make you happy."

"Spending my life with you will make me happy.

Watching our children grow will make me happy. Loving you will—"

He cut her off when his mouth captured hers. And from the smile that rose on her lips beneath his, there was no doubt she was the happiest woman in the Republic.

Epilogue

SLOAN STOOD WITH BAY AND CRICKET AND stared at the headstone that had just been erected beside Rip's. It had seemed appropriate to place the second headstone here, beneath the sheltering branches of the majestic live oak that had taken root long before there was a Republic, and would be here long after Texas had achieved greatness as a state of the Union.

The strong one, the gentle one, and the rebel all bowed their heads in respectful acknowledgment of what death had taken and what it had left behind.

The sound of children's laughter could be heard in the distance as the three women paid homage to their father by sharing this momentous occasion with him in the only way they could.

The three sisters weren't left alone for long. Cruz joined Sloan and handed her the tiny child that moved restlessly in his arms. "I think Ana María is hungry."

Sloan took her daughter and cradled her close to her breast. Cruz moved up behind her and slipped his arms around her to help support the child.

Long Quiet stepped up to Bay and circled her very pregnant body with his long arms. Meanwhile, Creed handed Cricket their sleeping daughter, Miranda, whom they had nicknamed Muffin, and slipped his arm around her slim waist, pulling her snug against him. Luke and Tomasita strolled over to join them, their fingers clasped and trailing occasionally across Tomasita's slightly mounded abdomen, their son Rafael in tow.

"Whose idea was it to put up the second headstone?" Cruz asked.

"Mine," Sloan admitted.

"But Bay found the marble," Cricket said.

"And Cricket found the man to carve it," Bay added.

"It's beautiful, and a fitting tribute," Creed said. "You should be proud of yourselves."

The three sisters shared smiles of remembered times as they leaned back into the shelter of their husbands' arms and read the messages they had left for posterity.

On Rip's gravestone had been carved:

RIP STEWART
Beloved Father

And on the second marble stone:

THE REPUBLIC OF TEXAS
1836–1845
LONG MAY SHE LIVE IN MEMORY

"Guess the Texas flag is coming down at Washington-on-the-Brazos about now," Luke said, "and being replaced by the Stars and Stripes. President Anson Jones will be handing over power to the new governor, Pinckney Henderson, and Sam Houston and Tom Rusk will be on their way to Washington as Texas's first two senators. Hard to believe it's really happening."

"It's happening, all right," Sloan murmured. "It's just too bad Rip—"

Whipp's gleeful shout, "Pick me up!" as he discovered where his father, Long Quiet, had disappeared to, startled Ana María, who began to cry with all the strength of a lusty six-week-old. Meanwhile, Cisco cheered in triumph as he discovered a bag of cherry sticks amid the several baskets of food, while Cricket's three-year-old daughter Jesse trailed in his footsteps, babbling with excitement, her eyes wide with wonder at this unexpected delight.

Sloan laughed at the cacophony of children's demands and said, "I guess that's about all the peace and quiet we're going to get today."

Cricket agreed with a chuckle. "I just heard Jesse begging for a cherry stick. If I hope to get that child to eat anything wholesome at all on this picnic, I'd better intercept that candy."

"You are wise to make sure she grows up strong," Long Quiet said. "For as the children grow, so grows the new state of Texas."

"Are you saying we women hold the future in our dainty hands?" Sloan asked with a teasing smile.

Luke grinned. "In your *dainty* hands, and your *burgeoning* bellies." He swept Tomasita into his arms and swung her in a circle. Her delighted laughter was interrupted by his quick, hard kiss.

Smiling, her face aglow with happiness, Sloan turned to Cruz and took the hand he held outstretched to her. They walked together toward the blankets that had been laid out for the picnic. She sat down and leaned back against the lightning-scarred trunk of the live oak, unbuttoning her dress to nurse her child.

Sloan looked up into the adoring eyes of her husband, then let her gaze drift to the sight of her family gathered around her. Life was beautiful in Texas. Life was sweet. There was no doubt the future belonged to the sisters of the Lone Star.

AUTHOR'S NOTE

_____

On July 4, 1845, the Texas Congress voted at Washington-on-the-Brazos to accept the American offer of annexation and to begin work on a state constitution. Of the men who drafted the Texas constitution, only one was born in Texas. Eighteen writers came from Tennessee, eight from Virginia, seven from Georgia, six from Kentucky, and five from North Carolina. The constitution was approved, along with annexation, by a vote of 4000 to 200 on October 13, 1845.

Texas entered the Union on December 29, 1845, when American President James Knox Polk signed the annexation proposal. The actual transfer of power from the officers of the Republic to the state's new leaders didn't occur until a ceremony held on February 19, 1846.

Before the annexation treaty was even ratified, President Polk sent General Zachary Taylor to Texas with a small army from the United States. It was not a wasted effort. As predicted, Mexico and Texas went to war. In fact, hostilities had commenced by April 1846.

By the Treaty of Guadalupe Hidalgo, ratified in July 1848, the United States made peace with Mexico. For $15 million and an agreement to assume all Mexican debts, the United States purchased from Mexico the areas now comprising California, New Mexico, Arizona, Utah, Nevada, Wyoming, and a part of Colorado, and Mexico relinquished all claims to Texas, with its boundary set, as it is today, at the Rio Grande.

Dear Readers,

Texas Woman is the final book in the Sisters of the Lone Star trilogy, which also includes *Frontier Woman* (Cricket's story) and *Comanche Woman* (Bayleigh's story). I hope you've enjoyed reading about these three unique sisters—and the wonderful men in their lives—as much as I've enjoyed writing about them.

If you'd like to read about the modern-day Creeds, Coburns and Guerreros, be sure to pick up my Bitter Creek series *The Cowboy, The Texan,* and *The Loner.*

I always appreciate hearing your comments and suggestions. You can reach me through my Web site, www.joanjohnston.com.

Happy reading,
Joan Johnston
October 2003

ABOUT THE AUTHOR

New York Times bestselling and multi-award-winning author Joan Johnston has written fifteen historical romance novels and twenty-two contemporary romances. She received a master of arts degree in theater from the University of Illinois and was graduated with honors from the University of Texas School of Law at Austin. She is currently a full-time writer who lives in South Florida.